D1585654

"NO READER WILL EASILY FORGET IT."
—JAMES PATTERSON

"NOT TO BE MISSED!"
—LEE CHILD

"A RIVETING RIDE FROM START TO FINISH."
—JAMES ROLLINS

"IT'S SCARY GOOD."
—MARTIN J. SMITH

"SENSATIONAL."
—THOM RACINA

SOME HAVE ALREADY
DISCOVERED THE SECRET...

NOW IT'S YOUR TURN.

Titles by Chris Kuzneski

SWORD OF GOD
SIGN OF THE CROSS
THE PLANTATION

THE
PLANTATION

CHRIS KUZNESKI

BERKLEY BOOKS, NEW YORK

THE BERKLEY PUBLISHING GROUP
Published by the Penguin Group
Penguin Group (USA) Inc.
375 Hudson Street, New York, New York 10014, USA
Penguin Group (Canada), 90 Eglinton Avenue East, Suite 700, Toronto, Ontario M4P 2Y3, Canada
(a division of Pearson Penguin Canada Inc.)
Penguin Books Ltd., 80 Strand, London WC2R 0RL, England
Penguin Group Ireland, 25 St. Stephen's Green, Dublin 2, Ireland (a division of Penguin Books Ltd.)
Penguin Group (Australia), 250 Camberwell Road, Camberwell, Victoria 3124, Australia
(a division of Pearson Australia Group Pty. Ltd.)
Penguin Books India Pvt. Ltd., 11 Community Centre, Panchsheel Park, New Delhi—110 017, India
Penguin Group (NZ), 67 Apollo Drive, Rosedale, North Shore 0632, New Zealand
(a division of Pearson New Zealand Ltd.)
Penguin Books (South Africa) (Pty.) Ltd., 24 Sturdee Avenue, Rosebank, Johannesburg 2196,
South Africa

Penguin Books Ltd., Registered Offices: 80 Strand, London WC2R 0RL, England

This is a work of fiction. Names, characters, places, and incidents either are the product of the author's imagination or are used fictitiously, and any resemblance to actual persons, living or dead, business establishments, events, or locales is entirely coincidental. The publisher does not have any control over and does not assume any responsibility for author or third-party websites or their content.

THE PLANTATION

A Berkley Book / published by arrangement with the author

PRINTING HISTORY
Paradox Publishing trade edition / April 2002
Berkley mass-market edition / July 2009

Copyright © 2002 by Chris Kuzneski, Inc.
Excerpt from *The Lost Throne* by Chris Kuzneski copyright © 2009 by Chris Kuzneski, Inc.
Front cover photos: *Wrought Iron Gate* © Agence Images/Beateworks/Corbis; *Path* © Yossan/
Corbis; *Spanish Moss* © Philip Gould/Corbis; *Rusty Chain* © Nathan Griffith/Corbis. Stepback
photo: *Cypresses at Sunset* © David Muench/Corbis Edge.
Cover design by Diana Kolsky.
Interior text design by Kristin del Rosario.

ISBN: 978-0-425-22237-9

BERKLEY®
Berkley Books are published by The Berkley Publishing Group,
a division of Penguin Group (USA) Inc.,
375 Hudson Street, New York, New York 10014.
BERKLEY® is a registered trademark of Penguin Group (USA) Inc.
The "B" design is a trademark of Penguin Group (USA) Inc.

PRINTED IN THE UNITED STATES OF AMERICA
10 9 8 7 6 5 4 3 2

Foreword

A few years ago I nearly gave up. Like many writers, I had a tough time breaking into the industry. Agents ignored me, and publishers rejected me. My life was like a bad country song, only I didn't have a mullet. To make matters worse, my savings were almost gone, which meant I was *this* close to doing something desperate—like getting a "real" job.

Back then, the only thing that stood between me and the workforce was a novel I had just written called *The Plantation*. It featured two main characters that I really liked, Jonathon Payne and David Jones, and a plot that was pretty original. In hindsight, maybe *too* original. At least that's what I was told in several rejection letters. Editors and agents loved the book but weren't sure how to market it. And in the book business, that is the kiss of death. No marketing means no sales. No sales means no book deal. And no book deal means it's time to search the want ads.

Thankfully, I came across an article about a company called iUniverse and a new type of technology called print on demand. Simply put, copies of a book could be printed *after* a book order was placed, thereby eliminating large print runs that a struggling writer like myself couldn't afford.

vi   FOREWORD

Suddenly I had the freedom to print a small quantity of books that I could sell to family and friends. And if I was really lucky, total strangers would buy it, too.

Long story short, my plan worked. I sold enough copies out of the trunk of my car to ward off starvation, plus it gave me the confidence to take things one step further. I figured since readers loved *The Plantation*, maybe writers would as well. So I wrote letters to many of my favorite authors, asking if they'd be interested in reading my book. Incredibly, most of them agreed to help, and before long they were writing letters to me, telling me how much they enjoyed it. And I'm talking about famous authors like James Patterson, Nelson DeMille, Lee Child, Douglas Preston, and James Rollins. Each of them willing to endorse my novel.

Seriously, how cool is that?

Anyway, even though I had their support, I still didn't have a publisher. But all of that changed when Scott Miller, an agent at Trident Media, bought one of my self-published copies in a Philadelphia bookstore and liked it enough to e-mail me. At the time I had a folder with more than one hundred rejection letters, yet the best young agent in the business bought my book and contacted me. Not only did I get a royalty from his purchase, but I also got the perfect agent.

By then I had written my next novel, a religious thriller called *Sign of the Cross*, which Scott wanted to shop immediately since *The Da Vinci Code* was dominating the bestseller lists at that time. It proved to be a wise decision. Within months, he had sold the American rights to Berkley and the foreign rights to more than fifteen publishers around the world.

Finally, I could throw away the want ads.

Next up was *Sword of God*, which became my second international bestseller. In my mind, it was book three in the Payne/Jones universe. But to most readers, it was only book two because *The Plantation* was never released by a major publisher.

That is, until now.

Several years have passed since I wrote the first draft of

The Plantation. The original version was much longer and contained several mistakes that rookie writers tend to make. With the help of my good friend Ian Harper, I tried to eliminate as many of those as possible—while keeping the plot intact. After a lot of tweaking, I'm thrilled with the final product.

To me, *The Plantation* is my first love. It's the book that allowed me to write for a living.

Hopefully, you'll fall in love with it, too.

CHAPTER 1

ROBERT Edwards hurdled the fallen spruce but refused to break his frantic stride.

He couldn't afford to. They were still giving chase.

After rounding a bend in the path, he decided to gamble, leaping from the well-lined trail into the dense underbrush of the forest. He dodged the first few branches, trying to shield his face from their thorny vegetation, but his efforts were futile. His reckless speed, coupled with the early-morning gloom, hindered his reaction time, and within seconds he felt his flesh being torn from his cheeks and forehead. The coppery taste of blood soon flooded his lips.

Ignoring the pain, the thirty-two-year-old struggled forward, increasing his pace until the only sounds he heard were the pounding of his heart and the gasping of his breath. But even then, he struggled on, pushing harder and harder until he could move no farther, until his legs could carry him no more.

Slowing to a stop, Edwards turned and scanned the timberland for any sign of his pursuers. He searched the ground, the trees, and finally the dark sky above. He had no idea where they had come from—it was like they'd just materialized out of the night—so he wasn't about to overlook anything. Hell, he wouldn't have been surprised if they'd emerged from the underworld itself.

Their appearance was *that* mystifying.

When his search revealed nothing, he leaned against a nearby boulder and fought for air. But the high altitude of the Rockies and the blanket of fear that shrouded him made it difficult to breathe. But slowly, the pungent aroma of the pine-scented air reached his starving lungs.

"I . . . made . . . it," he whispered in between breaths. "I . . . fuckin' . . . made . . . it."

Unfortunately, his joy was short-lived.

A snapping twig announced the horde's approach, and without hesitation Edwards burst from his resting spot and continued his journey up the sloped terrain. After a few hundred feet, he reached level ground for the first time in several minutes and used the opportunity to regain his bearings. He studied the acreage that surrounded him, looking for landmarks of any kind, but a grove of bright green aspens blocked his view.

"Come on!" He groaned. "Where . . . am . . . I?"

With nothing but instinct to rely on, Edwards turned to his right and sprinted across the uneven ground, searching for something to guide him. A trail, a rock, a bush. It didn't matter as long as he recognized it. Thankfully, his effort was quickly rewarded. The unmistakable sound of surging water overpowered the patter of his own footsteps, and he knew that could mean only one thing. Chinook Falls was nearby.

Edwards increased his speed and headed for the source of the thunderous sound, using the rumble as a beacon. As he got closer, the dense forest that had concealed the dawn abruptly tapered into a grass-filled clearing, allowing soft beams of light to fall across his blood-streaked face. Suddenly the crystal clear water of the river came into view. It wasn't much, but to Edwards it was a sign of hope. It meant that things were going to be all right, that he had escaped the evil presence in the woods.

While fighting tears of joy, the athletic ski instructor scurried across the open field, hoping that the campground near the base of the falls would be bustling with early-morning activity, praying that someone had the firepower to stop the advancing mob.

Regrettably, Edwards never got a chance to find out.

Before he reached the edge of the meadow, two hooded figures dressed in black robes emerged from a thicket near the water's edge, effectively cutting off his escape route. Their sudden appearance forced him to react, and he did, planting his foot in the soft soil and banking hard to the left. Within seconds he'd abandoned the uncovered space of the pasture and had returned to the wooded cover of the thick forest. It took a moment to readjust to the darkness, but once he did, he decided to climb the rocky bluff that rose before him.

At the top of the incline, Edwards veered to his right, thinking he could make it to the crest of the falls before anyone had a chance to spot him. At least that was his plan. He moved quickly, focusing solely on the branches that endangered his face and the water that surged in the distance. But his narrow focus prevented him from seeing the stump that lay ahead. In a moment of carelessness, he caught his foot on its moss-covered roots and instantly heard a blood-curdling snap. He felt it, too, crashing hard to the ground.

In a final act of desperation, Edwards struggled to his feet, pretending nothing had happened, but the lightning bolt of pain that exploded through his tattered leg was so intense, so agonizing, he collapsed to the ground like a marionette without strings.

"Shit!" he screamed, suddenly realizing the hopelessness of his situation. "Who the hell are you? What do you want from me?!"

Unfortunately, he was about to find out.

CHAPTER 2

Mars, Pennsylvania
(13 miles north of Pittsburgh)

THE alarm clock buzzed at 10:00 A.M., but Jonathon Payne didn't feel like waking up. He had spent the previous night hosting a charity event—one that lasted well past midnight— and now he was paying for his lack of sleep. Begrudgingly, after hitting the snooze button twice, he forced himself out of bed.

"God, I hate mornings," he moaned.

After getting undressed, the brown-haired bachelor twisted the brass fixtures in his shower room and eased his chiseled, 6'4", 230-pound frame under the surging liquid. When he was done, he hustled through the rest of his morning routine, threw on a pair of jeans and a golf shirt, and headed to his kitchen for a light breakfast.

He lived in a mansion that he'd inherited from his grand-father, the man who raised Payne after the death of his par-ents. Even though the house was built in 1977, it still had the feel of a brand-new home due to Payne's passion for neatness and organization, traits he had developed in the military.

Payne entered the U.S. Naval Academy as a member of the basketball and football teams, but it was his expertise in hand-to-hand combat, not man-to-man defense, that eventually got him recognized. Two years after graduation, he was selected to join the MANIACs, a highly classified special operations unit composed of the best soldiers the Marines, Army, Navy, Intelligence, Air Force, and Coast Guard could find. Established at the request of the Pentagon, the MANIACs' goal was to complete missions that the U.S. government couldn't afford to publicize: political assassinations, antiterrorist acts, etc. The squad was the best of the best, and their motto was fitting. *If the military can't do the job, send in the MANIACs.*

Of course, all of that was a part of Payne's past.

He was a working man now. Or at least he tried to be.

THE Payne Industries complex sat atop Mount Washington, offering a breathtaking view of the Pittsburgh skyline and enough office space for 550 employees. One of the executives—a vice president in the legal department—was exiting the glass elevator as Payne was stepping in.

"Morning," Payne said.

"Barely," the man replied, as he headed off for a lunch meeting.

Payne smiled at the wisecrack, then made a mental note to dock the bastard's wages. Well, not really. But as CEO of his family's company, Payne didn't have much else to do, other than showing up for an occasional board meeting and using his family name to raise money for charities. Everything else, he left to his underlings.

Most people in his position would try to do more than they could handle, but Payne understood his limitations. He realized he wasn't blessed with his grandfather's business acumen or his passion for the corporate world. And even though his grandfather's dying wish was for Payne to run the company, he didn't want to screw it up. So while people with MBAs made the critical decisions, Payne stayed in the background, trying to help the community.

The moment Payne walked into his penthouse office, his elderly secretary greeted him. "How did last night's event go?"

"Too late for my taste. Those Make-A-Wish kids sure know how to party."

She smiled at his joke and handed him a stack of messages. "Ariane just called. She wants to discuss your plans for the long weekend."

"What? She *must* be mistaken. I'd never take a long weekend. Work is *way* too important!"

The secretary rolled her eyes. Payne had once taken a vacation for Yom Kippur, and he wasn't even Jewish. "D.J. called, too. In fact, he'd like you to stop down as soon as you can."

"Is it about a case?" he asked excitedly.

"I have no idea, but he stressed it was *very* important."

"Great! Give him a call and tell him I'm on my way."

With a burst of adrenaline, Payne bypassed the elevator and headed directly to the stairs, which was the quickest way to Jones's office during business hours. When he reached his best friend's floor, he stopped to admire the gold lettering on the smoked glass door.

DAVID JOSEPH JONES
Private Investigator

He liked the sound of that, especially since he'd helped Jones achieve it.

When Payne inherited the large office complex from his grandfather, he gave Jones, a former lieutenant of his, a chance to live out his dream. Payne arranged the necessary financing and credit, gave him an entire floor of prime Pittsburgh real estate, and provided him with a well-paid office staff. All Payne wanted in return was to be a part of his friend's happiness.

Oh, and to assist Jones on all of his glamorous cases.

Plus he wanted business cards that said *Jonathon Payne, Private Eye*.

But other than that, he just wanted his friend to be happy.

Payne waved at Jones's receptionist, who was talking on the phone, and entered the back office. Jones was sitting behind his antique desk, a scowl etched on his angular face. He had short hair, which was tight on the sides, and cheeks that were free from stubble.

"What's up?" Payne asked. "Trouble in Detectiveland?"

"It's about time you got here," Jones barked. His light mocha skin possessed a reddish hue that normally wasn't there. "I've been waiting for you all morning."

Payne plopped into the chair across from Jones. "I came down as soon as I got your message. What's the problem?"

Jones exhaled as he eased back into his leather chair. "Before I say anything, I need to stress something to you. What I'm about to tell you is confidential. It's for your ears only. No one, and I mean *no one*, is allowed to know anything about this but you. All right?"

Payne smiled at the possibilities. This sounded like something big. He couldn't wait to hear what it was. Maybe a robbery, or even a murder. Jones's agency had never handled a crime like that. "Of course! You can count on me. I promise."

Relief flooded Jones's face. "Thank God."

"So, what is it? A big case?"

Jones shook his head, then slowly explained the situation. "You know how you have all those boxes of gadgets near my filing cabinets in the storage area?"

"Yeah," Payne replied. He'd been collecting magic tricks and gizmos ever since he was a little boy. His grandfather had started the collection for him, buying him a deck of magic playing cards when Payne was only five, and the gift turned out to be habit-forming. Ever since then, Payne was hooked on the art of prestidigitation. "What about 'em?"

"Well," Jones muttered, "I know I'm not supposed to mess with your stuff. I know that. But I went in there to get some paperwork this morning, and . . ."

"And what? What did you do?"

"I saw a pair of handcuffs in there, and they looked pretty damn real."

"Go on," Payne grumbled, not liking where this was going.

"I brought them back here and tried to analyze them. You know, figure them out? And after a while, I did. I figured out the trick."

"You did?"

"Yeah, so I slipped them on to test my theory, and . . ."

Payne stared at D.J. and smiled. For the first time, he realized his friend's hands had been hidden from view during their entire conversation. "You're handcuffed to the desk, aren't you?"

Jones took a deep breath and nodded sheepishly. "I've been like this for three freakin' hours, and I have to take a leak. You know how my morning coffee goes right through me!"

Laughing, Payne jumped to his feet and peered behind the desk to take a look. "Whoa! That doesn't look comfortable at all. You're all twisted and—"

"It's not comfortable," Jones interrupted. "That's why I need you to give me a hand."

"Why don't you just break off the handle? Or aren't you strong enough?"

"It's an antique desk! I'm not breaking an antique desk!"

Payne smiled. "Wait a second. I thought you could pick any lock in the world."

"With the proper tools, I can. But as you can plainly see, I can't reach any tools."

"I see that," Payne said, laughing. "Fine. I'll give you some help, but . . ."

"But what?" Jones snapped as his face got more flushed. "Just tell me the secret to your stupid trick so I can get free. I'm not in the mood to joke here."

"I know. That's why I don't know how to tell you this. I've got some bad news for you."

"Bad news? What kind of bad news?"

Payne patted his friend on his arm, then whispered, "I don't own any fake handcuffs."

"What? You've got to be kidding me!" Jones tried pulling free from the desk, but the cuffs wouldn't budge. "You mean I locked myself to my desk with a real set of cuffs? Son of a bitch!"

"Not exactly something you'll put on your private eye résumé, huh?"

Jones was tempted to curse out Payne but quickly realized that he was the only one who could help. "Jon. Buddy. Could you please get me some bolt cutters?"

"I could, but I'm actually kind of enjoying—"

"Now!" Jones screamed. "This isn't a time for jokes! If my bladder gets any fuller, I'll be forced to piss all over your office building! I swear to God, I will!"

"Okay, okay. I'm going." Payne bit his lip to keep from laughing. "But before I leave . . ." He placed his hand on the cuffs, and with a flick of his wrist, he popped off the stainless steel device—a trick he'd learned from a professional escape artist. "I better grab my handcuffs so I know what type of bolt cutters to get."

Jones stared in amazement as his best friend walked across the room. "You bastard! I thought you said they were real?"

Payne shrugged. "And I thought you promised not to mess with my stuff."

CHAPTER 3

PAYNE'S schedule was free until an afternoon meeting, so he decided to return his girlfriend's message in person.

Ariane Walker had recently been named the youngest vice president in the history of the First National Bank of Pittsburgh, an amazing accomplishment for a twenty-eight-year-old female in the boys' club of banking. She was born and raised in nearby Moon Township, a fact that she and Payne were often kidded about since he grew up in Mars, Pennsylvania. Both of them took it in stride. Normally, they just replied that their relationship was out of this world, and they meant it. They'd been dating for over a year and had *never* had a fight—at least none without pillows.

As Payne strolled to Ariane's office, a journey he tried to make a few times a week, he peered down at Pittsburgh's gleaming skyline and smiled. Even though he grew up disliking the place, a city that used to be littered with steel mills, industrial parks, and the worst air this side of Chernobyl, his opinion had slowly changed. In recent years Pittsburgh had undergone an amazing metamorphosis, one that had transformed it from an urban nightmare to one of the most scenic cities in America.

First, the steel industry shifted elsewhere, leaving plenty of land for new businesses, luscious green parks, and state-of-the-art sports stadiums. Then Pittsburgh's three rivers—the Allegheny, the Monongahela, and the Ohio—were dredged, making them suitable for recreational use and riverfront enterprises. Buildings received face-lifts. Bridges received paint jobs. The air received oxygen. This mutt of a city was given a thorough bath, and a pure pedigree had somehow emerged, one that had been voted "America's Most Livable City."

"Hey," Ariane said the moment Payne knocked on her open office door. "I called you earlier. You get my message?"

"Yep, and since I had nothing else to do, I figured I'd pay my favorite girl a visit."

"I don't know where she is right now, so I guess I'll have to do until she gets back."

Payne sighed as he moved closer. "Oh well, I guess you're better than nothing."

The chestnut-haired executive grinned and gave him a peck on the cheek. "We've got to make this quick, Jonathon. With a long weekend coming up, I've got a lot of work to do."

"But you still have tomorrow off, right? Or am I going to have to buy the bank and fire you?"

"Oh, how romantic!" she teased. "No, that won't be necessary. Once I leave here at five, I'm officially free until Tuesday morning. The next one hundred and eleven hours are all yours."

"And I'm gonna use every one of them. I swear, woman, I don't get to see you enough."

"I feel the same way, *man*. But one of us has to work, and I know it's not going to be you."

Payne grimaced. "It certainly doesn't look like you're working too hard. I mean, here you are, a highly paid bank official, and instead of doing something productive, you're sitting at your desk, undressing me with your eyes."

Ariane blushed slightly. "Please!"

"And now you're begging for me. Damn, get a hold of your passion. You're embarrassing yourself."

She smacked him on the arm and ordered him to calm down. "What is it that you want?"

"Hey, you called me. Remember?"

"Please don't remind me of my bold and desperate act."

"I can't help it that you're easy."

"That's true," she joked. "I think I get that from my grandmother. She used to run a brothel, you know."

"Really?"

"No, not really." She laughed at the thought. "So, what are we going to do tonight?"

Payne shrugged. "Some of the new holiday movies come out today. I guess we could grab some dinner and catch a flick."

"Your treat?"

"I don't know," he scoffed. "You claim I don't even have a job. Why should I pay?"

Ariane faked a growl. "That wasn't a question, Jonathon. That was an order. Your treat!"

He loved it when she called him Jonathon. He really did. For some reason she was the first person he'd ever met that made it sound sexy. With anyone else, the name gave him flashbacks to the days when his parents were alive and he was just a boy. Jonathon was the name his mother used when he was in trouble. Like the time he accidentally ran over the neighbor's cat with a lawn mower. The cat's tail healed quickly, but Payne's ass was sore for weeks.

"Of course it's my treat!" He laughed. "I pay for all the women I'm currently dating."

"Well, we can talk about your hookers later. In the meantime, do you have time to take me out to lunch? I think this place could do without me for a little while."

"It would be my pleasure," he said, smiling.

Within minutes, they were strolling hand in hand above

the city, enjoying the summer sun and each other's company. In fact, they were so lost in their own little world that neither of them noticed the black van that started following them the moment they left the bank.

CHAPTER 4

Longview Regional Hospital
Longview, Colorado
(109 miles southwest of Denver)

TONYA Edwards sat in the ob-gyn's office, nervously waiting for her test results. Normally, Tonya was an optimistic person, someone who always looked at the bright side of life, but a first-time pregnancy has a way of changing that. Anxiety and fear often replace calm and joy, and as she waited for her doctor, the tension gnawed away at her very large stomach.

When the exam room door finally opened, Tonya wanted to jump up to greet the doctor, but it was physically impossible. She just wasn't in the condition to make any quick movements.

"How are you feeling, Tonya?" asked the middle-aged doctor as he pulled a chair next to her. "Any better?"

"Not really, Dr. Williamson. I'm still nauseous, and I have a slight headache."

"And how's the little fellow doing today?"

She grinned and patted her belly. "Robert Jr. is doing fine. He's been kicking up a storm while I've been waiting for the results, though."

"Well, I've got good news for both of you. Everything looks perfect. No problems at all."

Relief flooded Tonya's face. After taking a deep breath,

her lips curled into a bright smile. "That is such good news, doc. You wouldn't believe how worried I've been."

"Actually," he said, "I probably would. I've been doing this for many years, and I've seen this happen many times before. Tension tends to bring on flulike symptoms. First-time mothers have it pretty rough. Especially someone like you. Since you no longer have your own mother to talk to, you really don't have anyone to help you through this. Sure, Robert is there, but this is all new to him, too. And he certainly has no idea about the physical changes that you're going through, now does he?"

Tonya smiled as she wiped the moisture from her eyes. "He's kind of clueless on the physical stuff. In fact, I had to tell him how he got me in this condition to begin with."

Dr. Williamson let out a loud laugh. "Well, I must admit I expected him to know at least that much."

"Oh, don't get me wrong. Robert is a wonderful husband, and he's going to make a great dad, but you're right. He's clueless when it comes to my body and this baby."

"I'm sure he's doing the best he can, so take it easy on him."

When her appointment was over, Tonya waddled down the corridor toward the elevators. After pushing the down button, she leaned against a nearby wall and rested.

"Are you all right?" asked a man in a powder blue nurse's outfit.

The voice startled her. "What? Ah, yeah, I'm fine. Just tired."

"How many months are you?"

She laughed as she touched her belly. "Eight down, one to go."

"I bet you're excited, huh?"

Tonya nodded her head. "I don't know what I'm looking forward to the most: having a baby or getting my body back to the way it used to be."

The black man grinned. "Well, I admire you women. You go through so much in order to bring something so precious into the world. I got to hand it to you."

"Well, somebody's got to do it, and it certainly isn't going to be a man."

He nodded. He couldn't agree with her more. "So, what were you doing here?"

"I just had an appointment with Dr. Williamson. He wanted to run a few tests to make sure I'm fine."

"And everything went well, I hope?"

"Perfect."

"Good," the man said. "I'm glad to hear it."

As he finished his statement, the elevator door slid open, revealing an empty car. Tonya took a few steps forward, but she appeared a little unsteady on her feet.

"Wow," she muttered. "I really don't feel very good."

The man grimaced, then patted her on the arm. "I'll tell you what. If you hold the door for me, I'll get something that will help you out. Okay?"

She stared at him, a look of confusion on her face.

"Just trust me, all right?"

Tonya nodded, holding the door open button. The man jogged halfway down the hall and grabbed a wheelchair that had been abandoned in the corridor. Pushing it as quickly as he could, the man returned to the elevator. "Your chariot, madam."

She smiled and settled her wide frame into the seat. "Normally you wouldn't catch me in one of these for a million bucks, but to be honest with you, I think the rest will do me good."

"I was heading outside anyway, so it would be my pleasure to assist you to the parking lot."

"Thanks," Tonya said. "I appreciate it."

As the elevator door slid shut, the smile that had filled the man's face during the entire conversation quickly faded. Reaching into his pocket, he grabbed the hypodermic needle that he had prepared ten minutes earlier and brought it into view. After removing the cap, the man inched the syringe toward the exposed flesh of the unsuspecting woman.

"Don't worry, Tonya," he whispered. "The baby won't feel a thing."

Before she had a chance to question his comment or the use of her name, he jabbed the needle into her neck and watched her succumb to the potent chemical. The elevator door opened a moment later and he wasted no time pushing the sleeping woman through the lobby, right past the security staff at the front desk.

"Is she all right?" asked one of the guards.

"Dead tired," he answered as he rolled her toward the black vehicle that waited outside.

LATER that night, Payne and Ariane went to the movies. Unfortunately, the theater was so packed they were actually relieved when the film ended.

"Well, what do you think?" he asked as they walked outside. "Did you like it?"

"Like what?"

"Um, the movie we just saw."

Ariane smiled, giggling at her atypical behavior. "I'm sorry. I should've been able to figure that out. I've got a slight headache from that darn crowd. I guess I'm kind of out of it right now."

"No problem, as long as you aren't trying to back out of tomorrow."

"No chance there, mister. In fact, I think I have our entire weekend planned."

"Oh, you do, do you? Well, what do I have to look forward to?"

Ariane glanced at him and smiled. "I figured we can start off tomorrow morning with breakfast and a round of golf. Then, when I'm done kicking your butt, we can grab some lunch before heading back to your pool for some skinny-dipping and a variety of aquatic activities that will never be in the Olympics."

"I don't know." Payne laughed. "The TV ratings would

go through the roof if the Olympics used some of the events that I have in mind."

She blushed slightly. "Then on Saturday, if you're not too tired, I figured we can work on perfecting our routines."

Payne threw his arm around her shoulder and pulled her close. "That sounds pretty good to me. But one question still remains: What's on the itinerary for tonight?"

Ariane frowned. "Nothing but sleep. As I mentioned, I've got a slight headache, and I think it has to do with a lack of rest. If it's okay with you, I just want to go home and snooze."

"Sure, that's fine." In truth, he was disappointed, but he didn't want to make her feel guilty. "I guess I'll just go home and do some paperwork. You know me. My job always comes first."

CHAPTER 5

Friday, July 2nd
Plantation Isle, Louisiana
(42 miles southeast of New Orleans)

THE cross was ten feet high, six feet wide, and built with a sole purpose in mind. The carpenter had used the right kind of wood, soaked it in the ideal fuel, and planted it into the ground at the appropriate angle. The Plantation had one shot to do this right, and they wanted it to go smoothly. It would set the perfect tone for their new guests.

"Torch it," Octavian Holmes snarled through the constraints of his black hood. The wooden beams were set aflame, and before long fiery sparks shot high into the predawn sky, illuminating the row of cabins that encircled the grass field.

Ironically, the image brought a smile to Holmes's shrouded face. As a child, he had witnessed a similar scene, a cross being burned in his family's front yard, and it had evoked a far different reaction. It had terrified him. The bright glow of the smoldering wood. The sharp stench of smoke. The dancing specters in white hoods and sheets. The racial taunts, the threats of violence, the fear in his father's eyes. All of it had left an indelible mark on his young psyche, a scar that had remained for years. Now things were different. He was no longer a scared boy, cowering with his family, seeking strength and protection. Now the roles were reversed. He built the cross. He lit the flame. And he controlled the guest list.

Finally, a chance to exorcise some of his personal demons.

Over the roar of the blaze, he continued his commands. "Bring the prisoners into formation!"

A small battalion of men, dressed in long black cloaks and armed with semiautomatic handguns, burst into the cramped huts and dragged the blindfolded captives toward the light of the flames. One by one, the confused prisoners were placed into a prearranged pattern—three lines of six people—and ordered to stand at attention while facing the cross. When the leader of the guards was finally happy with the setup, he let his superior know. "We're ready, sir."

"Good," Holmes replied as he settled into his black saddle. "Drop your hoods!"

In unison, the entire team of guards covered their faces with the thick black hoods that hung loosely from the back of their cloaks. When they were done, they looked like Klansmen in black robes. Their eyes were all that remained uncovered, and they burned like glowing embers in the Louisiana night.

"It's time to show them our power!"

With sharp blades in hand, the guards charged toward the prisoners and swiftly cut small holes in the white cotton bags that had been draped over the heads of the captives.

"Ladies and gentlemen," Holmes barked as he trotted his stallion to the front of his guests. "Welcome to the Plantation."

He paused dramatically for several seconds before continuing his monologue. "I'm sure each of you would like to see your new surroundings, but there is something blocking your sight. It is called duct tape, and it will be quite painful when you pull it off. . . . Don't worry. Your eyebrows will eventually grow back." Holmes laughed quietly. "I realize that your hands are currently bound, but I'm quite confident you'll be able to remove the tape without our assistance."

Slowly and painfully, the prisoners removed the adhesive

strips from their faces, tearing flesh and hair as they did. Then, once their eyes had adjusted to the light from the intense fire, they glanced from side to side, trying to observe as much as they could. The sudden realization that each person was a part of a large group gave some captives comfort and others anxiety.

"Impressive!" Holmes shouted in mock admiration. "I'm quite pleased with the guts of this group. Normally my prisoners are weeping and praying to me for mercy, but not you guys. No, you are too strong for that." He clapped sarcastically, slamming the palms of his black leather gloves together. "Now that you've dazzled me with your inner strength, it's time for me to show you how weak you really are. While you are guests on my plantation, there are strict rules that you must follow. Failure to follow any of them will result in severe and immediate punishment. Do I make myself clear?"

The prisoners remained quiet, too scared to speak.

"My God! I must be going deaf! Why? Because I didn't hear a goddamned word from any of you." He rode his horse between the lines of prisoners. "Let's try this again, but this time I want you to scream, *Yes, Master Holmes!*" He glared at the captives. "Are you ready? Failure to follow my rules will result in severe and immediate punishment. Do I make myself clear?"

Fewer than half of them answered. An act of disobedience that pissed off Holmes.

"Yesterday you had the right to do what you wanted, say what you wanted, think what you wanted. But all of that is gone now. Your freedom has faded into the air, like smoke from this burning cross." The prisoners glanced at the clouds of ash that slowly rose into the darkness. "You are no longer members of a free society. You are now possessions. You got that? And as my possessions, you are now governed by the rules that I'm about to share with you. Failure to comply with *anything* will result in swift and decisive action on my part. Do you understand?"

"Yes, Master Holmes," mumbled most of the crowd.

Holmes shook his head in disgust, disappointed that he

would have to damage some of his property so early in the proceedings. "Bring out the block," he ordered.

Two guards ran to the side of the field and lifted a four-foot wooden cube onto a small cart. Then, as the prisoners stared in confusion, the guards dragged the large chunk of wood to the front of the crowd.

"Thank you," Holmes said as he climbed off his horse. "Before you hustle off, I'd like you to do me a favor."

"Yes, sir!" the guards said in unison.

"Do you see the tall man at the end of the front row?" Holmes pointed at Paul Metz, a father of two from Missouri. "Please bring him to me."

"Me?" Paul shrieked as he was pulled from the line and dragged to the front of the group. His family, who'd been standing next to him, trembled with fear. "What did I do?"

"So you *can* talk! See, I wasn't sure if you had the ability to speak until now. Why? Because a moment ago I asked the group to answer a question, and no sound came from your lips."

"I answered, I swear."

Holmes slammed his gloved hand onto the wooden block, and the sound echoed above the roar of the fire. "Are you calling me a liar?"

"No," Paul sobbed. "But I swear, I answered you. I yelled my response."

"Oh, you yelled your response, did you? I was staring right at you, focusing solely on you, and I saw nothing! No sound, no head movement, not a goddamned thing!"

"I screamed, I swear."

Holmes shrugged his shoulders at the claim. He had no desire to argue with a prisoner. It would set a very bad precedent. "Put your hands on the block," he said calmly.

"What?"

Holmes responded to the question by slapping Paul in the face. "Don't make me tell you again. Put your hands on the fucking block."

He closed his eyes and eased his bound hands onto the wood. He quivered as he did.

"Now, choose a finger."

Paul opened his eyes and stared into the hooded face of his captor. "Please, not that," he begged softly.

In a second flash of rage, Holmes threw a savage punch into Metz's stomach, knocking the breath from him. On impact, Paul collapsed to the ground in front of the wooden block.

"Choose a finger or lose them all."

From his knees, Paul reluctantly placed his hands on the chopping board, then extended the pinkie of his left hand. As he wiggled it, announcing his choice, he sobbed at the impending horror. "This one, Master Holmes."

Holmes smiled under his hood, enjoying his moment of omnipotence. This was the type of respect he would demand from all of his prisoners. And if they failed to comply, he would make sure that they had a very unpleasant stay.

"Now," he shouted at the transfixed crowd, "I would like you to observe the following." With the viselike grip of his left hand, he grabbed Paul's wrist and pinned it painfully to the wood. "This man chose to ignore a direct order from me, and because of that, he will be severely punished."

With his right hand, Holmes grabbed his stiletto, then paused to enjoy the surreal nature of the moment. In the presence of the dancing flames, the length of the five-inch steel shaft gleamed like Excalibur in the regal hands of King Arthur. The crowd gaped in awe at the spectacle they were witnessing. Wailing from his knees, Paul waited for his punishment to be executed.

"Let this be a lesson to you all!"

With a quick downward stroke, Holmes rammed the razor-sharp blade into Paul's knuckle, just below his fingernail, immediately severing the tip. A flood of crimson gushed from it, glistening in the firelight. Paul screamed in agony while trying to pull his damaged hand off the block, but Holmes was too strong for him. After lifting the knife again, he plunged the blade into Paul's finger a second time, severing it just below the middle knuckle.

"Stop!" Alicia Metz shrieked above her husband's wails.

A guard instantly silenced her with a ferocious backhand.

"Not yet!" Holmes answered. He pulled the embedded blade from the block again, and this time buried it into the edge of Paul's palm, dislodging the last section of his little finger with a sickening pop.

"Why?" she sobbed as she slumped to the ground. "Why are you doing this? What have we done to deserve this?"

Holmes glanced at the three chunks of finger that sat on the chopping block in front of him and smiled, admiring his handiwork. "I'm sick of her babbling. Gag her."

Two guards grabbed the fallen woman and wrapped her mouth in duct tape.

"Anything else, sir!"

"Yes," Holmes sneered. "Get this man some gauze. It seems he's had an accident."

CHAPTER 6

The Kotto family estate
Lagos, Nigeria
(Near the Gulf of Guinea coast)

HANNIBAL Kotto stared into his bathroom mirror and frowned at the flecks of gray that had recently emerged. Although he was fifty-one years old, he didn't look it. In fact, people always assumed that he was ten years younger than he actually was.

After opening his plush purple curtains, Kotto gazed across the man-made moat that encircled his majestic grounds and observed a team of workers as they pulled weeds from his impeccably maintained gardens. All of them were new employees, and he wanted to make sure that they were following his orders. Unfortunately, before he had an opportunity to evaluate their performance, his phone rang. "Damn," he muttered. "There's always something."

Kotto reached into the pocket of his robe and pulled out his cellular phone. "Kotto here."

"Hannibal, my dear friend, how are things in Nigeria?"

For the first time that day, Kotto smiled. It had been a while since he'd spoken with his business partner, Edwin Drake, and that was unusual. They normally spoke a few times a week. "Things are fine. How about South Africa? Is Johannesburg still in one piece?"

"Yes, and I still own most of it." Drake, an Englishman who made the majority of his money in African diamond mines, laughed. "However, with the civil unrest in this bloody city, my holdings are not as impressive as they used to be."

"That is a shame, but a common drawback to life in Africa. Governments come, and governments go. The only thing that's constant is conflict."

"A more accurate statement has never been spoken."

Kotto smiled. "Tell me, Edwin, where have you been hiding? I thought maybe you were getting cold feet about our recent operation."

"Not at all. I couldn't be happier with our partnership. The truth is I had some last-minute family business to attend to in London, and I honestly didn't want to call you from there. I never trust those bloody hotels. You can never tell who's listening."

After a few minutes of small talk, Kotto steered the conversation to business. "I was wondering what you thought of the last shipment of snow you received. Was it to your liking?"

"*Snow*? Is that what we're calling it now? I like the sound of that."

"I'm glad. I felt we needed a code name for the merchandise, and I hate the term they use in South America."

"You're right. *Snow* is so much simpler to say than *cargo blanco*."

"Exactly. And since both of us speak English, I figured an English word was appropriate."

"Why not something Nigerian? Couldn't you come up with something colorful from your native tongue?"

Kotto laughed loudly. He always got a kick out of the white man's unfamiliarity with Africa. "Edwin, I *did* come up with a word from my native tongue. English is the official language of Nigeria."

"Really? I didn't know that. I'm sorry if I offended you."

"It's all right. I'm used to your ignorance by now," Kotto teased. "But I hope you realize I don't walk the streets of Lagos in a loincloth while carrying my favorite spear."

Drake couldn't tell if his friend was lecturing or joking until he heard Kotto laugh. "Hannibal, I must admit you had me going for a while. I thought I hit a nerve."

"Not at all. I just thought a moment of levity was in order before we continued our business."

"Yes, it was rather pleasant. Thank you."

"So, what did you think of your last shipment of snow? Did it meet the expectations of your buyers?"

"In some ways yes, and in some ways no."

Kotto frowned. It wasn't the answer he was hoping for. "What do you think needs to be improved?"

"Honestly, the overall quality. I think my buyers were hoping for something better than the street product that I sold them. They wanted something purer. You know, upper-class snow."

"Well," he replied, "the last batch was just a trial run. From what I understand, the next shipment we receive will be the best yet."

CHAPTER 7

WITH such a diverse group—an equal mix of young and old, male and female—there appeared to be no link between the prisoners of the Plantation. But Harris Jackson knew that wasn't the case. He knew the reason that these people had been pulled from their lives and brought to this island. He understood why they were being humiliated, abused, and tortured. And he relished the fact that they were stripped of their homes, their possessions, and their pride. All of it made sense, and he was going to enjoy his authority over them for as long as it lasted.

In the flickering firelight, Jackson stared at the seventeen people in front of him and savored how each of them was shaking, literally trembling with fear. God, how he loved that! It made him feel indestructible. "Ladies and gentlemen, my name is Master Jackson, and my job on this island is leader of the guards. When you address me, you shall use the name *Master Jackson* or *sir*. Nothing else is acceptable. Nothing else will be tolerated."

Under his black hood, he smiled. When he'd worked as a lawyer during his short-lived legal career, he loved addressing the jury—trying to get them to listen, hoping to catch their eye, convincing them to believe—and for some reason, his orientation speech made him think back to his days in the courtroom. The days before his disbarment.

"As you can probably tell, none of you were given an opportunity to change your clothes after you received your invitation to the Plantation. Some of you are filthy, and some of you are clean. A few of you are dressed warmly, and others are not." He stared at Susan Ross, a sixteen-year-old who'd been abducted from a community pool in Florida, and appreciated the way her teenage body looked in her bikini. He made a mental note to pay her a visit later. "In an attempt to make everybody equal, I'd like each of you to disrobe."

Despite his command, nobody moved. They just stared straight ahead in absolute shock.

Like Holmes before him, Jackson shook his head in disappointment. "What a shame! I assumed that each of you had a pretty good understanding of your situation by now. I figured the Ginsu display from earlier was going to keep you in line for the rest of your visit." Jackson shrugged his broad shoulders as he walked toward the prisoners. "I guess I was wrong."

Jackson stopped in front of Susan, his six-foot frame towering above her. "I'm looking for a volunteer," he roared in the voice of a drill sergeant. "And I think *you* will do nicely."

Despite her cries of protest, he lifted her half-naked, 110-pound body over his shoulder and carried her toward the chopping block. Two guards offered to assist him, but he quickly ordered them to stay back. He was enjoying himself far too much to let them share in the fun. When he reached the wooden cube, he set her gently on the ground, then put her in a stranglehold so she couldn't run away.

"What do you want from me?" she cried through the cloth of her white hood.

"You'll find out soon enough," he whispered into her left ear. "And I must admit I'm looking forward to it." He pushed his groin against the small of her lower back, and she immediately felt his excitement start to grow. "Can you feel how hard I am? That's because of you, you know. All because of you."

Susan tried squirming free of his grip, but Jackson was simply too strong for her. As she tried to pull away, he laughed at her feeble attempts.

"Are you done?" he asked in a civil tone.

After one more try, she nodded her head.

"Good, because I'm dying to begin."

Like a tarantula, Jackson's black fingers crawled down her nubile flesh, gradually creeping across her firm stomach, then sliding under her bathing suit. "Do you like my magic fingers?" he whispered. "Do you like when I touch you?"

Before she could respond, he lifted her off the ground and forced her to stand on the bloody chopping block. Within seconds, her bare feet were coated with the red fluid that had gushed from Paul Metz's finger.

"As I told you a moment ago, I would like each of you to take off your clothes. Apparently, you're not as threatened by me as you were by Master Holmes. Now, because of your ignorance, this young girl has to suffer."

"Please don't hurt me," she sobbed. "I was being good. I didn't do anything wrong. I was being good."

With a mischievous smile, he placed his dark hand on the back of her leg and slowly, sexually, stroked her inner thigh. "I know, my dear, but it's not my doing. You should fault your fellow inmates for ignoring my instructions. They're more to blame than I." His hand crept higher and higher on her smooth leg until it stopped on her ass. "Remember, I'm not to blame for this. Bear me no ill will."

Taking his stiletto from the folds of his cloak, Jackson slowly raised the blade behind the unsuspecting female, inching it toward his target. The sharp steel glistened in the light of the raging fire.

"I want you to kneel for me," he purred. "And I want you to take your time."

Without a word of complaint, the girl dropped to her

knees. His unblinking eyes followed the curvature of her cheeks on their downward path. When she reached the block, he heard her groan as she sank into the cherry liquid that coated the surface. The sound brought a smile to his lips.

"Now raise your hands above your head, and hold them there."

She did as she was told, and her movement electrified him—her unquestioning compliance literally made his heart race faster.

"Remember," he breathed, "no ill will."

Jackson placed his hand on the girl's bare back and searched for the perfect spot to make his incision. Once he found it, he lifted the knife to her flesh, tracing the ridges of her spine with the broad side of his cold, metal blade. As he did, he noticed the emergence of goose bumps, not only on her skin but on his as well. Gathering his emotions, Jackson inched the stiletto to the midsection of her back, the spot directly between her shoulder blades, then paused.

This was where the cut would be made.

Turning the blade to the appropriate angle, Jackson gazed at the crowd to make sure that they were watching. They were. The entire throng was focused on the hypnotic movements of his knife, like he was an ancient Mayan priest preparing for a ritual sacrifice. Pleased by the attention, he redirected his gaze to his target.

"It's time!" he whispered.

With a quick slash, Jackson sliced the strap of her bikini top. Then, before she had an opportunity to flinch, he carved her swimsuit bottom as well, exposing her entire body to the audience and the humid Louisiana night.

A wave of humiliation flooded over the girl. She tried to cover herself by crouching into a tiny ball on the wooden cube, but Jackson wouldn't allow it. He yanked her from her bloody perch and forced her to retake her position with the rest of the prisoners.

He would've preferred to wrap her in his arms but knew this was no time to be playing favorites. He had to treat everyone the same in order to set the rules, in order to get their respect.

Besides, he'd have a chance to make things up to her later—when they were alone.

CHAPTER 8

**Wexford, Pennsylvania
(11 miles north of Pittsburgh)**

DESPITE the early hour, Jonathon Payne managed to smile as he drove to Ariane's apartment. Normally a grin wouldn't make an appearance on his lips until much closer to noon, but since he was spending the entire day with her, he woke up in an atypically good mood.

Years of predawn calisthenics had soured his opinion of the morning.

Dressed in khaki shorts and a white golf shirt, Payne pulled his Infiniti SUV into the crowded lot outside of her building. After parking, he walked under the maroon awning that covered the complex's entrance and pressed the button to be let in. When she didn't reply, he tried the system a few more times before he walked back to the parking lot to make sure that her car was in her assigned space. It was there, and in his mind that meant she was definitely home.

Slightly frustrated, Payne strolled back to the intercom system and tried the buzzer again, yet nothing changed. He was still unable to get her attention.

Come on, he thought. *I know you're scared to face me on the golf course, but this is ridiculous.*

Standing in the entryway, pondering what to do next, he noticed a thin strip of duct tape sticking to the frame near the automatic lock of the security door. Moving closer, he realized that the tape started outside the frame and ran inside the building, purposely keeping the door open.

"Oh," Payne mumbled, figuring the intercom system must be broken.

Thankful to be inside, he jogged up the carpeted stairs to the second floor and noticed that the thick fire door at the top of the steps was propped open with a large stick.

Without giving it much thought, Payne continued his journey down the hallway toward Ariane's apartment. That's when he noticed something he couldn't dismiss. A piece of duct tape had been placed over the peephole of her door. Tape that wasn't there when he dropped her off the night before.

Suddenly, a wave of nausea swept through Payne's stomach. He wasn't sure why, but he knew that something had happened to Ariane.

Payne pounded on her door loudly, hoping that she had overslept or had been in the bathroom when he was buzzing her. But somehow he knew that wasn't the case. He knew that something was wrong. Very seriously wrong.

"Ariane!" he yelled. "It's Jon. Open the door!"

When his pleas went unanswered, Payne reached into his pocket and pulled out his cell phone. He hit the speed dial and watched as her name and number appeared on the screen. "Come on! Answer the damn phone!"

After four rings, Payne heard a click on the line. It was her voice mail.

Payne cursed as he waited to leave his message. "Ariane, if you're screening your calls or you're still in bed, pick up the phone." There was no response. "I'm really worried about you, so *please* call me on my cell as soon as you hear this message, okay?"

He hung up the phone, worried. "Think, goddamn it, think! Where could she be?"

Payne racked his brain for possibilities, but couldn't

think of any logical explanations. Most stores weren't open at that hour, and even if they were, she would have taken her car to get there. Most of her friends would still be sleeping or getting ready for work, so they wouldn't have picked her up. And her family lived out of state, so she wasn't with them.

No, something had happened to Ariane. He was sure of it.

PAYNE wasn't the type of guy who waited around for news. He was the aggressor, a man of action. Someone who followed his instincts, despite the odds. In the military, his gut feelings were so accurate that they were treated with reverence, like a message from God.

And in this case, he sensed that time was precious.

Without delay, Payne took a step back and launched his right leg toward the door. His foot met wood with a mighty *thump*. It echoed down the hallway like a gunshot. The sturdy frame splintered in several places as the door swung open with so much force that the lower hinge snapped a bolt. Adrenaline was a wonderful thing.

In his former career, Payne would've been armed and whispering orders into his headset. But today he was alone and empty-handed, worried about what he might find inside.

Cautiously, he walked into Ariane's apartment. The place was immaculate. No overturned tables, no broken lamps. And most importantly, no dead bodies. Payne wasn't sure what he was expecting to see, but he felt a certain sense of relief when he found nothing.

The only damage he noticed was the damage that he had done himself.

Taking a deep breath, Payne realized that he needed a second opinion. And when he needed help, he turned to his best friend. Payne hit his speed dial and waited for Jones to answer.

"Yeah?" Jones croaked, obviously sleeping in on his day off.

"D.J., it's Jon. Something's happened, and I need your help."

That was all that Jones needed to hear.

FIFTEEN minutes later, Jones pulled up next to Payne's SUV and studied the parking lot, but nothing seemed out of place. "Have you heard from her?"

Payne shook his head as he jogged over to Jones's car.

"Don't worry. That doesn't mean something bad has happened. I'm sure there are a thousand possibilities that could explain where she is, so tell me everything you can. I'm sure we can figure something out."

Payne nodded while shaking his friend's hand. "I appreciate you coming over so early. I feel better just having you here."

"No problem. It's the least I can do for free office space."

Payne smiled, but his body language told the real story. He was scared. "You know how I used to get gut feelings back when we were in the MANIACs?"

Jones nodded. "Your gut saved my ass more often than Preparation H."

"I don't know why, but I'm getting the same bad feeling right now. I know that something's happened to Ariane. I don't know what, but something."

"Jon, listen. We've been out of the military for a while now, so the tuning fork in your stomach is bound to be rusty. Right? Besides, you're not used to being awake at this time of day, so I'm sure your system is out of whack."

Reluctantly, Payne agreed.

"Why don't you fill me in on everything, and we can come up with some kind of solution."

Payne nodded. "I walked Ariane to her door last night. She had a headache and said she needed to get some sleep. We made plans for this morning, then I went home."

"You didn't stay the night?"

"If I had, do you think I'd be out here?" he snapped.

"Sorry, I just—"

"No," Payne apologized. "I'm the one who should be sorry. I didn't mean to yell at you. It's just, I don't know. . . ." He paused for a minute, trying to gather his thoughts. "I would've stayed the night, but she had a headache and thought it would be best if she got some rest."

"So, you didn't have a fight or anything?"

Payne shook his head. "I was supposed to pick her up at seven thirty. We were going to grab a light breakfast, then head straight for the golf course. She told me that she'd made an eight thirty tee time."

"Fine. Now walk me through this morning."

"I woke up early and showed up on time. I tried buzzing the intercom, but there was no reply. Next I checked the lot, and her car is here." Payne pointed toward it. "I went back to the front door, and that's when I noticed the duct tape."

"What duct tape?" The two of them walked to the entry-way, and Jones studied the way the tape had been placed over the lock. "Well, if something has happened to her—and I'm not saying that it has—I doubt we're dealing with professionals."

"Why do you say that?"

"Look at the placement of the tape. Instead of running the strip over the lock in a vertical fashion, they placed it horizontally, allowing us to see it."

"And in your opinion, is this lack of professionalism good or bad news?"

Jones shrugged. "To be honest with you, it could be either. If something has happened to Ariane—and it's still a big *if* in my mind—then there's a good chance that other mistakes have been made as well. And that'll increase our opportunity to find her."

"That sounds good to me. So, what's the bad news?"

"If this isn't a professional job, there's a better chance that someone will panic, and if that happens . . ." Jones didn't have the heart to finish the sentence.

"Understood," Payne grunted. "Let me show you up-stairs."

The two men jogged to the second floor. Jones shook his

head when he saw the stick used as a door prop. "Definitely not professionals," he muttered as they walked toward Ariane's front door. "You tried calling her, right? Maybe she's just sleeping and can't hear the door from her bedroom."

"Trust me, she's not in her bedroom."

"How can you be so sure?"

"I went *into* her bedroom."

"You had your key with you?"

Payne shook his head. "Not exactly."

Jones noticed the splintered door frame before he reached Ariane's apartment. The door hung there, slightly tilted, like it had been battered by a tropical storm.

"Let me guess," Jones quipped. "Hurricane Payne."

"She wouldn't answer the door."

Jones shrugged as he walked inside. "Seems like a reasonable response."

"Listen," Payne said, "I realize everything I've showed you is marginal at best. But this is the thing that really got me going." He pointed to the tape that covered Ariane's peephole. It was the same type of tape that covered the lock on the front door. "There's nothing innocent about this. And I guarantee that this tape wasn't here last night. No way in hell."

Jones grimaced. It did seem suspicious. But he didn't touch it, just in case there were fingerprints on it. "What kind of security system does her apartment have? Didn't you pay to have it upgraded?"

"Yeah, they installed alarms on all the windows and the two doors. I also had a camera mounted inside the peephole, but they must've known about that."

"Not necessarily. Just because they put tape on the door doesn't guarantee that they knew about the camera. They could've been trying to prevent her from seeing into the corridor. Shoot, for all we know, maybe her neighbor across the hall was doing something illegal, and he wanted to guarantee his privacy."

"But how does that explain the fact that she's missing?"

"I have no idea," Jones admitted. "But I'm trying to keep

as many options open as possible. Have you tried talking to her neighbors? Maybe they saw something."

"I was reluctant to bug them so early, but now that it's after eight o'clock and you're beginning to see my point of view, I'm willing to try anything."

Jones nodded his approval. "Why don't you handle this floor while I head downstairs?"

"Fine. But if you find anything, please let me know immediately."

"Will do," he assured Payne. "And Jon? Keep the faith. We'll find her."

CHAPTER 9

KNOCKING on each door, Payne started with Ariane's neighbor across the hall and slowly made his way down the corridor. Everyone that he talked to was friendly and immediately knew who Ariane was—females of her beauty tended to stand out. Unfortunately, no one saw or heard anything out of the ordinary. And no one could account for the duct tape over the front lock.

After speaking to the last of her neighbors on the second floor, Payne heard Jones running up the stairs in an obvious state of excitement.

"I think I've got a witness," Jones exclaimed. "He's waiting downstairs in the hall." Within seconds, the two men were standing in front of the open door of apartment 101. "Mr. McNally, this is Jonathon Payne, Ariane's boyfriend. Jon, this is Mr. McNally."

Payne shook the hand of the elderly man while trying to observe as much as he could. McNally appeared to be in his mid-eighties, walked with the aid of a metal cane, and closely resembled Yoda from *Star Wars*—minus the green color. His apartment was cluttered with heirlooms and antiques, yet for some reason a framed *Baywatch* poster of

Pamela Anderson hung near the entrance to his kitchen. "Mr. McNally, D.J. tells me that you might've seen something that could help me find Ariane?"

"Who the hell is D.J.?" the old man snapped. "I didn't talk to any bastard named D.J."

Jones looked at Payne and grimaced. "Sir? Remember me? I talked to you about two minutes ago. My name's David Jones, but my friends call me D.J."

"What the hell kind of person has friends that refuse to use his real name? You kids today. I just don't understand your damn generation."

"Sir, I don't mind. D.J. is just a nickname."

"A nickname?" he shrieked. "You think that's a nickname? Horseshit! It's just two capital letters. Why don't you just use B.S. as your nickname instead? Because that's what your nickname is: bullshit! When I was growing up, people used to have nicknames that said something about them, like Slim or Cocksucker, not pansy names like D.J."

"Sir," Payne interrupted, "I don't mean to be rude, but I was wondering what you saw this morning. David said you saw something that could help me find my girlfriend."

"Your girlfriend? Who's your girlfriend?"

Payne rolled his eyes in frustration. This was getting nowhere. "Ariane Walker. She lives upstairs in apartment 210."

McNally pondered the information for a few seconds before his face lit up. "Oh! You mean the brunette with the dark eyes and the nice cha-chas? Yeah, I saw her bright and early, about an hour ago. She was wearing a red top and a short skirt. It was so small I could almost see her panties." The elderly man cackled in delight as he pondered his memory of the beautiful girl. "That gal's a real looker."

Payne couldn't agree with him more. She was the prettiest woman he had ever seen. The first and only person who had literally left him speechless, which was unfortunate since he was in the middle of a speech at the time.

A few years back, Payne had volunteered to speak to a group of convicted drunk drivers about the tragic death of his parents. The goal of the program was to make recent offenders listen to the horrors of the crime in order to make them think twice about ever drinking and driving again. Payne was in the middle of reliving his nightmare—describing the devastation he felt when he was pulled from his eighth-grade algebra class and told about the death of his parents—when his eyes focused on Ariane's. She was standing off to the side, watching and listening with complete empathy. In a heartbeat, he could tell that she'd been through the same horror, that she'd lost a loved one in a similar nightmare. It didn't matter if it was a brother, sister, or lover. He knew that she *understood*.

Payne managed to finish his heart-wrenching tale without incident, but when he started his conclusion, he found himself unable to take his eyes off of her. He knew he was there to make a point, but suddenly he was unable to focus. There was just some quality about her, something pure and perfect that made him feel completely at ease. In his mind, something good had finally come from their loss. His parents' accident and her parents' accident had brought them together.

And the realization stole his ability to speak.

"Jon?" D.J. whispered. "Do you have some questions for Mr. McNally, or do you want me to ask him?"

Payne blinked a few times, which brought him back to the moment at hand. Turning toward the elderly man, he said, "Where did you see Ariane?"

"In my bedroom," McNally muttered.

Payne and Jones exchanged confused glances, trying to figure out what the man meant. "Ariane was in your bedroom?"

The man cackled again. "If she was in my bedroom, do you think I'd be out here talking to you bozos? Hell, no! I'd be popping Viagra like it was candy corn."

"Then why did you mention your bedroom?" Jones asked.

McNally inhaled before replying. "Do I have to spell everything out for you whippersnappers? I was in my bedroom when I saw her outside my window with a bunch of fellows. And let me tell you . . ." He tapped Payne on his chest. "You need to get your woman on a leash because she looked pretty darn snookered. They were practically dragging her."

"She was being dragged by a bunch of guys? What did they look like?"

McNally pondered the question for a few seconds, then pointed at Jones.

"They were black?" Payne asked.

"No, you dumb ass, I mean they were butt ugly and had stupid nicknames! Of course I mean they were black."

"Could you tell us anything else? Were they tall? Short? Fat? Anything?"

"They were black. That's it. Everything about them was black. Black clothes, black hoods, black shoes. I don't even know how many there were because they looked like shadows, for God's sake. Shoot, they even drove a black van."

Payne grimaced at the news. "Did you happen to see a license plate on the van?"

"As a matter of fact, I did!" McNally declared. "It was the only thing that wasn't black."

"You saw it? What did it say?"

"I have no damn idea," he answered. "The numbers were just a big ol' blur. But I do know one thing. The plate was from Louisiana."

Skepticism filled Payne's face. "How do you know that?"

"I got me a lady friend that lives down in Cajun country, and every year I visit her for Mardi Gras. When the van first pulled up, I saw the Louisiana plate and thought maybe she was coming here for a little lovin', but obviously, when I, um . . ." The old man furrowed his brow as he tried to remember his train of thought. "What was I talking about again?"

"Actually," Jones lied, "you had just finished. Is there anything else that you can tell us about this morning?"

"I'm kind of constipated. But I ate some prunes, so I'm hoping—"

"That's not what he meant," interrupted Payne. Even though he was sympathetic to McNally's advancing age, he didn't have the time to listen to him ramble about his bowel movements. "David wanted to know if you had anything else to tell us about Ariane?"

McNally pondered the question, then shook his head.

"Well, I'd like to thank you for your information." Jones handed McNally a business card, then helped him back inside his apartment. "If you think of anything else, please don't hesitate to call me."

Once Jones returned to the hall, he said, "I have to admit things are looking worse for Ariane, but I don't think we can go to the cops quite yet."

"Why not? You heard what he said. A group of guys dragged her to their van early this morning, and no one's heard from her since."

"True, but Mr. McNally is not exactly what you would call an ideal witness. Don't get me wrong, I don't think he's lying or anything, but you have to admit he lost touch with reality a couple of times during our conversation."

"Shit!" Payne thought they had enough information to go on, but Jones knew a lot more about police procedures than he did. "So what do you recommend?"

"Honestly, I think we should go upstairs and snoop around Ariane's apartment a little more. Plus we can see if the peephole video camera recorded anything before they covered the lens."

CHAPTER 10

INSIDE the plantation house, Theo Webster stared at his computer screen as he scrolled through page after page of painstaking research. After removing his wire-rimmed glasses, Webster rubbed his tired eyes and stretched his skinny 5'8" frame. The track lighting above him reflected off the ebony skin that covered his ever-growing forehead and highlighted the dark bags that had recently surfaced under his drooping eyelids.

After cracking his neck, Webster settled back into his seat and resumed his research, studying the in-depth genealogy of the island's most recent arrivals. As he scrutinized Mike Cussler's family, Webster heard a creak in a floorboard behind him.

"Shit," he muttered as he reached inside his oaken desk.

Without looking Webster fumbled through various items until his hand made contact with his gun. Slipping his fingers around the polymer handle, Webster slowly pulled the .38 Special from his desk while staring at his computer screen.

The floorboard whined again, but this time the sound was several feet closer.

It was time to make his move.

In a sudden burst, Webster dropped to the hardwood floor and spun toward his unsuspecting target. The move stunned the trespasser so much that he dropped the cup of coffee he was carrying and shrieked like a wounded girl.

The pathetic wail brought a smile to Webster's face. "Gump, what the hell are you doing sneaking up on me? Don't you know we have nearly two dozen prisoners on this island that would like to see me dead? You got to use your head, boy! God gave you a brain for a reason."

Bennie Blount lowered his head in shame, and as he did, his elaborate dreadlocks cascaded over his dark eyes, making him look like a Rastafarian sheepdog. "I sorry 'bout that. I was just trying to bring you something to wakes you up."

Webster glanced at the brown puddle that covered the floor and grimaced. "Unless you have a straw, I think it's going to be tough for me to drink."

The 6'6" servant stared at the steaming beverage for several seconds before his face broke into a gold-toothed smile. "For a minute, I thought you be serious, but then I says to myself, Master Webster ain't no dog. He ain't gonna drink his drink from no floor, even with a straw!"

"Well, that's awfully clever of you, but before I congratulate you too much, why don't you run into the other room and get a mop?"

"That's a mighty good idea, sir. I guess I shoulda thought of it since it's my job to clean and all." Blount slowly backed away from the spill as he continued to speak. "Don't ya worry now."

Blount had been hired by the Plantation for his strong work ethic and knowledge of the local swamps. Nicknamed Gump for his intellectual similarities to Forrest Gump, the dim-witted character from the movie bearing his name, Blount lived in the guest wing of the white-pillared mansion. During the course of the day, he spent most of his time cooking and cleaning, but twice a week he was allowed to journey to the mainland for food and supplies.

When Blount returned to Webster's office, he was disappointed to see his boss working again. He liked talking to his superiors whenever he could, even though they often got upset when he interrupted their top-secret duties.

"Gump," Webster asked without turning around, "what are we having for breakfast?"

The question brought a smile to his lips, and his gold teeth glistened in the sunlight. "Well, I figure since this be a big week for y'all, I should fix a big Southern meal likes my momma used to make. I makes eggs 'n' bacon 'n' ham 'n' grits 'n' biscuits 'n' fresh apple butter, too. Ooooooooweeeeee! I think my mouth is gonna water all day!"

Webster nodded his head in appreciation, at least until Blount's statement sank in. He turned from his computer and faced the dark-skinned servant. "What exactly did you mean when you said this was a big week for us? What do you know about this week?"

With the soiled mop in his hand, he shrugged. "Not much, sir, but I can tell somethin's up. There an excitement in the air that's easier to smell than the magnolias in May. I figured maybe it's your birthday. Or maybe it's 'cause the Fourth of July is coming!"

Webster studied Blount as he spoke, and it appeared that he was telling the truth. "I think it's just the holiday that has everybody excited," he lied. "I know I'm looking forward to it."

"Well, I be, too! In fact, I was wondering if I can go to the city for the fireworks show on Saturday night. I don't know why they on the third, but they is!"

"Let me ask the other guys at breakfast, then I'll let you know. But as far as I'm concerned, that's fine with me."

"Thank ya, Master Webster! Thank ya! That'd be nice of ya!" Blount picked up his bucket and backed toward the open door. "Oh! Speaking of breakfast, I almost forgets to tell ya that it's ready to eat."

CHAPTER 11

ARIANE'S place appeared to be in order, with the exception of her splintered door. An off-white sofa sat against the wall to the left and faced a tasteful entertainment center that held a television, stereo, and DVD player. A leather chair rested in the corner of the room under a halogen lamp.

Jones walked to the security panel near the front door and pushed the button for a system check. Within seconds, the unit beeped and a digitized voice filled the room. "The crime alert system is operational. Current status is deactivated. Push one to activate the system."

"The unit is working, which means she probably turned it off to answer the door. Either that or she forgot to turn it on last night."

Payne shook his head. "When I walked her to the door last night, I made sure she got in and turned the system on before I left. In fact, I always wait until the damn thing beeps."

"Then she turned it off for some reason. And my guess is to open the door."

Payne swallowed deeply while opening the tiny black box that was mounted to the inside of Ariane's front door.

He removed the recordable DVD from the peephole surveillance system and carried it to the player. "I don't know if we'll see anything, but it's worth a look."

After slipping the disc inside, he hit play and waited for it to begin.

"How does this thing work?" Jones asked.

"It's activated by movement in the hallway. That way it doesn't record hour after hour of nothing." Payne pointed to the black screen to show Jones what he meant. "Since the opening is blocked, the camera interpreted that as someone standing directly in front of the door." Payne glanced at his watch, then looked at the electronic counter on the DVD player. "What time did Mr. McNally say he saw Ariane?"

"He said it was about an hour before we talked to him."

"Well, I got here about seven thirty, and there was no black van in the parking lot, so I'd guess we're talking about seven or seven fifteen, right?"

Payne skipped back several minutes until his own face filled the screen.

"When was that filmed?" Jones asked.

Payne studied the image and recognized the clothes he'd worn the previous evening. "That was from last night, but I'm not sure if it was before or after my date with Ariane." The faint beeping of the security system could be heard through the TV's speaker as Payne's image turned and walked away from the door. "See, I told you she set the damn system last night. I told you!"

Jones started to defend himself when a figure flashed across the screen. "Whoa! What was that?"

"I don't know," Payne said as he hit the pause button, then frame advance.

The picture crept by at a sluggish pace. After several seconds of nonaction, a gloved hand emerged from the right side of the screen. Moving an inch at a time, the arm eventually reached the lens of the peephole, and once it did, the picture immediately went black.

"Damn!" Payne cursed. "Not a goddamned thing!"

"Be patient." Jones grabbed the remote from Payne and

slowly rewound the image to the moment before the tape was applied to the door. "Just because we didn't see a face doesn't mean it's a total loss. There's more here than you think."

"Like what?"

"What color was the man who put the tape on the door?"

Payne stared at the screen. "I can't tell. He's wearing black gloves and long black sleeves."

"True," Jones muttered as he placed his finger on the image. "But look closer. There's a gap where the glove ends here, and the sleeve begins there."

Payne moved closer to the screen and stared. "I'll be damned! You're right. I can see the edge of each garment."

"You thought they overlapped because of his skin. Whoever put the tape on the door is black. Not coffee and cream like me, but pure black. I'm talking *hold the milk, hold the sugar, hold the freakin' water* black."

"Hey," Payne interrupted. "What's that on his arm?"

"Where?"

"Right between the glove and sleeve. Is that a tattoo?"

Jones crouched in front of the TV and considered the question. Unfortunately, the image was too dark to see things conclusively. "Hang on a sec. Let me change the brightness on the TV. It might help."

Payne stared at the screen as it brightened. "It might be a tattoo, but I honestly don't know."

"Don't worry. I know a way we can find out. I have a computer program at my office that lets me blow up video images, alter color schemes, manipulate contrast, and so on. I'll take the disc over there and see if I can learn anything else."

"Sounds good to me." Payne reached for the eject button, but before he pressed it, Jones grabbed his arm.

"Listen," he said in a sympathetic voice, "I wasn't going to mention this, but I have to be upfront with you. There's still one thing we need to check. I was going to wait until later, but I feel you deserve to be with me when it's done."

"What are you talking about? What do you need to check?"

Jones placed his hand on Payne's broad shoulder and squeezed. "The peephole camera records image and sound, right? I mean, we heard the alarm system beeping, didn't we?"

"Yeah, so?"

Jones swallowed hard. "The video of what happened this morning is obviously unwatchable because of the duct tape, but there's a good chance that we might be able to hear this morning's events after the peephole was blocked."

"Oh, God, you're right! Put it on!"

"Jon, keep in mind if something did happen to Ariane, it might be painful to—"

"Put it on! I've got to know what happened."

Jones nodded, then hit the appropriate button on the remote. After several seconds of silence, the faint sound of a doorbell could be heard from the blank TV screen. It was followed by a loud, rhythmic knock.

"You're early," Ariane complained. "I'm still getting ready."

A brief silence followed her comment before a faint giggle emerged from the speaker.

"First you're early, now you're covering the peephole!"

Beeps from the security system chimed in the tape's background.

"I'll tell you what, Jonathon, I'm going to kick your butt all over the golf course. There's no doubt about that!"

Her comment was followed by the click of a deadbolt, the twist of the door handle, and—

Jones pushed the pause button and glanced at Payne, whose face was completely ashen. "Are you sure you want to hear this?"

"Yeah," Payne muttered, his voice trembling with emotion. He didn't really want to, but if he was going to help Ariane, he knew he had no choice. "Play the disc."

"Are you sure?"

Payne shook his head from side to side. "But play it anyways."

With the touch of a button, Ariane screamed like a banshee, sending chills through Payne and Jones. As her wail echoed through the room, it was quickly replaced by heavy footsteps, muffled squeals, and then the most frightening sound of all.

Silence.

CHAPTER 12

WHILE Holmes, Jackson, and Webster had breakfast in the mansion, Hakeem Ndjai, an unmerciful man who'd been hired as the Plantation overseer, took control of the captives.

Even though he was a valuable part of the Plantation team, his foreign heritage excluded him from the decision-making hierarchy. He had been handpicked by Holmes, who had heard several stories of Ndjai's unwavering toughness in Nkambé, Cameroon, where Ndjai had been an overseer on a cacao plantation. Like most workers from his country, he had labored in unbearable conditions for virtually nothing—his average income was only $150 per year—so when Holmes offered him a job in America, Ndjai wept for joy for the first time in his life.

But that was several months ago, and Ndjai was back to his old ways.

In a cold growl, Ndjai reinforced the instructions that Jackson and Holmes had given during their cross-burning party, but he did it with his own special touch. "I am the overseer of this Plantation, and out of respect for my job, you shall refer to me as *sir*. Do I make myself clear?"

"Yes, sir!" the naked group shouted.

"Each of you has been brought here for a reason, and that reason will eventually be revealed. Until that time, you will become a part of the Plantation's working staff, performing the duties that will be assigned to you." Ndjai signaled one of the guards, who ran forward, carrying a silver belt that shone in the sun. "While you are working, you will be positioned on various parts of our land, and at some point, you might be tempted to run for freedom."

He smiled under his dark cloak. "It is something I do not recommend."

Ndjai grabbed the metal belt and wrapped it around a cement slab that rested near the bloodstained chopping block. After clicking the belt in place, he handed the cement to a nearby guard, who immediately carried it fifty yards from the crowd.

"When you are given your uniforms, you will have one of these belts locked to your ankle. It cannot be removed by anyone but me, and I will not remove it for any reason during your stay on this island." He reached into the pocket of his robe and pulled out a tiny remote control. He held the gadget in the air so everyone could see it. "This is what you Americans call a deterrent."

With a push of a button, the cement block erupted into a shower of rubble, sending shards of rock in every direction and smoke high into the air.

"Did I get your attention?" he asked. "Now imagine what would have happened if your personal anklet were to be detonated. I doubt much of you would be found."

A couple of the guards snickered, but Ndjai silenced them with a sharp stare. He would not tolerate disrespect from anybody.

"I know some of you will try to figure out how your anklets work, and some of you will try to disarm them. Well, I will tell you now: Your efforts will fail! We have buried a small number of transmitters throughout the Plantation. If at any time your anklet crosses the perimeter, your personal bomb will explode, killing you instantly. Is that clear?"

"Yes, sir."

"Oh, one more thing. If your device is detonated, it will send a signal to the anklets that are being worn by several other prisoners, and they will be killed as well. Do you understand?"

They certainly did, and the mere thought of it made them shudder.

CHAPTER 13

JONES returned to his scenic office and locked himself in his massive technology lab. The room cost a staggering amount of money and was filled with high-tech equipment that many police departments would love to have. The most important piece of hardware was the computer, but it was the instrument that cost Jones the least. Built by Payne Industries, the computer was a scaled-down version of the system used at FBI headquarters in Langley, Virginia, and had been given to Jones as an office-warming gift.

Placing the surveillance disc into the unit, Jones quickly broke the footage into manageable data files. He was then able to select a precise frame from the video and put it on his screen in microscopic clarity.

"What should I look at first?" he mumbled to himself.

Then it dawned on him. He wanted to examine the assailant's right wrist to see if the black mark was, in fact, a tattoo.

Jones scrolled through a number of frames until he found the scene that fit his specific needs. The suspect's arm was centered perfectly on the monitor, and the gap between the glove and the sleeve was at its widest. Then he zoomed in and sharpened the image.

A few seconds later, Jones smiled in triumph when an elaborate tattoo came into view. The three-inch design was in the shape of the letter *P*, and it started directly below the palm of the suspect's hand. The straight edge of the symbol was in the form of an intricately detailed sword, the blade's handle rising high above the letter's curve. At the base of the drawing, small drops of blood fell from the weapon's tip, leaving the impression that it had just been pulled from the flesh of a fallen victim. Finally, dangling from each side of the sword was a series of broken chains, which appeared to be severed near the left and right edge.

As Jones printed several copies of the image, his speakerphone buzzed, followed by the voice of his secretary. "Mr. Payne is on line one."

With a touch of a button, Jones answered his call. "Jon, any news?"

"I was about to ask you the same thing. I went to the police like you suggested and filled out the appropriate paperwork. It turns out that I knew a few of the officers on duty. They assured me that Ariane would get top priority."

"Even though she's only been gone a few hours?"

"Her scream on the surveillance tape and Mr. McNally's testimony have a lot to do with it. Normally, they'd wait a lot longer before they pursued a missing person, but as I said, the evidence suggests foul play."

"Did they give you any advice?"

"I wouldn't call it *advice*. I think a warning would be more accurate. These cops know me, so they automatically assumed that I would do something stupid to get in their way. Why would they think that?"

Jones smiled. The cops had pegged him perfectly. Payne was definitely the intrusive type. "Instead of giving you the obvious answer, let me tell you what I discovered." He described the image in detail, then filled him in on a theory. "I think we're looking for a Holotat."

"A Holo-what?"

"Holotat."

Payne scrunched his face. "What the hell is that?"

"Back in World War Two, German guards used to tattoo their prisoners with numbers on their wrists in order to keep track of them. After the war, the people who survived these camps had a constant reminder of the Holocaust, marks that eventually became a source of inspiration."

"What does that have to do with Ariane?"

"About five years ago, members of Los Diablos, a Hispanic gang from East L.A., decided it would be cool if they tattooed their brothers in a similar fashion, marking them on their wrists. Before then, gangs used to get their tattoos on their arms, chests, or back, but suddenly this trend caught on. Holocaust tattoos, known as Holotats, started popping up everywhere."

"And you think the *P* tattoo is a Holotat gang emblem?"

Jones nodded his head. "That's what it looks like to me. Of course, I could be wrong. It could be a jailhouse tat or the initial of his girlfriend, but my guess would be a Holotat."

Payne considered the information, and a question sprang to mind. "You said it might be his girlfriend's initial. Does that mean we're sure it's a guy?"

"That would be my guess. The thickness of the wrist suggests a masculine suspect, but to be on the safe side, I wouldn't completely rule out a female. Of course, she'd have to be a Sasquatch-looking bitch."

Payne laughed for the first time in a long time. He felt better knowing that Jones was helping him through this. "So, what now?"

"Why don't you come down here? I have a few more tests I want to run on the video. But I want you to look at the tattoo to see if you notice anything that I didn't."

"Sounds good to me. I'll be there in a few minutes."

IT took Payne nearly an hour to reach Mount Washington, and the drive was a miserable one. Holiday traffic was starting to pick up even though it was only midday. Payne used his master key to enter Jones's technology lab and found his friend hard at work on the computer.

"Any new developments?" Payne asked as he picked up a printout of the tattoo and studied it.

"There wasn't much visual data to work with on the disc, so I focused on the audio. I know it's hard to believe, but sound can tell you so much."

"You mean like her scream?"

"No, I mean like background noise. You know, stuff that's there, but isn't really obvious."

"Such as?"

Jones walked to the far side of the room and tapped his hand on a small metallic unit. "I call this device the Listener, and for the last half hour, it's been our best friend."

Payne crossed the room for a closer look and watched as Jones typed a specific code into the unit's keypad. The Listener responded by extending its front tray six inches forward.

"This unit was designed to analyze sound and place it into specific categories. Since we were dealing with a stable environment with little background noise I had the machine focus on a couple of things. The first was her voice. I wanted to see if I could understand what she tried to say after her initial scream."

"You mean when her voice got garbled."

"Yeah. My guess is they were probably gagging her at the time, but I was hoping the machine might be able to isolate the sound and clean it up for us."

"Did it work?"

"Actually, it worked beautifully. Unfortunately, it won't help our cause very much."

"Why not? What did she say?"

Jones picked up the transcript and read it aloud. "She said, 'Help me. Somebody help me.'"

Payne closed his eyes as Ariane's words sank in. He had managed to stay relaxed while Jones explained the features of his computer equipment, but now that the focus of the conversation was back on Ariane, Payne felt the nausea return. What would he do if he couldn't track her down? Or worse yet, if someone had already killed her?

"Jon?" Jones said. "Are you okay? I asked you a question."

Payne opened his eyes and turned to his friend. "Sorry. What was that?"

"I wanted to know if you told the cops how many people were involved."

He thought for a moment, then shook his head. "I told them that Mr. McNally saw more than one person, but wasn't sure how many."

"Well, thanks to the Listener, I'd say that there were probably three of them."

Payne sat up in his chair. "How did you figure that out?"

"Simple. I programmed the device to filter out everything but the footsteps, and after listening to the disc, I could hear three distinct sets. But, as they were leaving, I could only hear two."

"You mean someone stayed inside Ariane's apartment?"

Jones shook his head. "At first, that's what I thought, too, but as I listened to the disc again, I noticed a scratching noise in the background. I filtered out all the other sounds, isolating the scratch, and this is what I got." He pushed his mouse button once, and a rough grating sound emerged from his system's speakers. "What does that sound like to you?"

"Feet dragging on a carpet?"

"Bingo!" Jones was impressed that his friend had figured it out so quickly. It had taken him several minutes to come up with a hypothesis. "Remember what McNally said? It looked like your girlfriend was snookered because they were practically carrying her to the van? Well, my guess is she was drugged or knocked out. The three sets of footsteps that the Listener originally detected were Ariane and the two assailants. They broke into her place, gagged her, drugged her, then dragged her out. That's the only thing that fits."

"But I thought you said there were three guys involved. Where was the third guy while the abduction was going on?" Before Jones had a chance to answer, the solution popped into Payne's head. "Oh, shit! They probably needed a driver to stay outside in the van."

Jones nodded. "That's what most criminals would do."

CHAPTER 14

PAYNE and Jones gathered all of the information they'd accumulated and took it directly to the police. When they entered the local precinct, Payne headed for Captain Tomlin's office. He had met Tomlin a year earlier at a charity golf event that Payne Industries had sponsored, and they had stayed in touch since.

"Do you have a minute?" Payne asked as he tapped on Tomlin's glass door. The captain, who had curly hair and thick arms, waved him in. "Have you ever met David Jones?"

Tomlin introduced himself, shaking Jones's hand with a powerful grip. "Jon has told me all about you. I almost feel like we've met. I understand that you served under him in special ops."

"Yeah," Jones answered as he took a seat next to Payne. "We relied on each other so much we ended up attached in the real world."

"That happens all the time. There's something about life in the military that draws soldiers together—a kindred spirit that bonds all warriors."

Payne winced at the suggestion. "I don't know about that crap. I think D.J. stuck with me so I could get him a job."

Jones nodded. "To be honest, he's right. I actually can't stand the bastard."

Tomlin laughed loudly. "So, I take it from your comedy that Ariane's all right? Where was that gal hiding?"

The comment drained the humor from the room.

"Don't let our joking fool you," Jones declared. "It's just our way of dealing with things. The truth is we're still looking for her."

Payne held up his cell phone, showing it to Tomlin. "I'm having all of my calls forwarded. If she tries to contact any one of my lines, it'll ring here."

"Good, then you won't have to sit at home, killing time."

Payne took a deep breath and nodded. To him, waiting was the hardest part. "How are things on your end? Did you have a chance to send any officers to her apartment?"

"I sent a small crew over. Unfortunately, we didn't notice anything new. You guys must've done a pretty thorough job this morning."

"We did," Payne said. "I hope we didn't step on any toes by entering the scene."

"Heavens no. I would've done the same thing if a loved one of mine was involved in something like this. Of course, my answer as a police officer would've been different if I didn't know you. But you're professionals, so I trust your judgment when it comes to a crime scene."

Jones stood from his chair and handed the captain all of the information he had acquired from Ariane's DVD. "We did get some data on one of the suspects that entered the apartment. He had an elaborate tattoo on his right wrist. Looks like a Holotat to me."

Tomlin pulled a close-up of the tattoo from the large stack of papers and studied it. "It could be, but very few gangs in Allegheny County use them. They're a lot more common on the West Coast and down south."

"That makes sense," Payne said, "since this person's probably from Louisiana."

Tomlin furrowed his brow. "I'm not so sure of that. If I were a criminal, I wouldn't use my own van as a getaway vehicle. And if I did, you can bet I wouldn't use my own license plate. I'd bet there's a good chance we're going to get a report of a stolen plate or an abandoned black van somewhere in the area. And when we do, we can go from there."

That wasn't what Payne wanted to hear. He was hoping the captain supported his theory on the van's origin. When he didn't, he felt an unexpected burst of betrayal. "What are you saying, that these clues are a waste of time?"

"No, I'm not saying that at all. Every little bit helps. However, I'm not going to blow smoke. I respect you way too much for that."

"Good! Then tell me where we stand. I need to know."

Tomlin leaned back in his chair and searched for the appropriate words. "In a standard kidnapping, there's little we can actually do until we get some kind of ransom demand. Sure, we'll continue to search for evidence and witnesses, but without some kind of break, the odds of us finding her *before* they call are pretty slim."

Jones glanced at his friend and waited to see if he was going to speak, but it was obvious he was done talking for the moment. "Captain? In your opinion, do you think this abduction was done for money?"

Tomlin didn't want Payne to feel responsible for the kidnapping, but there was no denying the obvious. "To be honest, that would be my guess. Payne Industries is a well-known company, and Jon is recognized as one of the wealthiest men in the city. Since Ariane doesn't have a history with drugs or any other criminal activities, I can think of no other reason for her abduction."

"Thank you for your honesty," Payne said. Then, to the surprise of Jones and Tomlin, he stood up and headed for the door. "If you find anything at all, please let me know."

"I promise," Tomlin called out. "The same goes for you. Call me day or night."

* * *

WHEN they reached the parking lot, Jones questioned Payne. "Jon, what's going on? First you snapped at the man, then you bolted from his office without even saying goodbye. What's going on in that head of yours?"

Payne shrugged. "I'm not really sure. But I'll tell you one thing. I'm not going to sit at home, waiting for some ransom demand."

"I kind of assumed that. You aren't exactly the sit-on-your-ass type."

Payne nodded as he pondered what to do next. Even though he valued Captain Tomlin's advice, there was something about his opinion that bothered him. He couldn't place his finger on why, but he knew he didn't agree with Tomlin's assessment of the black van.

While thinking things through, Payne pulled from the crowded police lot and turned onto a busy side street. He maneuvered his vehicle in and out of traffic until he got to McKnight Road, one of the busiest business districts in the area. As he stopped at a red light, Payne reached across Jones's lap and pulled a small book out of the Infiniti's glove compartment.

"What's that?" Jones asked.

"It's my address book. I'm checking to see if I know anyone from Louisiana. I figure maybe a local would know something about the Holotat. You don't know anyone down there, do you?"

"Sorry. My roots are up north, just like yours. Why, do you have someone in mind?"

"No, but—" The light turned green, and as it did, the word *green* clicked in Payne's mind. "I'll be damned! I just thought of someone from New Orleans."

"Who?"

"Did I ever introduce you to Levon Greene?"

Jones's eyes lit up with excitement. Levon Greene was an All-Pro linebacker for the Buffalo Bills before a devastating knee injury knocked him from the NFL. Before getting chop-blocked by Nate Barker, a guard with the San Diego

Chargers, Greene was a fan favorite. He was known throughout the country for his tenacity and his colorful nickname, taken from a famous Bob Marley song. "The Buffalo Soldier? You know the Buffalo Soldier?"

Payne nodded. "He lived in Pittsburgh for a year after the Bills cut him. The Steelers signed him and kept him on their injured list for over a season. Our paths crossed on more than one occasion on the b-ball courts. He liked to play hoops for therapy."

"But that doesn't mean you *know* him. I see Steelers and Pirates all of the time, but that doesn't mean they're my boys."

"True, but I know Levon." He handed Jones the address book and told him to look for a phone number. Jones quickly flipped to the *G*s and was stunned when he saw Greene listed.

"Holy shit! You do know him."

"I told you I knew him. What's Levon's home number?"

Jones glanced at the page for the requested information. "You don't have a home number. You only have a cell listed."

"Yeah, that makes sense. When he gave me his info, he was just getting ready to move back to New Orleans and didn't know his new number."

"He was moving to Louisiana, and he gave you his number? What, were you guys dating or something?"

Payne laughed. "Jealous?"

Jones shook his head and grinned. He'd always been amazed at Payne's ability to keep his sense of humor in the most tragic times. Sure, his buddy would have the occasional flare-up and reveal his true emotions during a crisis, but on the whole Payne was able to conceal his most personal feelings under a facade of levity.

Originally, when the two first met, Jones had interpreted Payne's frivolity as a lack of seriousness, and he actually resented him for it. After a while, though, he learned that Payne's sense of humor was simply his way of dealing with things. He realized that Payne never mocked the tragedy of a situation. Instead, he tried to use humor as a way of coping with the fear and adrenaline that would otherwise overwhelm him. It was a good trick, and eventually Jones and several other MANIACs learned to do the same thing.

"Seriously, what's the deal with you two? Have you known him long?"

"I met him in North Park playing basketball. We were on the same team, and the two of us just clicked on the court. He was rehabbing his knee, so he couldn't move like he used to on the football field. But he was strong as an ox. He set some of the most vicious screens I have ever seen in my life, and most of the time he did it to get me open jumpers."

Jones laughed at the description of Greene. "It sounds like Levon plays hoops with the same intensity he showed in the NFL."

"Hell, yeah! Even though we were in the park, he had a serious game face on. In fact, some people were afraid to play against the guy."

"I bet, but that still doesn't explain why he gave you his number."

"We ended up making it a daily thing. We'd meet at the courts at the same time every day, and we'd take on all comers. Kicked some serious ass, too. Unfortunately, right before Steelers camp started, he failed his physical and was released from the team. But he told me if I was ever in New Orleans I should give him a call."

"Wow, I'm kind of surprised. I thought I knew most of your friends, and now I find out you've been keeping a celebrity from me. So, are there any movie star chums that I should know about?"

"Did I ever tell you about my three-way with the Olsen twins?"

Jones laughed at the comment. "What are you going to do about Levon?"

"It's not what I'm going to do. It's what you're going to do." Payne handed him his cell phone. "I want you to dial his number for me."

"You want me to call Levon Greene? This is so cool!" Jones dialed the phone, then looked at Payne when it started to ring. "What should I say to him?"

Payne snatched the phone from Jones's grasp. "Not a damn thing. He's my friend, not yours."

"You are such a tease!"

Payne was still laughing when Greene answered the phone. "Who's this?"

"Levon, I don't know if you'll remember me. My name is Jonathon Payne. I used to run ball with you at North Park when you were living up in Pittsburgh."

"White dude, nice jump shot?"

"Yeah, that's me."

"Yo, man, wazzup? I haven't heard from your ass in a long time. How ya doin'?"

"I'm fine, and you? How's the knee?"

Greene winced. It was one topic that he didn't like dwelling on. "Still not a hundred percent, but it's better than it used to be. I'm still hoping some team needs a run-stuffing linebacker and gives me a look in camp. But I don't know. It's getting kind of late."

"Well, they'd be crazy not to take you, Levon. You're as fierce as they come."

"Thanks, man. I appreciate it. So, wazzup? Why the call out of the blue? Are you coming to New Orleans? I got a big-ass house. I can hook you up with a room. Won't charge you much, neither," he joked.

Payne wasn't sure what he was hoping to find out from Greene, but he figured the only way to learn anything was to be up-front with the man. "Actually, Levon, the reason I called is an important one. You know how I told you I was doing fine?"

"Yeah?"

"Well, I lied. Something's going on up here, and I was hoping you could give me a hand."

"I don't loan people money, man. You're gonna have to ask someone else."

Payne grinned. If Greene knew how much money Payne actually had, Levon might be asking him for a loan. "No, it's not about cash. Nothing like that. I promise."

"What is it then? What's the deal?"

Payne exhaled, trying not to think about Ariane. "I was hoping to get some information about a gang that might be operating in Louisiana, and I figured since you play a lot of street ball, you might be able to find something out on the courts."

"Is that all you need? Shit! No problem, man. What's the name of the posse?"

"Actually, that's what I was hoping you could tell me."

"All right, but you gotta give me something to go on, 'cause there's a lot of motherfuckin' gangs down here. And every day a new crew pops up."

"Damn," Payne mumbled. He had been naively hoping that New Orleans was a one-gang town. "Do any of the gangs have Holotats? You know, tattooed gang emblems on their wrists?"

"Hell, yeah. A lot of crews do. Just tell me what it looks like, and I'll tell you what I know."

"The letter *P*, with a bloody knife sticking out of it."

Greene thought about the information for a moment, then responded. "Off the top of my head, there's nothing I can think of. But if you give me some time, I can ask around. If anything turns up, I'll let you know immediately."

"That sounds great," Payne replied. "And I'd really appreciate anything you can come up with. It's a matter of life or death."

"Give me an hour, and I'll give you a buzz at this number. I know a couple of brothers that know about this type of shit. Let me get ahold of them, then I'll get ahold of you."

"Levon, thank you! I'll be awaiting your call."

Jones, who'd overheard the entire conversation, questioned Payne the minute he hung up the phone. "So, he's going to hook you up?"

"He's going to try."

"And what if he does? What are you gonna do?"

Payne smiled as he put his hand on Jones's shoulder. "How does Fourth of July in New Orleans sound to you?"

CHAPTER 15

**The Kotto Distribution Center
Ibadan, Nigeria
(56 miles northeast of Lagos)**

MOST aspects of the sprawling complex were recognized as legitimate. Hundreds of Nigerian-born workers came to the center each day to unload massive shipments of cacao, palm oil, peanuts, and rubber that had been brought in from Hannibal Kotto's various businesses. Because of these ventures and the numerous employment opportunities that he offered, Kotto's name was known and respected throughout Africa.

And it was this respect that allowed him to take advantage of the system.

As he sat behind his mahogany desk, Kotto waited for his assistant to give him the go-ahead to start the conference call. When the woman nodded, Kotto knew that everybody was ready.

"Gentlemen," he said into the speakerphone, "I realize that English is not the strongest language for all of you, but since I'm dealing with several clients at once, I feel it is the most appropriate selection." Kotto took a sip of Oyo wine, a local beverage made from the sap of palm trees, then continued. "In order to give everybody a sense of who they'll be bidding against, I'd like each of you to name the country that you're representing. Each of you has been assigned an auction number. When your number is called, please tell the group where you are from."

As Kotto's assistant read the numbers, heavily accented voices emerged from the speakerphone, each announcing his country of origin. Algeria, Angola, Cameroon, Ethiopia, Kenya, Libya, Namibia, and the Democratic Republic of the Congo were all represented.

"If you were listening," Kotto stated, "I am sure each of you realizes that Africa is the only continent that Mr. Drake and I are dealing with. We've had several offers from Asia and South America as well, but we're not ready to deal with their politics. At least, not yet."

"When do you expect to broaden the operation?" asked the Ethiopian delegate.

"That's a decision we haven't made. If all continues to go well, there's the possibility of expansion within the next few months." Kotto took another sip of wine while waiting for further questions. When none came, he changed the course of the discussion. "I realize that some of you were disappointed with the last shipment. Mr. Drake and I discussed the issue, and I apologize for any problems it might've caused. I would like to assure you that you will have no such problems with the next delivery. It is the best quality we've ever prepared."

The Kenyan spoke next. "What will that do to the price? I imagine we will have to pay more for the increase in caliber, will we not?"

Kotto grinned. "I would imagine, like in any business, that an increase in quality will cause an increase in price, but to what extent the price will rise, we'll find out shortly."

JONES settled into the soft leather seats of the Payne Industries jet and closed his eyes for a moment of retrospection. During his military career, he'd been on hundreds of life-threatening missions, but this was the first time he'd ever felt hopeless before a flight. For one reason or another, he knew he was completely unprepared for what he was about to do.

And it was a feeling that he didn't like.

When he was a member of the MANIACs, they were always given advanced reconnaissance before they were dropped into enemy territory. Maps, guides, safe houses, and specific objectives were always provided before they were put into danger. But not today. No, on this mission Jones was willing to ignore every protocol he had ever been taught because his best friend needed his help. He was flying to a city he'd never visited to look for a girl who probably wasn't there, and the only thing they had to go on was a tattoo of the letter *P*.

"This is crazy," he said to himself.

As he opened his eyes, he saw Payne hang up the phone at the front of the cabin and return to his seat, which was across the aisle from Jones.

"Go on. Get it off your chest," Payne said, knowing his friend wasn't happy.

"Are you sure this trip is wise? I mean, don't you think it's a little bit impulsive?"

"Not really. As I told you before, Levon talked to some of his boys in the city, and they assured him that Holotats are used by several of the local gangs."

"Yeah, but that doesn't guarantee that Ariane is going to be down there. For all we know, the gang could have members in cities across America like the Bloods or the Crips. It could be a local thug from the Hill District that we're looking for. Heck, the *P* could stand for *Pittsburgh*."

"True, but that doesn't explain the Louisiana license plate, now does it?"

Jones shook his head. He wasn't really sure how to explain that. "But don't you think that this is jumping the gun? We have no idea what we're getting ourselves into."

Payne smiled. If he didn't know better, he would've assumed that his friend was afraid of flying. "What's troubling you, D.J.? We've been to thousands of places that are more dangerous than New Orleans, and I've never seen you act like this."

"Well, I've never felt like this," Jones admitted. "I don't

know how to explain it, but I can tell we're about to walk into a hornet's nest. And the fact that we weren't allowed to bring any weapons into the airport makes me feel unprotected."

"I figured you'd feel that way. That's why I just gave Levon another call. Since he has a number of contacts on the street, I assumed that he'd have some gun connections."

"Does he?"

"He said he'd see what he could do, but I think that's his way of saying he'll get it done."

A few hours later, the jet landed on an auxiliary runway at Louis Armstrong International Airport in Kenner, Louisiana, which spared Payne and Jones from dealing with the hassle of the main terminal. After grabbing their bags from the plane, they walked to the nearest rent-a-car agency, where they picked up the fastest rental available, a Ford Mustang GT convertible.

The airport was only fifteen miles west of the Crescent City, so the drive to New Orleans was a short one. Following Interstate 10 all the way into Orleans Parish, Payne followed the directions Greene had given him. Before long they were navigating the streets of the central business district.

As Payne and Jones expected, the contrast between the tourist areas and the outlying neighborhoods was disheartening. Hurricane Katrina had ravaged the entire city in August 2005, and since that time most of the governmental funds had been funneled into the city's businesses and infrastructure, not the residential sections or suburbs. In many ways, the reasoning was sound. Tourists were the lifeblood of the region, and the only way to get them to return was to restore the areas that they wanted to visit.

One of those places was the Spanish Plaza, the spot where they would meet Greene.

Donated by Spain in 1976 as a bicentennial gift, the plaza was one of four foreign squares that paid tribute to the roles that France, Italy, England, and Spain played in the history and culture of New Orleans. The focal point of the site was a man-made geyser, encircled by an elaborate cut-stone deck and illuminated by a rainbow of lights that lined the scenic monument.

As Payne and Jones strolled down the plaza's steps, they saw Greene, wearing a pair of white Dockers and an ice blue Tommy Hilfiger shirt, looking even larger than he did during his NFL playing days.

"Levon," Payne called as he neared his friend. "Thanks for meeting me."

Greene, 6'3" and 275 pounds of muscle, stood from the bench where he'd been resting his knee. "No problem, my man." He grabbed Payne's hand and pulled him close, bumping his shoulder while patting him on the back with his free hand. It was a greeting that was quite common in the sports world. "You're looking good. You still playin' ball?"

"Not as much as I used to. But I manage to work out whenever I can. Of course, I still have a long way to go before I'm a badass like you."

Greene smiled and turned his attention to Jones. "By the way, my name's Levon Greene. And you are?"

Jones grabbed Greene's hand and replicated the greeting Greene had given Payne—except Jones did it with much more vigor. He was thrilled to meet one of his biggest sports heroes. "I'm David Jones, a friend of Jon's and a big fan of yours."

"That's always nice to hear, especially since I'm a huge fan of yours as well. I can hardly believe that I'm actually talking to the lead singer of the Monkees!"

Payne couldn't help but laugh. He occasionally teased Jones about his name's similarity to Davy Jones, and it was something that D.J. couldn't stand. However, Payne had a feeling that the remark would produce a much different reaction coming from Greene.

"Oh, I get it!" Jones said as he playfully punched Greene on his arm. "The Monkees! That's pretty damn funny. I bet I used to look a lot whiter on TV, huh?"

Greene laughed, then returned his attention to Payne. "Have you guys eaten yet? There are a number of places in this city where we can get traditional Louisiana food, like jambalaya or gumbo. Or, if you prefer, we can just head over to the French Quarter for a beer and some naked breasts. Trust me, whatever you want, I can deliver. Just name it, and it's yours."

Payne glanced at Jones, then back at Greene. He'd been less than forward with Greene on the phone and decided it was time to give him a few details about their mission. "Levon, I have to tell you something. This isn't going to be a pleasure trip. We're down here for one reason and one reason only: to find out about your local gangs."

Greene grimaced, confused. "Man, what is it about this damn tattoo that brought you guys down here? What could possibly be so important?"

Jones noticed the anguish on Payne's face, so he decided to answer for him. "Early this morning Jon's girlfriend was kidnapped from her apartment building. On the surveillance video, we noticed the tattoo that Jon described on one of the criminals. There was a witness who saw his girlfriend thrown into the back of a van that had Louisiana plates. We're down here to try and find her."

Greene grunted. "Damn, I had no idea. What did the police say?"

"Not much," Jones answered. "They're doing everything they can in Pittsburgh, but until we receive a ransom demand or find some conclusive evidence about the gang, they aren't willing to contact the FBI or any other law enforcement agency."

"So, you two are here to snoop around? What are you planning to do to get her back?"

With determination in his eyes, Payne rejoined the conversation. "Whatever it takes."

CHAPTER 16

BECAUSE of his size, Greene claimed the shotgun seat of the cramped Mustang, forcing Jones to sit in the back. Normally Jones would've bitched and moaned about losing his front-seat status, but since Greene would've needed the flexibility of a Russian gymnast to contort his 275-pound frame into the backseat, Jones didn't mutter a single complaint.

After getting into the car, Greene spoke first. "I was able to purchase the artillery that you guys wanted, but it cost me a pretty penny. If you want, we can pick it up now."

Payne agreed, and Greene directed him to the nearby parking garage where his black Cadillac Escalade was parked. The SUV was equipped with a gas-guzzling 400-plus-horsepower engine, limousine-tinted windows, and enough speakers and subwoofers to register a 3.5 on the Richter scale. "This here is my pride and joy," Greene exclaimed. "It was the last extravagant gift I bought myself before my injury. Ain't she sweet?"

"She's a nice ride, and it certainly looks like you take care of her."

Greene nodded as he opened his hatch. "My daddy always used to say, if you take care of your car, your car will take care of you."

Jones slid up next to the ex-linebacker and glanced inside the spacious cargo hold. "My God, your trunk's bigger than the seat you're making me ride around in."

Payne rolled his eyes at Jones's remark. "What did you get for us, big man?"

"You said you needed some reliable handguns, so I picked you up a couple of Glocks. I didn't know which model you'd prefer, so I got a 19 and a 27. The 19 uses standard nine-millimeter ammo, which many people like. Personally, I prefer the 27. In fact, it's the kind I carry for protection. It's chambered in forty-caliber Smith & Wesson, which I think is ballistically better than the nine-millimeter."

Payne smiled his approval as he picked up the charcoal gray Glock 27 from Greene's cargo hold. The ridged polymer handle fit snugly into his experienced hand, and as he held it up to the overhead lights, he stared at the gun with the wide-eyed fascination of a kid with a new toy. "You made a nice choice. No external safeties to worry about. It's light, dependable. Perfect."

"I guess that means I'm stuck with the 19, huh?" Jones didn't have a problem with the weapon, but after riding in the cramped backseat, he was in the mood to complain about something. "Did you get us anything else?"

Greene leaned into the trunk and pulled out a large maroon suitcase. As he fiddled with the case's combination lock, he spoke. "You told me that money wasn't an object and that you needed a couple of weapons with some serious firepower, right? Well, I hope this is what you had in mind." Greene opened the case, revealing a Heckler & Koch MP5 K submachine gun and a Steyr AUG assault rifle.

Jones reacted quickly, grabbing the MP5 K before Payne could get his hands on it. "My, my, my! What do we have here? German-made, three-round burst capability, nine hundred rounds a minute. A nice piece of hardware."

"That's not all," Greene declared. "I picked up the optional silencer as well."

"Great!" Payne said. "That means he can kill a librarian without disturbing any readers."

"Not that I'd *ever* kill a librarian," Jones assured him. "They're special people."

Greene ignored their banter, focusing on Payne instead. "Jon, this Steyr AUG is one of the best assault rifles on the market. It has an interchangeable barrel, so you can use it accurately from a distance like a sniper or up close like a banger. And the cartridges—five-point-five-six by forty-five millimeters—can be bought in department stores, for God's sake! It's very versatile."

Payne picked up the rifle and attached the scope with the skill of a soldier. Once it was in place, he held the eyepiece to his face and put a fire alarm across the garage in his sight. He held the weapon steady, sucked in a deep breath, then paused. "Bang!" he mouthed before dropping the AUG to his side. "You're right. This is a fine choice, and all the weapons appear to be in pretty good shape. What did the purchase run you?"

Greene pulled a handwritten invoice out of his pocket and gave it to Payne.

Payne glanced at the sheet and smiled. "What kind of a street dealer writes out receipts? Does he have a return policy if we're not completely satisfied?"

"Actually, I wrote the stuff down so I wouldn't forget. I'm not that strong with numbers."

"Me, either," Payne admitted. "That's why I try to avoid them at work."

"Oh, yeah? What do you do for a living?"

"I'm the CEO of a multinational conglomeration. We specialize in everything from new technologies to clothes to food products."

Greene laughed in a disbelieving tone. "Okay, whatever. If you don't want to tell me, that's fine. Besides, I'm too hungry to worry about it. Why don't we get out of here?"

Jones agreed. "Sounds good to me. Should we take one car or two?"

"Why don't we take two?" Payne said. "There's a good chance that we're going to be putting ourselves in danger before the end of the night, and I'm not comfortable asking

Levon to help us any more than he already has. It's one thing to ask him for guns and a place to stay, but it's entirely different to put his life in danger for two guys he barely knows."

"Yeah, you're probably right," Jones seconded. "Things could get a little bit nasty if we meet up with the wrong people."

"Come on, D.J., let's put our stuff in the back of the Mustang, then we can follow Levon to dinner." Jones nodded, then walked toward the car with a handful of weapons.

"Hold up a fuckin' minute!" Greene roared. "I can't believe you had an entire conversation about me and didn't bother to ask my opinion. What kind of Yankee bullshit is that?"

"Yankee bullshit?" Payne muttered. "I don't remember talking about baseball."

"I don't think you did. He must've misheard you. The acoustics down here aren't that great."

"Enough already! Would you guys please shut up before I'm forced to use a Glock on your ass? Damn!" Greene shook his head in disgust as he walked toward Payne and Jones. "Listen, I realize that I don't know you guys very well, but I'll be honest with you: This shit intrigues me. When I was still playing ball, I used to live for the adrenaline rush that I got on game day. The crowd calling my name, the speakers blasting my Bob Marley theme song, the feel of a quarterback sack. Man, those were the days."

Greene's eyes glazed slightly as he thought back to his All-Pro seasons with the Bills.

"Unfortunately, that shit has changed. Since Barker blew out my fucking knee, I haven't been able to get too excited about anything. I've done my best to rehab and run and lift, but the truth is, my career is probably done."

"So, what are you saying?" Payne asked.

"For the first time in almost three years, I can feel the adrenaline pumping again. When you called and told me that you wanted me to round up some weapons, I nearly got a hard-on. Then, when you told me the reason for your visit, I got even more excited—an excitement I haven't felt in a long time. Anyway, I guess this is what I'm saying: If you don't mind, I'd like to come along for the ride. I'd like to help you find your girlfriend."

Payne turned to Jones and grinned. He'd been hoping Greene would offer his services. "I don't know, man. I just don't know. D.J., what do you think?"

"Well, a New Orleans native with street connections might come in handy, and his nickname is the Buffalo Soldier after all."

"Good point." Payne smiled and shook Greene's hand. "Okay, Levon, you're on. But if at any time you feel like we're leading you somewhere you don't want to go, just say the word and we'll understand."

Jones nodded his head. "Yeah, there's no sense getting killed in a fight where you have nothing to gain."

"That sounds pretty fair," Greene exclaimed. "But before we begin, I need to ask for one small favor."

"You got it," Payne said. "Just name it."

"Well, since there's a good chance that you might die on this trip, I was hoping you could pay me for the guns before you got killed."

CHAPTER 17

ROBERT Edwards lay on the dirt floor of the small cabin, trying to hold back tears. He had never felt more exhausted in his entire life, yet the waves of agony that engulfed his body hindered his ability to slip into a painless sleep.

His face was still scarred and scabbed from his unsuccessful escape attempt through the Colorado woods on Thursday morning. The flesh on his back was sunburned and slashed from the numerous whippings he had received in the field as punishment for alleged misbehavior. His hands were sore from pulling weeds, and his arms ached from crawling through the untilled soil.

But all of that paled in comparison to the pain that he felt in his injured left leg.

The swelling in Robert's foot and ankle was so severe that his limb no longer looked like a normal appendage, but instead appeared to be a severe birth defect or some kind of laboratory mutation. The bloated and deformed leg had turned such a deep shade of purple that its hue bordered on black instead of the peach color of his uninjured leg. And enough blood had pooled in the lower extremity that the subsequent pressure was cutting off his foot's circulation.

His toes were ice-cold, and his foot tingled as if it were on the verge of falling asleep. Robert knew something needed to be done, but his limited knowledge of first aid was not advanced enough to deal with the severity of his injury. Without ice or an analgesic to reduce the pain and swelling, he did the only thing that he could. He elevated his leg by resting it on the cabin's lone bench.

As he closed his eyes, trying to get the rest that his body required, he heard the rattling of the cabin's lock. He turned his head and watched the door inch open. He stared at it with unblinking eyes until he recognized the shadow that slid into the room. It was Master Holmes, and he was holding a sledgehammer.

"What's that for?" Robert cried. "I've done everything you've asked of me! I haven't caused any problems!"

"That's not what I've heard," Holmes growled. "My guards assured me that you were lagging behind in the field, you needed assistance on more than one occasion, and you objected to being beaten. Those sound like serious problems to me."

"I swear I was doing my best! The pain in my leg was unbearable, and it slowed me down at times, but I never quit. I never gave up. I swear to God I did everything I could! Please don't hit me. I swear I'll get better. Oh, God, I swear!"

Holmes considered Robert's plea, then shrugged as he moved closer. "But I don't see *how* you can get better. You claim you were doing your best today, but my guards told me that your efforts weren't good enough. If you were already doing your best, I don't see how you could improve."

Robert tried to sit up, but he was unable to budge his leg. "I promise I'll get better. Just give me a painkiller and I could work harder. I just need something for the pain."

Holmes shook his head and sneered. "It's always something with you. This morning you were complaining to the guards. Now you're claiming you can do anything if we get you some drugs. As far as your pain goes, I don't give a fuck! Pain is something everyone must deal with, and those that deal with it the best will succeed the most. Obviously, you're one of those people that can't cope."

"I can, Master Holmes. I swear I can cope with the pain."

Holmes grinned as he tightened his grip on the wooden handle. "All right," he stated, lifting the sledgehammer high above Robert's head. "Let's see if you can deal with this!"

Screaming like a medieval warrior, Holmes shifted his weight forward and swung the mallet's iron head. Robert raised his hands and tried to deflect the blow, but his reflexes were too slow and Holmes's efforts were too determined. The hammer smashed into the bridge of Robert's nose, splintering the delicate bones of his face, not stopping until the cold steel collided with the blood-soaked floor.

"Can you handle that?" Holmes mocked. "Or do you need something for the pain?"

Gasping for air, Robert opened his eyes and lifted his head from the floor with a terrified shriek. He gazed around the room, searching for Holmes with every ounce of energy that remained in his body, but the powerful man was nowhere to be found. The tiny cabin was empty, except for the sound of a feminine voice that was urging him to lie down.

"Honey," Tonya Edwards pleaded as she stroked her husband's damp hair, "you were just dreaming! It was just a bad dream."

Robert tried to catch his breath as he glanced at his wife's face, but the image of Holmes's hammer still lingered. The dream had been so intense, so real, that his entire body was dripping with perspiration and his heart was pounding with urgency.

"Shhh," she begged, "let me take care of you."

It took a moment to settle him down, but Robert finally did as she requested. He eased his weary head to the cabin's floor, then stared into Tonya's dark eyes, searching for answers. "How did you get in here? How did you find me?"

Tonya continued to stroke her husband's hair, doing everything in her power to calm him. "You collapsed when the guards brought you back from the field, and they didn't want you to die. They brought me here to help you. I've been waiting for you to wake up ever since."

Robert's eyes filled with tears as he tried to make sense of it all. The abduction, the brutality, the labor. What had he done to deserve this? He had never lived the life of a saint, but he had never done anything to warrant this. He had never killed, robbed, or harmed anyone. In fact, he had never purposely hurt anybody in his entire life. And what about his wife? Why was she here? She was pregnant, for God's sake! What could she have possibly done to merit her imprisonment on the Plantation?

"Sweetie, did you hear me?" Tonya sobbed. "Can you hear what I'm saying?"

Robert did his best to focus on her lips, yet he had no idea what she had said. "How did you get in here?" he repeated, not remembering his earlier question.

She swallowed deeply, trying to stay strong for him. "The guards brought me in to take care of you. They want me to try and fix your leg."

"But you're not a doctor."

Tonya smiled, and the small movement of her lips temporarily lifted his spirits. "I know I'm not a doctor, but I'm the only person who's allowed to help. The guards told me what needed to be done, but I didn't want to do it until you woke up. I wanted to get your approval first."

"My approval?" Robert didn't like the sound of that. If it was a simple medical procedure like putting on a bandage, Tonya would've done it while he was asleep. Since she wanted to ask his permission, he knew it was something serious. "What do you have in mind?"

Tonya clambered to her feet—a difficult task because of her pregnancy—and waddled to the bench where her husband was currently elevating his leg. Carefully, she sat next to his swollen limb, trying not to jostle the bench with her body weight. Then, with the tenderness of a new mother, she placed her left hand on his injured ankle.

"Robert, the guard told me you have a displaced fracture. That means your bone was broken and the pieces shifted away from each other."

"The guard told you? Is he a doctor?"

His wife shook her head as she pointed to his leg. "No, he's not a doctor, but if you look at it, it's kind of obvious." Tonya took a deep breath before continuing. "Your leg's pointing straight ahead, but your foot is turned way to the right."

Robert didn't need to look at his injury. The severity of his pain let him know that something was seriously wrong. "How are you supposed to fix it?"

Tonya gulped before answering. "The guard told me if you want the bone to heal properly, I need to . . . um . . . straighten it out."

He was going to ask how she was going to do that, but he knew the answer. She had to twist his foot until everything was aligned in his leg. "Do you trust his advice?"

She nodded. "Remember when I slipped on the ice and broke my finger two years ago? The first thing the doctor did was pop it back into place. That way, it was able to grow back together." She bent her right index finger back and forth. "And see? It turned out just fine."

Robert agreed with her logic. If he wanted the ability to walk without a limp, he knew that something needed to be done immediately. "Do you think you can handle this? I know how squeamish you can be."

"Yeah, I can handle it," she said, smiling. It was a smile that said, *If I'm doing it for you, I can handle anything.*

Robert appreciated the sentiment. "I want you to promise me something, though. When you do this, do it quick, like removing a Band-Aid. Just make one decisive move and get it over with, okay?"

"You got it." Tonya stared at him, wanting to say something to her husband, but the appropriate words escaped her. "Are you ready?"

"Not really." He laughed through gritted teeth, "but I have a feeling I could never be ready."

She grinned, admiring his courageous sense of humor. "I think this will be easier if we did it on the flat ground. That way, I'll be able to anchor your upper leg with my body weight."

Robert closed his eyes as his wife lifted his swollen limb off of the bench and lowered it to the cabin's dirt floor. He winced as she placed it on the hard ground, but the pain wasn't nearly as bad as he had expected. "So far, so good."

Tonya leaned forward and gently kissed her husband on his forehead. After whispering soft words of encouragement, she turned away from him, resting her weight on his left knee, anchoring his upper leg in place. Without stopping to think, she leaned toward his broken limb and grabbed his foot. Then, with a quick burst, she rotated his foot to the left. The violent twist filled the cabin with a series of sounds—first the grotesque snap of his leg as his bones shifted back into place, then the heart-stopping shriek of a man in agony.

It was a sound that would be repeated by several prisoners in the coming days.

CHAPTER 18

THE last thing on Payne's mind was dinner, but Greene insisted that they stop for something to eat. They had to, he said. His stomach demanded it. As a compromise, Payne pulled into the first drive-through he could find and ordered several ham and cheese po'boys, a local specialty.

"So," said Payne as they waited for their food, "where to next?"

Greene thought about it for several seconds. "The first thing we're gonna have to do is talk to some of my boys from the Quarter. They'd be more aware of things on the street than me."

"What kind of things?" Jones asked.

"Everything. If it happens in the city, they'll know about it. They'll be able to fill you in on the tattoo you're looking for. Plus, if you're lucky, they might be able to tell you something about the kidnapping. Of course, since that didn't happen down here, details might be limited."

Payne considered Greene's words carefully. "Will your friends be willing to talk to us?"

Greene shrugged. "That's something I don't know. Most of the time, they're pretty receptive about helping me, but in your case, I don't know. You have two things working against you."

"And those are?"

"You're white, and you're from the North. Some people down here don't take kindly to those two things."

Payne nodded. "I can understand that, and I figured as much. But at the same time, I have two things that will help my cause."

"Like what?" Greene asked.

"First of all, I have you guys on my side, and since both of you are black, that might help us with some of the bigger racists we come across."

"That's true, but it might not be enough."

"And secondly," he said as he laid a thick wad of cash on the dashboard, "I'm willing to spend my entire fortune if it helps get Ariane back."

Greene eyed the stack of bills that sat before him and grinned. "You know, I think you'll get along with my boys just fine!"

"I had a feeling I would."

"But before we go anywhere, there are still a few ground rules I'm gonna have to insist on before we meet my people."

Payne scooped up his money and nodded. "I'm listening."

"This is my hometown, the place I've chosen to live for the rest of my life. So I don't want you doing anything that's going to hurt me after you guys leave. That means I don't want you roughing up any of my contacts, and I don't want you making me look bad in any way. I have a reputation to uphold in this city, and I don't want it tarnished. Okay?"

Payne and Jones agreed to his conditions.

"And finally, if I'm going to help you out, you need to promise me one more thing: absolutely no police involvement of any kind."

"Why not?" Jones asked, slightly suspicious.

"The people that we'll be dealing with aren't exactly friends of the law, and if word gets out that I'm teaming up with the local authorities, then my sources will dry up. And trust me, that won't help you find the girl, and it won't help me after you've left."

"No cops, no problem," replied Payne, who was willing to agree to just about anything. "Now, unless there's something else, can we get this show on the road?"

AFTER arranging a meeting with his best source, Greene directed his friends through the narrow streets of the Vieux Carré, the historic neighborhood also known as the French Quarter.

"Some people get confused when they come down here because the term French Quarter is misleading," Greene said. "Most of the architecture around here is Spanish in design, built in the eighteenth century. Most of the original French settlement was burned during a rebellion a little more than two hundred years ago. And thankfully, much of it survived Katrina."

From the backseat, Jones glanced at the buildings and noticed nothing but bars, strip clubs, and T-shirt shops, and none of them looked very old. "Levon? Are you telling me that Spain had nude dancing back in the seventeen hundreds?"

Greene laughed. "If they did, I doubt the conquistadors would've ever left. No, this is the one part of the French Quarter that has been ruined by modern-day greed. If you want to experience the true character of this area, you need to explore the side streets. That's where you'll find the flavor of the early settlers."

Payne suddenly looked at Greene in a whole new light. He always knew that Greene was intelligent, but he never realized the ex-linebacker had a passion for history. In the past, their playground conversations never got beyond street basketball and life in the NFL. "I have to admit, Levon, I'm kind of surprised. You never seemed to be the type of person who cared about the events of early America. Now you sound like a tour guide."

"I'm not sure if that's supposed to be a compliment or not."

"Yes," he assured Greene, "it's a compliment."

"Thanks. I guess ever since I hurt my knee I've had the opportunity to do a lot of things that I wouldn't have done earlier in my career. One of those things is historical research. I've been reading a lot of books on the past, trying to picture what life used to be like down here before the nineteen hundreds. As you can imagine, it was a much different place."

Payne nodded as they pulled up in front of the Fishing Hole, a nightclub where the marquee boasted "the Prettiest Girls in *Nude* Orleans." After parking, the three men walked to the front door and were quickly greeted by a bouncer who recognized Greene. With a slight nod, he allowed the trio to enter the club for free. Payne and Jones followed Greene into the smoke-filled lobby and were immediately taken aback by the first thing they saw: the couch dance room.

Similar in design to the orgy rooms of the Roman Empire, the room consisted of ten couches scattered around a spacious chamber. For a twenty-dollar tip, a naked vixen led an eager man to one of the black leather couches. During the course of a song, she would attempt to seduce him by rubbing, sliding, and grinding against his fully clothed body. Her goal was simple: convince him to purchase another song. And it wasn't a tough sale. Mix horny men with inexpensive alcohol, naked women, and heavy petting, and there's a better chance that a guy will file for bankruptcy before saying no to a beautiful stripper.

Strolling between the couches, Payne and Jones gaped at the erotic scene that unfolded around them while Greene chuckled with childlike delight.

"It's kind of hypnotic, isn't it?" asked Greene. "I always enjoy watching the crowd that stands along the walls. You'll see an awful lot of perverts with their hands in their pockets, if you know what I mean."

Both men knew what he meant, but that didn't mean they wanted to watch it.

"What are we doing here?" Payne asked. "Is it for the

scenery, or did we come here to meet somebody in particular?"

"Actually, both. The main guy I wanted you to speak to is the owner of this club. And since I didn't want you fellas to come to New Orleans without having a chance to experience Bourbon Street, I told him that we would meet him here. I hope that doesn't bother you."

Jones continued to stare at the naked females and shook his head. "Nope, doesn't bother me at all. In fact, I'm tempted to borrow twenty bucks."

Payne grabbed Jones by the arm and pulled him into the hallway. "Come on, D.J., get your mind in the game. If we start to lose focus, we could miss something important."

"Sorry," Jones muttered, his face flushed with embarrassment. "But the only time I see stuff like this is late night on Cinemax."

Greene led Payne and Jones through a back corridor, and before long they were strolling through the dancers' dressing room. Surprisingly, none of the undressed women were bothered by the men's presence. When they reached the back corner of the room, Greene spoke to the security guard who stood outside of a private office. "Let Terrell know I'm here. He's expecting me." The guard quickly opened the thick metal door to get authorization from the club's owner but noticed that he was on the phone.

"It'll be one minute, Mr. Greene. Mr. Murray is finishing up a call."

Greene nodded, then returned his attention to Payne and Jones. It was time to supply them with some background information on the man they were about to meet. "Terrell Murray is one of the most influential men in New Orleans, even though you'll rarely hear his name mentioned in high society. He tends to stay out of politics and high finance and prefers to deal with the seedier side of the city—strip clubs, prostitution, gambling, and so on. Very few things of an illegal nature get done in Orleans Parish without his permission or knowledge, so there is a very good chance that he'll be able to point us in the right direction."

Payne nodded. "And I take it you'll do all of the talking?"

"Since he doesn't know you, he won't help you. Fortunately, he's an avid football fan and has a place in his heart for me, so I'll be able to ask him anything that you guys want to know. I obviously understand the basics of your case, so I'll get him to talk about the tattoo and the kidnapping, but is there anything else you want to find out?"

Payne shook his head before they were led into Murray's private office.

The well-lit room was immaculately maintained and outfitted with French Neoclassical furniture from the late seventeen hundreds—definitely not what Payne and Jones were expecting to find. Four Louis XVI chairs, possessing the classic straight lines of the period, encircled a round wooden table that sat in the middle of the hardwood floor. Gold trim lined the walls, ceilings, and picture frames of the chamber, matching a chandelier that dangled above the sitting area. The room's artwork was obviously influenced by the Roman Empire, a motif that reflected the French's interest in the designs of the ancient cities of Pompeii and Herculaneum. A marble bust of Tiberius, the second emperor of Rome, sat proudly on a pedestal in the far corner.

An elderly black man, dressed in a pale gray suit and an open-collared shirt, stood from his seat behind his Louis XVI desk and greeted his visitors with a warm smile. "Please come in. Make yourself at home."

"Thank you," Payne replied as he soaked in the office's decor. "This is an impressive setup you have here. It's like a museum."

Murray shook Payne's hand and thanked him for the compliment. "First of all, enough with the formalities. If you're a friend of Levon's, there's no need to call me *sir*. Please, my name is Terrell." Payne nodded in understanding. "And as far as this room is concerned, antiques are a hobby of mine. I own a number of shops on Royal Street, but I'm afraid I deny my customers the opportunity to buy the best items. I tend to keep them for myself."

"And you've done a wonderful job," Jones added. "You truly have."

"Good, I'm glad you like it." Murray motioned for the men to be seated in the Louis XVI chairs and eagerly joined them. "So, Levon, what brings you here on a Friday night to see an old man like me? I know it can't be companionship because most of the lovely ladies of the club would be more than willing to go home with you."

Greene smiled at the thought. "Actually, I've come for your knowledge of the city. My friends and I are in search of a particular gang that operates in the area, and we were hoping that you could point us in the right direction."

Murray furrowed his wrinkled brow before speaking. "And am I to guess the name of the gang, or would you like to give me that information?"

"That's one of the reasons I came to you. The only thing we know is the design of their Holotat. It's in the shape of the letter *P* and uses a bloody dagger in the image."

"Yes," Murray replied with the blank face of a gambler. "I know that tattoo, and its appearance is a recent one to this city. Unfortunately, I know little about the men who wear them. I am sorry I cannot tell you more."

Without saying a word, Payne turned toward Greene and pleaded for him to dig deeper. Payne sensed that the old man was holding something back, and Greene picked up on the nonverbal request to continue.

"Terrell, I know that you try to stay out of other people's business, but in this case, I'm hoping you'll make an exception. Earlier today a man bearing that Holotat burst into the apartment of Jon's girlfriend and abducted her. So far, there's been no ransom demand and very little police activity. We're afraid if we don't do something immediately we may be too late. Please, any lead that you can give us would be appreciated."

Murray considered Greene's plea for several stress-filled seconds before nodding. "Above Rampart Street near St. Louis Cemetery #1, there is a small tattoo shop. It is operated by a man known as Jamaican Sam. He's the most popular skin artist in the area, and I would bet he's the man responsible for designing that Holotat. Go to him, and see where it leads you."

CHAPTER 19

Galléon Township Docks
Galléon, Louisiana
(37 miles southeast of New Orleans)

THE driver of the Washington Parish ambulance stopped near the narrow dock, then made a three-point turn in the gravel driveway. Once the vehicle pointed away from the Gulf of Mexico, he backed it carefully to the edge of the secluded pier. Satisfied with its positioning, he turned off the motor and stepped under the wharf's lone streetlight.

Tension was evident on his face.

While listening to the lapping water, he checked his watch and realized he was a few minutes early. To kill time, he pulled a cigarette from his pocket and lit it with a paper match. He took a deep drag, then blew a puff of smoke into the nighttime air.

This would be his last delivery for a while, and for that he was quite thankful. He didn't know why, but he'd grown more and more anxious with each mission that he'd completed for the Plantation. At first, he blamed his uncomfortable feelings on the recent death of his aunt. He assumed her passing had caused some sort of subconscious guilt since his after-hours duties centered on the shipment of cadavers for medical experiments. But lately, his concerns were a little more tangible. Snippets of overheard conversations, copies of phony death certificates, and deliveries that were scheduled for the dead of night.

All of which made him nervous.

But that was only part of it. What freaked him out more than anything were the sounds. On more than one occasion, he could've sworn he heard noises coming from the back of his ambulance—loud thumps emerging from the sealed containers, muffled screams leaking from the crates of the dead. God, the thought of it made him shudder.

To calm down, he took another drag on his cigarette and stared at the warm waters of the gulf. Something about this didn't seem right.

As he continued to wait, he pondered his role as a deliveryman, thinking back to the day he was first hired. A well-dressed black man spotted him washing his ambulance and asked him if he was interested in making some extra cash. The man claimed he was operating a private medical center off the coast in Breton Sound and was looking for the quickest way to deliver his research from Lakefront Airport to his new facility. Since emergency vehicles were given special privileges on the roadway, he felt that an ambulance would be the most efficient mode of transportation. Plus, he pointed out, he was looking for someone who would be comfortable around dead bodies and felt a medical worker would be perfect.

The driver glanced at his watch again and realized he still had a few minutes until the workers from the Plantation would arrive. If he hurried, he figured he could sneak into the back of his ambulance and investigate the crates that had been loaded for him at the airport.

"Screw it," he said aloud.

He emphasized his statement by slamming his cigarette into the water.

With quiet determination, he opened the door of the ambulance and climbed across the front seat. Sliding through the narrow entryway, he crept into the back and quickly grabbed the paperwork that had been attached to the top of the first wooden container. It read:

WALKER, ARIANE
28 YEARS OLD
WEXFORD, PA
JULY 2

Wow, he thought to himself. She died earlier today. That's pretty quick for someone to be moved across state lines.

He continued to flip through the documents, hoping to find a cause of death or the reason she was going to be examined, but the sheets were filled with numbers and other data that he was unable to comprehend.

Taking a deep breath, he glanced at his watch again. They would be here soon. And the last thing he wanted was to be caught snooping. Not only would they refuse to pay him, but he realized he might end up in one of the coffins as well.

AFTER leaving the ambulance, the small boat navigated the narrow channel of the cypress swamp, carefully avoiding any logs or stumps that would puncture its bow. As it eased against the moss-covered dock, the captain of the vessel tossed a rope to one of the guards, who quickly attached it to its anchoring post.

The craft was now secured.

Octavian Holmes emerged from the shadows of the stern and shouted terse orders to the men on cargo duty. The workers, dressed in black fatigues and carrying firearms, hauled the two wooden crates to a waiting truck. Once Holmes climbed into the back of the vehicle, the driver started the motor and maneuvered the shipment through the thick camouflage of the island's foliage. A short time later, the flatbed truck burst from the claustrophobic world of leaves into the neatly manicured grounds of the Plantation.

"Stop here," Holmes growled with authority.

The workers lifted the wooden crates from the vehicle and placed them on the charred remains of the burned cross. As Holmes watched closely, they tore into the crates with crowbars and within seconds the boxes were reduced to shreds. Cautiously, the men lifted the two unconscious prisoners from the dismantled containers and placed them in the cool grass.

"They're all yours, sir."

Holmes nodded while studying the paperwork of his new arrivals. Satisfied, he bent over to examine their sleeping forms and immediately liked what he saw. The first captive was an elderly man with a strong jaw, thinning white hair, and a deep surfer's tan. He was in amazing physical shape for his age, possessing great muscle tone despite his seventy-one years of life. His wrists were thick, his shoulders broad, and his stomach carried little flab.

"Jake Ross," he mumbled as he nudged the man's hip. "I bet you're still a pit bull, huh?"

When he was done with the senior citizen, he turned his attention to the drugged female, and her beauty instantly overwhelmed him. Her chestnut hair flowed over her rosy cheeks, cascading down her neck and onto her slender shoulders like a tropical waterfall. Her bosom, concealed under a bright red golf shirt, danced with each life-sustaining breath, and the image stirred something deep within Holmes. Her legs, tanned and athletic, were in full view since her white skirt had been torn during her cross-country journey. But even in rest, they possessed the fragile grace of a master ballerina's.

And her face—her gorgeous face—was the most beautiful he had seen in a very long time.

After catching his breath, Holmes dropped to his knees and kissed the girl on her lips. "Ariane Walker," he whispered, "it's a pleasure to have you on my island."

With a smile on his face, Holmes scooped her off of the turf and gently folded her frame over his left shoulder. As her arms dangled against his muscular back, he carried the unconscious girl toward her cabin with little effort. His eighteen years of work as a mercenary, which required stamina, strength, and discipline, guaranteed a level of physical conditioning that few men could ever hope to achieve. His missions had taken him through the severe warmth of the equator, the extreme cold of the Arctic Circle, and all the milder climates in between. In the process, he had learned how to survive anything that this world was capable of throwing at him.

And because of that, invincibility radiated from him like heat from a flame.

When he reached Ariane's cabin, he paused briefly, letting one of the guards unlock the exterior deadbolt. "You go in first," Holmes ordered. "Make sure her roommates are facing the wall in the back corner of the room." The guard did what he was told, threatening Tonya and Robert Edwards until they were properly positioned.

"All clear, sir."

Holmes walked into the cabin and eased Ariane onto the hard ground. Then, before either captive could see his face, he turned from the room and disappeared into the dark night, leaving Tonya to take care of another family member.

This time, her unconscious baby sister.

CHAPTER 20

IN New Orleans, St. Louis Cemeteries #1 and #2 are referred to by locals as "cities of the dead." Designed in the eighteenth century, both graveyards feature elaborate aboveground vaults and French inscriptions that are both poetic and charming. Unfortunately, a nighttime visit to either burial ground is liable to add to the body count of the sacred lands. Located west of Louis Armstrong Park, this area is known as one of the most dangerous in the city. Gangs and criminals control the territories to the north of Rampart Street, and they use the popularity of the graveyards to ambush unsuspecting tourists.

Before leaving the safety of their Mustang, Payne, Jones, and Greene gazed at the terrain like antelopes surveying a water hole. They carefully searched the shadows of the land, looking for predators that lay in wait, hunting for a clear passage to their intended destination. When they were satisfied, they crept cautiously from their vehicle.

"If I'm not mistaken," Greene stated, "the tattoo shop should be right ahead of us."

The men continued their walk in silence until they found

a small shop with a flickering neon sign that said *Sam's Tattoos* in the window. Like most tattoo parlors, this one stayed open after midnight to cater to the bar crowd. Glancing at a historical plaque that was fastened to the building's front, Greene pushed the door aside. Chimes from a small bell announced their presence.

A tall white man, dressed in an elaborately tie-dyed shirt and baggy denim shorts, emerged from behind a wall of dangling beads and greeted his customers with a nod of his head. As he did, his braided orange hair fell across his pale green eyes while his shaggy beard bunched up in the folds of his neck. Tattoos covered the tanned flesh of his arms and legs.

"What can I do for you dudes?" he asked in the syntax of a stoner.

As Payne studied the employee, he realized it looked like a box of Skittles had thrown up on the guy. "We're looking for a man named Jamaican Sam. Can you tell us where to find him?"

"Dude! You're in luck. Sam, I am!"

The three men looked at each other in confusion. They were expecting their contact be a little more Jamaican and a little less Dr. Seuss.

"You mean you're the owner?" Payne asked. "You don't look like I pictured you."

"Is it the nickname, dude? People always get thrown by my nickname." The three men nodded at the walking rainbow. "Damn! I gotta get me a new nickname."

Jones knew he was going to regret asking it, but for the sake of curiosity, he had to know. "How did you get the name Jamaican Sam?"

"Well, dude, the Sam part was easy because, you see, that's my name. But the Jamaican part, well, that's a little more complex. A couple years ago, a bro from the islands came in to get some ink done. I did this bitchin' drawing of a naked hottie and put it on his back. Once I was finished, he was pretty stoked. In a heavily accented voice, the dude said, 'Ja makin' Sam's name known t'roughout da city, mon!' Well, some customers overheard it, and they lumped *ja makin'* with the *Sam*, so people started calling me Jamaican Sam." He punctuated his story with a huge grin. "Pretty sweet, eh?"

As fascinating as the story was, Payne didn't come to this part of town to learn Sam's history. He had more important things to find out—things that could possibly save his girlfriend. "I don't mean to be rude, but I was hoping you could give us some help."

With his left hand, Sam brushed his braided orange locks from his eyes. "Like I said in the beginning, what can I do for you dudes?"

"Actually, you can help me with a tattoo. I recently saw an elaborate design on this guy on the bus. The moment I saw it, I knew I wanted to have it. I just knew it! Unfortunately, before I had a chance to ask him where he got it done, we arrived at his stop and he disappeared. Do you think you could tell me who drew it for him?"

Sam shook his head violently, trying to clear his head. "Hold up. Let me see if I understand your quandary. You spotted a slammin' tat, and you expect me, even though I've never seen it, to picture it in my mind and tell you who did it? That's some challenge, dude."

"But can you do it?" Payne demanded.

It took thirty seconds for Sam to reply, but he finally shrugged his shoulders. "I don't see why not. But it'll cost ya twenty bucks." Payne handed him the money, and Sam quickly stuffed the bill into his multicolored boxers, which could be seen above the waistline of his shorts. "What did this Picasso look like?"

"It was in the shape of the letter *P*. The straight part of the *P* was a dagger, and—"

"Whoa!" Sam gasped, sounding like Keanu Reeves. "Was there, like, blood dripping from the dagger?"

Payne stared at the guy—he couldn't have been older than twenty-two—and nodded. "So, you're familiar with it?"

Sam walked over to his counter and flipped through a picture album of some of his most impressive designs. When he reached the page he was looking for, he handed the book to Payne. "The tat you're looking for is one of mine. How cool is that? Kind of a small globe, eh?"

"Yeah," Jones grunted, who suddenly didn't like the precision of Terrell Murray's off-the-cuff recommendation. "Way too small for my taste."

Payne picked up on Jones's tone and instinctively touched the gun that he'd concealed under the flap of his shirt. "What can you tell me about its design?"

Sam scratched his bright orange beard for a moment, pondering his position, then shook his head from side to side. "It just ain't worth it, dude." He reached into his boxer shorts and withdrew Payne's twenty dollars. "You can take your money back. I've got nothing for ya."

Payne looked at the money with disapproval. He wasn't willing to touch something that had been stored in Sam's underwear. Nor was he about to let him off the hook that easily. "A deal's a deal. You accepted the cash, now it's time to give me some info."

"Sorry, dude, but I just can't do that!" Sam laid the money on the counter and slowly backed away. "I made a previous deal with a group of brothers that requested my work for that particular job. I told them my lips were *el sealed-o* if anyone asked me about that tat."

"How many people were in the group?" Jones asked.

Sam shrugged, then let out a weasely little laugh. "Sorry, bro. I don't remember getting any money from you, so I don't owe you any info. You dig?"

Payne grinned at Sam and waited for the orange-haired freak to return his smile. When he did, Payne pulled his firearm into view and nestled it under the artist's hairy chin. "First, you referred to a bunch of black men as 'brothers,' and then you referred to my friend as your 'bro.' Now you're going to test my patience even further by refusing to answer a simple question? Sorry, bro, that's not the way my friends and I operate."

"Wait a second," Sam gulped, as the color drained from his face. "Did you guys come in together? Oh, dude, I didn't know that! If I had known that, I wouldn't have been so shady!"

Payne nodded, but refused to lower his gun. "Tell us about this group, Sam, before my finger gets a twitch and I add some red to your obnoxious shirt."

"Well, a bunch of brothers . . . uh, I mean, Africans came here a couple weeks ago—"

Jones quickly corrected him. "The appropriate term is African Americans."

"No, dude, not in this case. These dudes were African."

Payne raised an eyebrow. "Continue."

"Anyways," Sam stuttered, "they were looking for a Holotat. They told me the name of their gang and what they were looking for, then left the rest up to me. They gave me some cash and told me to have a tat design by the next day." Sam pointed to the picture in the album. "This is what I came up with, dude. Honest!"

"What was the name of the gang?" Payne demanded.

"Dude, I can't tell ya that. I just can't."

Payne pushed the barrel of his gun even harder against Sam's throat, and as he did, he noticed Sam start to tremble with fear. "Sammy? I have a policy that prevents me from killing the mentally challenged, but since we're in a hurry, I might be willing to make an exception."

Sam took a trouble-filled breath, then answered. "I've got a problem, dude. When the group got their tats, they threatened to kill me if I told anyone about their posse. Now, here you are, and you're threatening to kill me if I *don't* tell you about their posse. Well, you don't have to be Alex Trebek to see that I'm in jeopardy."

"Jeez," Payne said. "That jeopardy comment was pretty funny."

"Did you like that?" Sam asked, hoping to lighten the mood. "I just made that up."

"You did?" Payne grunted. "Well, unless you want it to be the last clever thing you say, I think you should start talking. What's the name of the gang?"

Sam closed his eyes in thought. After thinking about all

of the consequences, he figured it was better to possibly die later than to definitely die now. "The Plantation Posse."

Payne lowered his weapon. "And what can you tell us about this Posse?"

"I don't know," Sam mumbled. "They were young, black, and very athletic-looking."

"Wow," Greene remarked. "You just described every team in the NBA. You gotta do better than that."

"And some of the guys had thick African accents."

"Come on!" he objected. "My NBA comment is still accurate."

Sam glared at the ex–football star. After a moment, a flash of recognition crossed his face. "Whoa, dude, I know you. I know who you are!"

Greene cursed under his breath. He knew going into this partnership that there was a good chance that he was going to be recognized. Now it was just a matter of how he was going to handle it. "Who I am is not important, you box-of-crayons-looking motherfucker! What *is* important is my boy's question. What did these guys look like?"

The rage in Greene's voice was enough to silence Sam. There was no way he wanted to piss off the Buffalo Soldier. "Okay, dude, I'll tell you anything you want to know, just don't hurt me! I've got a low threshold for pain."

Greene nodded. "I appreciate your honesty. In return, I promise not to test that threshold. But instead of talking to me, I want you to talk to my friends. Okay? And while you're telling them everything that they need to know, I'm gonna go in the back and use your bathroom." He turned toward Payne and Jones, looking for permission. "That is, if you guys can handle things alone for a couple of minutes."

Payne patted Greene on his shoulder. "Thanks, I think we can take over from here."

"While you're back there," Jones added quietly, "check to see if anybody is hiding or if there's another way into this place. I'm not in the mood for any surprises."

Greene hustled into the back and did what was requested.

"Things look fine," he yelled to Payne and Jones. "There's nothing back here that can hurt you."

Payne grinned as he leaned against the counter. "Sorry, Sam. Since you're all out of allies, it appears that you're kind of stuck. You have no choice but to tell us about the Posse."

"Dude, I swear, I can't describe them any better than I have. The only thing in my brain is their black clothes and the large roll of bills they were toting. Other than that, nothing!"

Payne nodded, beginning to believe Sam's claim. He realized that it would be tough for anyone to remember specific details about a group of men who had visited him several weeks ago, especially if they were foreigners. One face would blend in with the next. "Fine, let's get off their appearance. Why don't you tell me about the tattoo? What did the image symbolize?"

Sam scratched his beard while studying the picture from his album. "Well, dude, the *P* obviously stands for *Plantation Posse*, but I bet you figured that out, huh?"

"Come on," Payne mumbled. "Tell us something that might actually be useful."

"Fine!" Sam growled. "I'll tell you what you want to know, but I'm warning you dudes, you're forcing me to sign my own death warrant. My blood's gonna be on your hands!"

And in a blink of an eye, Sam's words became prophetic.

CHAPTER 21

THUNDER echoed from across the street as the sniper pulled the trigger on his rifle. His first shot shattered the window of the tattoo shop, sending thousands of knifelike shards in every direction. As they fell to the floor in a melodic song, the bullet entered the right eye of its victim, obliterating Sam's brain and skull in a single flash.

Without pausing to think, Payne and Jones reacted to the situation like it was an everyday occurrence. Their experiences with the MANIACs had prepared them for far worse. Payne dashed for cover in the front corner of the shop, which was away from the broken window and allowed him to take a clean shot at anyone who entered the front door. Meanwhile, Jones headed in the opposite direction, taking refuge behind the front counter.

"Are you all right?" Jones yelled as he pulled out his Glock.

"I'm not perfect, but I'm better than Sam."

Jones glanced around the corner and stared at the near-headless victim. Crimson gushed from the gaping hole where his face used to be. Hair, brain, and bone clung to the back wall like chunky spaghetti sauce.

"We're dealing with a serious weapon, Jon. Whatever it is tore right through his skull."

Payne surveyed the scene before offering his summation of the kill. "From the looks of it, the shooter has an elevated position."

"Why do you say that?"

"Look at the window if you can. The top is the only part that's broken, and the only way a bullet can do that and hit a man in the head is if it was discharged from above."

Jones nodded in agreement. "If that's the case, this wasn't a drive-by. The bastard's probably on a roof or in a tree. No way we'll be able to nail him from this angle."

"You're probably right. That's why we're going to have to go outside and get him."

Jones put his finger in his ear and tried to unclog it. "Sorry, I must've misheard you. Did you say we should go out there and get him?"

"Yes, princess, that's what I said."

The statement didn't sit well with Jones. "But we don't know what we're up against! Hell, we don't know a damn thing, and you want us to go outside with our weapons blazing? Am I Butch or Sundance?"

Payne chuckled at Jones's reaction. He expected something more soldierly from an ex-MANIAC. "Wow, wait until I tell the fellas about this at our next squad reunion. They won't believe how quickly you've lost your nerve!"

"I haven't lost my nerve, Jon. I've gained common sense. What good is it to go outside and face a sniper?"

"What good? Going out there could save Ariane's life!"

"How do you figure?"

"Think about it! Why was Sam killed? What purpose could that have served?"

Jones shrugged. "I don't know. Somebody wanted to keep him quiet."

"Exactly! Sam must've known something, and it must've been pretty damn important."

"Like what?"

"I have no idea. Maybe he could identify someone, or has

a billing address in his files, or maybe, just maybe, he knew something about Ariane. Truthfully, I don't know. But if we don't go outside, our odds of getting an answer go down considerably. And you know it!"

"Shit," Jones grumbled, realizing what Payne had in mind. "You're hoping to take this guy alive, aren't you?"

Payne nodded. "How else is he going to be useful?"

Jones knew that Payne was right, that they needed to talk to the guy, but he also realized the level of danger that would be involved. If the sniper was still outside, he was probably waiting for them to make a move. And the moment they did—bang! Because that's how snipers operated. They patiently waited for their targets to do something stupid, then they took full advantage.

"So, are you coming or not?" Payne asked in a less than pleasant tone. " 'Cause if you aren't, I gotta start looking for a new best friend."

"Ah, man, why did you have to go there? Anytime you need a favor, you always pull out the best-friend card. Fine, I'll help you out, but I'm not doing this because of your stupid threat. I'm doing this because I need the exercise."

Payne grinned in appreciation. "The first thing we need to do is figure out how we're going to get out of here. Since the door is glass, he'll pick us off before we even open it. We'll need to find a different exit."

"How about the window? If I knock out the bottom half, we could slip behind one of the cars outside with little exposure time. Plus, it'll let this guy know we're armed."

"Sounds good. But before we go, let me get the lights. The less this guy sees, the better."

Jones liked the idea. Darkness would improve their odds even more. "Can you reach 'em from there, or are you going to have to shoot 'em out?"

Payne leaned out from his hiding place and stared at the small panel of switches near the door. It would take some doing, but he felt he could reach the buttons without risking his life.

"No problem," he lied. "Piece of cake."

THE PLANTATION 111

Moving quickly, Payne dropped to his hands and stomach and crawled across the vinyl floor. He did his best to avoid the broken glass, but since there were chunks of it everywhere, he found himself bleeding immediately.

"Looking good," Jones whispered as he peered out from behind the counter. "In about two feet, you'll be directly under the switch. Okay, stop."

Payne tilted his head back and tried to reach the metal panel above him, but the damn thing was a foot too high. That meant he'd have to leave the safety of the floor to reach it. Of course, the advantage he'd gain with darkness outweighed the risk of going for the lights. While keeping his torso parallel to the floor, he stretched his bloody hand upward, inching it slowly along the wall until he felt the cold surface of the switch.

"Let's see if you like the dark," Payne said as he turned off the lights.

The gunman replied with a blitzkrieg that tore through the tiny shop. Glass, wood, and plaster erupted into the air as the sightless sniper relied on blind luck and sheer volume to hit his targets. A second wave followed quickly, which shattered the front door and showered the room with a stream of razor-sharp confetti, but Payne remained calm, keeping his face covered and his body against the base of the thick front wall.

"I guess not," he sneered.

When the violence subsided, Payne risked a quick peek into the back of the shop. Things were blurry at first because of the lack of light and a cloud of dust, but after a few seconds, he realized the counter that shielded Jones had taken more hits than a hippie at Woodstock.

"D.J.," Payne whispered, "are you all right?"

"Yeah, and very lucky. I don't know how that last batch missed me."

"Me, either." Payne glanced around the shop and realized they couldn't stay there much longer. "We have to get out of here. If we stay put, he's going to hit us eventually."

Jones agreed. "He did us a favor by knocking out the

door and window. If you want, I can fire a few clearing shots so you can bolt outside."

Payne nodded. Even though Jones wouldn't be aiming at the sniper, he would minimize the risk of return fire, which would allow him to slip outside. Of course, the drawback to the plan was the possibility of more than one gunman. If someone was waiting near the door, he'd shoot Payne rather easily.

But it was a chance they had to take.

"Are you ready?" Payne asked as he peered through the darkness. "On the count of three, shoot through the window as I head for the door."

"You got it."

"One," Payne whispered as he adjusted the Glock in his sweaty right hand.

"Two," muttered Jones as he peered at his glassless target.

"Three!" they yelled in unison.

With a burst of adrenaline, Payne leapt from the ground and sprinted out the door while Jones aimed his gun at the window and fired. Or at least tried to. Unfortunately, nothing came out when he squeezed the Glock's trigger, which left his friend in a very precarious position.

The concrete under Payne's feet exploded in wispy puffs of smoke as the gunman opened fire from the roof across the street. With nowhere else to go, Payne cut sharply to his right and dove behind the closest car he saw, a maneuver that tore most of the skin from his knees. In Payne's mind, it was a fair trade. He definitely preferred scabs to bullet holes.

"Are you all right?" Jones called from inside.

"I'm fine!" Payne snarled. "Where the hell was my cover fire?"

"Sorry. I had a misfire. The damn gun wouldn't shoot."

"What do you mean it wouldn't shoot? You have to pull the trigger, you know."

Jones grinned, countering the insult with a fact that Payne had overlooked. "Don't be mad at me, be mad at the source. Remember, you got your gun from the same place as me."

Growling softly, Payne focused his attention on the weapon in his hand. If it had the same malfunction as Jones's, he wouldn't have a chance against the sniper. The truth was he had slim odds to begin with, but with a broken firearm, he would be in serious trouble.

"Shit," he mumbled to himself. There was only one way to find out.

Payne pointed his Glock toward the building across the street and squeezed the trigger. But nothing happened. No explosion. No discharge. Just a quiet click.

In situations like this, Payne was taught to use a simple corrective technique known as "tap, rack, bang." He tapped the bottom of the handle to make sure his magazine was properly engaged. Then he racked the gun, ejecting the mis-fired round and chambering the next one. Finally, he pulled the trigger again, hoping to hear a bang.

But in this case, the only sound he heard was another click.

"Well?" Jones called from inside the shop. He had tried the same technique without any luck.

"We're so screwed we should be wearing condoms."

Jones grinned. "Don't give up hope yet. What kind of shot is this guy? Any good?"

Payne glanced at the holes in the sidewalk and sighed at the damage that had been done. "Not really. If he was, I wouldn't be talking to you right now."

"And he's probably working alone, huh?"

"If he wasn't, his partner would've nailed me by now."

"If that's the case, then what are we afraid of? Are we going to let some redneck knock off two of this country's best soldiers, or are we going to come up with a plan to take this guy out?"

"If I was a betting man, I'd put my money on the red-neck."

"I'm serious! We've been in several situations worse than this, and we've always made it out."

Payne grunted as he stared at his broken Glock. "Fine, let's list everything that we have, and maybe a plan will become obvious."

Jones nodded. "As far as I can tell, we have two defective handguns and . . ."

"And?" Payne muttered, hoping that he was forgetting something important.

"And that's about it! As far as I can tell, we have two broken Glocks."

Payne leaned his head against the Chevy Celebrity that protected him and groaned. Their current inventory wouldn't stop a mugger, let alone a well-placed sniper. "Is there anything else in there that can be used? A gun behind the counter? A telephone? A flashlight?"

"Oh, shit!" Jones suddenly shrieked. "I just thought of something big!"

"Oh, yeah? What's that?"

"Levon!"

The answer stunned Payne. Somehow he had completely forgotten about Greene. "Holy hell! Why don't you see where that badass is hiding?"

"Be back in a flash."

Payne snuggled up against the car the best he could, trying to conceal his body under the maroon frame. He realized if the sniper attempted a ground assault, the only way he could protect himself was by hiding under the car. Thankfully, before that was necessary, Payne detected a sound in the far-off distance. At first he wasn't sure if he was imagining it or not, but after a few seconds of listening, he knew that he wasn't. It was the wail of sirens, and they were headed his way.

"Jon?" Jones shouted from the back of the shop. "Is that what I think it is?"

Payne peered underneath the Chevy and saw several squad cars pulling onto his street. "Yes, Mr. Jones, the cavalry has arrived!"

"Thank God."

"You said it." Payne leaned back on the sidewalk, his

legs still underneath the car for protection. "By the way, how's Levon doing?"

Instead of shouting his response, Jones scrambled out of the store and took a seat next to his friend. Once he was safely behind the car, he turned toward Payne and looked him dead in the eye. "You're not going to believe this. You're really not."

"What now?"

"I don't even know how to start, but . . ." Jones struggled for the right words to break the news to his friend. "Levon is gone."

Payne sat upright, the color draining from his face. "Oh, my God! How did he—"

"No," Jones said as he grabbed Payne's arm. "He's not *dead* gone. He's *gone* gone. I don't know how he did it, but that slippery son of a bitch managed to escape."

CHAPTER 22

AS the police pulled to a screeching stop in front of Sam's Tattoos, Payne stared at Jones, trying to determine if his best friend was serious. After several seconds, Payne decided that he was. "Levon has disappeared?"

"Yep. He's gone."

Payne shook his head in disbelief. "How is that possible? He's, like, eight feet tall and weighs five hundred pounds, yet you managed to lose him in an empty room."

"That's what I said."

"I thought you were supposed to be a professional detective."

"I am. And in my professional opinion, I'm telling you he's not in there."

Payne leaned closer to Jones and tried to smell his breath. "Have you been drinking?"

Jones grinned. "I wish I was."

Payne was about to reply, but before he had a chance, a booming voice shattered the stillness of the night.

"We see you behind the car," announced a patrolman through his bullhorn. "Put your hands where we can see them and come out very slowly."

The two of them did as they were told and were frisked by a team of gun-toting officers.

"Gentlemen," barked Sergeant Rutherford, the lead officer at the scene, "I'm sure you realize y'all have a lot of explaining to do."

Rutherford was in his mid-forties and possessed the face of an ex-boxer. His nose was crooked, his teeth were fake, and his face was dotted with several scars. His thick black hair was splashed with gray, but his police hat covered most of it.

"Before I throw you guys in cuffs and haul your asses to the station, you need to tell me what happened here."

Payne cleared his throat and began to speak before Jones had a chance to say anything. "My buddy and I just flew in to New Orleans earlier tonight for a little R & R. We rented a car, got something to eat, and decided to do something out of the ordinary. A local told us that Jamaican Sam drew the best tattoos in the whole darn state—"

"A lovely state, I might add."

"It sure is, D.J. Anyway, we decided to come here to check out his craftsmanship."

"We were impressed. Very colorful stuff."

"But we were here for less than ten minutes when somebody shot Sam from across the street."

"We think from that rooftop there," Jones said, pointing. "With a sniper rifle."

"We wanted to fight back."

"But we didn't have any weapons."

Payne nodded. "I hid in the corner for protection, and D.J. dove behind the counter."

"When I was back there, I found two guns. I tossed one to Jon and kept the other for myself."

"We tried to use them when the madman started shooting at us."

"But neither of them worked."

"I left mine on the sidewalk," Payne volunteered.

"And mine is inside."

"You can check for yourself. Neither of them is capable of firing a round."

"Yep," Jones seconded. "I squeezed the trigger, but it wouldn't make a bang or nothing."

Payne paused in thought. "Anything else you can think of?"

Jones shook his head. "Nope. I think that covers it."

Payne nodded in agreement. "That's about all we've got, sir. Hopefully that makes your report pretty easy to write."

Rutherford studied the two men and smiled. He wanted to comment on the conversation but was simply too fascinated to speak. Even though Payne's and Jones's statements were coming from two different voices, it was like they were coming from the same mind. When Payne started a sentence, Jones finished it. If Jones started, Payne ended it. Rutherford had been on the job for over twenty years and had never seen anything like it.

"Okay," the cop muttered as he emerged from his trance. "We'll take a look around and see if your story checks out. If it does, y'all have nothing to worry about. I'll have you back on your vacation by sunrise. However, if it doesn't, then you might be staying here in our state"—Rutherford turned his head toward Jones and smirked—"pardon me, our *lovely* state, for a lot longer than you were planning. In the meantime, why don't you guys show me some ID? That'll give me a chance to see if y'all have escaped from a mental health facility, which is a distinct possibility in my book."

AFTER examining the scene for an hour, Rutherford decided that Payne and Jones were telling the truth. But before he let them go, he decided to discuss the facts with his second in command. "Richie, can you think of any reason to hold these two any longer?"

The second cop, white and overweight, glanced at his notes and shook his head. "Nah. From what we've found, these guys couldn't have been the shooter. The bullet that killed Sam matched the size of the casings from the roof across the street. The two Glocks found at the scene have no serial numbers, probably bought by Sam for protection. And just like the guys said, the damn things appeared to be un-fired. We couldn't smell discharge."

"On top of that," Rutherford added, "the two suspects are covered in cuts and scratches, which were probably caused by flying glass. That means they were in the shop when the shooting started."

"Yep, and the initial 911 call mentioned a sniper as well."

"What about their histories? Any warrants?"

"We checked their backgrounds, and neither of them have any prior convictions. Both of them have military academy educations, and both are currently employed by a reputable company, Payne Industries. In fact, the white guy in your car is CEO of the corporation."

"You mean it's *his* corporation?" Rutherford asked.

"Yes, sir. He's the head honcho. Flew down here on his private jet."

"I'll be damned. What the hell is a rich corporate type doing in a New Orleans ghetto in the middle of the damn night?"

"Apparently getting a tattoo."

Rutherford laughed at the suggestion. "Kind of unlikely, huh?"

"Yeah, but I'll be honest with you. I don't think he flew all the way down here to kill Jamaican Sam, either. A rich man like that doesn't commit his own crimes. A millionaire pays to have them done for him."

Rutherford nodded. "True, but we've already decided that Payne and Jones didn't kill anyone, right? So what brings them here at this hour?"

"Drugs?"

"I doubt it. I ordered a background check on Jamaican Sam Fletcher, and he had no record other than a few busts for marijuana. The guy was a smoker, not a seller. The cops that patrol this neighborhood claim he ran a clean place. In fact, his artwork was so admired by the local gangs that thugs went out of their way to protect him."

"Where does that leave us?"

Rutherford didn't want to admit it, but he had no choice. "Honestly, it leaves us without a case. We can't charge these two without just cause, and we can't prove that these guys did anything wrong. We could hold them for twenty-four hours of questioning if we wanted to, but I guarantee that Payne would have a fancy-pants lawyer down here in the blink of an eye causing a big stink about something. No, thank you! It just wouldn't be worth it."

"Then we're kinda forced to let them go, huh?"

"It looks that way, but that doesn't mean we're gonna forget 'em."

The cop looked at his superior and grinned. "What do you have in mind? Some kind of tail?"

Rutherford laughed at the suggestion. "Nothing that drastic, at least not yet. I'm gonna do some digging when I get back to the station and see if I can turn up anything that makes sense. If I do, I'll nail these guys before they know what hit 'em." Rutherford groaned as he stared at the captives in the back of his squad car. "Let 'em loose, but tell 'em I want to have a brief chat with them before they leave."

While waiting for the duo, Rutherford leaned against a nearby building, ready to verbally pounce on the men at the first opportunity. Payne and Jones barely had time to stretch their legs before the veteran cop started his lecture.

"Gentlemen," he said sternly, "y'all should know better than to be roaming this type of neighborhood in the middle of the night. Violence is pretty common here, and the idiot that told you to visit Sam's shop at night should've known better. Y'all are lucky to be alive."

Payne nodded his head in agreement as he walked toward the sergeant. "Thanks to you, we are. If you guys didn't show up when you did, we would've been killed by the sniper for sure."

"Don't thank me," admitted the cop. "Thank the person who called 911. He was the one that made us aware of the shooting."

"Actually, I'd like to. Is the guy around?"

Rutherford shrugged while staring at the crowd that had

gathered across the street. "Probably, but I don't know where to find him. He used a pay phone to report the incident, but refused to leave his name."

Jones smiled to himself, wondering if Levon Greene was the person who'd made the call. If he had, they probably owed the Buffalo Soldier their lives. "If you manage to find out who it was, thank him for us, okay?"

Rutherford shook Jones's hand and smiled. "You got it." Then he turned to shake Payne's. "In the meantime, stay out of trouble, all right? Keep in mind if I hear your names mentioned at the station in connection with any other suspicious events during your vacation in New Orleans, I might be forced to reconsider your involvement. Do I make myself clear?"

Both men nodded even though they realized that their trouble was far from over.

In fact, it was just beginning.

CHAPTER 23

LIGHTNING bolts. The pain felt like lightning bolts surging through her brain.

Ariane did her best to ignore it—tried to open her eyes, tried to fight through the jackhammer that thumped inside her skull—but the agony was overwhelming. God, she wondered, what's wrong with me? She'd never felt this bad before. Ever. She'd suffered through hangovers, migraines, and a skiing accident that left her with a severe concussion, but in all her years, she had never come close to feeling like this.

Hell, it felt like she was giving birth through her nose. The pain was *that* intense.

To escape the pounding, Ariane was tempted to fall back asleep. She figured if she got a little more rest she'd have to feel a whole lot better than she did now. Then, if all went well, she'd roll out of bed like she had planned and whip Jonathon's butt in a round of golf.

Golf? Wait a second. Something about that didn't seem right. She tried to figure it out, struggled to put her snippets of memory together in an orderly fashion, but was unable to. She could vaguely remember waking up and brushing her teeth and getting a shower and . . . the door. Something about the door. She could remember someone pounding on her door.

Or was the pounding in her head?

Wow! She honestly didn't know. The details were hazy, like a painful childhood incident that had suddenly crept back into her consciousness. Why couldn't she remember the door? What was it about her door?

Ariane tried to open her eyes, fought to pry her lids apart, but the pain was too intense. Wave after wave crashed inside her head, causing her to lurch forward into the fetal position. As she did, the maelstrom surged toward her gut, inducing the worst muscle spasms of her life. To her it felt like her innards were exploding upward. Like her gallbladder, liver, and intestines were inching their way toward her mouth, swimming ever so slowly up the back of her throat on a viscous river of bile.

"What's wrong with me?" she called out, hoping God would provide her with an answer.

"Shhh," a motherly voice replied. "Just relax. The pain will soon pass. I promise."

The sound of a strange voice sent shock waves through Ariane.

"Who are you?" she shrieked, now trying to open her eyes with twice the urgency of before. "What are you doing in my bedroom?"

The voice sighed at the query. "You're not in your bedroom."

That was news to Ariane. She honestly couldn't remember leaving her apartment. "I'm not? Where am I, then? What's wrong with me?"

"I'm not sure where we are. I wish I knew. And as to what's wrong with you, you're having a reaction to the drugs. But don't worry, it'll pass quickly."

"Drugs?" Ariane mumbled.

"Yeah, sis, I said drugs." The female paused to let the information sink in.

Sis? Did she say *sis*? Why the hell would this person call her *sis*?

Oh, God! The reason suddenly dawned on her.

"Tonya? Is that you?"

Tonya Edwards looked down at Ariane and attempted to smile. "Of course it's me—unless you have another sister that you've been hiding."

"No, but . . ." The presence of her pregnant older sister only added to Ariane's confusion. Tonya lived in Colorado. What in the world was she doing in Pittsburgh? "Why are you here? Is something wrong?"

It was the understatement of the year.

"Yeah, sis, I'd say something is wrong."

Ariane swallowed, the bitter taste of bile still in her mouth. "Is it the baby?"

"The baby, Robert, you, me. Pretty much everything." Tonya tried to lower herself to the floor, but her belly prevented it. "I'm not sure why, but our family's been kidnapped."

SLIGHTLY banged up but happy to be alive, the two friends walked to their rented Mustang in total silence. As they strolled past the ancient cemetery, Payne shuddered slightly, realizing how close he'd come to his own funeral. If the sniper had been a little more accurate, Payne and Jones would've been returning to Pittsburgh in wooden crates, not in the comfort of a private jet.

"You're awfully quiet," Jones said, studying his silent friend. "Are you all right?"

Payne nodded as he slid into the car. "As good as can be expected."

After strapping himself in, Payne allowed his mind to drift back to the incident at the tattoo shop. Even though the shooting was unexpected, Payne knew that Ariane's kidnappers were bound to become aware of his presence. But the big question was, how? How did they find out about him so quickly? Was there a spy at the airport? At the Fishing Hole? Or was the late-night gunplay an unlucky coincidence? Maybe Sam's death had been ordered several days before, and the sniper just happened to show up at the same time they did. Sam was the first one eliminated, so maybe he was the number one priority of the hit. Maybe the Plantation Posse, or some unrelated gang, had been planning to silence him for an entirely different reason. Even though it seemed unlikely, it was a possibility.

Shit, in New Orleans, anything was possible. One trip to Mardi Gras would prove that.

"By the way," Jones asked, "where are we going? Or are you planning on driving around this city until someone starts shooting at us again?"

"That's not what I had in mind, but now that you mention it, that's better than anything I can come up with."

"Stumped already?"

"I wouldn't say stumped, but I'm pretty confused. There are simply too many variables floating around in my mind right now. And I can't figure out which ones are important."

"I was thinking the same thing. There are lots of questions and very few answers."

"You're right about that. However, two things are bothering me more than anything else. I can't figure them out for the life of me."

"And they are?"

"Number one, if Ariane was kidnapped for money, why the hell would the Posse try to kill me? I'm the one with the bank account. Why eliminate me? My death would instantly take away their chance of a big payday."

Jones nodded. It was a thought that hadn't entered his mind. "You're right. That's a pretty big issue, one that I can't answer. What's number two? Maybe I can help you with that."

"That one's even more confusing. Where the hell is Levon?"

CHAPTER 24

BECAUSE of his size and the weapon he carried, Levon Greene showed no fear as he walked through Louis Armstrong Park. Like most American cities, New Orleans had a policy against large, gun-toting black men walking in its city parks after midnight. But Greene knew he was in no danger of being stopped since most cops were at Sam's Tattoos, trying to solve that shooting.

As he emerged from the darkness of the tree-lined sidewalks, Greene tucked his pistol in the waistband of his Dockers, concealing it completely under his shirt. Despite the early-morning hour, up-tempo funk leaked from Donna's Bar and Grill, a famous jazz club off of St. Ann Street. A group of well-dressed men and women waited to show the bouncer their IDs. Greene didn't have the patience to linger in line, so he shook the hand of the starstruck guard and slipped inside without delay.

Celebrity had some privileges.

Since the sniper had prevented him from using the bathroom at Sam's, Greene quickly made his way to the rear of the club while trying to conceal his identity from as many people as he could. He simply didn't have time to sign autographs for anyone at the moment. There were more pressing matters on his mind—and his lower colon—to deal with. After making his way into the restroom, Greene found himself angered by his phone, which started to ring the moment he turned the lock on his stall door.

"Who's this?" he demanded.

"This is D.J.," Jones said, relieved. "Are you all right?"

The call was completely unexpected, like hearing the voice of a ghost, and it took Greene a moment to catch his breath. "Am *I* all right? I think the better question is, are *you* all right? I thought you were dead for sure! I can't believe you're alive! Did Jon make it, too?"

"He's fine. He's sitting next to me."

"I'll be a son of a bitch," Greene muttered. From the number of bullets fired, he assumed nobody in the front of the shop could've survived. And if someone had, he figured they'd be bleeding all over intensive care by now. "How about Sam? Did he make it?"

"I'm afraid not. The first shot took him out clean. He didn't have a chance."

"What about the next one hundred shots? What the hell did they hit?"

"Everything but us," Jones admitted. "I guess our military training helped us escape."

"Training? What kind of training teaches you to dodge bullets? Are you guys fucking ninjas?"

"I swear I never fucked a ninja in my life." Jones chuckled, hoping that Greene understood his joke. "The truth is, luck played a bigger role in our safety than I'm willing to admit."

"Man, how lucky can two guys get?"

"Speaking of lucky, how did you get out of there? I could've sworn we left you in Sam's bathroom. When we went to save you, you weren't in there. How did you pull that one off?"

Greene smiled as he thought about his easy escape, but it

was a secret that he wasn't ready to share. He wanted Payne and Jones to ponder the mystery for a little while longer. "I'll tell you in a little bit, okay? But I'm in a public restroom as we speak, and I don't know if there are people in the other stalls listening."

"What did you do? Flush yourself to another part of the city?"

Greene laughed. "No, nothing like that, but you'll have to wait a few more minutes for the details. Where are you guys now?"

Jones asked Payne for details. "We're somewhere in the French Quarter. Jon thinks it's called Conti Street."

"That's pretty close to me." Greene gave Jones directions to Donna's Bar and Grill and told him that he'd be waiting outside when they got there. "But first," he insisted, "I've got some urgent business to attend to, and I'm not willing to do it while we're on the phone."

THE Mustang stopped in front of the crowded club and pulled away with its new passenger. As the car picked up speed, Greene greeted Payne and Jones, warmly shaking their hands. "Military? You guys never told me you were in the military. What branch were you in?"

Payne answered first. "I went to the Naval Academy. After that I got selected by the government to work on a special forces unit."

"That's where I met him," Jones added. "I was assigned to the same team as Jon, even though I was from the Air Force. And we've been side by side ever since."

"I'll be damned," Greene muttered. "I'm sitting here with two Rambos. No wonder you guys were able to escape the tattoo parlor. I'm surprised you didn't kill the shooter in the process. What, are you guys rusty or something?"

"Actually, we wanted to get the bastard but weren't able to because of you."

Greene looked at Payne, confused. "Because of me? What did I do?"

"It's what you didn't do. You didn't get us guns that worked."

"They didn't work? What do you mean they didn't work?"

Jones jumped into the fray. "Just like he said. We pulled our triggers several times, and nothing came out. Like a guy with a vasectomy."

Payne grinned at the analogy. "Tell me more about your gun dealer. Has anything like this ever happened before?"

"No," Greene assured them. "He's got a first-class rep on the streets."

"Maybe so, but his faulty products almost got us killed." Payne slowed to a stop at a red light and turned toward Greene. "I'd love a chance to meet this guy. You know, to see if I get a good feeling about him. Do you think you could set something up?"

Greene glanced at Payne and shrugged. "I could, but it won't do you any good. You guys already met him, and you trusted him just fine."

"Terrell Murray?" Payne asked. "The owner of the Fishing Hole?"

Greene nodded. "The one and only."

"Why didn't you mention that before we talked to him?" Jones demanded.

"Terrell is very hush-hush about his activities. Sure, he owns and operates some skin clubs, but those things are legal and can't get him into trouble. What he refuses to do, though, is flaunt the things that could get him busted. If he sells something illegal, he deals with a restricted list of clientele, and if they betray him, he cuts them off immediately. That's why I purchased the weapons by myself and why I didn't mention his name earlier. Can you understand that?"

"Sure," Payne admitted. "That makes plenty of sense to me. So, why tell us now? If Terrell is so secretive, why risk his confidence by mentioning his name?"

"Sometimes you gotta betray one trust to gain another."

Payne and Jones pondered the comment, nodding their

heads in admiration. For an ex-jock, Greene possessed a pretty good understanding of human nature.

"And besides," he continued, "when we go to get your refund, I want you to do the talking. I'd feel safer if you pissed him off instead of me."

CHAPTER 25

AS they drove to the Fishing Hole, Jones patiently waited for Greene to answer the question that he'd asked earlier, but it was apparent that Greene had completely forgotten about it—or was trying to avoid it. "Levon, since you're out of the john now, can you please tell me how you managed to escape from Sam's? That's been bugging me for the past hour."

Payne glanced at Jones and smiled. "You must've been reading my mind. I was getting ready to ask him the same thing."

Realizing that he was the center of attention, Greene grinned mischievously, his eyes twinkling like a small child's at a birthday party. When he could hold it in no longer, he blurted the secret. "I went through the back wall."

Jones laughed in a disbelieving tone. "Who are you, the Kool-Aid guy? I don't remember seeing any Negro-shaped holes in the back room."

But Greene stuck by his story. "How hard did ya look?"

"Pretty damn hard."

"Apparently not hard enough, because I got my ass out."

Payne joined Greene in laughter. "He's got you there,

Sherlock. I guess you aren't the infallible detective after all."

Jones leaned forward to object. "Yeah, but—"

"Actually," Payne interrupted, "why don't you let him explain things? Maybe you can learn a thing or two from the big man."

Jones rolled his eyes while he waited for Greene to begin.

"Thank you, Jon. I'd love to help him out. When I got into the back, I did as you asked. I looked for anything suspicious, but there was nothing there but a bathroom and a closet."

"Right," Jones blurted. "That's what I found, too."

"So, like I said, I went into the bathroom to take care of my business, and—*boom! crash!*—I heard a gunshot then glass breaking in the front. I wanted to come out to check on things, but my pants were around my ankles, and that slowed me down a bit."

"I bet it did," Jones muttered.

"By the time I got my pants up, I heard a number of shots. Glass was breaking, walls were shattering, chaos! At that point, I assumed you guys were dead. I mean, come on! How was I supposed to know that you were commandos in a former life? Anyway, I figured I needed to get out of the place without going out the front door, right? I remembered from when I walked into the shop that there was a historical landmark plaque on the front wall, and it said the building used to be a part of the Underground Railroad."

"Seriously?" Jones asked.

Greene nodded. "Like I told you guys, I've been doing a lot of research on my hometown, and one of the things that fascinates me was New Orleans' role in the slave trade. A number of ports on the Gulf of Mexico were notorious for bringing slaves into this country, but at the same time, a number of ports were used to smuggle slaves out. Shit, there was so much diversity in this city during the eighteen hundreds that people often confused slaves with their masters. In fact, there was one period, in 1803, when ownership of New Orleans passed from Spain to France to the United

States in less than a month's time. If a city doesn't even know what country it belongs to, how's it gonna keep track of the people?"

Jones tried to absorb all of the information. Historical facts and local folklore normally fascinated him, but in this case, he wanted to get to the important stuff. He wanted to know how Greene got out of the damn shop without being seen. "Levon, not to be rude, but—"

"I know, I know. You want to know how I did it. Fine, I'll tell you. The landmark plaque clicked in my mind, and I remembered going on a tour or two where there was a trapdoor or a hidden set of steps that allowed fugitives to slip out of the place undetected. And guess what?"

Payne answered. "You found something."

"Exactly! The rear wall of the closet was actually a door. A well-concealed door."

"Once you got outside, did you try to get the shooter?"

"To be honest with you, no. My nickname is the Buffalo Soldier, but I don't have much experience with killing people. And the truth is, I thought you guys were already dead."

"We probably should've been," Jones admitted. "A well-trained gunman would've picked us off clean. *If* that was his goal."

Greene frowned. "What does that mean? You don't think he was aiming for you?"

"At this point, we don't know. What would be the purpose of killing Jon if he hasn't paid a ransom yet? If the kidnappers want his millions, they better not kill him. Right?"

The comment took Greene by surprise. "You've got millions? I thought you were some kind of unemployed street baller. You really got that many bucks in the bank?"

"I have a nice nest egg, yeah."

"I'll be damned! A rich Rambo! What the hell did you do? Auction your soldiering skills to the highest bidder? Or did you just sell a stolen warhead?"

"Nothing that dramatic. When my grandfather died, he left the family business to me."

"Like a family restaurant or something?"

Payne shrugged, trying not to brag. "Something like that."

Greene nodded his approval. "As I was saying, I didn't have the expertise to take out the shooter, so I did the next best thing. I called the cops."

"So, that was you!" Jones said, happy that Greene had come through for them. "The police said someone had reported the crime to 911, but they weren't willing to give a name."

"I told you, I don't like dealing with the cops. Plus, I don't want to read tomorrow's newspaper and see my name linked to a bad part of town. That wouldn't be good for my image."

"Amen!" said Payne as he thought about the irony of Greene's statement. "Now let's go inside this strip club and bitch to the owner about the defective guns that you bought for us."

DESPITE the approach of daylight, the Fishing Hole was still crawling with semiaroused men and naked women, a sight that surprised Payne and Jones. Neither man was a huge fan of the skin club scene, so they weren't aware that most dancers usually did their best business just before closing time— due to the horniness and intoxication of their fans.

"Let me see if Terrell's still here," Greene stated. "It's nearly four A.M., so there's a good chance he's already gone home for the night."

"Should we go with you?" Jones wondered.

"Probably not. Terrell's pretty skittish around new people. If the three of us go charging back there, he's liable to get pissed. And trust me, you don't want to see him pissed."

Payne nodded while receiving a skeptical glance from Jones. Once Greene had entered the club's back corridor, Jones spoke up. "What's your gut say about Terrell Murray?"

"It's undecided. Earlier tonight he seemed pretty hospitable, but it could've been an act. I find it pretty suspicious that he sold us defective weapons and recommended our visit to Sam's shooting gallery within a twenty-four-hour period. That's a pretty big coincidence, don't you think?"

"But what would he gain from our deaths? Like you mentioned, if the kidnappers want your money, they need to keep you alive."

"I know. That's why my gut is undecided. I don't know why he'd want to eliminate us. Shoot, maybe all of this was just a fluke."

Jones pondered Murray's role as he watched the Fishing Hole's crowd. "You know, maybe he doesn't want to kill us. Maybe he has to."

"How so?"

"In a perfect world, the people who took Ariane would want to take your money, but maybe our presence in New Orleans has everyone spooked. Maybe the kidnappers figure it's better to cut their losses before they get caught. You know, live to play another day."

"Possibly," Payne admitted. It was a thought that hadn't crossed his mind. "But to be honest with you, I didn't get the sense that Murray was surprised by our visit. If he is, in fact, the ringleader of this crime, you'd think that our appearance would've flustered him."

"You're right, but if Levon had mentioned our names when he purchased the guns earlier in the day, Murray would've had plenty of time to gather his senses. Right?"

"Right."

"And get faulty weapons for us."

"Yep."

"And arrange our death."

"I see what you're saying. But for some reason that last part just doesn't seem to click. If Murray wanted us dead and he knew that we had broken guns, then why didn't he have someone walk into Sam's shop and shoot us at close range?"

"That's a good point. So where does that leave us?"

Payne shrugged. "Confused and very tired. I'm sure there's something staring us in the face, but I can't think of it."

"Then let's get out of here," Greene said from behind. His approach had been so silent he startled both Payne and

Jones. "Terrell's not here, so I think our refund is going to have to wait."

"That's okay," Jones muttered. "I think all of us could use some sleep before we face our next round of confrontations."

Payne nodded. "Trust me, my gut tells me that there are some big ones headed our way."

CHAPTER 26

WITH the help of several guards, Hakeem Ndjai ordered the captives out of their cabins at the first sign of daylight. He led the bruised and battered group across the dew-covered grass to the far end of the field. The walk was a brisk one, forcing the prisoners to maintain a pace that they were barely able to keep, but at no point were they tempted to complain since their journey was far better than the backbreaking labor that Ndjai usually put them through. Furthermore, a complaint would have resulted in a swift and vicious beating at the hands of the guards.

Not exactly the way the prisoners wanted to start their day.

When they neared the tree-lined edge of the field, Ndjai ordered the group to stop, then waited for everyone to gather around him. After clearing his throat, the African native spoke to the prisoners, lecturing in his thick accent on the torture device that they were about to see, an invention that he had constructed himself.

"What I am about to show you is a contraption that I was never allowed to use on the cacao plantations of Cameroon because the landowners felt it was too destructive to the morale of the workers. Thankfully, Master Holmes views things differently and has given me permission to use some of my toys on the people that need to be disciplined the most." Ndjai paused, staring into the scared eyes of his prisoners. "I like to call it the Devil's Box."

Ndjai started walking again, leading the group along the edge of the forest, taking them even further from the cabins where they spent their terror-filled nights.

As their journey continued, the sights, sounds, and smells of nature were more prevalent than on the cultivated land near the plantation house. Ducks, geese, and brown pelicans waddled on the marsh's edge, carefully avoiding the foxes that guarded the land and the alligators that patrolled the water of the swamps. White-tailed deer darted among the fallen timber like a scene from a Disney movie, while nutrias scoured for food on the hard ground. Doves, egrets, and wild turkeys squawked and sang in the dense groves of oak trees to their left, which dripped with thick blankets of Spanish moss. Small pockets of flowers—lilies, orchids, honeysuckle, jasmine, and azaleas—dotted the terrain, filling the air with a sweet fragrance that overpowered the horrid stench that covered the skin and clothes of the prisoners, temporarily giving the group a reason for hope.

But five more minutes of hiking ended that.

The soft sounds of nature that had calmed them a moment before had been replaced by the distant howl of a man. The echoing scream was muffled at first, but it slowly increased in volume and intensity with every step that the group took.

"A little farther," Ndjai said as he enjoyed the sound of torture. "Then you will see why my friend is so unhappy."

With tired legs and shortness of breath, the group mounted a man-made slope that had been built decades earlier to prevent flooding. A few of the prisoners struggled with the climb, stumbling on the loose sand and gravel that covered the mound, but the guards showed them no mercy, flogging the fallen captives across their backs with punishing blows from their braided whips. The loud cracks of cowhide, followed by the sharp shrieks of pain, only added to the horrific sound of terror that came from the crest of the hill. In unison, the combination of cruelty, agony, and torment created a noise that was so sinister, so evil, that some of the guards shielded their ears from the heinous symphony.

When the last captive reached the top of the ridge, Ndjai ordered the prisoners to study his invention. He wanted their full attention when he explained the torture device. But his command wasn't necessary. Members of the pilgrimage had never been more wide-eyed in their entire lives. The concentration of each person was focused solely on the wooden cube that had been anchored into the hilltop. Trembling, they waited for a detailed explanation of Ndjai's masterpiece, the Devil's Box.

Standing four feet tall and four feet wide, the cube did not appear threatening at first glance. Made out of thick slabs of oak, the device was secured in place by a number of sturdy metal cables that had been pounded into the rocky turf. The outside surface of the box had been sanded to a smooth finish, then painted with several coats of black waterproof sealant, giving the device the look of a giant charcoal briquette. The box was solid on all sides but one; the center of the top layer had been carved in an intricate lattice pattern, allowing fresh air into the cube without giving the occupant any view except of the hot sun above.

"I know what you are thinking. The Devil's Box does not appear dangerous, but do not let its simplicity fool you. It can be nasty in so many ways. And if you do not believe me, you can always ask Nathan." Ndjai put his face above the box and laughed. "Isn't that right, Nathan? You thought you were tough when you were out here, but now that you have been in there for a while, you do not feel very tough, do you?"

The prisoner answered with a torture-filled grunt, but his words were indecipherable.

"You will have to excuse Nathan. He has been in my box since long before your arrival on the Plantation, and it seems dehydration has swollen his tongue to twice its normal size. Unfortunately, that makes words very difficult to pronounce." Ndjai turned his attention back to Nathan. "Isn't that right? You are a little bit thirsty, aren't you? Well, you should have thought of that before you hurt one of my bosses, you stupid man!"

The guards laughed in amusement as they watched the taunting continue.

"But do not worry. I will not let you die of thirst. I will keep you like this for as long as I possibly can, teetering on the edge of life and death."

Once again the captive screamed in agony, but this time with a far greater intensity. It caused each prisoner to shiver with fear and hatred for the man who had put him there.

"Before you get the wrong idea," Ndjai continued, "and start to think that this device is simply used to bake the bad attitude out of a troubled inmate, let me point out your error. The Devil's Box is not used for dehydration, even though I must admit the severe loss of fluids is a pleasant side effect to my invention. In fact, that is why I painted it black to begin with, to draw in the intense heat of the sun. You would be surprised at how uncomfortable a person can get when they run out of liquid."

He moved closer to the group so they could see the emotion on his face.

"In the beginning you feel an unquenchable thirst, but from there the human body falls apart quite quickly. The tongue starts to balloon, followed by the drying of the throat lining and nasal passages, making it difficult to talk or even breathe. Lips start to crack, and skin starts to separate, painfully pulling apart with the slightest movement of any kind. Intense cramps surface in your arms and legs, causing spasms of agony that you cannot stop. Your bladder swells from the lack of moisture in your body, making you suffer through the severe urge to urinate, but the joke is on you because there is no liquid in your system to squeeze out. From there your kidneys fail, followed by the rest of your body, including your brain. All in all, not a pleasant way to go."

Ndjai caught his breath while enjoying the horrified look of the crowd that surrounded him—children clinging to their parents, strangers holding hands for comfort and unity, fear and desperation in the eyes of everyone. It was a sight that he truly loved.

"But as I pointed out to you, dehydration is not the main intent of the Devil's Box. It is merely a bonus, heightening the effects of its original purpose. And what purpose is that, you may ask. Well, let me tell you. The purpose is agony!"

Ndjai approached the box again, but this time one of the guards handed him a plastic container that was no larger than a carton of tissues.

"When we put Nathan in here several weeks ago, he was covered in cuts and scratches, wounds that I personally administered with the aid of a metal-tipped whip. Since that time his body has been unable to heal the torn flesh because of his severe thirst and his lack of a balanced diet. In fact, I would guess that his wounds are in worse shape now than the day I created them due to the infections that have developed. Tsk-tsk. It is really a shame. Nathan used to be such a large man. We even had a difficult time squeezing him inside the box because of his girth. But now, due to his lengthy stay in my device, he has been sapped of his size and strength—like Superman in a kryptonite cage!"

Ndjai grinned as he held the small container above the opening in the top of the box, taunting the imprisoned man by swooshing the object back and forth. This increased the intensity of Nathan's screams, turning his moans and wails into terrified shrieks of torment. The sound, which filled the air with a sense of dread, quickly brought gooseflesh to everyone on the ridge.

"One of the most difficult things to deal with in the Devil's Box is the loneliness. The heat is bad, the thirst is horrible, but the solitude is what gets you. Without companionship, the mind tends to wander, leaving sanity behind while looking for ways to amuse itself. It is a terrible thing, but it eventually happens to each of my victims."

Ndjai peeled open the container's cover and slowly started dumping its contents into the box.

"Since I worry about my friend's sanity, I do my best to occupy him with tangible things. Instead of allowing his mind to drift into a fantasy world, where it is liable to get lost, I try to keep his brain focused on real-life issues. Each day it is something new, and each problem gets more and more difficult for Nathan to solve. You are probably wondering, what is today's problem?" He laughed softly while answering his own question. "Fire ants!"

Ndjai drained the container into the Devil's Box, glancing through the cube's tiny slits to see how Nathan handled it. His intense screams proved that he wasn't happy.

"As you can tell from his reaction, the sting of the fire ant is very painful. The poison is not life threatening—unless, of course, a person gets stung by several dozen ants in a short period of time. Did you hear that, Nathan? Do not let them sting you, if you can help it!"

Ndjai chuckled as he redirected his attention to the group. "Unfortunately, his task might be difficult. You see, fire ants are actually drawn to the taste of blood, and since he has a number of open wounds, they are going to get pretty wound up, like sharks in a sea full of chum. Oh, well, look on the bright side. If he is able to eat the ants before they eat him, he will get his first dose of protein since his capture."

The guards smiled at the remark, showing their approval of Ndjai's presentation.

"At this point of my lecture, I am sure you are wondering why I brought you up here to start this day. That is what you are wondering, isn't it? Well, the reason is quite simple. I wanted to show you how good you currently have it." Ndjai paused for a moment to let that comment sink in. "Is the heat of the summer sun intense? Sure it is. Is working all day in the field tough? Definitely. Is sleeping on the ground of your cabin uncomfortable? Of course."

Moving closer to the group, Ndjai narrowed his eyes to tiny slits. "But keep this in mind. If you mess with me or my staff, I will make things so much worse for you. I will make your stay a living hell."

CHAPTER 27

DRAPED in a Tulane University blanket, Payne opened his eyes and gazed around the room. Wearing nothing but boxers, he had spent the night on Greene's couch but barely got any sleep. Thoughts of Ariane had kept him awake way past daybreak.

Payne felt much better after a quick shower. His body was reenergized, and his mind was suddenly clear. Some people needed caffeine in the morning, but Payne relied on a bar of soap. After getting dressed, he looked for Jones, finding him downstairs in the living room.

"What time is it?" Payne asked.

"Almost noon. I would've woken you up earlier, but I know you didn't sleep much."

"You got that right."

"Don't worry. Levon and I were busy while you were getting your beauty rest."

"Doing what?"

"Discussing last night. And after careful analysis, we came to the conclusion that Levon messed up bad."

"How so?"

"He neglected to tell us something about our guns. Something important."

"Such as?"

"They were loaded with dummy bullets."

Payne shook his head as he sat on the couch next to Jones. "How did *that* slip his mind?"

"Apparantly, on the rare occasion that Terrell sells a weapon to a new customer, he likes to load them with dummy bullets—substituting sand for powder. That way his weapons can't be used to rob him."

"And Levon knew this?"

Jones nodded. "But since he was buying the guns for us, Levon assumed that they'd be loaded with regular ammo."

"You realize his assumption could've gotten us killed."

"You're right, and he knows it. The big baby's been pouting all morning."

"Why? There's nothing he can do about it now. Besides, it's not like we could've saved Sam, even if our guns had worked."

"That's what I told him, but he's still taking it hard."

"Don't worry, he'll be fine once I talk to him. Speaking of which, where is he?"

"At Terrell's. While you were sleeping, he made an appointment to get us some new guns. This time, loaded with *real* bullets."

"That should help. When will he be back?"

Jones pointed to a nearby security monitor. "Actually, I think that's him now."

Payne glanced at the screen and saw an Escalade pull through the front gate. A minute later, Greene walked through the front door.

"Guys!" Greene shouted. "Where are you?"

Payne and Jones made their way to the foyer, anxious to see why Greene was so excited.

"What's gotten into you?" Jones asked. "You seem happier than before."

"That's 'cause I am! You know how I went to get you

guns? Well, I came back with more than that. Something *much* better."

"I hope you didn't buy a missile, because Jon doesn't carry that much cash."

"No." Greene laughed. "I got some news on the Posse!"

"On the Posse?" Payne demanded. "How did that happen?"

"Well, I went to the Fishing Hole to talk to Terrell about the dummy bullets. I figured if I bitched enough I could get him to cut us a deal on some new guns. Unfortunately, he was on the phone when I rolled in, and his boys said he'd take a while to finish. So instead of waiting by his office, I strolled out front to check out the talent. And that's when I saw him!"

"Him?" Jones asked. "What the hell were you doing watching a guy dance?"

Greene rolled his eyes. "The guy I saw was a customer."

"Was he cute?"

"Anyway," Greene said, ignoring Jones's teasing, "I saw this guy leaning against one of the brass railings, his hand and arm just dangling over the side. And guess what I noticed?"

Payne guessed. "A Posse tattoo."

"Give that man a prize! Can you believe my luck?"

"Did you talk to him?"

"I tried, but he saw me staring at his wrist. I don't know how he noticed me—I mean, I was being really careful—but he did. Next thing I know, he's whispering something to the buckwheat next to him, then bolting from the club. Thankfully, the buckwheat at the bar knew everything we needed to know. Well, not everything, but he knew a lot."

"And trust me," Jones said, "I want to hear every last word. But first, you've got to explain something for me. You keep saying *buckwheat*. What the hell does that mean?"

"Sorry, man, it's a Southern term. You remember that Little Rascals character, Buckwheat? You know, the one that Eddie Murphy played on *Saturday Night Live*?"

"O-tay," Jones chuckled, using Murphy's famous expression. "I remember."

"Well, there are brothers around this part of the country that are *really* rural. Nappy-looking hair, old work clothes, messed-up backwater language. Well, we call those brothers buckwheats. And trust me, this guy was a buckwheat and a half. Fucked-up dreadlocks, gold teeth, taller than me. Shit, I almost felt bad for the punk."

"Buckwheat, huh? I'll have to remember that term."

"Guys!" Payne yelled, unable to wait any longer. "What did he tell you, Levon?"

"Sorry, Jon." Greene gathered his thoughts before continuing. "I went up to him all cool-like, just watching the girls for a while. After a couple of minutes, he turns to me and starts talking. As luck would have it, he recognized me from my playing days, and we started bullshitting about football. After this goes on for five minutes or so, I decided to push my luck. I asked him about the guy with the tattoo."

"And what did he tell you?"

"He said he worked with the guy. He wouldn't give me many details but said all the brothers he worked with had the same kind of tattoo. It was a requirement for their job."

Jones frowned. "I didn't know gangbangers had jobs, other than shooting each other."

Greene shrugged. "Apparently, these guys do."

"Or," Payne added, "maybe they aren't bangers. Maybe the tattoo isn't what we think it is. Maybe it isn't a Holotat."

"Well, that gets me to the next part. This guy is pretty quiet about his friend, but he's unable to shut up about himself. He keeps rambling on about his job and stuff. He says he cooks and cleans for a bunch of people every day, and the only time they let him leave is to pick up supplies. Then he mentions the guy with the tattoo is the one who brought him to New Orleans. I guess he's the buckwheat's driver or something."

Jones groaned. "They're not from New Orleans? That's gonna make our job a lot more difficult. Or did this guy let the name of the town slip?"

"Nah, I wasn't that lucky. I asked him where he worked and what kind of place it was, but he got rattled. Said it was top-secret stuff. Said he could get into all kinds of trouble from the state if he blabbed about it."

Payne frowned. "From the state? What does that mean?"

"You've got me," Greene admitted. "Louisiana might be a little backward, but I've never heard of any state workers getting inked for employment. Or any top-secret facilities that would hire a dumb-ass buckwheat like this guy."

"What kind of place was he talking about?"

"I don't know, Jon. I asked him, but he said he had to shut up. I even offered to buy him a drink for his trouble, but he quickly turned me down. He said he had to buy a bunch of supplies before it got too late, that he wanted to get his work done before the fireworks started."

Jones raised an eyebrow. "Fireworks? Isn't it a day early for that?"

"You'd think so, huh? But the local shows are gonna be held on the third this year. So if you fellas want to see fireworks in New Orleans, you better be looking at the sky tonight."

Payne didn't care for fireworks—the loud bangs and bright lights brought back memories of Iraq. But due to the circumstances of that night's show, he was suddenly a fan. "I'm sure I'm asking for a miracle here, but did this guy happen to say where he'd be watching the fireworks? Because I'll tell ya, I'd love to talk to him."

Greene smiled at the inquiry. Not a sly smirk, but a big, *I got a secret* grin. "As a matter of fact, he did. He'll be watching them at Audubon Park."

CHAPTER 28

PAYNE dropped off his friends on opposite ends of the park, then focused his attention on finding a nameless witness in a sea of sixty thousand people. Sure, he realized his chances were slim, but he knew he had three things going for him—his target's unique appearance (very tall, gold teeth, and more dreadlocks than a Bahamas barbershop), his unwavering determination to find Ariane, and his two kick-ass partners.

Together, they made the Three Musketeers look like Girl Scouts.

With cell phone in hand, Payne parked his car on the Tulane University campus, then jogged for several blocks until he reached the spacious grounds that he had been assigned. Greene had told him that the center of Audubon Park would be packed with partygoers, but when Payne arrived, he was greeted by the exact opposite. The scenic grove was empty.

Confused, he pulled his gun and inched along the concrete walkway, suspiciously searching the green boughs above him for signs of a potential ambush. A cracking branch. A glint of color. The smell of human sweat. Yet the only thing he noticed was insects, dozens of chirping insects wailing their summertime song. Next he examined the massive trunks of the live oak trees that surrounded him, the decorative cast-iron benches that lined the sidewalks, and the Civil War fountain in the center of the park. But everything in the vicinity seemed clear.

Too clear for his liking.

Puzzled by the lack of activity, Payne paused for a moment and considered what to do next. He was tempted to call Greene for advice, but before he did, he heard the faint sound of horns seeping through the trees several hundred yards to the south. Relieved, he strolled toward the music and eventually found the scene that Greene had described. Thousands of drunken revelers frolicked on the banks of the Mississippi River, enjoying the hell out of the city's Third of July extravaganza.

"Damn," Payne grumbled. "This place looks like Gomorrah."

Clowns with rainbow-colored wigs trudged by on stilts while tossing miniature Tootsie Rolls to every child in sight. A high-stepping brass band blared their Dixieland sound as they strutted past an elaborate barbecue pit that oozed the smoky scent of Cajun spareribs and grilled andouille. Vendors peddled their wares, ranging from traditional plastic necklaces to fluffy bags of red, white, and blue cotton candy. And a group of scantily clad transsexuals, dressed as Uncle Samanthas, pranced in a nearby circle, chanting, "We are gay for the USA."

But Payne ignored it all. With a look of determination on his face, he blocked out the kaleidoscope of diversions that pleaded for his attention—the gleaming streaks of light as kids skipped by with sparklers, the sweet smell of funnel cakes that floated through the air, the distant popping of firecrackers as they exploded in the twilight like Rebel cannons on the attack—and remained focused on the only thing that mattered: finding the Plantation witness.

Unfortunately, Payne had little experience when it came to tracking civilians on American soil. He was much more accustomed to finding soldiers in murky swamps than buck-wheats at carnivals, but after giving it some thought, he re-alized his basic objective remained the same.

He needed to locate his target as quickly and quietly as possible.

To do so, he tried mingling with the locals, slyly shifting his gaze from black man to black man as he made his way through the festive crowd. But his efforts to blend in were almost comical. No matter what he attempted, the scowl on his face made him stand out from the lively cast of charac-ters that surrounded him. He tried smiling and nodding to the people that he passed, but the unbridled intensity on his face made him look like a serial killer.

After making a few children cry, Payne realized he needed to change his approach. Drastically. So instead of trying to hide in the crowd, he decided to stand out in it, making his anxiety work for him instead of against him.

Why be cautious when there was no risk in being bold? The Plantation witness had never seen his face, so it made little sense for Payne to slink through the crowd, hiding. He figured, why not approach every Rastafarian in sight and just talk to him? To do so, he simply needed an excuse, one that would allow him to talk to strangers without raising their suspicion. But what could he use? What could he ask anyone that would seem so harmless that a person wouldn't flinch at the query? The question needed to be simple, yet something that explained the frazzled look on his face, a look with so much intensity that it actually scared kids.

Kids! That was it! He could pretend he'd lost his kids. He could move from person to person, pretending to look for his lost kids, while actually searching for the Plantation wit-ness. Heck, in the few seconds it took for a person to re-spond to his query, Payne could study the man's face, hair, teeth, and height. And if that wasn't enough, Payne could listen to the man's voice and see if it possessed the backwa-ter accent of a buckwheat.

Damn! Payne thought to himself. The plan was inge-nious.

It was bold, daring, creative . . . and completely unsuccessful.

Payne talked to every black man he saw, every single one, but most of them turned out to be way too short to be his suspect. And the few he found who actually stood over Greene's height of 6'4" didn't have the Fort Knox dental work or the redneck speech pattern that Greene had described. In fact, nobody in the crowd even came close.

Yet Payne remained undeterred. He had waited his entire life to find someone like Ariane—intelligent, witty, beautiful—so he wasn't about to give up hope after an hour. If it was necessary, he would stay in New Orleans for the rest of his life, spending every cent of his family's fortune, searching for the one witness that could bring her back into his arms.

But as it turned out, none of that was necessary.

His best friend was having a lot more luck on the eastern end of the park.

Payne hardly noticed it at first. The sound was too soft, too timid, to be heard above the cacophony of the boisterous crowd. But when it repeated itself a second and third time, it grabbed his attention. It was his cell phone.

"Hello?" he mumbled.

"Jon, it's D.J. You're not going to believe this, but I nabbed the bastard!"

"You what?"

"You heard me! I found him!"

A huge smile formed on Payne's lips. "Are you serious? I was beginning to think this was a waste of time."

"Me, too," Jones admitted. "But I got the Bob Marley wannabe right here." There was a brief pause on the line before he spoke again. "Say something, you little prick."

For a minute, Payne thought he was being scolded. Then he heard a meek squeal on Jones's end of the phone. "Howdy, sir. How is you?"

The accent brought a smile to Payne's lips. "What's your name?"

"Bennie Blount."

"Well, Bennie, it's nice to meet you. Now do me a favor and put my friend back on."

Jones got on the line a second later. "Polite sucker, isn't he?"

Payne ignored the question. "Where are you? I want to chat with this guy *now*."

"We're near the main road, about five minutes from the basketball courts where you dropped me off. How about you?"

"Not too far." Payne paused to collect his thoughts. "Listen, get to the courts as quietly as possible. I don't want our conversation to draw a crowd, and the courts should be deserted."

"No problem. And I'll give Levon a buzz on my way there."

"No," he growled. "I'll call Levon. I want you to keep two hands on this guy at all times."

Jones laughed at the indirect order. "Don't worry, Jon. This boy ain't going anywhere. I've got a gun shoved in his back. Plus, I'm using his hair as a leash."

Payne chuckled at the image. "Well, don't hurt him too much, you big bully. I want Bennie to be talkative, not comatose, when I meet him."

After calling Greene, Payne ran to the basketball courts, hoping to survey the territory before his partners arrived. As he'd hoped, the courts were completely deserted. Plus they were far enough from the festivities to attract unwanted attention, which would come in handy if they had to pacify Bennie with force.

As for the area itself, it was divided into two contrasting regions. Three concrete basketball courts with tattered nets and bent rims sat off to the left, next to a jungle gym and an old swing set that had clearly seen better days. A sandbox sat dormant, decorated with a number of sandcastles that crumbled like many of the structures in the surrounding neighborhood.

Meanwhile, the second region was in impeccable shape. Finished in smooth black asphalt and recently painted with bright white lines, the full-length basketball court was tournament ready. It was surrounded on all sides by metal bleachers and a large barbed wire fence, designed to keep the ball in and vandals out. To get inside the compound, a person normally had to file past an armed park guard, but on this night, the only people who were armed were Payne and his friends.

"Yo, Jon!" called a voice in the night.

Payne turned from his perch on the metal bleachers and saw the massive form of Levon Greene jogging toward him. "Over here, Levon."

Greene lumbered closer, a limp fairly obvious in his stride. "Where is he? I want to make sure you got the right guy."

Payne shrugged as he watched Greene enter the main gate and approach the bleachers. "D.J. was the one who found him, but he hasn't shown up yet. I hope he didn't run into any problems."

"None at all," Jones bellowed from the shadows. Payne and Greene whipped their heads sideways, searching for the source of the sound. "I was just waiting to make a big entrance."

Payne struggled to see him, but after a while, two dark faces emerged from the night.

"Gentlemen," Jones announced, "let me introduce you to our new best friend and a future witness for the prosecution, Mr. Bennie Blount."

CHAPTER 29

PAYNE had seen thousands of people in his life, folks from dozens of different lands and cultures, yet despite all of his experiences, he could not remember seeing a more unique character than Bennie Blount.

Standing 6'6" with an elaborate web of dreadlocks that added an additional three to five inches of puffiness to the top of his head, Blount looked like an exaggerated stick figure, created in the mind of a warped cartoonist. He lacked muscle mass of any kind; instead, he resembled a limbo pole turned vertically, topped off with a poorly crocheted black wig. Gold front teeth were the only remarkable thing about his face, and his dark eyes revealed absolutely nothing, like the lifeless props often found in a taxidermist's shop.

"How'd you find him?" Payne asked as he watched them enter the court.

"It wasn't very tough," Jones joked. "Some kids were using him to break open a piñata."

Payne smiled despite the seriousness of the situation. "And does our new friend know why you've brought him here?"

"Not yet." Jones released Blount's hair and pushed him forward. "I figured you'd want to provide him with all the details."

Payne nodded as he walked toward the witness. "Do you know why you're here?"

Blount raked the dreadlocks from his eyes with his E.T.-like fingers, then responded. "I gets the feeling it ain't to play basketball."

"You got that right," Greene growled from the bleachers. "You're lucky I'm resting my knee, or I'd come down there and kick the shit out of you."

Blount trembled as he cowered from the angry voice. "Mr. Greene, is that you? My lord, that is you! Did I do somethin' bad that I don't remember?"

"It's not what you did," Payne interjected, "it's what you didn't do. You failed to tell Levon the things that he wanted to know during your earlier conversation."

Blount glanced at Payne and frowned. "Do I knows ya, sir? I don't mean to be rude none, but ya don't looks like someone I knows."

"My name's Jonathon Payne, and we talked on the phone a few minutes ago." He pointed to Jones before continuing. "And that over there is David Jones."

Blount instinctively massaged the top of his sore scalp. "Oh, yes, I knows him. We's already been introduced."

Payne tried not to laugh as he pictured Jones using Blount's hair as a leash. "Bennie, as I mentioned, the reason that Mr. Greene is angry with you is because of your behavior earlier today at the Fishing Hole."

"But I didn't do nothin' wrong! I didn't drinks too much or cause no problems! Mr. Murray warns me about touching the gals, and I swears I didn't do none of that today! I swears!"

"That's not what I'm talking about. Mr. Greene is upset because you weren't willing to answer his questions about the man with the tattoo. He asked you some simple questions, and you refused to answer."

Blount glanced at Greene and shivered slightly. "Is that

why you's mad at me, Mr. Greene? 'Cause I wasn't in a talkin' mood?"

"I gave you an autograph, Bennie, and you weren't willing to give me any information. That was kind of disappointing."

"More like rude," Jones chimed in. "You should be ashamed, Bennie."

"Real ashamed," Payne added.

As Blount considered his actions and studied the men that surrounded him, guilt flooded his face. "I'm so sorry, Mr. Greene! I didn't know that it meant that much to ya! If I'd known things was that important, I'd've told ya everything I known. I promise I woulda!"

Grinning, Payne slowly reached out his hand and placed it on Blount's rail-thin shoulder. "Well, Bennie, maybe it's not too late to make amends. If you act nicely, I bet Mr. Greene would give you a second chance. In fact, I know he would."

"Does ya think so, Mr. Payne?"

"I know so, Bennie." Payne stepped aside, allowing Blount to get a full view of Greene. "Go ahead, Bennie. Apologize to my friend."

Blount lowered his head in shame and looked at Greene's feet as he spoke. "Mr. Greene, I swears I didn't do nothin' wrong on purpose. If you gives me one mo' chance, I promise I make things up to ya!"

Greene sighed deeply, as if he actually had to weigh the consequences of Blount's apology. "All right, kid. I'll let this one slide. But you better tell us everything that we want to know, or I'll never forgive you. Ever!"

Blount's face erupted into a wide smile. "Anything, Mr. Greene. Just ask it and I'll tells ya. I promise, Mr. Greene. I don't wants ya to be mad at me. Really I don't!"

Greene grinned with satisfaction, enjoying every moment of this mini drama. "I'm glad, Bennie. That's what I was hoping you'd say."

"Me, too," Payne interjected. He led Blount to the metal bleachers and asked him to sit down. "I've got a number of questions that I'd like to ask you, Bennie, and some of them might seem a little bit strange. But trust me, each of them is really important to me and my friends."

"Okay," he mumbled, slightly confused.

"First of all, what can you tell me about your friend with the tattoo? How do you know him?"

"Ya mean the *P* tattoo? I met him at work, Mr. Payne. Most of the people have it."

"And where do you work, Bennie?"

Blount paused for a second, not sure if he should answer the question.

"Come on, Bennie," Greene urged. "You promised you'd help us."

"That's true, I did. But it's not as easy as that, sir. Ya see, I promised other peoples that I wouldn't talk about this none."

Greene moved forward on the bleachers, flexing his massive arms as he did. "But those other people can't hurt you right now, can they?"

Blount gulped. "I guess you's right. The place is called the Plantation."

The word piqued the interest of all three men, yet Greene was the first to speak. "The Plantation? What exactly is the Plantation?"

Blount gazed at Greene. It was obvious that the Plantation was one of the things he wasn't supposed to talk about, but all it took was one glare from Greene and he started to speak. "The Plantation is the name of the place that I be working. It's a special jail that the state put in less than a year ago."

"A jail? What kind of jail?" Payne demanded.

"The *secret* kind."

"What the hell is a *secret* jail?"

Blount exhaled. "You know, the kind that people is sent to for special crimes."

Payne grimaced. This was getting nowhere. "Special crimes? What the hell are they?"

"You know," he whispered, "the kind that people ain't suppose to talk about."

Payne glanced at Jones, looking for an explanation, but it was obvious that he was just as confused. "Bennie? Can you please tell me what type of people commit special crimes?"

"Not really, Mr. Payne. There've been too many people for me to keep track of over the past months."

"Men? Women? Old? Young?"

"Yes, sir. All of them."

"Is there anything else that you can tell us about this place?"

Blount considered the question for a moment, then brushed the hair from his face. "Yes, Mr. Payne, there be one more thing I could tell you about the people at the Plantation."

"And what's that, Bennie?"

Blount pointed a long, bony finger at Payne. "All the people look like you."

It took a moment for Blount's comment to sink in, but once it did, none of the men knew how to respond. After a moment of silence, Jones spoke. "All of the people look like him? You mean everybody at the Plantation is ugly?"

The joke brought a smile to Blount's face. "That's not what I meant, sir. What I be tryin' to say is they white. Everybody at the jail is white."

"Levon?" Payne said in a soft voice. "Do you have any idea what he's talking about?"

"I wish I did, but I'm clueless." Greene turned his attention to Blount. "Bennie? What do you mean everybody's white? You're telling me there aren't any black people at the Plantation?"

"No, I ain't sayin' that. There be plenty of black people at the jail. All the workers be black."

"What?!" Jones demanded. "The prisoners are white and the guards are black? Holy parallel universe, Batman!"

Payne glanced at his friend. Sometimes he wondered if Jones was still a teenager. "Bennie, don't you think that's a little bit strange? Why are all of the prisoners white?"

"I don't know, sir, 'cause I ain't in charge of no prisoners. I just be in charge of the taters and grits. My bosses don't allow me to get near the people. They keeps me far away."

"And why do you think that is, Bennie?"

"My bosses tell me it be for my safety, but sometime I don't know. I just don't know."

"Why's that?" Payne wondered. "Why do you doubt them?"

"'Cause some of the prisoners ain't that scary. I ain't afraid of no girls, and I sure as heck ain't afraid of no kids."

Nausea quickly built in Payne's belly. "Kids? What kind of kids, Bennie?"

"White ones."

"No, that's not what I meant. How old are the kids?"

"Well," Blount mumbled, suddenly realizing he had probably already revealed too much information, "it be hard to say. I ain't too good at guessin' no ages."

Payne moved closer, trying to intimidate Blount with his proximity. "This isn't the time to quit talking. How old are the damn kids?"

"I don't know," he whined. "I really don't. I just know that some of them have to be young 'cause I have to make them different chow. I have to cut up their food 'cause they don't got big teeth yet."

"Jesus," Payne groaned. That meant the Posse had kidnapped kids under the age of five. "And you don't find that strange? Come on, Bennie, you can't be that dumb! What kind of prison holds toddlers?"

Blount lowered his head in disgrace, too embarrassed to answer the question.

"Levon," Jones whispered, trying to take the focus off of Bennie, "what do you think? Could a place like this exist?"

Greene chuckled at the thought. "A state-run facility with black guards and white inmates? Hell, no! The government couldn't get away with a place like that in Louisiana. There are way too many David Dukes down here to oppose it."

"How about privately?" Payne wondered. "Do you think a black-run facility, one that imprisons and punishes white people, could secretly exist in this state?"

"Now that's another story." Greene sighed, closing his eyes as he did. "Racial tension has always been a huge concern in this state. For one reason or another, there are still thousands of people that are upset about the Civil War. I know that sounds ridiculous to a Northerner, but trust me, it's true. White supremacists run some towns, while black militants control others. Then, to complicate things further, there are places in this state that no one controls. The swamps, the forests, the bayou. Shit, I guarantee you there are entire communities in Louisiana that don't know what year it is—or even care. Those are the areas where a place like the Plantation could exist. No visitors, no cops, no laws. That's where a place like that could *thrive*."

The possibility didn't make Payne happy. He had secretly hoped that Bennie Blount was a simpleton who mumbled to strangers about fictitious places in order to get attention, but that seemed less likely now. If someone like Greene was willing to believe that the Plantation could exist, then there was a good chance that it actually did.

And if that was the case, then it was up to Payne to find it.

CHAPTER 30

Sunday, July 4th
Independence Day

THE leaders of the Plantation had waited several years for this day to come, and now that their plan had come to fruition, they could barely contain their enthusiasm. The special ceremony they had planned was originally slated to begin an hour before dawn, the same time they had held the symbolic ritual of the burning cross, but now that their big day was actually here, they realized that their adrenaline wouldn't let them wait another four hours.

Their big announcement would have to be pushed forward.

Holmes notified Hakeem Ndjai, who told the rest of the guards. Within minutes, the Plantation's tattooed battalion began assembling the prisoners into formation, forcing the tired captives into a very specific order:

GROUP ONE:	**GROUP TWO:**	**GROUP THREE:**
The Metz and Ross families	The Potter and Cussler families	The Edwards and Walker families

Before Holmes, Jackson, and Webster made their appearance, the guards double-checked the prisoners, making sure everyone was where they were supposed to be.

Then, like a shadow through a sea of black, Master Holmes and his raven-colored steed charged through the night. The only thing announcing their presence was the sound of hooves tearing up the soft turf in rhythmic bursts and the occasional crack of a leather whip against the horse's dark flesh. The sound brought chills to the recently flogged prisoners.

Once he reached the three groups, Holmes stared through the holes of his black hood and sighed. "Well, well, well! What do we have here? A bunch of frightened white people! The sight warms my heart!" He turned his attention to Ndjai. "Is everyone here, Hakeem?"

"Everyone except Master Jackson and Master Webster."

Holmes nodded as he thought back to the days when he was the scared victim, when he watched members of the Ku Klux Klan ride in on horseback and terrorize his family with burning crosses and threats of violence. Shit, he could still remember the pounding of his heart and the knot in his gut. The way he trembled while clinging to his mom for safety.

"Will they be joining us?" Ndjai asked.

Holmes nodded, refusing to take his eyes off of the prisoners. He loved the way they quivered in the firelight. "My friends wouldn't miss it for the world."

BLOUNT gawked at the interior of Greene's mansion as he walked down the hallways, glancing into every room he passed. He had never been in such a large house before and wanted a chance to snoop around. Unfortunately, his hosts had other ideas.

"Bennie!" Payne shouted. "Where are you hiding? Levon got off the phone five minutes ago, and we've been waiting for you ever since!"

"I sorry, Mr. Payne!" He jogged toward the sound of Payne's voice. "I guess I gots a little bit lost when I left the toilet. I sorry!"

Payne grinned at Blount's lanky form and easygoing
country manner. "That's all right. But if we're gonna finish
our preparations, we've got to get back to work." He threw
his arm around Blount's shoulder and squeezed. "And you're
our star!"

The concept made him smile. "Let's gets to it then! I
been waitin' my whole life to be a star!" Blount and Payne
joined Greene and Jones at the massive dining room table.
Maps and sketches were scattered all over the wooden surface. "So tells me, what does ya need to know?"

Jones, who possessed the strongest background in military strategy, glanced at the information in front of him. He
had graduated from the U.S. Air Force Academy, where he
had studied computers at the Colorado Springs campus. After receiving the highest score in Air Force history on the
MSAE, the Military Strategy Acumen Examination, he
earned his entrance into the MANIACs after a short stint in
the military police. Once in the MANIACs, he served several years under Payne, planning a variety of successful
missions.

"Now that we know about the Plantation itself, we need
to talk about points of entry. How are we supposed to get
onto the island?"

Blount answered. "The only way to gets onto the island
is from the western dock. Cypress swamps is gonna block
every other way to this place."

"Then tell me about the west. What do we have to worry
about before the dock?"

"There be a clean path, right down the middle, and you
needs to follow it to avoid trouble. If you goes to one side of
the path, boom! You hits some stumps. If you goes to the
other side, boom! You hits some trees. But, if you stays in
the middle—"

"Boom! The guards see us coming and blow our asses
out of the water."

Blount laughed at Jones's comment. "That's right! We's
gonna be gator stew!"

"If that's the case," Jones continued, "how do you recommend us getting there? If we can't use the dock without being seen, how can we get there undetected?"

"Why does you want to make this so complicated, Mr. Jones? There ain't no reason to find no back door when the front door is working just fine."

"But I thought you said that there'll be guards at the western dock."

"Yep," he chuckled, "but the guards won't be expectin' what I has in mind."

"And what is that?"

Payne and Jones listened to Blount's idea and liked what they heard. Even though they had won dozens of military awards, had planned intricate missions through several of the world's most hostile countries, and had been in charge of the most elite fighting force in America's history, they were forced to admit that Bennie Blount, a dreadlocked, slow-talking buckwheat from the bayou, had bested their military minds by devising the perfect plan all by himself.

And most importantly, it was simple enough that even he couldn't screw it up.

DANCING slightly with every hill and crevice, the headlights of the all-terrain vehicles looked like giant fireflies as they skimmed across the landscape of the Plantation. When the motors could finally be heard, the three groups of prisoners turned and watched the arrival of the two men. Wearing black hoods and thick cloaks, Jackson and Webster soared through the darkness, looking like supernatural beings on a mystical quest, their ebony robes flapping in the great rush of air. It was the type of entrance that nightmares were made of.

After stopping his vehicle, Jackson climbed off his ATV and walked toward Holmes, who was impatiently sitting on his steed. "Sorry we took so long. Right after you left, we got a phone call that we had to deal with."

"Is everything all right?" Holmes asked.

Jackson nodded. "It seems that we're going to be getting a few more captives, but it's nothing to worry about."

Even though he wanted to hear about the new arrivals, Holmes realized this wasn't the time or place. He had more important things to deal with, like his announcement. "People, you have already met Master Jackson and myself. Now, it's time to meet the real brains of the Plantation. I want you to say hello to Master Webster."

Despite their hatred of the man, the group screamed in unison. "Hello, Master Webster!"

Webster laughed under his hood. When he'd started this mission of revenge, he had dreamed of this moment, but now that it was here, he no longer knew how to react. His reality had somehow intersected with his dream world, and he could no longer discern which was which.

"Soon the sun will rise on the Fourth of July. Independence Day. A day to celebrate the freedom of this great nation." Webster took a deep breath while staring at the attentive crowd, wondering if they would understand the irony of their situation. "Unfortunately, some Americans weren't given their freedom in 1776. In fact, thousands of men and women from the United States weren't given their emancipation until after the Civil War had concluded. Yet we as a nation celebrate our independence on this day and this day alone. Ironic, isn't it? A country celebrates its freedom on a day when only half of us were freed!"

He cleared his throat as the prisoners thought about his words.

"Wait! You want irony? Independence means freedom from control and restrictions. That's the basic concept, right? So what's the opposite of independence? Slavery! Back in the days, white people used to refer to slaves as indentured servants. Did you know that? That was the politically correct way to say *slaves*! *Indentured servants*. Has a nice ring to it, huh? Well, what does that term mean? If you're indentured, it means that you're bound to work for someone, literally forced to be a servant. *Forced.* In other words, slavery!"

Webster could tell that his guests were getting confused, so he simplified things for their benefit. "I'm sure you're wondering, what's so ironic about that? Well, look the two terms up in the dictionary, and guess what you'll find? The two words sit next to each other. First, you'll see indenture, then you'll see independence! Side by side, one after the other! Two words with completely different meanings, yet they're neighbors in the English language. Pretty damn amazing!" He shook his head at the irony. "And if you think about it, it's kind of like us. We're independent, but all of you are indentured!"

Holmes laughed loudly. He had never seen Webster so animated.

"And that brings us to the moment we've all been waiting for. The answer to the number one question on each of your minds . . . Why are you here?"

Under his dark hood, Webster smiled at the prisoners.

"That's what you're wondering, isn't it? Why you've been selected to join us at the Plantation? Why, out of all of the people in America, did we bring you unlucky bastards here?"

He smiled again, loving the tension in the slaves' faces.

"Why, you ask? We did it because of your past!"

CHAPTER 31

THE boat inched from the private dock, slowly making its way through the dark water that surrounded Plantation Isle. Dressed in a black robe, the muscular figure tied a rope around the white man's wrist, making sure that the knot was tight enough to pass inspection. He tested it twice just to be sure, and each time his handiwork held in place. Then, sliding toward the back of the boat, the black man repeated the process. After wrapping the thick cord around the next prisoner's arms, he completed his knot with a series of quick jerks, pulling the extra slack from the restraint with a firm tug.

"Watch it! That hurts!"

Levon Greene sneered at Jones, then yanked the rope even harder. "We're playing for keeps, D.J., and if that means you have to suffer a little bit, then so be it."

"Yeah," Payne seconded over the rumble of the boat's motor. "You didn't hear me complain when Levon tied me up, did you?"

"No," Jones cracked, "but you've always liked that kinky stuff."

After his comment, the joking stopped, giving everyone a chance to think about their duties. Since so much of the plan revolved around Blount, a simpleminded twenty-four-year-old, Payne was more concerned than usual. He turned to examine the eyes of the boat's captain and could tell the dreadlocked servant was very uptight.

"Bennie," Payne said, "we'll only get one shot at a surprise attack, so we need *everything* to go perfectly. If you don't mind, I'd like to talk about your plan one more time."

"Yes, sir. That's fine. I don't wanna be doing nothin' that gets no one hurt—especially me!"

"Don't worry!" Greene said as he moved next to Blount. "This will go smoothly."

Remarkably, as Payne stared at the pair, he suddenly realized that they were a study in contrasts. Even though both men were black, their appearances couldn't have been more different. Greene was thick and defined, muscle stacked upon muscle, veins literally bulging through his skin. His head was shaved, his nose was broad, and his teeth were pearly white. If he were a tree, he'd be the biggest, baddest oak in all the land.

Blount, on the other hand, looked like a sapling gone bad. His limbs sprouted from a thin torso and appeared too feeble to support even the smallest amount of weight. His face, long and narrow, was topped with a haircut that resembled a rotting fern, black stems and roots tangled in every direction. And his gold teeth were straight out of the Mr. T School of Dentistry.

"Like I told you earlier," Greene said, "as long as you stay by my side, you're not going to get hurt. I promise."

Blount smiled, but the action seemed forced. "If you says so, Mr. Greene."

"Yes," he asserted, "I say so."

When Payne was done watching their conversation, he turned his attention to the back of the boat. "Hey, D.J., come up here so we can discuss some things. I want to make sure everyone knows what's going to happen."

Jones hustled forward and took a seat.

"When we pull up to the western dock, Bennie said we should expect two guards. As long as we don't look suspicious, that's all we'll have to deal with. Unfortunately, if we don't make this look believable, they'll radio for backup, and our mission will get ugly before it even starts."

Payne glanced at Blount and saw confusion in his eyes.

"Do you know what I mean by believable, Bennie?"

"I think so, Mr. Payne. You just want me to play Bennie. Right?"

Payne grinned. Things couldn't be any easier. "That's correct. But I need to remind you of one little detail that you keep forgetting. You have to stop calling me Mr. Payne. I doubt that the prisoners are referred to in such a polite manner."

Blount smiled, and this time it seemed more sincere. "You's definitely right about that. I ain't even referred to in that polite a manner, and I works here."

Payne nodded, turning his attention to Greene. "Obviously, you have the most important role of all. You have to make the guards believe that you're one of them and you're bringing two new prisoners to the island. Bennie claims that your black cloak is similar to the ones they wear, but it's not a perfect match. So don't let them get a good look at it. Always keep moving, okay?"

"Don't worry. I will."

"And make sure your hood is up. If they're sports fans and they see your face, the game's over. They'll immediately know you're not a guard. Then, once we get past the dock, you'll need to borrow one of their vehicles to take Bennie's supplies to the main house and us to the holding area. But before we get there, you'll cut our ropes and leave us in the woods. That'll give us a chance to do some recon."

Jones asked, "When will we get our weapons?"

Payne answered. "One of Bennie's boxes has our guns. We'll take what we need and stash the rest in the trees. We don't want to be bogged down until we know what we're up against."

He turned back to Blount. "Bennie, this is when you execute your part of the plan. I want you to go into the house and start breakfast. While you're making food for the guards, I want you to mix in the drug that I gave you. Pour half the bottle in the coffee, the other half in the scrambled eggs. That way, everyone's bound to get some, whether they're eating or not."

"Okay, Mr. Payne, I will. . . . Oops! I mean, okay, prisoner."

Blount smiled with pride. He thought he'd done a good thing by remembering his line, but his momentary blunder would've been enough to get everyone killed.

"Keep working on it, Bennie." Payne sighed, praying that Blount would improve before the big show actually started. "Where was I? Oh, yeah, within ten minutes of breakfast, everyone should be unconscious. That's when D.J. and I will make our move. We'll emerge from the woods in serious S & D mode."

Greene frowned. He was unfamiliar with the term. "S & D mode?"

"We'll search for the prisoners and destroy anything that gets in our way."

"You mean, you's gonna kill people?" Blount asked.

Payne nodded. He'd already gone over this at Greene's house and during the car ride to the dock, and he didn't feel like discussing it again. Unfortunately, he didn't have a choice. He had to keep Blount as calm as possible. "We don't want to, Bennie, but we might have to. That's just the way it is. Sometimes, the only way to help one group is to hurt another, and that's the situation we're facing. In order to help my girlfriend and the innocent people on this island, we might have to hurt some of the guards. We'll do everything in our power not to, but if it's us against them, they're the group that has to lose. I won't settle for anything less."

"Okay," he whined. "I guess you's right. Just try not to hurt me."

"You got it, Bennie." Payne smiled at Blount, then settled into his seat for the next portion of the plan.

BECAUSE of his frequent trips to the Plantation, Blount knew the appropriate channel through the cypress swamp.

He carefully navigated the boat toward the moss-covered poles of the wooden dock until he could see the two guards.

"Is that you, Gump?" asked one of the guards as he stared at the captain of the boat. "We were expecting you a while ago."

"Yeah," said the other. "Did the fireworks run late or something?"

Before Blount could answer, Greene moved to the front of the boat and spoke for him. "It wasn't the damn fireworks!" he growled. "There's been a security breach! Now quit your small talk and take our damn line before there's trouble. I have two prisoners on board."

The guards glanced at the large figure in the black cloak and jumped to attention. After dropping their guns to the ground, they ran to the dock, offering their assistance in any way possible. Greene nodded at them, tossing them the boat's rope. The two guards snared the line and carefully pulled the craft against the side of the dock.

"It looks like they're buying it," Jones whispered. "We might pull this off."

Payne nodded slightly, but for some reason, he wasn't nearly as confident. His gut told him there was something fishy, and it wasn't just the stench from the murky water of the swamp. "I hate to say this, D.J., but—"

The confidence drained from Jones's eyes. "Don't tell me! Your gut?"

Payne nodded. But before he could explain, Greene approached the duo and ordered them to be quiet. "Things are going well. Don't blow it by talking."

Greene followed his command by forcing Payne off of the boat and onto the shore while one of the guards did the same with Jones. Once both of them were on the ground, Greene turned to the workers and spoke. "Bennie and I will watch them while you get me a truck. There are a lot of supplies out there, so start moving."

"Yes, sir!" they blurted, running to complete their tasks. Greene smiled at Blount, then glanced at the two captives at his feet. "How was that? Was I authoritative enough for you?"

Jones tried rolling onto his back, but his bound hands hindered his effort. In a strange way, he looked like an upside-down turtle that had trouble flipping over. "You sounded good to me, but I'm not the one you need to worry about. Ask Jon what he thinks. He's worried about something."

Greene turned his attention to Payne. "Is there something we need to talk about before the guards get back?"

"Not really," he groaned. "I can wait until they return, if you'd like."

"What do you mean by that?"

"I mean, you're just going to tell them anyway."

The smile faded from Greene's lips as his bewilderment grew. In order to sort things out, he lowered his black hood and knelt on the ground next to Payne. As he did, his bad knee cracked several times. "What are you talking about?"

"Yeah," Jones demanded. "What the hell are you talking about?"

Payne wanted to look Jones in the eyes, but the position of their bodies made it impossible. "D.J., I'm sorry to tell you this, but if my guess is correct, Levon is one of them."

CHAPTER 32

HOLMES and Jackson had planned on speaking to the prisoners, but since Webster was doing such an eloquent job, they allowed him to continue his lecture.

"Independence Day is a holiday that is supposed to symbolize freedom in this country. Freedom? In America? What a joke! A country that turned its back on my people, black people, for decade after decade believes in freedom? My black brothers and sisters were smuggled into America in the hulls of slave ships in the most unsanitary of conditions, brought here like cattle, then purchased by white men for their own personal use. And you call that freedom?"

The prisoners listened, trembling.

"Take a look around you! This plantation was built several decades before the Civil War. Nice, isn't it? It's probably hard to imagine, but the people who worked this soil were my ancestors. My *actual* ancestors! That's right! Through painstaking research, I have traced my family tree back to this plantation. Isn't that amazing? My forefathers worked this land! They slept here, ate here, and raised families in the tiny cabins that surround us!"

Webster shook his head at the thought, rage boiling inside of him.

"And because of you, my family was forced to die here, too!"

A slight murmur rippled through the crowd. What did Webster mean by *that*?

"For the past few days, you have been subjected to unpleasantries. Long hours in the hot sun, a scarcity of food and water, nothing to sleep on but the hard ground itself. But guess what? That pales in comparison to the hardships that my relatives had to endure. Back in the eighteen hundreds, slaves were forced to live in these tiny cabins year-round. Ten, twelve, sometimes as many as fifteen people were thrown together into one cabin and forced to make do, huddling in the center of the dirt floor for warmth. And if they bitched, they were beaten!

"During the rainy season, the ground became so saturated with water that the moisture would rise up into their cabins, forcing them to sleep in the mud. Like animals! These were my ancestors, for God's sake, and they were treated like beasts! Meanwhile, the Delacroix family, the white bastards that owned this property, slept in the comfort of the plantation house. They didn't work, but they lived like kings! Do you know what my relatives got to eat? At the beginning of every week, each person was given three and a half pounds of bacon from the smokehouse and enough corn to make a peck of cornmeal. That's it! For the entire week! Just bacon, cornmeal, and water for every meal, for a lifetime!"

Webster paused to catch his breath.

"And what about punishment? Do you actually think we've been rough on you? The punishment that occurred in the nineteenth century was far more brutal than anything we've implemented here. Back in the old days, slave drivers used to whip their niggers until they could see *ribs*. The gashes on their backs were so wide and deep you could see their lungs! Have we done anything like that to you? Anything that brutal? Tell me, have we?"

Despite his point-blank questions, the crowd remained silent. They were way too frightened to talk. But that didn't matter to Webster. He viewed the slaves' silence as insubordination, which needed to be dealt with. Turning toward Master Holmes, he said, "Can you believe that? They don't respect me enough to answer. Maybe you better show them what I mean about discipline."

Holmes grinned savagely under his black hood. He'd been on his best behavior since the finger-chopping incident, but now that Webster was encouraging him, he figured he could slide back to his sadistic ways.

He stepped forward, searching for a target, staring at the scared faces in the moonlight. Who should he choose? Which person would be the most beneficial to their cause? Then he saw him, the perfect victim. He was the finest specimen in Group One. A middle-aged male, father of Susan and two other brats. What was his name? Ross. Jimmy Ross. Yes, he would do nicely. An impeccable sacrifice.

Devastate the strong and the weak will crumble!

With unblinking eyes, Holmes focused on him, quietly selecting him as his prey. And Ross knew it. Holmes didn't even say a word, yet Jimmy dropped to his knees in fear. His entire body trembled with trepidation.

"Pick up the coward," Holmes growled.

And the guards obliged, pouncing on Ross like hungry wolves before they dragged him to the front of the crowd. Then, just as quickly as they had attacked, they backed away, leaving Ross at the feet of his master, with nothing between the two but a palpable wall of hate.

"Master Webster?" Holmes continued. "Why don't you tell our guests about the white man's temple? I think they'd enjoy that tale."

Webster readjusted his glasses, grinning. "In the nineteenth century, the white man considered his body sacred. It was a divine and holy temple that was not to be defiled by the dirty black man. Sure, it was fine for Massah to sleep with all the good-looking black women of the plantation. Famous men like Thomas Jefferson were reputed to have fathered many biracial children during their day. But if a Negro ever touched a white man for *any* reason, the slave could legally be killed. Can you believe that? The courts actually allowed it! Of course, that didn't make much financial sense to the slave owner, so it was rarely done. I mean, why murder someone who is doing your chores? So the white man was forced to come up with a better punishment than death."

Jimmy Ross gulped, waiting for Master Holmes to make a move. But the black man didn't budge. He stood like a statue, not blinking, not breathing. Silent. Completely silent. Listening to the words of his friend.

"No one knows where the idea of the post first came from, but its popularity spread across the Southern states during the early part of the eighteen hundreds. In fact, it spread like wildfire."

Suddenly, without warning, Holmes burst from his trance and lunged in Ross's direction. The prisoner instinctively flinched, raising his hands to protect himself, but it was a grave mistake.

"You tried to hit me!" Holmes screamed, stopping six inches short of Ross. "You white piece of shit! You tried to hit me!"

"I didn't, Master Holmes. I swear! I—"

"I don't give a fuck what you swear! I'm in charge of your sorry ass, so your words mean shit to me! If I say you tried to hit me, then you tried to hit me!" Holmes turned toward his guards. "Get me the post, now! I need to teach this cocksucker a lesson!"

"In fact," Webster continued, as if he was narrating an evil documentary, "even if the threat was an implied one—a swing that never landed, a tip of a cap to a white woman, or a hand being lifted for protection—slave owners were encouraged to administer this punishment."

The guards carried a six-foot wooden post, approximately six inches in diameter, to the front of the group and slammed it into the ground. After straightening it with a careful eye, they drove the long peg into the pliable turf with several swings of a sledgehammer. Once it was anchored in the ground, the device was ready for use.

"Now get him!" Holmes ordered.

The guards clamped onto Jimmy's arms much rougher than they had before and slammed him against the post. Then, before Jimmy could move, the larger of the guards forced Jimmy's cheek against the rough wooden surface, holding his face against the post with as much strength as possible. And Holmes was pleased by the sight.

While watching Jimmy tremble, Holmes slid in behind him while pulling a claw hammer out of the folds of his dark cloak. The sight of the savage tool brought a smile to his lips. Even though he enjoyed chopping fingers, there was nothing Holmes enjoyed more than the post. The fear. The blood. The disbelief in his victim's eyes. He loved it! For one reason or another, it satisfied something inside of him that most people couldn't understand.

The desire to be violent.

Reaching into his pocket, Holmes fumbled for a nail. Four inches in length, silver in color, sharpened to a perfect point. He lifted the tiny spike behind Jimmy Ross's head, then studied it with a suspicious eye. It was so small, yet capable of producing so much pain. God, it was beautiful. Holmes breathed deeply, thinking of the impending moment of impact. The smile on his face got even broader.

"The post," Webster said, "was a two-step process. Step one was the attachment phase. In order to prevent a messy scene later, the slave needed to be attached to the post in the most appropriate fashion. According to the journals that I've read, there was one method in particular that was quite popular."

Holmes raised the tip of the metal spike and ran it through the back of Jimmy's hair, tracing the ridges of his skull, looking for the proper insertion point. Once it was located, Holmes lifted his hammer, slowly, silently. The crowd, realizing what was about to be done, gasped with fear and shouted pleas of protest, but to Holmes, the murmur of shock sounded like a beautiful chorus, only adding to his enjoyment.

With a flick of his wrist, Holmes shoved the nail through the elastic tissue of Jimmy's outer ear, piercing the cartilage with a sickening snap. Before Jimmy could even yelp in pain, Holmes followed the attack with a swift swing of the hammer, driving the nail deep into the wood, anchoring the ear to the post.

After a moment of shock, Jimmy screamed in agony, then made things far worse for himself by trying to pull his head away from the wood. It was a horrible mistake. The more he pulled, the more flesh he tore, causing sharp waves of pain to surge through his skull. Blood trickled, then gushed down the side of his face. Warm rivulets of crimson flowed over his whiskered cheek, adding gore to the already vicious attack.

And the sight of it was too much for his family to endure.

In the crowd, Jimmy's sixteen-year-old daughter, Susan, fainted from the gruesome scene. The image of her battered father was simply too much for her to handle. Tommy and Scooter, his two boys, vomited, then dropped to their knees in a series of spasmodic heaves. They had never seen anything that horrible in their young lives.

Unfortunately, the brutal part was yet to come.

With his left forearm, Holmes slammed Ross's face against the post. "Stop your fuckin' squirming," he grunted. "You're just causing more pain."

"Okay," Ross sobbed, willing to do anything to stop the agony. "Okay!"

"I promise if you stop moving, I'll let you go. I'll free you from the post."

"All right, whatever you say!" He took an unsteady breath, wanting to believe the vicious man. "I will. I swear! I'll stay still."

Holmes nodded. Things were so much easier to complete with a calm victim.

"Good," he hissed, "because your squirming is ruining my souvenir!"

From the constraints of his belt, Holmes unsheathed his

stiletto, slipping the five-inch blade behind Ross's head. Then, while calming his victim with words of reassurance, Holmes lowered the razor-sharp edge to the tip of Jimmy's ear, pausing briefly to enjoy the scene. He truly loved this part. The quiet before the storm. The silence before the screams. There was something about it that was so magical, so fulfilling, that he couldn't put it into words.

Finally, when the moment felt right, Holmes finished the job. He removed the ear with a single slice, severing the cartilage from the side of Jimmy's head in one swift slash, like a movie on the life of Vincent Van Gogh.

A wave of pain crashed over Jimmy, knocking him to the ground. Blood oozed from his open wound, flooding his neck and shoulder with a sea of red. That, coupled with his loud screams, caused his wife to break from formation. She rushed to his side, crying, hoping to administer as much first aid as possible, but there wasn't much she could do.

Her husband was missing his ear, and she didn't have a sewing kit.

"The second part of this punishment, as I'm sure you've noticed, was the removal of the ear," Webster said. "As a sign of the white man's power, it was left hanging on the post right outside the slaves' cabins for several days. Not surprisingly, it was an effective way to get the master's message to his slaves. *If you do something wrong, you will pay for it in agony!*"

Holmes stared at his souvenir, left dangling from the pole like a freshly slaughtered pig. "And that, my friends, is how the Listening Post was born."

CHAPTER 33

PAYNE wasn't sure about Greene until that very moment, but one look into his eyes told him everything he needed to know. The Buffalo Soldier was a member of the Posse.

"Were you always with them, or did they get to you after we showed up in New Orleans?"

Jones's eyes widened when he heard Payne's proclamation. "What are you talking about?"

But Payne ignored him. "Just answer me that, Levon. From the beginning or just recently? I've got to know. To me, it'll make all the difference in the world."

Greene continued to stare at Payne, no emotions crossing his face.

"Come on, Levon, just one little answer. Which was it? Before we arrived, or after?"

Greene refused to dignify the question, and to Jones, the silence was maddening. Because of his current position, he couldn't see what was going on. "Bennie!" he called, trying to get involved in the conversation. He strained his neck, trying to find the dreadlocked servant. "Bennie! Help a brother out! Kick me closer to the action! Anything!"

"Be quiet," Payne ordered. "If my guess is correct, Bennie's one of them, too, so he won't help you. He's on Levon's side."

Jones's eyes got even larger. He had no idea where any of Payne's theories were coming from, but the mere possibility that they were true was mind-blowing. "Bennie? Levon? Guards? Will somebody tell me what the hell is going on? I'm supposed to be the detective here. Someone throw me a crumb."

Payne shook his head. "D.J., just shut up and listen. Levon's about to tell us everything."

Greene glanced at Jones, then returned his gaze to Payne. "I can't believe you, man. How can you think that after all the things I've done for you? I showed you my city. I let you sleep in my house. I let you eat my food—"

Payne interrupted him. "You gave us faulty guns. You tried to have us shot. You kidnapped my girlfriend. . . . Should I go on?"

"No," Greene growled, "you shouldn't. I've heard all that I'm gonna take. You called me up, and I went out of my way to help you guys. And this is how you're gonna repay me? You accuse me of trying to have you killed? Get fucking real!"

In a burst of rage, Greene kicked a nearby rock, then stormed away in anger. But that was fine with Payne, because it gave him a chance to talk to Jones.

"Do you believe me?" he asked.

Jones tried to shrug. "I know you too well not to believe you, but I'd love to hear something that supports your theory."

Payne nodded. "Bennie? Do you want to fill him in, or should I?"

Blount glanced at the two men near his feet, then stared at Greene in the distance. "I thinks you better do the talkin'. I don't wanna make Mr. Greene mad at me."

Payne smiled. Blount was a hard man to read, but if Payne's theory about Greene was correct, then Blount had to know more than he was willing to reveal. He simply had to.

"Okay, Bennie, have it your way. I'll do all of the talking. . . . Remember how things started bugging me on the boat? How my gut knew something was wrong? Well, it was the guards. The guards acted wrong when we showed up."

Jones scrunched his face. "The guards? I could barely see the guards from the boat, but you could tell that they did something wrong? What, are you psychic or something?"

"When we pulled up to the dock, they approached the boat expecting Bennie. They called to him, asking about the fireworks. Remember? But before Bennie could say anything, Levon told them about a security problem and started giving orders. Right?"

Jones nodded his head.

"What did they do after that?"

"They jumped to attention."

"And then?"

Jones thought back, trying to remember. He knew the guards ran onto the dock, following Greene's instructions, but he couldn't recall anything else. "I give up. Tell me."

"What did they do with their guns?"

It took a moment, but the solution eventually popped into his head. "I'll be damned. They threw them to the ground, didn't they?"

"Even though Levon should've been a stranger to these guys, he tells them that there's a security problem, and they throw away their guns. How in the hell does that make any sense? Come on, even mall security guards would know better than that! Unless . . ."

"Unless they were told what to expect ahead of time."

"That's what I figured."

Jones nodded, admiring his friend's theory. "I have to admit, that's pretty good. In fact, I'd give you a round of applause, but . . ."

"You can't because we let Levon tie us up?"

"Exactly."

"Probably not the brightest thing in the world that we could've done, huh?"

"Nope. Probably not."

"Right up there with being handcuffed to the desk, isn't it?"

Jones smiled. The last few days had suddenly become cyclical. "So, did you have doubts about Levon before the guards?"

"Nope. The guards woke me up, but then I started to think back over the past couple of days. The broken guns, his rule against police involvement, his escape through Sam's secret door, his discovery of Bennie, and so on. I figured all of that was too coincidental to be a coincidence."

"Yeah, you're probably right. Detective work should never be *this* easy. I mean, two days ago, we were in Pittsburgh with a license plate and a tattoo as our only clues, and here we are on the threshold of finding Ariane. Please! Things were too simple."

"To be honest, I wasn't one hundred percent sure about Levon until I mentioned it to him. There was a look in his eye that told me everything. He looked like a big ol' dog that was caught sleeping on the couch—guilt all over his face!"

"It wasn't guilt," Greene remarked. He had circled in behind them, trying to acquire as much information as possible. "It was shock. I couldn't believe that you caught onto me. I thought I'd done everything right."

"Don't kick yourself." Payne sighed. "It was the guards' fault. They ruined the entire scene. They should be fired immediately."

"I concur," Jones echoed. "In fact, I think you have a big future in acting, just like that other ex–football player from Buffalo. Hmm? What was his name? O.J. something."

"Nah, Levon's too good for that! He decided to skip O.J.'s second career and went right to his third . . . a life of crime!"

Jones laughed. Then, using the melody and the accent of the classic Bob Marley song, he began to sing. "He's just a Buffalo Convict . . . works for da Posse! He took a bunch of steroids . . . now he's their boss-y!"

"That was clever," Greene admitted. "Very clever indeed."

Jones gave him a big wink. "Thank you, Louisiana! I'll be here all week!"

"Actually, you will be. Might not be alive the whole time, but we'll worry about that later."

Payne twisted his head and glanced at Jones. "I don't know about you, but I'm going to worry about that now."

"Damn." Greene laughed. "You guys don't stop. I thought your black humor was just an act, but you guys are even like this in the darkest of situations."

Payne ignored the comment, opting to change the subject. "Hey, Levon? I gotta know. Did you sell us out before we came to New Orleans or after?"

A grin crossed Greene's lips. Since his cover was blown, he figured the answer to one question wouldn't do too much damage to his ruined reputation. He crouched to his knees so he could stare Payne in the eyes. The kindness that had been present during the past few days had been replaced by a cold, hard glare.

"Jon, if it makes you feel any better, I've been involved with the Plantation from the very beginning. And just so you know, if you had told me why you needed my help during your initial phone call, I wouldn't have invited you down here. Can you imagine my surprise when you finally told me why you were in town? I almost shit myself! But at that point, what was I to do? You were digging, and I had to stop you. It's as simple as that."

"Then why not kill us? Why take the time to lure us here?"

"Well, as you mentioned, I did try to kill you. I didn't want to personally pull the trigger, but I set things up at Sam's. Unfortunately, the damn sniper screwed that up. After that it would be too suspicious if you were killed somewhere else in the city this weekend. I figured getting you off the mainland was a better way to take care of things."

"And what about Ariane? Why did you bring her here?"

Greene sighed. He was getting bored with the inquisition and knew that the rest of his partners were waiting for him. "I'm afraid that's a question that will have to wait. They're about to make a big announcement, and I don't want to ruin their surprise."

CHAPTER 34

THE ringing telephone brought a smile to Harris Jackson's face. He'd been expecting a call for several minutes now, and when it didn't come, his anxiety began to rise. But now that the call was here, he was finally able to relax.

"Master Jackson, this is Eric down at the dock. Bennie and Master Greene just left our area, and they're headed your way."

"And the prisoners?"

"They're tied up and docile. I don't think they'll be causing you any problems."

"Good," sighed Jackson. Since Payne and Jones had been a nuisance in New Orleans, he figured they might continue the trend on the island, especially since he'd learned of their military background. But now that he knew they were under control, he felt a whole lot better about their presence at the Plantation. "Very good indeed!"

"What's good?" asked an eavesdropping Holmes.

Jackson hung up his cellular phone. "The two prisoners will be here shortly. No problems."

Holmes patted Jackson on the back. "Nice work, Harris. It seems your guards have everything under control."

"It seems that way, but we'll find out for sure in a moment." Jackson pointed to the truck as it emerged from the trees of the outer grounds. "Why don't you tell Ndjai to keep the captives busy while I check into things? Come on down when you're done."

Holmes agreed and went on his way.

"Master Webster!" Jackson shouted. "Join me for a minute, would you?"

The two men walked cautiously toward the truck, not knowing what to expect. When they saw the huge grin on Greene's face, they knew that things were fine. Holmes joined them a short second later, and the three of them finished the trip in unison.

"Gentlemen," Greene crowed, "Bennie and I should win an Oscar for this. We just put on a spectacular performance."

"Bennie helped out?" Jackson asked.

"He practically carried it by himself! You should've seen the performance he put on. Unbelievable! His acting is even better than his cooking." Greene signaled for Blount to get out of the truck, and he willingly obliged. "Come out here and take a bow. You deserve it!"

"We heard you did a great job!"

"Congratulations, Bennie!"

Blount was flabbergasted. He had never been treated nicely by his bosses before. "Thanks," he mumbled, barely smiling. He simply didn't know how to react to their compliments.

"So," Greene asked, "what are we going to do with them now?"

"You mean the new arrivals?" Holmes glanced into the flatbed of the truck and saw Payne and Jones, bound. "You know 'em better than we do. What do you think should be done?"

Greene considered the question, but it was obvious that he already had a plan in mind.

"For the time being, we need to keep Payne and Jones as far away from the other prisoners as possible. We don't want them mentioning my name or our location to anyone. Then, after you guys make your big announcement, I think it would be best if my friends were eliminated. I figure, why take any unnecessary chances with men like these?"

.

ONCE the foursome had finished their discussion, they walked back to the prisoners and allowed Webster to finish his speech. Earlier, he had prepared the captives for his announcement by lecturing them on the concepts of freedom, slavery, and punishment, yet there was no way that they could be ready for what he was about to reveal.

"The concept of the Plantation came to me several years ago, back when I was in college. As part of my major, I was required to take a class in American history. The topic we were discussing was the Civil War, and somehow my white professor managed to talk during the entire class without mentioning black people. In my opinion, the Civil War was fought over the concept of slavery, and that white bastard managed to steer clear of the topic. After class I approached him and asked him about his oversight. I figured he'd tell me that an upcoming lecture would be devoted to slavery, or I'd get to learn about the topic in a future reading. But do you know what he had the audacity to say? He said, *'Over the years, the impact of slavery in this country has become greatly overrated.'* Can you believe that? We're talking about the main cause of the Civil War, and my professor tells me that it was overrated! Well, right then and there, I knew what I wanted to do with my life. I decided to devote my life to the promotion of black history, emphasizing the cruel history of slavery in our so-called Land of the Free.

"But how does one do that? I wasn't really sure, but I knew I needed to get America's attention. That's why I immediately ruled out papers, studies, or projects. Why? Most people won't pay attention to academics. What I needed was something spectacular, something unforgettable, something that would get this issue noticed. But what?

"Before I made my decision, I thought it was best if I did

some extensive research on the topic. I read books and journals and manuscripts and diaries—anything that I could find
about the topic of slavery—and before long, one common
theme stood out: plantations! Everything I read about slavery
in America mentioned plantations as the focal point. Plantations were the place where slaves lived, worked, birthed, and
died. It's where they escaped from when they could and returned when they were caught. For better or worse, plantations were the center of the black man's world!

"Now, before you get bored with my ramblings, let's
move on to the good stuff. How does any of this involve
you? I'm sure you're asking that question right now. Why is
this bastard making us stand in a field in the middle of the
night to listen to this lecture? That's what you're thinking,
isn't it? You don't think there's anything in this world that I
could tell you that would justify your being here. You think
I'm just some kind of thug who abducted you and your
families on a whim. That's what you're thinking, isn't it?"

Webster paused to let the tension build. He wanted to see
the confusion and misery in his captives' eyes as it continued to grow.

"Then each of you is about to receive the shock of your
lives, because you were selected for a specific purpose!"

Harris Jackson moved forward, taking over the lecture.
"During Master Webster's research, he was able to compile
some extensive genealogy, an actual list of black family
trees. Why is this significant? Because it was nearly impossible to do. Unlike white people, whose history is well docu-
mented in public records, the history of the black man is
often shrouded in obscurity. Slaves rarely had last names,
marriages weren't officially recognized, kids were often
sold or given away as gifts. Shit, these were just a few of the
drawbacks that Master Webster had to overcome in order to
complete his work."

Octavian Holmes grinned. "And that's what brings us to
you. Why are you here? It's the question you've been wondering for a very long time. Trust me, I know. I've seen it in

your eyes. 'Why me?' you constantly wonder. 'Why us?' you plead! 'There has to be a mistake,' you assure us! 'We've done nothing wrong!'"

Holmes grimaced, his eyes narrowing to slits. "No! There have been no mistakes! Each and every one of you is guilty of crimes against the black race! Crimes that you are in the process of being punished for!"

The captives glanced at each other, panicked. The sound of Holmes's voice told them that he truly believed what he said. Holmes actually believed that they were guilty of something terrible.

"Group One," Holmes shouted as he pointed toward them, "step forward!" Members of the Metz and Ross families glanced at each other, then reluctantly inched ahead. "Jake Ross, age seventy-one, make yourself known."

The old man emerged from the center of the pack.

"You are the father of Alicia and Jimmy Ross, are you not?"

Jake Ross nodded his balding head. "Yes, Master Holmes, I am."

"After marrying Paul Metz, Alicia gave birth to Kelly and Donny Metz. Is that correct?"

"Yes, sir," Jake agreed. "They're my grandkids."

"And your son, Jimmy? He married Mary DaMico, and she eventually gave life to Susan, Tommy, and Scooter. Right?"

Jake was mystified by the line of questioning, but he still answered. "Yes, sir."

"Now tell me, what was your grandfather's last name on your father's side?"

"It was Ross, same as mine. The Ross name has lasted for several generations now."

Holmes winced when he heard the pride in Jake's voice. The tone actually made him want to vomit. "According to our research, the Ross family first surfaced in America shortly before the 1800s. They settled in Massachusetts, but slowly migrated south as this country expanded in that direction.

Eventually, your great-great-grandfather purchased a large chunk of land in Georgia, where he grew peanuts to the ripe age of eighty-one."

Jake wasn't sure what Holmes was getting at, but he could tell that it was something big. "Yes, sir. That sounds about right."

Holmes nodded contentedly. The Plantation had located the right family.

"Group Two," Harris Jackson shouted, "step forward!" The Potter family took an immediate stride toward Jackson. "Richard Potter, as the oldest member of your family, I would like to speak to you!"

Richard groaned softly, then stepped ahead. "That's me, sir."

"If I am correct, you are fifty-eight and have three kids, Andy, Darcy, and Jennifer. Andy married Sarah Goldberg, and they have a three-year-old daughter named Courtney."

"Yes, sir."

"Your one daughter married Mike Cussler, and your other daughter, Jennifer, is single."

"Yes, sir. That's correct."

"Do either of your daughters have kids?"

"No, sir. Not yet."

Jackson was fairly certain that they were childless, but if they'd had any kids out of wedlock, he wanted to know about them, too. "Where did your maternal grandparents come from?"

"Mississippi, sir. I lived there myself until my parents died."

"Yes, I know." Jackson moved closer to the man, hoping to scare him with his proximity. "What did they do for a living?"

"They were farming people, sir. Cotton, mostly."

"And what was the name of their farm? Do you recall?"

"Yes, sir. I was forced to sell it after my folks died. It was called Tanneyhill Acres. Named after my mother's side of the family."

Jackson glanced at Holmes and nodded. Both of them were pleased with what they had learned. So far, Webster had made no mistakes in his research.

"I guess that leaves me," Webster muttered. "Group Three, step ahead and join the others."

Ariane Walker moved forward and was quickly followed by her sister, Tonya, and her injured brother-in-law, Robert Edwards.

"Since each of you is fairly young, you might not be able to help me with the questions that I would like answered. Therefore, I will give you a brief rundown on your family's history. If you disagree with anything I say, please let me know."

The three nodded, not knowing whose family he was referring to.

"Ariane, you're the closest, so you will be the spokesperson. Two years ago your sister married Robert Edwards from Richmond, Virginia, and she is currently carrying their first child. Your parents, each of them an only child, died in a car crash. Each of your grandparents died at an early age, before you were even born. You have no cousins, aunts, or uncles. It's just the three of you and the fetus on the way. Is that correct?"

Ariane agreed with everything. "Yes, sir."

"Excellent," he mumbled. "Your father's parents were raised in a coastal town in North Carolina, but your father's grandparents had roots that extended much deeper south. In fact, they stretched all the way to Louisiana."

Ariane shrugged. "If you say so. I've never had the chance to research my family. As you've pointed out, most of my family is already dead."

Webster smiled. "And they're lucky they are. Because if they weren't, they'd be standing here right next to you!"

The statement made Ariane wince. She knew her presence had something to do with her family's background, but what? Her parents were both law-abiding citizens. Her sister was never in trouble, so it couldn't have anything to do with her. And as far as she could tell, her brother-in-law was one of the sweetest guys in the world. So what the hell could it be?

"I can tell by your face, Ariane, that you are deeply confused. Your face is flushed. Your eyes are darting. Anger is boiling inside."

In a moment of reckless courage, Ariane decided to voice her feelings. "Yes, sir, I'm angry. As far as I can tell, my family's done nothing wrong, yet we're here, suffering in this field for no apparent reason. So, if you would be so kind, I was wondering if you could tell me why! Why are we here? What possible explanation could you give me that would explain why we're here?"

Ariane could tell from Webster's eyes that she had spoken too harshly. In order to soften the request, she continued.

"That is, if you'd like to tell me, Master Webster, sir."

Webster glared at the girl for a tense moment, then eventually grinned. "As fate would have it, we were just getting ready to tell the entire group that very thing. And for that, you are quite lucky. Otherwise, I would've been forced to punish you severely."

Ariane nodded, relieved.

"Master Holmes?" Webster continued. "Would you care to tell old man Ross and the rest of his family why they are here?"

For a brief moment, Holmes thought back to his own childhood, one that was filled with racial threats against his family. This was finally his chance to pay the white man back for crimes against his ancestors, to get even for generations of pain and abuse. "With pleasure."

Holmes turned toward the seventy-one-year-old slave and grinned. "During our research, we stumbled across a fact that I found quite interesting. We located the name of the man who was responsible for much of the pain in my family's history. My ancestors, after they were forced to come to America in the belly of a wooden ship, were sold to a peanut farmer in rural Georgia. There, they worked, day after day, under some of the most horrible conditions imaginable. And what does any of that have to do with you? Their owner's name was Daniel Ross, and he was your great-great-grandfather!"

Jake's head spun as he took in the news. Even though he knew his family had a farm in the South, the thought that they had once owned slaves never crossed his mind. It should've, since it was a typical practice of the time, but it never did.

"And Group Two!" Jackson growled. "We've already discussed your heritage, but I left something out. Before your family owned and operated a warm and cuddly farm, they ran one of the strictest cotton plantations in the entire South. The Tanneyhill Plantation was known for its harsh guards and inhumane treatment of slaves. In fact, some modern-day black historians refer to it as the Auschwitz of Mississippi."

Richard Potter took a deep gulp as he waited for Jackson to finish.

"For the record, many of my kin were murdered on that plantation. Their innocent blood dripped from the hands of your relatives, and I will never forgive or forget."

Richard and the rest of his family lowered their eyes in shame. Even though they were never part of the horrendous events of the Tanneyhill Plantation, they still felt guilt for the actions of their ancestors. They had no reason to, because it was a different time, a time when they weren't even alive, but the feelings surfaced nonetheless.

"And that brings us to you, Ariane!" Webster glanced at Tonya and Robert, then looked around the land of the Plantation. "Remember how I told you that your ancestors stretched way down to Louisiana? Well, guess what? Your family, formerly named Delacroix, used to own this piece of land that we're currently standing on."

The color drained from Ariane's face. She had no idea if the information was accurate or not, but she knew that Webster believed it.

"That's right! The family that you claimed was so innocent used to own this plantation and all of the people that worked on it. A group of workers that included my ancestors!"

Breathing heavily, Webster moved closer to Ariane and whispered, "That's why you're here. To make up for their sins by giving us your lives."

CHAPTER 35

AFTER leaving the announcement ceremony, Hakeem Ndjai checked on Payne and Jones. The guards assured him that neither man had put up a fight while they were being transported, and both of them had been switched from rope restraints to handcuffs, as ordered. The news pleased Ndjai. Because of the prisoners' background, Ndjai realized that these two men would pose a special problem if they ever escaped from custody, a situation he'd rather not deal with.

Payne had been locked in the smallest cabin on the Plantation, one that was usually reserved for solitary confinement of the island's troublemakers. It possessed a low-beamed ceiling, a rock-covered floor, eight square feet of living space, and the lingering odor of urine and vomit. All things considered, it was like the hazing room of a typical fraternity house.

Jones, on the other hand, was given the Taj Mahal of slave cabins, a room usually used by the guards. A narrow mattress filled the left-hand corner of the room, nestled between a sink and a small lamp that had been mounted to the thick wooden wall. A white porcelain toilet sat next to the basin, giving Jones a luxury that no other captive was afforded. To make up for it, though, they'd strapped an explosive to his leg, the same device used on the other slaves.

"Hakeem?" called a voice from behind.

Ndjai turned and was surprised to see Levon Greene approaching. He wasn't used to seeing him on the Plantation. "Yes, Master Greene? Is there a problem?"

Greene shook his head. "I need to have a word with David Jones. Can you let me see him?"

The African nodded, inserting the key into the cabin's lock. "I will be outside. Just call if you need me."

"Don't count on it," he said dismissively. "This boy's all mine."

Greene pushed the door open with confidence and scanned the room for the captive, who was resting comfortably in the corner of the room, his hands bound behind him.

Sitting up on the makeshift bed, Jones spoke. "Levon, is that you?"

Greene nodded. "Are the guards treating you all right?"

"I'm still waiting for room service, but other than that, I can't complain. How about yourself?" Jones paused for a second. So much had happened during the last couple of hours, he wasn't sure if Greene's presence was good or bad. "Oh, yeah! That's right! You're one of them, you bastard!"

He ignored the insult. "I came to get you out of here."

Jones's eyes widened in the dim light. "Excuse me?"

"You heard me. I came to get you out. Let me see your hands."

This wasn't something that Jones was expecting. When Payne had first warned him about Greene, he was skeptical. He couldn't believe that the Buffalo Soldier was playing for the enemy. But after thinking things over, it started to make sense. The broken guns, Sam's death, Greene's escape. Everything fit into place. Greene had been pulling their strings from the very beginning, treating them like wealthy tourists in a game of three-card monte. And now this. One minute he's Benedict Arnold, the next he's a hero. "Are you serious?"

"You heard me. Turn around and let me see your hands. Be quick about it!"

Despite his skepticism, Jones leapt off the mattress and turned his back to Greene. "What's going on? What are you doing?"

"This!"

With a quick burst, Greene forearmed Jones in the back of the head, sending him face-first into the corner of the cabin. Before Jones could gather his senses, Greene pounced on top of him, pummeling him with a series of vicious blows to his ribs and kidneys. Punch after punch, elbow after elbow, landed solidly on Jones's back, causing him to gasp in agony.

"You have to be the most gullible brother I've ever met! Did you actually think I was gonna set you free?" Greene punched Jones again, landing another blow to the back of his head. "What good would it do if I let you go? As far as I can tell, you've already chosen a life of captivity. David Jones, house nigger for Jonathon Payne!"

Greene chuckled as he stood. "Of all the people in this world, I hate your kind the most. You've been given so many advantages that other brothers would kill for, yet you squander them by working for a white man. You take his charity. You call him boss. You kiss his ass!"

He cleared his throat and spit a giant wad of saliva on the barely conscious Jones. "You make me sick. Absolutely sick!"

The large man turned and walked back toward the door. When he opened it, he was surprised to see Ndjai standing nearby.

"Is everything all right?" Greene asked.

The African glanced past his boss and looked at Jones, who appeared to be a few blows short of a coma. "Did he cause you any problems?"

Greene glanced at his hands for a moment, then smiled. "My knuckles are sore, but other than that, things went fairly well."

Ndjai nodded his head in understanding. "Is there anything else I can do for you?"

"Yes. I understand that you currently have my good friend Nathan in the Devil's Box."

His eyes lit up with pride. "Yes, sir! Would you like to see him now?"

Greene shook his head. "How's he doing? I don't want him to die, you know."

"Yes, sir, I am quite aware of that. We monitor his health frequently, and he is very much alive. He is a little bit swollen from a run-in with some fire ants, but other than that, he is fine."

"Can he talk?"

"Not very well. He is too dehydrated to speak."

Greene pondered things, then grinned. "Pump him full of fluids over the next few hours. I want to talk to him later today, and it won't be fun if I can't understand him. All of the others had a chance to speak to their guests, and I want the same opportunity with mine."

"Yes, sir."

"One more thing. Why don't you move Payne to the Devil's Box while you're taking care of Nathan? It's supposed to be such a lovely day. I would hate to keep him away from the summer heat. He is a guest, you know."

Ndjai smiled at the possibility.

Let the torture begin.

CHAPTER 36

PAYNE had always loved the sun. Whether he was golfing, swimming, or reading, he always tried to catch as many rays as possible. He couldn't explain why, but there was something about the sunshine that made him feel good about himself, something that made him feel healthy.

Those views quickly changed as he baked in the Devil's Box.

"What the hell was I thinking?" he moaned. "Winter is so much better than this."

With his uncovered forearm, Payne tried to wipe the large beads of sweat that had formed on his cheeks and forehead. Unfortunately, since his hands were shackled to a metal loop in the floor, it was impossible, requiring the flexibility of a triple-jointed circus freak.

"Snow, ice, hypothermia. That stuff sounds *so* good!"

When Payne was initially dragged across the length of the island and up the slope of the hill, he wasn't sure what to expect. The possibility of a lynching entered his mind, but for some reason, he had a hunch that the Plantation was more about torture than death. He wanted to ask the guards who were towing him, but the four men weren't speaking English, mumbling instead in an African dialect.

After reaching the hill's summit, Payne was actually relieved when he saw the Devil's Box. No guillotine, no electric chair, no gas chamber. Just a box, a simple four-foot wooden box that had been anchored to the ground. Shoot, he figured, how bad could it be?

Then they opened it.

The figure that emerged was something from a horror movie, a grotesquely deformed zombie breaking from the constraints of his wooden tomb. Haggard and obviously dehydrated, the man's skin practically hung from his bones, like a suit that was two sizes too large. Payne wanted to turn from the scene—no sense getting a mental picture of the personal horror that was to come—but he knew it would be a mistake. He had to study the prisoner, investigate the guards, analyze the device. He needed to know what may be in store for him, if there were any loopholes in the system. It was the only way he could plan an escape.

The first thing Payne noticed was the prisoner's size. Despite his malnutrition, the man was quite large. It took three guards to lift his massive frame from the tiny device, and even then it took a concerted effort. In fact, the prisoner was so big, Payne was amazed that the guards had been able to squeeze him into the cube to begin with. His limbs seemed too thick, too long to contort into such a confined space, but it brought Payne some optimism. He figured if they could fit the giant in there, then there should be plenty of room to maneuver.

Once hauled from the box, the victim tried to stand on his own, but it was a foolish mistake. He had been imprisoned far too long to stand unaided. Atrophy and disorientation took over, forcing him to the ground with a sickening thud, his once-proud body melting into the rocky soil that surrounded him.

The memories of the tortured man, shivering and trembling at the feet of the guards, made Payne flinch. So much so that it snapped him back to the real world.

He had been in the device for several hours, and the intense heat of the Louisiana sun was already forcing his mind to wander. And he knew things would only get worse as time wore on. The more he sweat, the more dehydration would occur. The more dehydration, the higher his body temperature. The more heat, the more illusions. And so on. It was a vicious ride, one that he desperately wanted to avoid.

"Hello!" he yelled, hoping to find a savior. "Can anybody hear me?"

But the only reply was the sound of the breeze as it coyly danced around the Devil's Box.

Payne leaned his head against the oaken interior and stared at the bright sky above. The tiny slits of the lid's lattice pattern gave him a limited view of the world, but he wasn't about to complain. He figured things could be worse. He could be rotting in a freshly dug grave right about now. Still, his current situation didn't offer much hope.

At least until he heard the sound.

At first, Payne thought it was his imagination playing tricks on him, his lack of liquid causing the synapses of his brain to misfire. A heat-induced hallucination. But then he heard it a second time. And a third. Each more clear than the last. The sound, like a memory coming into focus, grew more distinct with each occurrence. Hazy, then muffled, then clear.

It was footsteps, the sound of footsteps.

Someone was coming.

Payne stretched his neck as far as it could reach, trying to peer through the intricate grate of the Devil's Box. But the tiny slits in the device prevented it.

"Who's there?" Payne called. "Hey, I'm in the box. Can you give me a hand?"

But there was no reply. In fact, the only sound that he heard was the whistling wind as it whipped over the crest of the hill, which was baffling to Payne. He knew he had heard movement only seconds before. No doubt about it. Someone was definitely out there.

In order to listen effectively, Payne turned his head to the left and placed his ear against the grate. From this position he hoped to hear things clearer, praying that it would somehow make a difference. And it did. Despite the constant rumble of the wind, Payne was able to hear the sound again. But what the hell was it? It was loud, then quiet. Close, then distant. It sounded like breathing, labored breathing, like a fat man's in aerobics class.

"Hello," Payne yelled, his voice cracking from thirst. "Who's out there? I want to know who I'm talking to."

After a short pause, the movement started again, this time with calculated strides. But instead of approaching the box, the footsteps circled it, like a hawk examining its prey, patiently waiting for its moment to strike. Payne took a deep gulp, pondering the possibilities.

What the hell was going on?

To find out, he shoved his ear closer to the grate, his lobe actually sticking through one of the air holes in the box. Someone was out there. Payne could hear him. Breathing and footsteps, nothing but breathing and footsteps. Why wouldn't he say something? Someone was circling the device, faster and faster, building himself into a frenzy. What was this guy doing? Payne strained to catch a glimpse of him, struggled for any clue, but the only thing he could hear was breathing and footsteps, multiple footsteps.

Then it dawned on him.

"Oh, shit!" he screamed, pulling his head from the lid a split second before the attack.

The beast, a snarling mixture of teeth and sinew, landed on top of the box. Drool sprayed from its mouth like it was a rabid coyote. Hoping to get inside, the animal clawed and chewed at the sturdy lid, but the device held firm.

For the first time all day, Payne was happy to be inside the box. He was actually thrilled that the contraption was so damn sturdy. Crouching as low as he could, he tucked his head between his legs like a passenger anticipating an airplane crash. As he did, he felt the creature's saliva coating the back of his neck with drop after drop of slobber.

"Close your mouth, you drooling bitch!"

With his heart pounding furiously, Payne twisted his neck, hoping to identify the animal without getting in harm's way. He wasn't sure if it was a wolf or a dog, but it was, without question, the sleekest animal he had ever seen. Covered in a sheer white coat, the level back and lean muscular frame of the creature glistened in the bright sun as it frantically clawed at the Devil's Box, trying to rip Payne into tender, bite-sized morsels. Its face, thin and angular, revealed a full set of spiked teeth, each quite capable of inflicting serious damage, and a pink nose, one of the few instances of color on the entire beast. The most prominent of its features, besides its ferocity and propensity for drool, were its ears. Long and light pink, they stood at attention like an antenna on an old TV.

As the attack continued, Payne gained confidence in the cube's sturdiness, which allowed him to take a relaxing breath. If the animal had somehow entered the box, Payne realized he would've been screwed. Since his hands were bolted to the floor and his legs were severely restricted, he wouldn't have had a chance to defend himself.

"Bad doggie!" Payne yelled, cowering from the lid. "Go home! Return to Satan!"

Surprisingly, the command worked. Just as quickly as the attack had started, it stopped. The animal suddenly leapt from the box and scurried away.

Payne's eyes grew wide from the surprising turn of events. He had never expected his request to work. In fact, he'd said it simply in jest. "Wow! Is my breath that bad?"

Before he could answer his own question, a voice interrupted him.

"Hello, Mr. Payne. How are you doing today?" The words were English, but they were tinted with an African accent.

Payne looked above but couldn't tell where the voice was coming from. He strained his neck in all directions but was unable to see who approached. "God? Is that you?"

"Master Greene told me you were somewhat of a jokester. I guess he was right."

Payne grimaced. "Actually, I'm not *somewhat* of a jokester. I *am* a jokester! There's a big difference, my African friend."

Hakeem Ndjai leaned his face over the top of his box and smiled, revealing a set of decaying teeth that had been neglected for some time. "Yes, I guess you are a jokester. Quite comical, especially for someone in your predicament."

"By the way, I meant to talk to you about that. You know, you have to do something about this box of yours. Your wooden-mesh roof is seriously messing up my sunlight. If I'm not careful, it's going to look like I tanned my face in a waffle iron."

Ndjai grinned. "All you have to do is write down your request and put it in the suggestion box at the main house. Oh, I forgot! You are unable to get to the house. Too bad! I guess you will just have to deal with it."

Payne sighed. "I guess so."

"Now, if we are done with the fun and games, I would like to ask you a question. How did you enjoy your introduction to my pet?"

"Your pet? You mean the albino pit bull? Oh, yeah, it was swell. I bet it's great around kids. Just make sure you get a head count beforehand."

Ndjai sat on the edge of the black device and chuckled. "Surprisingly, he is wonderful around children. He is only hostile when I want him to be. That is why he backed away from the box when I called him. He is very obedient."

"You called him? Damn! I was hoping it obeyed *my* commands. That would make my escape so much easier."

"Yes"—he laughed—"I guess it would. Unfortunately for you, Tornado only listens to me."

"Tornado? That's a pretty stupid name for a dog. How the hell did you come up with that?"

Ndjai sneered. "If you did not notice, Tornado circles his prey again and again until he is ready to attack. It is how he whips himself into a frenzy."

"Boy, that's kinda weird, don't you think? Why not call him Dizzy? That's a good name for a dog. Or how about Retardo? That seems to fit. I mean, let's be honest, how smart can the dog be if it has to run in a loop to attack?"

"Quite intelligent," Ndjai argued. "Ibizan hounds are some of the smartest dogs in the world. They were originally bred for Spanish royalty."

"Well, some of them might be smart, but I don't think yours qualifies. Did you get it at a clearance sale? Because that would explain a lot."

Ndjai stood from the box. He wasn't used to arguing with his prisoners. Normally, they were too scared to even speak. "You have a lot of nerve for someone who is about to die. Trust me, I will make sure you go slowly and painfully."

"You mean, like your teeth? You know, if you started brushing now, you might be able to save the last few you have left." Payne's words hit his mark, and Ndjai responded by slamming his fist into the top of the box. "What? Was it something I said? If so, why don't you let me out of here and kick my ass like a real man? Then again, you'd probably have to run around me like your fucked-up mutt. By the time you were done, you'd be too dizzy to hit me."

Ndjai took a deep breath, finally understanding the game that the prisoner was trying to play. Payne wanted Ndjai to become so infuriated that he'd do something irrational, like opening the box to get at him. It was a nice try, but Ndjai was too smart for that.

"Do not worry about my aim, Mr. Payne. If I were to let you out of your cage—something I am not going to do—I would be able to strike you. In fact, let me prove my accuracy."

Payne sat up in the box, trying to view the exhibition that Ndjai was going to put on for him. Unfortunately, as it turned out, it was a show in which he was forced to participate.

With a grin on his face, Ndjai climbed on top of the cube and lowered the zipper on his pants. "The reason for my visit, Mr. Payne, was to give you your daily dose of water, but seeing how uncooperative you have been, I have decided to alter your menu."

A sudden stream of golden liquid fell from above, surging through the slits of the cube like a warm waterfall. By lowering his head and closing his eyes, Payne did his best to avoid the downpour, but his restricted mobility prevented much success.

"What do you think of my aim now?"

Payne wanted to answer, desperately wanted to scream insults at the sadistic guard, but he couldn't risk saying a word. The possibility of the yellow liquid seeping past his cracked lips and into his mouth was far too great. Besides, he knew that he would somehow escape from the Devil's Box and make Ndjai pay for his actions.

And when he did, he would pay for them with his life.

CHAPTER 37

IT was hard for Ariane to believe, but her seemingly perfect life was spiraling out of control. Two days earlier, she was a successful bank executive, preparing to spend a relaxing holiday with the man she loved. The only activities on her itinerary were golfing, swimming, and fooling around. No business. No stress. Just pleasure. She'd been looking forward to it all summer and had done everything in her power to plan the perfect weekend.

Unfortunately, her plans were altered.

In a matter of forty-eight hours, she'd been drugged, kidnapped, and smuggled to Louisiana, where she was being tortured for the sins of relatives she'd never even known existed. Her days, which used to be filled with meetings and paperwork in an air-conditioned office, were now occupied with grueling field labor and the stinging crack of leather whips in the sweltering Southern sun.

If it wasn't for her inner strength, a trait that was tested and fortified when her parents died several years before, she would have broken down. As it was, she stubbornly clung to hope, realizing that things were never as bad as they seemed.

Well, almost never.

Her current situation offered little hope, and because of that she decided to push her luck. While pulling weeds from the untilled ground, Ariane glanced around the spacious field, searching for someone to talk to. She knew that conversation of any kind was forbidden by the guards, but she had the feeling if she didn't do something soon, there was a very good chance she was going to end up dead. And she wasn't about to let that happen without a fight.

A young woman, no more than eighteen years old, stood fifty feet away from Ariane, busily plucking rocks from the dark brown dirt. She tried to signal the girl from a distance, hoping to catch her eye, but the teen remained focused on her task.

Undaunted by the threat of punishment, Ariane moved her wicker basket to the east, carefully approaching the teenager.

"Hello," she mumbled under her breath. "My name's Ariane."

The athletic-looking girl was stunned at first, surprised that someone had the guts to speak under the close watch of the guards. After suppressing her shock, she whispered back.

"Kelly Metz." She wiped the dirt from her hands on her orange work pants, then brushed the brown hair from her eyes. "Where you from?"

Ariane glanced around. The closest guard was over one hundred feet away. "Pittsburgh. What about you?"

"Farrell, Missouri." As she spoke, she continued ripping rocks from the soil. "Heard of it?"

Ariane shook her head. There was no sense speaking when a gesture would do. "How old are you?"

Now it was Kelly's turn to be cautious. Like a student trying to cheat on a test, she made sure the coast was clear. "Seventeen." She carefully checked a second time, then continued. "Are you new? I don't remember seeing you in the field before."

"I think I got here yesterday. I'm not sure, though. Everything's kind of foggy."

Kelly nodded in understanding. "The drugs'll wear off, you know. Don't worry. Just hang in there. You'll get through this."

Ariane smiled at the optimism. She found it amazing that a girl Kelly's age was holding up so well in such adverse conditions. "You here alone?"

Kelly searched for the guards. They were busy hassling one of the male slaves. "Me and my family are a part of Group One. Ten of us in all."

Ariane thought back to earlier in the day, back when it was still dark. If she remembered correctly, Kelly was in Master Holmes's group. "Are you the one with the cute little brother?"

For the first time in a long time, Kelly wanted to laugh. "I've heard my brother called a lot of things, but certainly never cute." She looked over her shoulder, paranoid. "The cute one is Scooter. He's my cousin."

"But you have a brother, don't you?"

"Yeah," she whispered. "His name's Donny."

Something about Kelly's voice worried Ariane. She wasn't sure why, but she could tell something was wrong. She quickly looked for the nearest guard, who was still occupied with the men. "What's going on, Kelly? Is something wrong with your brother?"

She brushed the hair from her face one more time. "He's not what you would call tough. I get the feeling that he isn't holding up too well."

Ariane found that hard to believe. If Donny was anything like his sister, he was probably cutting down trees with his bare hands. "Are you sure? 'Cause you seem to be doing great."

"I play sports year-round, so physical stuff doesn't bother me. Donny, on the other hand, is in the band. The most exertion he gets is playing his trumpet."

"So, he's breaking down physically?"

"And mentally. My dad was tortured the first night we were here. I think that got to him."

Ariane tried to picture the members of Group One. She

distinctly remembered a middle-aged man with a bandaged hand. "What did they do to him?"

Kelly took a deep breath. "They cut off his finger. He didn't even do anything wrong, but they still chopped it off. Probably to prove that they were in charge."

Ariane was surprised that Kelly was handling it so well. Ariane knew there was no way she could have witnessed a loved one tortured and remained so calm—especially back when she was a teenager.

"How about your cousins? Have you talked to them?"

"Not really, but I can tell Susan's on the edge. She's real close to losing it."

"Which one is Susan?"

"She's a year younger than me. She's petite, blond hair. Very pretty."

Ariane tried to place the girl in her mind but couldn't. Too many faces, too little time.

"She was abused on the same night as my dad. Master Jackson cut off all of her clothes in front of everybody. I think that rattled her something good."

"He cut off her clothes? What did he do that for?"

Kelly shrugged. "She was wearing a bikini, so she kind of stood out."

"And you think she's in bad shape?"

She nodded. "I don't think she's gonna make it."

DESPITE her best effort, it took Ariane over an hour to cross the field—her basket of weeds and the guards' careful scrutiny made her movement difficult—but in time she eventually made her way to Susan Ross.

As she approached the teen, the first thing she noticed were her eyes. They were striking, the color of the perfect summertime sky. But it was more than their light blue hue that made them stand out. It was also the tears.

Apparently, Kelly Metz was right. Her cousin was close to losing it.

Ariane inched closer, hoping to comfort the girl with a

word or two, but the move backfired. Susan sensed Ariane's approach and tensed with fear.

"Get away from me!" she shrieked. "Just leave me alone!"

The outburst stopped Ariane in her tracks. She assumed the plea was loud enough to be heard by the guards, and the last thing in the world she wanted to do was attract their attention. She had seen how rough they were with the other slaves and desperately wanted to avoid that.

"Calm down," Ariane whispered. "You don't have to be afraid of me. I just wanted to see how you're doing."

"I'm fine!" she screeched, not giving a damn if the guards heard her or not. "Are you happy? Now get away from me!"

Ariane was flabbergasted by Susan's behavior, but under the circumstances she was willing to cut the kid some slack. "You've got to be quiet."

She glanced over her shoulder, half expecting a stampede of guards to be headed her way, and felt a great sense of relief when she realized their attention was still focused on the men.

"I realize you don't know me and probably don't trust me, but your cousin Kelly sent me over here to check on you."

The frightened girl stared at Ariane coldly. Her body language and icy glare suggested that trust was no longer in her vocabulary.

"You know, I saw you and Scooter at the ceremony this morning. He sure is a cutie."

Susan blinked a few times but didn't respond.

"How old is he?"

She licked her parched lips, giving the question some thought. "Eight."

Ariane grinned, relieved that the girl was willing to talk. "Well, he's just about the cutest eight-year-old I've ever seen. He looks like a little athlete."

Susan nodded, but refused to comment.

"How's he holding up? He seems like he's doing pretty well considering the circumstances."

She shrugged, never shifting her eyes from Ariane's face.

"And you? What about you? How are you doing?"

Susan breathed deeply, sucking in the air through her dry mouth. "What do you want? There has to be some reason you're talking to me. You don't even know me."

Ariane smiled warmly. "Like I said, your cousin wanted me to check on you."

The answer didn't sit well with Susan. "Then why didn't Kelly come over here herself? Why'd she send you?"

Ariane moved closer, hoping her proximity would lower the volume of Susan's voice. "No reason. I'm trying to talk to as many people as possible, and when I talked to your cousin, she mentioned that she was worried about you."

"She's worried about *me*? That would be a first from my family."

"Come on! Don't be silly. Your family's worried about you. They've got to be."

The statement brought a new batch of tears to the teen's eyes. "You don't know my family very well, do you? None of them have even asked how I'm doing. Not one of them."

"Well, I'm asking you. How are you doing, Susan?"

"How the hell do you think I'm doing? Every time I turn around one of the guards is touching me. Last night I saw my dad's ear get cut off. And when I do get to see my family, all my parents care about are my younger brothers. I mean, would it kill them to ask how I am?"

Ariane couldn't believe what she was hearing. Despite the gravity of their situation, Susan was showing signs of sibling jealousy. How petty could someone be? "Don't take it personally. I'm sure your parents are paying them more attention because they feel they need it. You're older. They probably figure you can handle things by yourself."

Susan wiped the moisture from her face. "Great! You're on their side, too."

"It's not about sides. It's about—"

"Just get away from me! I don't want to hear it."

"Susan."

"Get away from me!" she repeated louder. "I don't want to talk to you!"

Ariane pleaded for her to calm down, but the teen refused to listen. "Susan, if you keep making noise, the guards are going to come over and punish us."

"Good! At least that'll get you away from me!"

"Susan, I'm just trying to help."

"I told you. I don't want your help." Susan picked up her wicker basket and began walking away. "And if you follow me, I'll scream for the guards. I swear to God. I'll scream."

Despite the threat, Ariane was tempted to run after her. In her mind, she figured Susan wasn't a bad kid. She was just a traumatized teen, one who was looking for someone to cling to. And if Ariane could be that person, she'd love to be able to help.

Unfortunately, the Plantation wasn't the best place to make friends, so Ariane's act of kindness would have to wait for another day. That is, if both of them could last that long.

CHAPTER 38

AFTER waking from his nap in the plantation house, Master Jackson strolled into the field to check on the current group of slaves. As leader of the guards, he had many important duties at the Plantation, but most of them occurred before guests were even brought to the island. Jackson was in charge of training the guards, a task he shared with Ndjai since several of the men were straight off the boat from Africa. If it hadn't been for the language barrier, Jackson would've preferred training the guards by himself, but as it was he didn't really have a choice. He was forced to work with Ndjai, even though the African gave him the creeps.

Ironically, Jackson often elicited the same reaction from women, sending off a dangerous vibe that females instinctively disliked. It hadn't always been like that. The bad vibe was more of a recent thing for Jackson. As a youngster, he'd been very effective with the fairer sex. He was suave, polite, and romantic. But all of that changed in a heartbeat, one misstep that altered Jackson's life and his attitude toward women—and white people—forever.

He'd been a young associate at one of New Orleans's top law firms, and as his friends used to say, he had the world by its balls. He was handsome, intelligent, and personable. People often confused him with Wesley Snipes, but he was quick to point out their mistake. No, he used to tell them, my name is Harris Jackson, and before long, people will say *he* looks like *me*. And he believed it, too. Jackson was on the fast track to success, and he knew in his heart that he was ultimately destined for greatness.

Until he met her.

A month before that fateful day, Jackson left his law firm to start his own business. The Harris Jackson Sports Agency. He figured that with his legal mind, quick wit, and black skin, he would be able to land professional athletes by the dozen. And he was right. Within two weeks, he had signed Levon Greene, a friend of his from college, and soon after several other stars in the world of sports started using his services.

As a token of his appreciation, Jackson invited his newest clients to New Orleans for a gala celebration and arranged everything that he needed to have a successful party: food, alcohol, strippers, and rap stars. Unfortunately, when he made the party arrangements, he didn't count on the presence of a she-devil. Sure, she looked like a harmless exotic dancer—shoulder-length blond hair, great face, see-through dress—but underneath that beautiful exterior lived the heart of the Antichrist.

At the end of the evening, she begged Jackson for a ride home, and before he could say no, she was riding him in his limo. At the time, he figured it was just a one-night stand, a meaningless night of sex with a drunken vixen, but it turned into something more. It became the event that ended his career. Unbeknownst to Jackson, the girl was young. Too young. An uninvited sixteen-year-old who had snuck into the party to meet some of the celebrities. After sobering up, she regretted her actions and quickly told the cops everything that had occurred. The liquor, the nudity, the sex, everything. In a flash, Jackson was arrested, convicted, and disbarred. Before he knew it, his legal career was over, and all because of some white bitch.

After his release from prison, Jackson realized that he needed to experience the sweet taste of revenge if he was ever going to put the past behind him, and he figured the Plantation was the perfect way to do that. One white whore had taken everything that he'd ever worked for, and in his mind, this was his opportunity to get even with her and everyone like her.

Theo Webster had academic reasons for the Plantation.

Octavian Holmes had a childhood trauma to overcome.

But Harris Jackson had something different. He was in it for personal revenge.

As he scrutinized the female slaves in the dying sunlight, he tried to choose the one he wanted to play with the most. But it was a tough process, a lot tougher than the last group that had been brought to the Plantation. In order to prepare for Webster's special group of slaves, the Plantation Posse abducted twenty-five homeless people for a trial run back in May. After practicing their kidnapping and transportation techniques on the vagrants, the Posse ironed out the kinks in the slaves' housing setup. They perfected the guards' work schedules and corrected any glaring errors in management strategy, guaranteeing that the real group of slaves would be handled as efficiently as possible.

Unfortunately for Jackson, the homeless group had only one good-looking female, a down-on-her-luck runaway, so he didn't have many playmates to choose from. But the current crop of slaves was different. As far as he could tell, there were five females in the bunch that would please him immensely. They were young, pretty, and white—just how he liked them. It was just a matter of time before he chose the one that he wanted to break first.

After figuring out the girls' names, Jackson spoke to one of the guards and told him to round up the following slaves: Kelly Metz, Jennifer Potter, Sarah Potter, Susan Ross, and Ariane Walker. As far as he was concerned, the other females were too old or too pregnant to mess with.

"Ladies," he said to the five, "I'm sure you're wondering why I've pulled you away from your work. Well, I'll explain that in good time. First of all, a question: How have you enjoyed working in this wicked heat?"

Not surprisingly, the women were too scared to speak.

"Ah," he sighed. "It seems that you have forgotten the policy that was established on day one. When I ask a question, you respond, or you will pay the price."

He looked at Susan, who trembled at his presence. She remembered how he had treated her on that first night: the sharp edge of his stiletto as it slid against her flesh, his erect penis as he rubbed it against the small of her back, his threatening words. The memory of it all made her wince in agony.

"So, let me ask you again. How have you enjoyed the heat?"

"We haven't liked it," Ariane admitted. "Not one bit."

The comment made Jackson grin. "Thank you! Even though no one else had the courage to speak, I'm sure each of you agrees with Miss Walker's statement."

The women nodded their heads.

"Finally, a sign of life!"

Jackson moved forward, glancing at the bodies and the faces of the slaves, looking for the tiniest of imperfections. Sarah and Ariane were older than he usually preferred, but they did have the nicest figures of the five. Full breasts, great legs, firm bodies. And Ariane definitely had the prettiest face. Shit, she could be a model if she wanted to be. Unfortunately, he knew that neither of them was a virgin. Good-looking women don't reach their age without screwing someone. And for Jackson, that was a turnoff. He preferred his victims innocent and pure, like the other three girls in front of him.

He wanted the opportunity to ruin them for the rest of the world.

He wanted a chance to destroy a piece of their life, just like that whore had done with him.

"What I'm about to offer to you might sound too good to be true, but it's an opportunity that is steeped in tradition. Plantations used to have house slaves, people that assisted inside the house instead of in the field. They cooked and cleaned and provided indoor services that were requested.

As payment they were given a bed to sleep in and a bath to soak in."

Jackson studied the faces of the women, trying to predict which one would jump at the chance. "Now, keeping in mind that this house has air-conditioning, I need one of you to volunteer for the position."

The females glanced at each other. Each of them had a feeling what the job was really about. Everyone, that is, but Susan Ross. After a momentary delay, she stepped forward.

"I'll do it," she said. "Take me."

"Splendid!" he remarked. In his mind, he figured that she would be the one to volunteer. Of all the females, she was the one who had struggled the most in the field. The tears in her eyes were another sign that she was looking for a way out. "Guards, take her inside so she can get cleaned up. I'll be in shortly to give her further instructions."

But as the guards moved toward the sixteen-year-old, Ariane did as well.

"Susan," she pleaded, "don't do it! This is about sex!"

Jackson jumped forward, viciously slapping Ariane in the mouth. "Get back in line, bitch, before I have you whipped."

"She's just a kid. If you need someone to abuse, take me. At least I can handle it."

"Oh, sure," Susan complained, not absorbing the extent of Jackson's ulterior motives. "Use my age against me to take my spot inside. First you talk to me in the field, and now this. That's just great!"

The moment the words sank in, Ariane took a step backward. She knew that Jackson was going to strike her again. He didn't have a choice. She had broken one of his major rules, and he would have to punish her. And he didn't let her down.

Jackson closed his fist into a ball and swung viciously, connecting with Ariane's face just above her jawline. It was a savage blow, one that knocked her unconscious before she even hit the ground. Then, as she lay there, he kicked her once in the stomach just to prove to the other women that he was still in control.

"Guards, while you're at it, take her in the house, too. Now that she's broken one of my commandments, we're gonna have to dispose of her. But before we do, I think she can provide all of us with some entertainment."

CHAPTER 39

THEO Webster answered the phone, smiling. If there was one thing in the world he could count on, it was Hannibal Kotto's punctuality. "Hannibal, it's nice to hear from you again. How are things in Nigeria?"

"They would be much better if America finally wised up and set its clocks to Nigerian time. It would make my sleeping habits much more routine."

Webster laughed. "I'll see what I can do. In the meantime, tell me about the auction."

"As I hoped, the winning bid exceeds your minimum price."

"By how much?"

Kotto smiled and told him the number.

"Holy shit," Webster mumbled as he did some calculations in his head. He had twenty-three units of snow on the Plantation. Throw in some extra cash for Tonya Edwards, the pregnant one, and they were going to make a lot more money than he had ever expected.

"How soon can you make the shipment?"

"The sooner the better."

"Excellent," Kotto said. "I'll notify the buyers at once."

Webster hung up the phone, stunned. The dollar amount that Kotto had quoted was beyond Webster's wildest dreams. Actually, in the very beginning, the concept of cash had never even entered his thoughts. He wanted to establish the Plantation for revenge, not money. He planned to smuggle people onto his island and treat them the way his ancestors had been treated. In his mind it would teach white people about the horrors of slavery while striking a blow for the black culture. Of course, since he'd never been an athletic person, he knew he needed help to make his plan a reality. He could control the bureaucracy by himself, but he needed someone to handle the brutality, someone who had been trained for it. But who?

While looking for assistance, Webster solicited the advice of Harris Jackson, his ex-roommate from college. Jackson wasn't very supportive of the idea at the time—this was before his legal problems had occurred—but he suggested the name of a client who might be willing to help. And it was the perfect recommendation.

Until that point, Octavian Holmes had made a good living as a mercenary, offering his military expertise to the highest foreign bidder, but he'd reached the point in his life where he was looking for a change of pace—guerrilla warfare in South America and jungle tactics in Africa were quickly losing their appeal. He was thinking about running a training camp for militia types or opening his own shooting range, but he'd never gotten around to it.

When Webster first called, Holmes was immediately intrigued with the idea. The concept of slavery was one that had always fascinated him, and the chance to actually participate in it was too great to pass up. Unfortunately for Webster, Holmes wasn't willing to do it for free. To coordinate something as large as the Plantation, Holmes wanted to be compensated in an appropriate fashion. But Webster didn't have that type of cash. He was willing to pay what he could, but it simply wasn't enough to please a professional soldier like Holmes. So, before it even got started, the Plantation had hit a snag, a problem that threatened its existence.

But not to worry. Holmes came up with a logical solution that saved the day. Why not make money while getting revenge? That way, they could get profits and vengeance at the same time.

It sounded good to Webster, but he wasn't quite sure how it would work.

Holmes quickly clued him in. He told Webster about an African who had hired him for some military exercises in Nigeria. The man's name was Hannibal Kotto, and he was reputed to be as powerful as he was wealthy. Holmes claimed that Kotto was loved and respected throughout Africa despite his tendency to operate outside the letter of the law. In fact, while Holmes was in Lagos, he had heard rumors of a white slavery ring that Kotto was attempting to start.

The concept intrigued Webster. If the rumors were true, then he would be able to take his slavery idea to a whole new level. Instead of just kidnapping and torturing white folks for revenge, he could actually sell them to the motherland for money. It would be the original slave trade, but in reverse: whites going to a black land instead of blacks going to a white one.

After checking with his sources, Holmes discovered that the rumors about Kotto were true. In fact, he had already laid the foundation for the business. Kotto and Edwin Drake, an Englishman who lived in Johannesburg, had cultivated a long list of African entrepreneurs who were interested in buying white-skinned slaves. Even though Africans could hire black servants at a minimal price, the idea of having a white slave was too compelling to pass up. To them, a white slave would be a status symbol, like owning a Mercedes or a Ferrari. *If I'm rich, I can hire a servant, but if I'm super rich, I can buy a white one.* On top of that, many men planned on using white women as concubines, fair-skinned mistresses to have at their disposal.

Still, the concept wasn't perfect.

After several failed experiments, Kotto and Drake realized it was difficult to find a reliable supplier of whites. Sure, the two men wanted to make money off of the slave trade, but neither of them wanted to get his hands dirty. They wanted someone else to do the hard stuff. Furthermore, even though there were thousands of white people scattered across Africa, neither man wanted to make enemies on the African continent. Kotto said it would be like defecating in his own backyard. In his mind, if they were going to get white people, they were going to have to smuggle them in from places where the two men had few ties: Australia, Europe, and North America.

And that's when the Plantation organizers stepped in and offered their services.

They were the suppliers. Kotto and Drake were the distributors.

A partnership was forged.

CHAPTER 40

IF there'd been food in his stomach, Payne was confident that he would've vomited; the strong stench of urine that engulfed him pretty much guaranteed that. But as it was, Payne was only forced to deal with dehydration, severe hunger pains, and intermittent episodes of dry heaves.

"Now I know what Gandhi must've felt like," he croaked, his throat burning from the act of speaking. Yet it didn't matter to Payne. He would continue to speak all night if he had to. It was the best way to stay in touch with reality. "Gandhi probably didn't smell like piss, though."

Payne leaned his head against the box, a position he had been in all day, when his right hamstring started to cramp again. He hastily tried stretching, doing anything to prevent the muscle contractions from striking, but the shackles on the floor made it impossible to move. He would be forced to ride out the wave of agony until the spasm passed.

As Payne suffered, Bennie Blount peered into the hole of the Devil's Box. "You ain't got enough *possium* in your body. That's why you crampin' like that."

The voice stunned him, yet Payne quickly replied. "No," he groaned. "I'm cramping like this because I'm locked in a

Rubik's Cube in the middle of a heat wave, not because I didn't eat enough bananas."

"I don't know. I still think it's the *possium*."

Payne continued fighting through his cramp, in no mood to discuss the merits of potassium. "Nothing personal, but I have a policy about talking to traitors."

Blount turned on a small flashlight and placed it under his chin. He wanted Payne to see his face as he talked. "I sorry about that, Mr. Payne, but I didn't have no choice. I wasn't allowed off the island unless I agreed to do it, and I really wanted to see the fireworks. . . . As it be, I didn't even get to see 'em."

Payne shook his head in pity. Blount was just a helpless pawn in this, caught up in something that he didn't know how to control or escape from. And even though Blount worked for the Plantation, Payne could tell he wasn't as sadistic as the others.

"Hey, Bennie, I don't want to get you into trouble, but I was hoping you could give me a hand."

"You mean free ya? They'd never trust me with the key. I'd probably lose it."

"That's okay. I don't need a key. There are other things you could do for me."

Blount lowered his face to the top of the box. "Like what?"

"Some food and drink would be nice."

Blount frowned, then suddenly stood from his perch.

Payne could hear the servant walking away and was afraid that he was abandoning him for a second time. "Bennie? What's wrong? Come back! Where are you going?"

The servant's face filled the top of the box one more time. "I wasn't going nowhere. When ya mentioned you could use some vittles, it helped me remember something. The reason I came up here was to bring ya some chow, but with all the talking I forgot to gives it to ya."

Food! Mouthwatering food! Payne couldn't believe his luck. The image of a thick, juicy steak suddenly popped into his mind, causing his stomach to rumble like a subwoofer. "Thank you, Bennie. I'm starving."

"First things first. I heard what Master Ndjai did to ya, and I thought ya could use a bath." The dreadlocked servant held up a big pot of liquid, explaining what he had in mind. "Now, don't ya be drinking this stuff while I pour it on ya. This ain't normal water."

"What the hell is it then?"

"Don't ya be worrying none. I mixed up an old family recipe, one that we use to bathe babies when they be young. Not only will it makes ya clean, but it'll make ya smell like an infant."

"Thanks, but I already smell like piss."

Blount smiled. "That's not what I meant. You be smellin' April fresh when I done with ya. I promise." He carefully tipped the pot until the liquid flowed over Payne, surging through the grate like a great flood, washing away the stale scent of urine and the lingering stench of sweat.

"I'll be damned!" Payne chuckled, suddenly feeling a lot better. He took a deep whiff, breathing in the fragrance. "You're right. I smell like the goddamn Snuggle Bear. What's in that stuff? It smells great!"

Blount's smile quickly faded. "Trust me, Mr. Payne. You don't wants to know. I know it made me sick the first time I found out. Yuck!"

Although he was curious about the secret ingredient, Payne quickly changed subjects. "Bennie, now that I'm clean, what do you have for me to eat?"

"I gots ya lots of stuff, but the most important stuff be the liquids. We gots to get ya full of fluid or you's gonna melt away like lard in a skillet."

Payne attacked his meal with zeal, smiling the entire time. Bennie Blount, the dreadlocked servant from the bayou, had saved his life—if only for the time being. Technically, Blount had only provided Payne with food, juice, and a much-needed shower, but in reality he had given Payne something even more important than sustenance. He had given him hope. "Bennie, I can't thank you enough. I can't even begin to explain how much I needed that."

Blount grinned as he tidied the area around the box. He

needed to make sure that there was no sign of his visit, or he'd get in serious trouble. "Well, I be feelin' bad about the trick that we played on you and Mr. Jones. I figure it be the least I can do."

"Speaking of D.J., how's he doing?"

Blount took a deep breath, pausing ever so slightly. "I don't mean to scare ya none, but I heard that Master Greene roughed him up somethin' fierce."

"What?"

"Before ya get too worried, I didn't get a chance to find out if that be true or not, but I just thought it be best if I done told ya what I had heard."

Payne considered the information. If it was true, it would make things doubly difficult.

"Where's he being held? Is he in the main house?"

"No, sir. He be in a utility cabin near the slaves. It kinda stands out from the others, though, since it has plumbing and be much larger than the rest."

"Is there any way you can visit him? You know, to bring him food and first aid?"

Blount shook his head. "Not without them knowing. The cabin is guarded, and it be locked from the outside. Since I ain't got no key, I can't get in with no permission. And I don't think I be gettin' any."

"Is there any chance of him getting out? A window? A trapdoor? Anything?"

"You be watchin' too much TV! There ain't no such thing as trapdoors in the real world."

Payne immediately thought of Levon Greene's escape from the tattoo parlor, but he didn't have time to explain it to Blount. "So, there's no way in or out without the key, right? How about Ariane? Is she still in the same place as before?"

Blount wrinkled his face in discomfort. When he originally briefed Payne and Jones about the Plantation, he had given them bogus information. It was all a part of Greene's master plan of deception. "I been wantin' to talk to ya about that. You see, the stuff that I done told you before was a little off."

Payne leaned his head against the Devil's Box and groaned. "How off?"

"Kinda completely off."

"Bennie," he said.

"I be sorry, but Master Greene wasn't about to let me tell ya the real stuff. He's one of the bosses of this place, so I didn't have no choice."

"Yeah, but . . ." Payne stopped his complaint in midsentence. He suddenly remembered that Blount had just saved his life, so there was no way he was going to make him feel worse about his earlier actions. "Okay, Bennie, you're probably right. You didn't have a choice. But I'd certainly appreciate it if you filled me in now."

Blount nodded. "We gotta be quick, though. I don't want to be gone too long from the kitchen. I might be missed."

"Fair enough."

"So, what do ya need to know?"

Payne grimaced. There were tons of things that he wanted to learn about the island, but before the opportunity passed, he needed Blount's assistance on something else. "Bennie, I know you've done a lot of nice things for me, and I really appreciate them all. But there's something I need that's even more important than information."

Blount brushed the braided hair from his face, gazing into the box. "Like what?"

"Well, I was wondering if you could scratch me."

"Huh?"

"I was hoping you could scratch me. I've been in here for a pretty long time, and I got a number of itches all over my body that I can't reach, so . . ."

"You's being serious, ain't ya?"

Payne nodded, trying to look as pathetic as possible.

"You's crazy! I want to help ya and all, but I ain't touchin' no man. Besides, there ain't no way my arms can fit in that thing. The holes on the top be too skinny."

Payne sighed, making sure that Blount could hear his disappointment. "Come on, Bennie, there has to be something you can do. These itches are driving me crazy! Every time I move, it feels like something is crawling on me—especially down there. It's horrible!"

Blount examined the grate of the box, but his suspicions were correct. There was no way for him to get his arm inside. "Why don't ya do it yourself?"

"If I could, I would. But as you can see, my hands are bound to the floor. I can't even crack my knuckles, let alone scratch myself."

Blount peered closer, shining the light inside. "Yeah, your hands is bound good. Unless . . ."

"Unless what?"

"Unless I can do somethin' with your hands."

Payne tried not to smile, but it was tough. Blount had just suggested the one thing that Payne was hoping for. In fact, it was the only reason that Payne had bitched to begin with. "Jeez, Bennie, what do you think you can do?"

Blount examined the shackles from several angles. Then he peered at the outside of the box. "You be in handcuffs, right? And the handcuffs is bolted to the floor?"

"That's right."

"And if I release the bolt from the floor, you'll still gonna be in cuffs, won't ya?"

Payne pretended to contemplate things. "Yeah. That sounds about right."

"And you can scratch yourself with cuffs, can't ya?"

"Definitely! And it wouldn't be like you were freeing me. I'd still be locked in this thing."

Blount mulled over the situation. He didn't want to do anything that would give away his role in this. "All right. I think I can unscrew the bolt from the outside. Once you pull your cuffs from the hook, I be putting the bolt right back. That way it looks like you did it on your own."

Payne lowered his head and smiled. The servant didn't realize it, but he had given Payne much more than an opportunity to scratch.

He had given him a way to escape.

CHAPTER 41

DAVID Jones had no idea where his best friend was being held or what was being done to him, but the racial overtones of the island suggested he was probably in bad shape.

Despite the pain in his ribs and back, Jones squirmed until his hands, which had been bound behind him, were stretched beyond his feet and repositioned near his stomach. Though his hands were still bound, he had a lot more freedom to move about the cabin and search for a way out. He quickly probed the floor, walls, and ceiling, but each of them proved to be solid. After several minutes, it became apparent that his only option was the heavily guarded front door. Made of oak and finished with a light lacquer, the door was thick, too thick to knock down. It sat in a matching oak frame and was sealed from the outside with a steel dead-bolt lock.

Frustrated, Jones lay on his mattress and pondered his situation. "What would MacGyver do?" he wondered aloud, referring to the TV character who had a penchant for creative solutions. "He'd probably make a grenade out of chocolate pudding and blow up the door."

He chuckled as he said it, but as he stared at the door

over his outstretched feet, two things became apparent. One, a doorway explosion was within the realm of possibility. And two, he wouldn't have to build a device because the guards had actually given him one.

The idiots had strapped it to his leg.

Forgetting the pain in his back and ribs, Jones leaned forward to study his anklet. The mechanism, attached below his shin, was encased in a silver, metallic shell that was no thicker than his hand. The gadget was streamlined and carried little weight; that meant the technology was pretty advanced.

Unless this is a dummy, he thought to himself.

Since the latest in incendiary gear was bound to be expensive, Jones wondered if the Posse had the finances to spend so much money on deterrents. If they didn't, he figured they might be tempted to put dummy devices on the legs of their captives. To him, it made sense. The prisoners would undoubtedly accept the guards' explanation of the anklets, and because of that they'd be too scared to run away or attempt to remove them.

To find out what he was dealing with, Jones looked for the safest way to penetrate the metal casing. He carefully explored the outside of the shell, realizing that there were only two practical choices. He could pick the lock on the front of the anklet, a difficult task without the proper tools, or he could pry the case open with some kind of wedge. The second option seemed the easier of two, but it also seemed much riskier. Even though there was a thin seam that ran along the top of the mechanism, one that could be pried apart with some effort, Jones figured it was bound to be booby-trapped. Most high-tech explosives were.

That meant he had to pick it.

The question was, how? If he had his lock-picking kit with him, Jones could open the clasp in less than a minute. Without it he had no idea how long the process would take— if he could do it at all. In order to try, he had to find something slender enough to fit in the lock but sturdy enough not to break. Jones scoured the walls for stray tacks or nails, but it was pretty obvious that there were none. Next, he examined his bed, hoping that there were iron springs on the inside, but the mattress was made of foam.

"Shit!" he grumbled. "What can I use?"

Jones glanced around the room for several seconds before his statement finally sank in.

He could use a part from the toilet.

With a burst of energy that masked his pain, he rushed to the porcelain throne and removed the back lid. Peering inside, he was glad to see the water in the tank was semiclear, tainted slightly with the orange residue of rust but better than he'd expected. Wasting no time, he plunged his shackled hands into the fluid, hastily searching for a tool that would fit into the lock of his anklet. After several seconds, Jones found the best possibility. The floater lever, which was shaped like an eight-inch-long barbecue skewer, was thin and made out of a hard plastic.

Dropping to his knees, Jones turned off the main water valve with a few rotations of his wet hands, then lowered the handle on the commode. With a quick flush, the murky liquid exited the tank, filling the white bowl like a wet tornado before dropping out of sight. Jones climbed to his feet, grunting slightly as he did, then removed the plastic rod with a twist.

Wasting no time, Jones closed the lid on the toilet seat and sat down. After taking a deep breath, he crossed his legs, bringing the anklet as close to his face as possible. Then, with his hands chained, he tried sliding the slender piece into the lock.

Thankfully, it fit.

With his limited view of the anklet, Jones couldn't identify the type of lock he was dealing with. He knew it could be opened with a key, that much was certain, but he wasn't sure about its internal safeguards. If it was a spring lock, he was confident he could pop it rather quickly. Spring locks have very few safeties, making them a criminal's dream. They can often be picked with a credit card or another thin object in a matter of seconds. If, however, the lock was tubular, then Jones was out of luck. The multiple pins of the cylinder and the dead-bolt action of the cam would require something more sophisticated than a sharpened piece of plastic.

Working like a surgeon, Jones jiggled the floater lever back and forth until he got a feel for the internal mechanism of the lock. A smile crept over his face when he realized what he was dealing with. It was a spring lock, just as he had hoped. After wiping his hands on his shirt, he slowly manipulated the lock in a circular fashion until it popped open with a loud click.

"Damn!" he said to himself. "Why are women never around when I do something cool?"

After sliding the device off of his leg, Jones was able to study the casing of the anklet in greater detail. The shell was silver in color, shiny and quite reflective, yet possessed an abrasive texture that was rough to the touch. It carried very little weight—one or two pounds at the most—but was durable, holding up to the rigors of his probing. The alloy was unfamiliar to him, possibly a mixture of titanium and a lesser-quality metal, but definitely expensive.

Too expensive for it to be a hoax.

"Ladies and gentlemen, we've got ourselves a bomb."

Now that he knew what he was dealing with, he had to decide the best way to use it. Sure, he could strap the explosive to the door and blow the sucker off its hinges, but what would that get him? Probably killed, that's what. The moment he ran outside, the guards would be all over him.

No, in order to escape, Jones needed a way to take out the guards and the door at the same time. But how? Jones went to work on the device as he planned a scenario in his head.

CHAPTER 42

EVEN though Payne was still trapped in the Devil's Box, he felt good about his situation. His hunger was gone, his thirst had vanished, and he smelled kind of pretty. As soon as Bennie left the hill, Payne went to work on his shackles.

When his hands were bound to the floor, there was no way for him to remove his handcuffs. The thick bolt had prevented it. But as soon as it was disengaged, he was able to use the maneuver that he'd learned from Slippery Stan, an escape artist whom he befriended while at a magic exhibit. Unlike most magicians, escape artists rarely use optical illusions in their trade. Instead, they learn to manipulate their bodies to escape from straitjackets or multiple layers of chains. And in the case of handcuffs, Payne was taught to turn his hands and wrists at a very precise angle, which allowed him to slide from the restraints like a hand from a glove.

Of course, the cuffs were only half the battle. The next part of Payne's escape would be more difficult, and he knew it. In order to get from the box itself, he had to rely on outside help. He wasn't sure where that was going to come from—perhaps Bennie, or a guard, or even an escaped captive—but he knew he was stuck until someone showed up.

And it took nearly an hour before someone did.

The instant Payne heard movement outside he slid his hands under his chains, hoping to maintain the appearance of captivity.

"Are you still alive?" asked Ndjai with his thick African accent. "I bet you are bored up here all by yourself." He lowered his face to the grate, smiling with his nasty teeth. "Do not worry. I have some company for you."

The wheels in Payne's head quickly started to spin. Was it Jones, Ariane, or maybe even Bennie? None of the possibilities pleased Payne, and the grimace on his face proved it. "Who is it?" he croaked, trying to pretend he was dehydrated. "Who's out there with you?"

"The question should not be *who*. The question should be *what*."

Payne scrunched his face in confusion. He couldn't hear Tornado's panting so he knew it wasn't him. In fact, he didn't hear anything except Ndjai's laughter. "Okay, *what* is out there?"

"A couple of playmates to keep you company."

Payne didn't like the sound of that. "I appreciate the offer, but I'm actually all right. I've kind of enjoyed the solitude."

"Is that so? You might get bored later, and I would hate for you to think of me as a bad host." Ndjai lifted a large shoe box above the grate then shook it a few times. An angry squeal emerged from the cardboard structure. The creature, whatever it was, did not like to be jostled. "Hmmm, he sounds mad. I hope you will be able to calm him down."

"I hope so, too."

Ndjai rested the cardboard container on the top of the box. "Then again, that might be tough for you to do. My little friend tends to get upset around the other playmate that I brought for you." Ndjai lifted a large duffel bag into the air, then set it down with a loud thump. "You see, this second guy is hungry, and when he is hungry, he has a nasty habit of wanting to eat the first guy, which makes the first guy nervous."

"Wait," Payne mumbled. "Am I the first guy or the second guy? You went so fast I got confused. Please say that again."

The African was ready to explain when he realized that Payne was making another joke, a reaction he hadn't expected. "I must admit, I admire your courage. Too bad it is a weak attempt to mask the fear underneath."

"It wasn't weak," Payne argued. "I thought it was a pretty good effort on my part."

Ndjai ignored the comment, moving to the business at hand. "So, Mr. Payne, I will now give you a choice. Which would you prefer first? The bag or the box?"

"Well, it'd be a lot easier if you told me what they contained."

"But that would take away the mystery."

"Who cares? Mysteries are overrated. I prefer comedies."

Ndjai laughed. "In that case, let us do something fun. How about both at once?"

With a gloved hand, Ndjai reached inside the small box and tried to grab the animal.

Payne listened closely, trying to figure out what Ndjai had in store for him, but all he could hear was the scratching of sharp claws and tiny squeals of anguish from the trapped creature. "I would like to introduce you to the plantation rat, a breed that is indigenous to Louisiana."

Holding it by its tail, Ndjai dangled the rodent above the Devil's Box. Payne, who'd never heard of the species, marveled at its size. It was sixteen inches in length, not including its tail, and must have weighed close to two pounds. It had a short snout, small ears, and was covered in coarse fur.

"Is that your son?" Payne asked.

"No, that is your new roommate."

"Then I expect this and next month's rent in cash, plus I'll need him to sign a few waivers. Can the squirrel write?"

Ndjai smiled while lowering the rat to the box's grate. As he did, the rodent squirmed, trying to free itself from the

Ndjai's grasp. To punish the rat for its escape attempt, Ndjai squeezed its tail quite hard, causing the creature to snap its teeth and brandish its claws in anger.

"You are going to have fun with him. He is not very happy."

Payne shrugged. "That makes two of us."

With his free hand, Ndjai reached into his pocket and removed a full set of keys. After choosing the correct one, Ndjai inserted the key into the lock and opened it with a soft click. He removed the padlock with his left hand while dangling the shrieking rat with his right. "Are you ready?" he asked as he threw open the lid of the Devil's Box.

"Actually, I was about to ask you the same thing."

Before Ndjai could react, Payne leapt from his crouched position and struck his captor on the bridge of his nose. The African stumbled backward, dropping the rat into the box as he staggered, but Payne couldn't have cared less. Before the rodent could attack, Payne pounced from the wooden cage, landing next to Ndjai, who raised his hands in defense but could do little against Payne. With a quick burst, he pummeled Ndjai with several shots to his face, beating him repeatedly until blood gushed from his nose and mouth.

Once the African had submitted, Payne grabbed his legs and dragged him roughly toward the box. "Let's see how you like this thing. Maybe you can get the rat to calm down."

He pulled Ndjai to his feet and bent him over the edge of the box, dangling his upper body inside. The rat, still angry from before, reacted instantly, jumping and nipping at the crimson liquid that dripped from Ndjai's face.

"Oh, isn't that cute! I think he likes you."

Payne punctuated his comment by dumping Ndjai upside down next to the appreciative rat and slamming the lid shut. As he reached for the lock, he suddenly noticed Ndjai's duffel bag out of the corner of his eye.

"Well, well, well! What other toys did Santa bring for me?"

Payne tried lifting the bag with one hand but was caught

off guard by its weight. "Wow, I can't even imagine what's in here. But that's okay, since you're such a fan of mysteries."

After emptying the bag into the Devil's Box, Payne closed the lid and broke the key in the lock. Then, as he pocketed Ndjai's key ring, Payne took a moment to watch the terrified rat as it scurried over Ndjai, both of them trying to avoid the jaws of the angry python.

CHAPTER 43

MOVING silently in the darkness, Payne glided across the open fields of the Plantation, constantly searching for guards. Since he was unaware of Ariane's current location, he decided to head straight for Jones, hoping that his friend was in good enough health to assist him. If he wasn't, Payne realized he would have to handle the Posse by himself. He had faced longer odds in the military, so he knew he was capable of doing it again, but all things considered, he'd love to have his former lieutenant by his side.

When the cabins finally came into view, rising out of the flat ground like wooden stalagmites, Payne dropped to his belly and scouted for patrol patterns and sniper placements. He watched for several minutes, studying the tree lines and roofs, the bushes and walkways, but he was unable to detect any movement.

His hazel eyes continued to scan the darkened landscape, probing every crevice and shadow of the compound, but the waning crescent moon and the lack of overhead lights made it difficult to see from his distance. Reluctantly, he moved closer.

Payne sprang from his stomach and charged forward at

top speed, the breath barely escaping his mouth, his feet rarely creating a sound. It was as if he was moving on a cushion of air that silenced each of his strides, softening the impact of his steps as he hustled across the hard turf. After closing the gap to forty feet, Payne found cover behind a large rock, pausing for a moment to feed his hungry lungs. When his breath returned, he carefully peeked over the boulder and searched the immediate area for patrolmen.

"Come out, come out, wherever you are," he mumbled softly.

But no one did. The grounds were devoid of Posse members, leaving the front door of the nearest cabin without protection.

Taking a deep breath, Payne placed his hand in his pocket and removed Ndjai's keys so they wouldn't jingle when he ran. Next, after looking around one last time, he sprinted forward, heading straight toward the cabin that was closest to him. Upon reaching it, he crouched near the ground and made himself as small a target as possible while double-checking the terrain. When he was sure that no one was around, he shoved the first key in the lock, but it didn't work. The same problem occurred with the next key, and the one after that, and the one after that. Finally, on his fifth attempt, with sweat dripping off his forehead from tension and physical exertion, he found the one that did the job.

With a sigh of relief, Payne opened the door as quietly as he could and slid into the cabin with nary a sound. It took his eyes a moment to adjust to the darkened interior of the room, but when they finally focused, he realized his mission had just become a whole lot easier.

He had been hoping to find Ariane or Jones.

Instead, he had hit the mother lode.

STILL in handcuffs, Jones opened the silver shell of the explosive and carefully probed the interior of the bomb for booby traps. He found several. If he had removed the anklet's casing without care, the device would've exploded in his face, triggered in a millionth of a second by a series of trip wires that protected the outer core of the mechanism.

Thankfully, he noticed them in time.

After neutralizing the safeguards, Jones dug deeper, examining the high-tech circuitry that filled the unit. "I'll be damned," he said, impressed. He had never seen a portable explosive filled with so much modern technology: data microprocessors, external pressure sensors, satellite uplink antennae—which he broke off—and digital detonation switches. The kind of stuff that couldn't be bought at Radio Shack. "This is some serious shit!"

Using the sharpened lever from the toilet, Jones continued to explore, searching under the electronic hardware for the actual explosive. In order to take out the door, Jones needed to understand how much force the device was capable of producing. He assumed that the component was filled with a relatively stable explosive, something that could handle sudden movements and exposure to body heat or static electricity, but he wasn't sure what. C-4, a commonly used plastic explosive, was a possibility, so were RDX, TNT, and pentolite. Because of the high-tech craftsmanship of the anklet, Jones figured that the manufacturer would use something newer, sexier. Perhaps a synthetic hybrid.

When Jones finally discovered what he was dealing with, he gaped in fascination. The device was unlike anything he had ever seen before. Two vials, three inches in length, sat tucked underneath the circuitry. Each plastic cylinder was filled with a liquid—one red, the other clear. They were connected to a third vial, which was twice as wide as the others, through a series of slender plastic tubes. Each one was color-coded and approximately the width of a pencil.

The cylinders, the liquids, the tubes. All of them were new to Jones.

"What the hell am I supposed to do with this?"

As the words left his mouth, his problems actually worsened because he heard the distinct sound of keys rattling directly outside. Someone was about to enter the cabin.

Jones hastily looked around for a hiding place but found

nowhere to stash the equipment. The mattress was probably his best possibility, but Jones knew if he was forced to sit on the bed, there was a chance that his weight could detonate the device, and the thought of shrapnel being launched up his ass was a bit unsettling.

Finally, with no other options in mind, Jones scooped up as many parts as he could and ran toward his bed. After setting the explosive on the floor, he turned his mattress on its side and angled it across the back corner of the room like a child's fort. He figured, if he timed things just right, he could throw the explosive at the guard the moment he entered the room, then duck behind the bed for protection.

The knob twisted with a squeak.

Jones knew the plan wasn't perfect, but he also realized that this could be his only chance to escape. That was why he was willing to risk everything on this plan. His entire life on one moment.

The door swung open.

Making things tougher, Jones had to throw the explosive with his hands bound together, forcing him to use an overhead soccer toss. And on top of that, his ribs still ached from the beating that Greene had given him earlier.

A man wearing black fatigues entered the cabin.

Jones had no choice. This had to be done.

In one swift motion, he launched the explosive at the dark figure and dropped to the floor behind his protective foam shield. In anticipation of a powerful blast, he covered his face and ears, curling into the fetal position against the back corner of the room. He was lucky he did. The cylinders ruptured on contact, creating a bright ball of flame that tore across the cabin in a tidal wave of heat and light. Thunder ripped through the enclosed space with the ferocity of a jackhammer, stinging Jones's ears despite the presence of his hands. Shards of metal sliced through the mattress, narrowly avoiding the exposed flesh of his back.

Slightly dazed from the jolt, Jones peeked over the tattered barrier to see how much damage had been done. Large streaks of red and orange danced from the far wall toward the unprotected surface of the beamed ceiling. Billowy puffs of smoke filled the enclosed space, making it tough for him to breathe. The door, shaken free from the concussion of the blast, sat unhinged and heavily dented, covered in debris and awash in flames. And the guard was . . .

Wait, where was the guard?

Jones knew he'd hit him—he *had* to have hit him, didn't he?—so, despite the crackling flames that raged throughout the cabin, he climbed over the mattress and searched for a body. It didn't matter that the fire was quickly becoming an inferno, shooting tiny embers into the air like bottle rockets. He *needed* to find the guard. He had to get the man's gun and take his keys. He had to question the bastard about Payne and Ariane before it was too late.

Hell, he had to do something to even the odds.

Unfortunately, the blaze was making his mission impossible. The smoke grew thicker and blacker every second, limiting his vision to a scant few feet. And the heat was so intense that Jones felt like he was standing in the core of an active volcano, one that was getting angrier by the minute. But still he searched, heroically digging through scraps of plastic and wood, hunting for the guard until he could take no more, until the hair on his arms literally started to sear like ants under a magnifying glass.

At that point he decided to flee the firestorm before he fried in its wake.

Covering his eyes with both hands, Jones ran from the burning cabin, shielding his head from the flames as he burst through the smoldering doorway. The nighttime air brought him instant relief, but he wasn't able to enjoy it. Jones realized that the Posse would be there any moment to investigate, and when they arrived he needed to be long gone. Using the orange glow of the cabin as his torch, he probed the area for cover, but his plans to flee were quickly altered. Before he found a hiding place, Jones noticed the guard sprawled on the nearby sod, a weapon sitting on the ground next to him.

No time to waste.

He rushed to the man's side and grabbed his TEC-DC9 pistol. Then, in a moment of greed, he frisked him, looking for anything that could help, and as he did he made a startling discovery.

The injured man was Payne.

CHAPTER 44

BECAUSE of the black fatigues and face paint that Payne had found in the first cabin, he looked like a Posse member in the darkness. It wasn't until Jones stared at Payne's face in the light of the fire that he recognized his best friend.

"Is there a reason you tried to blow me up?" Payne asked. He staggered to his feet, shaken from the powerful blast but injury free.

"I thought you were a guard," Jones argued.

"If you don't want to hang out anymore, that's fine! But you don't have to blow me up."

Payne shook his head in mock anger, then jogged away from the cabin. He knew the Posse would be arriving shortly, and he didn't want to be there when they did. Once they were far enough away from the scene, he turned back toward Jones and unlocked his handcuffs.

"What was that stuff anyway? It had some serious kick."

"Some kind of high-tech chemical explosive. Some African guy with bad teeth strapped the sucker to my leg to prevent my escape."

"Hakeem did that?" The thought of Ndjai in the Devil's

Box made him laugh. "Locking a soldier in a wooden cabin with a firebomb? Pretty good thinking on his part, huh?"

"That was more than just a firebomb. That was a first-rate piece of hardware. I'm not sure what we've stumbled onto, but the Posse isn't hurting for cash. Not with that kind of technology lying around."

"You don't know the half of it. Let me show you what I found."

Payne led Jones to the first cabin that he had explored. Instead of containing prisoners like he thought it would, it was filled with military accoutrements: rifles, pistols, ammunition, explosives, detonators, camouflage paint, etc. All labeled and packed in crates for shipping.

"Whoa!" Jones glanced at the gear, smiling. There was enough equipment to start a war. "This is some kind of collection."

Payne corrected him. "This is more than a collection. This is a business."

"They deal arms? Where'd they get this stuff?"

"Where do you think?" Payne pointed to one of the invoices on the wall. The initials *T.M.* were highlighted at the top. "Does that ring any bells?"

Jones glanced at the sheet. "Terrell Murray? Mr. Fishing Hole?"

"You got it." Payne strolled through the stacks of weapons, looking to add to his personal stock. He needed as much firepower as possible if he was going to rescue Ariane and the others.

"What are you saying? The Posse sells Terrell all of his weapons?"

Payne shook his head. "From the looks of Murray's office, he's too established to be buying from a new group like the Posse. So I'm guessing it's the other way around. The Posse gets their guns from Terrell."

Jones furrowed his brow while glancing through the crates. "But why would they need to buy all of this stuff? I mean, this is like an armory."

"Not *like* an armory. It *is* an armory. If my guess is correct, the Posse doesn't own these weapons. They're probably just holding them for Terrell as a favor. Remember what Levon said? Nothing goes on in New Orleans without Murray's involvement."

Jones pulled a Steyr AUG assault rifle from a crate. "Boy, this looks familiar, huh?" It was identical to the one that Greene had supposedly purchased from Murray. "So this is where Levon got his stuff? That son of a bitch! I can't believe he played us like that! I can't wait until I see him again. I really can't."

"Well, you'll have to wait a while. The first thing we have to do is find Ariane. Once I know she's all right, we can get as much revenge as we want."

Jones nodded, thinking mainly of Greene. "Who do you have in mind?"

Payne walked toward the cabin door. "There are too many on my list to name."

CHAPTER 45

OCTAVIAN Holmes roared through the trees on his ATV while two truckloads of guards followed closely behind. Out of all the men on the Plantation, Holmes was the best equipped to handle military situations, since he was a professional soldier. He had worked for nearly two decades as a mercenary, renting out his services to a variety of causes, but this was the first time his skills would be used to protect something of his own.

The Plantation was a part of him. He would not let it be destroyed. Not if he could help it.

Holmes stopped his vehicle near the burning cabin and watched his men attack the blaze. There was little hope of saving the structure since fire equipment was very scarce on the island, but they needed to prevent the flames from spreading. The other cabins were nearby and susceptible to damage.

As Holmes watched their effort, he sensed a presence sneaking up behind him. He turned quickly, raising his gun as he did, but his effort was unnecessary. It was Jackson and Webster, checking out the damage.

"Any ideas?" Holmes asked calmly.

Webster nodded, slightly nervous. "It was the new guys. I was in my office and saw one enter the door with a key. Moments later it blew up."

Holmes frowned. "Which of you lost your keys?"

Both men showed Holmes their personal sets, proving they weren't to blame.

"Fine. Where's Hakeem? He's the other possibility."

Webster shrugged. "I tried paging him on the radio, but he didn't answer the call. I tried all of you the moment I saw the guy enter the cabin, but there was nothing else I could do from my office. I swear, I did my best."

"Theo, don't worry about it." Holmes's voice possessed a scary type of calm. His presence was almost stoic. "You aren't here to do the dirty work. You're here to handle our finances. We'll handle the rest."

Holmes moved closer to the blaze, still examining it. There was something about the flames that interested him. The way they moved. The way they danced. He had seen it before. "Theo? You saw the explosion, right? Tell me, what did it look like?"

"It was a big, mushroom-type blast. A big flash of light burst from inside. Flames spread quickly across the door and roof. An unbelievable amount of thick, black smoke."

Holmes grinned at the description. Things finally made sense. "Well, if my guess is correct, we don't have to worry about escapees. The blast you described sounds like one of the anklets was detonated."

Webster disagreed. "Actually, I saw both of them survive. One of them went in, but two of them came out."

Holmes's grin grew wider. That meant the prisoners had discovered a way to remove the anklet without getting killed. The thought of two worthy adversaries piqued his interest. He'd take great pleasure in hunting them down. "What do you know about these men?"

Jackson answered. "Levon said they were ex-soldiers. They called themselves the Crazy Men or something weird like that. If you talk to him, I'm sure he can tell you more. He babysat the bastards for two days."

"Crazy Men?" Holmes had never heard of a group that went by that name, and he considered himself an expert on the military. "Could it have been something else? Perhaps the MANIACs?"

"Yeah, that was it. Have you heard of them?"

"Yeah," Holmes muttered as the smile on his face disappeared. "I've seen their work. They're clean. Real clean. Some of the guys I worked with called them the Hyenas."

"Hyenas? Why's that?"

"They liked to ravage their victims. I mean, rip 'em to fucking shreds from very close range. Then they'd leave the scene in packs, laughing, like their job was the easiest thing in the world." Holmes shivered at the thought, an equal mixture of fear and excitement surging through him. After all these years, he would finally get to see how good he was. "They're the best-prepared soldiers in the world."

"Come on, how tough can they be?" Jackson asked naively. "We've got dozens of armed men, and we're fighting against these guys in a confined space, right?"

Holmes nodded gravely. The stories he had heard about the MANIACs bordered on legend. "True, but if these guys are who you claim, we might be outnumbered."

AFTER stealing gear from the armory, Payne and Jones hustled into the nearby trees to establish their attack strategy. Unfortunately, their planning would be difficult since they still lacked one major piece of information: Ariane's current location.

Payne updated his friend on everything he'd learned about the guards and the landscape. Then he filled him in on what he didn't know. "I searched a few of the cabins before I reached you. All of them were empty."

"Empty? Then where is everybody? Bennie said there were twenty to twenty-five captives."

"I didn't check all the cabins, but none of them are being guarded. Therefore, either the prisoners are being kept elsewhere, or they've been moved off the island."

"Or," Jones added, "there are several people in one cabin. In the old days, slaves used to sleep ten to a room, and I have a feeling the Posse isn't trying to make their guests comfortable."

Payne nodded in agreement. "So tell me, what should we do?"

Jones smiled at the question. "I thought you'd never ask."

For as long as they'd known each other, this was how their partnership worked. Payne would name a place, and Jones would lead him there. It didn't matter if it was a top-secret mission into Cuba or a beer-filled trip to a Steelers game, Jones was the navigator. He was the planner. A strategy prodigy. It was his specialty. He was the best there was.

Payne, on the other hand, was the finisher. The closer. The military's equivalent of a baseball relief pitcher. He would come in when everything was on the line and finish the job. In truth, it was rarely pretty. Most of the time his work was bloody, even borderline savage. But things always worked out in the end. Always.

Give him a quest, and he'd make it a conquest. Guaranteed.

Together, they were an unstoppable duo.

Let the games begin.

CHAPTER 46

THERE was no reason for the duo to wage battle in the open fields where a lucky shot could take them out. No, it was better to do their dirty work in the dark underbrush of the island, where they could control the game. The woods would be their playground. Search and kill, jungle style.

Without speaking, Payne and Jones communicated their ideas through hand signals. It wasn't traditional sign language, but for them it was just as effective. They knew exactly what the other meant without saying a word, and that was critical. During night runs, sound was the biggest enemy.

On the other hand, sound could also be quite useful, the ultimate ally. By making a noise on purpose, a soldier could divert his enemy's attention. The crash of a thrown rock could confuse a tracker. A snapping twig or a well-placed scream could quickly draw attention away from an endangered colleague. And occasionally, it could be used as a lure, a way to bring several people into an area at one time. It was a difficult thing to accomplish, but when done right, it was very effective.

Cows to the slaughterhouse, as Payne liked to say.

Eventually, this was the technique that Jones settled on.

In order to make it work, they placed some charges near a small clearing that they found in the middle of a thick grove. A boulder, partially buried on a nearby plateau, would be used as the duo's nest. The goal was to draw as many men as possible into the open area below the large stone before Payne and Jones used their elevated position to commence target practice.

After climbing the bluff, Jones settled into position next to Payne. Normally, they would've spread far apart, attempting to surround their victims in hopes of cutting off their escape routes, but in this case it was completely unnecessary. This assault would be child's play, a complete bloodbath. Two experienced soldiers facing a team of untrained men was as lopsided as a battle could get. Besides, the landscape didn't allow them to fan out over a wide range. The terrain dictated that both of them sit in the crow's nest from the get-go.

When Payne was ready, he glanced at Jones and nodded. It was time to begin.

BOOM!!! An explosion shook the earth, and a flash of light brightened the nearby sky. Everyone near the burning cabin flinched and turned their heads toward the trees. The prisoners were apparently in the woods. Holmes gave orders to pursue them.

Tat-tat-tat-tat-tat!!! Payne and Jones squeezed off a few rounds for additional attention, plus they wanted to make sure that their weapons were functional. The last time they'd used Terrell Murray's guns they were very disappointed with the results.

BOOM!!! A second charge exploded. Payne and Jones tried to lure the guards to a specific spot in the woods. They couldn't afford to have any strays sneaking up behind them. It would ruin their plans and cost them their lives. No, they needed everyone to appear in the open area below the boulder, right where the guards would be most vulnerable.

BOOM!!! The last of the small charges was detonated. Neither Payne nor Jones wanted the woods to be too bright when the guards arrived. They wanted a soft glow, just enough light to see their targets, but not enough light to give away their own location. Candlelight to kill by.

"Do you hear that?" Payne whispered as he screwed the silencer onto his MP5K. His weapon was capable of spitting out nine hundred rounds a minute, and now that its silencer was in place, it would make less noise than an iPod.

Jones smiled. He heard several footsteps approaching through the grove. "Here come the first contestants on *The Price Is Life*."

Nodding, Payne focused on the area below, but he wouldn't fire his submachine gun until the small pocket of space was completely filled with guards. He needed to make sure he could get everyone at once.

One by one, the black men emerged from the trees. Two, then five, then ten. Thirteen in total. Unlucky thirteen. They glanced around, looking for the source of the commotion, but found nothing. They stood there, confused, unable to choose their next move, for none of them had the experience or the authority to take control.

"Like cows to the slaughterhouse," Jones mumbled, stealing Payne's line.

Payne nodded again, his face devoid of emotion. "Moooooo!"

Pfffft! Pfffft! Pfffft! Pfffft! The guns hissed, spraying in silence.

Pfffft! Pfffft! Pfffft! Pfffft! Their venom flew, striking its mark.

There wasn't any time for the guards to react or fire back. Hell, they never even knew what hit them. One minute they were standing, searching for the escaped prisoners. The next they were sprawled on the ground, marinating in each other's blood.

There were no screams, no tears, and no pleas of mercy. Death had been silent and swift.

ANTICIPATING an easy victory, Jackson and Webster followed the guards at a leisurely pace. Thirteen men against two. With odds like that, they figured it would be a massacre, an absolute slaughter. And it was—just not in their favor. When they arrived at the scene, they found nothing but bodies. All of them black. All of them dead. Victims of gunfire. Head shots. Heart shots. Limbs tattered. Pistols still holstered. Rifles unfired. The smell of war lingered in the air. Crimson poured from gaping wounds, flooding the forest's floor. Death was everywhere.

And Webster couldn't handle it.

When he realized what had happened, he dropped to his knees and vomited. It was the first time that he'd seen a corpse outside of a funeral home, so the sight of the baker's dozen was too much for him to handle. He was the brains, not the brawn. He took no part in the actual torture and disposal of the bodies. All of that was outside of his realm.

"They killed them! They killed them all!" He staggered to his feet, wanting to confront Jackson, but was unwilling to walk among the gory remains of his fallen comrades. "Octavian was right! These guys are the best! Look what they did to your guards! Just look!!"

"Be quiet!" Jackson whispered sternly. "They might still be around."

The thought hadn't crossed Webster's mind. The killers could be in the trees, watching him at that very moment. He gagged as more vomit rose from his belly.

Jackson rolled his eyes in disgust. He didn't have time to babysit. He needed to focus all of his attention on the battle site. He needed to look for clues while the trail was still warm. "Don't worry. I might not have their training, but I can be a warrior if I have to be."

As Jackson finished speaking, his radio squawked, causing him to flinch in fear.

The incoming voice said, "This is Octavian. What's going on out there?"

Jackson whispered. "Dead. Everyone's dead. Payne and Jones killed them all. Theo and I showed up one minute behind the guards, and we found corpses. Thirteen fuckin' corpses. Blood everywhere. No sign of the prisoners, but our guys are dead!"

"You're sure."

Jackson kicked one of the men in front of him. He didn't move. "Yep."

Holmes felt his pulse quicken and noticed the hairs on his arms stand at attention. Thirteen kills in less than ten minutes. *My lord, these guys were good.* "What did they use for weapons?"

"Guns," Jackson answered. "I don't know what kind, but they have rapid-fire capability. I don't see any shells near the guards, so I guess they didn't have time to fire back."

"Where the hell did they get weapons like—"

Holmes stopped before he finished his statement. Nervously, he glanced at the cabin on the far end of the row. The door looked closed from a distance, but there was only one way to know for sure.

"Guards!" he shouted. Two men left the burning cabin and ran to his side. "Check the armory and tell me if anything's missing!"

The men saluted crisply, then ran off.

As he watched them approach the storage shed, Holmes felt the tension rise in his body. If Payne and Jones had located the artillery, there was a good chance that they'd stolen enough equipment to wipe out the entire island. Instead of seizing the Plantation one guard at a time, they could do it one acre at a time.

Within seconds, the guards reached the cabin and studied the partially opened door. The armory had been violated. Drawing their weapons, the two men kicked the door aside and prepared to fire at the perpetrators. It was the last move they would ever make. Because of their inexperience, the men failed to notice the wire that had been tied to the base of the door. When they bumped the cord, it triggered a fragmentation grenade, which exploded in their faces. The fragger, designed to launch razorlike pieces of metal over an extended area of space without the impact of a large explosion, tattered the men with shrapnel, killing both men instantly.

Holmes grimaced as he heard the muffled blast, followed by the guards' silence. The sounds proved what he already knew in his gut. The Plantation's artillery had been compromised.

"Damn!" he muttered.

He wasn't the least bit concerned about his men, but he was worried about the missing weapons. It was going to make his job much harder to accomplish.

He grabbed his radio once again. "Harris? Theo? Are you there?"

"What do you need?" Jackson whispered. He was walking through the trees with Webster, trying not to make a sound. "We're on our way back now."

"That's probably a good idea. Not to alarm you, but Payne and Jones got into Terrell's gear. There's no telling what other surprises they have in store for us."

"What do you mean by surprises?"

"I don't know," Holmes admitted. He still needed to get someone inside of the armory to check the inventory. "Land mines, flame throwers, grenades, rocket launchers. Shit, they could have anything."

Without responding, Jackson and Webster increased their stride significantly.

CHAPTER 47

WHEN Greene saw the site of the explosion, it hit him like a punch in the gut. It was Jones's cabin, and there was nothing left of it. The wooden frame had collapsed, succumbing to the intense heat of the fire. Debris, spread from the power of the initial blast, littered the manicured yard. Clouds of smoke lingered in the air, making it tough to breathe or even see.

"Damn," he muttered as he removed his mask and cloak. "This can't be good."

Holmes, Jackson, and Webster saw Greene's approach and rushed to his side. Before they even said a word, Greene tried to assess the severity of the situation but was unable to do so because of their wide range of emotions. Holmes had the cold glare of a terrorist. Blank face, intense eyes, neither a frown nor a smile on his lips. He had seen this type of shit before and wasn't fazed by it. Jackson, though not as polished as Holmes, was still under control. His eyes showed some concern, like a sick man waiting for test results in a hospital, but he did his best to mask it with a broad grin. This was his first combat, and overall, he was holding up well.

Then there was Webster. He was the complete opposite of the other two men. In fact, if he had been a horse, Elmer's would've been negotiating for his glue rights. His face was pale and sweaty. His body trembled. And his eyes were as big as pancakes. If not for the tragic possibilities of the situation, Greene would've laughed at him.

Hell, he was tempted to do it anyway.

"Why are you here?" Webster asked. "Who's watching the boat of prisoners?"

"Don't worry about it. The passengers are chained and surrounded by water. They aren't going anywhere." Greene turned toward Holmes. He knew this was the man who would give him the facts he was looking for. "What happened?"

"Your friend blew up the cabin and managed to escape in the process."

"Jones escaped? How is that possible? Where was Hakeem when this happened?" The three men looked at each other but didn't respond. "Shit, where's Hakeem now?"

Holmes shrugged. "We don't know, but we're assuming he's dead. He's been missing for quite some time, and Theo saw one of the prisoners with his set of keys. We figure that—"

"Prisoners?" Greene blurted. "Are we talking plural?"

Holmes nodded. "It seems your other friend, Payne, unlocked the cabin door before Jones blew it up. At least that's what we've pieced together. Theo watched the escape from the house and thinks Jones made the bomb from his anklet."

All eyes turned to Webster, who just stared at the flames in the distance.

Holmes shook his head at Webster's high level of anxiety. "I'm still trying to figure out why they blew up the cabin. It just doesn't make sense to me. I mean, why blow it up if you have a set of keys to get out quietly? Wouldn't the explosion just draw attention to your escape?"

Greene considered the question. "Maybe that's what they wanted. Maybe they blew the cabin up for attention. You know, draw us to this part of the Plantation for some reason." He paused as he fleshed out the theory in his mind. "What were the other blasts I heard?"

"Actually," Jackson answered, "you may be on to something there. Three charges were set off in the trees for just that purpose. Your friends lured thirteen of my guards to a spot in the woods, then waited for their arrival. When they showed up . . ." He finished his statement by running his thumb across the base of his throat in a slashing motion.

"They killed all thirteen?" Greene asked. "How the hell did they do that?"

Webster groaned, and Jackson cleared his throat. Neither of them wanted to tell Greene about the carnage they had witnessed. But Holmes didn't mind talking. In fact, he wanted Greene to know what kind of trouble he'd brought to the island. "It seems our escapees aren't your average, everyday army grunts. These are two very talented men, special forces plus."

Greene furrowed his brow. "Special forces plus? What does that mean?"

"It means that they're the best. They're capable of doing anything they want."

"Anything?" said a doubtful Greene. He'd fought Jones a few hours before, and his opponent barely put up a fight. He certainly didn't think of him as a killer. "Come on, they're just men! Two injured men! How tough can they be?"

"You don't understand. I've known about the MANIACs for a very long time. These guys aren't human. They're machines. Military supermen."

"Get real!" Greene laughed. "Don't you think you're exaggerating just a little bit?"

Holmes's face finally showed some emotion—not much, just a slight flare-up in his eyes. "Exaggerating? They slipped out of bondage, located Terrell's armory, stole a shitload of weapons, killed thirteen guards in the woods and two with a booby trap, then mysteriously disappeared into the night. Now you tell me, do these guys sound normal to you?"

Greene took a deep breath. He didn't want to admit it,

but from Holmes's description it did seem like Payne and Jones were pretty talented. Hell, he'd underestimated them at Sam's Tattoos and they had escaped. Maybe these guys *were* something to worry about.

"So, they're still out there, huh?"

"Yeah," Holmes answered. "They're still on the loose, doing God knows what."

"And what about Payne's girlfriend? Where's she? She's our insurance policy, you know."

Holmes turned toward Jackson. "Didn't you have her in your possession?"

"She's in the guest bedroom. I left her tied to the bed."

"Jesus!" Greene growled. "You left her in the house this entire time by herself, and you didn't say anything! She's what they want!"

The thought of Ariane's escape made Greene tense with fear. She was his best chance at safety, and he knew it. As long as he had her, he had lots of bargaining power.

"We better get the bitch before they find her. If we lose her, we're in deep shit."

Holmes nodded in agreement. "I'll come with you, Levon. I think we should bring the young blonde out of the house as well. The less spread out we are, the better."

WITH a hollow reed in his mouth and a bag on his shoulder, Payne took a breath of fresh air and slipped into the warm water of the gulf. He wouldn't have to swim far, but the distance he'd travel would be done underwater in complete darkness, so the reed would guarantee a supply of oxygen if he needed it.

Using his hands as his only guide, Payne swam blindly through the intricate web of wooden poles that supported the western dock, making his way toward the heavily guarded boat. After circumnavigating the bow, he breathed through his reed and continued forward, hugging the underbelly of the ship as he successfully wove through a series of ropes before he emerged along the edge of the stern.

The toughest part was over. He was where he needed to be.

WHILE peering through the scope of his Heckler & Koch PSG1 semiautomatic sniper rifle, Jones swung his gun from side to side, searching for targets. He found several. It was a good thing that his weapon offered a deadly combination of precision and speed, or he wouldn't have a chance against so many men. And if he failed to complete his mission, Payne would probably die.

Thankfully, he had plenty of experience dealing with pressure.

The first blast echoed in the night as the bullet struck the guard. His skull exploded in a mixture of blood, brain, and bone. Before the victim's partners could react, Jones lined up his second target and repeated his performance.

Another shot. Another corpse. Blood everywhere.

Shot three eliminated one more guard. Shot four did the same.

And for some reason, the guards weren't hiding. They just stood there, scanning the trees for the source of the gunfire, hoping to see the discharge in the distant night. Jones couldn't believe his luck and their stupidity, but he was going to take advantage of both while they lasted.

"*Adios.*" Guard five, killed.

"*Sayonara.*" Guard six, dead.

If he'd had the chance, Jones would've continued shooting all night, but a few of the guards finally wised up and dashed into the woods to find him. That was his cue to leave. Before he departed, though, Jones blasted a few shots into the water—his signal for Payne to begin—then slipped deeper into the trees for safety.

He had done his part. Now it was up to his partner.

AND Payne was ready.

He'd been waiting for several seconds in the water, trying

to remain completely silent near the stern, but now that Jones had signaled him, he knew he could spring into action. Using a rope that hung from the deck, Payne quickly scaled the back edge of the ship. He slipped his hand into his shoulder bag and grabbed his Glock. The powerful handgun, fitted with a silencer and a full clip of ammo, would allow him to kill with stealth. And that was crucial. He couldn't risk drawing attention to himself before he had a chance to leave the area.

As water dripped off his damp clothes, Payne crept around the small boat, looking for the enemy. One stood by the instrument panel, his back facing the water. Another rested by the bow. And neither sensed the presence sneaking up behind them.

Pffft! the Glock whispered.

Pffft! Pffft! Both men were dead.

The prisoners saw the guards fall and immediately turned toward the sound of the muffled gunshots. Payne, covered in slime and water, raised his finger to his lips to silence them.

"I'm one of the good guys," he whispered.

Ten mouths dropped in wonderment. They couldn't believe that someone had found them.

"Are there any other guards on board?"

Ten people shook their heads in unison before a masculine voice rose from the back of the crowd. "Jon? Is that you?"

The sound of Payne's name made his heart leap. He realized it wasn't Ariane—the voice was too deep to be hers—but the question meant someone else on board knew him. But who? He frantically searched through the faces, looking for the source of the sound, but couldn't figure it out until the man spoke again.

"Jon Payne?"

Payne nodded and moved closer to the man, desperately trying to recognize him, but the guy's battered appearance made it difficult. Bruises covered his face and neck. Blood and dirt covered everything else. A makeshift splint was tied to his leg. "Do I know . . . Robbie?"

Robert Edwards, Ariane's brother-in-law, nodded his head with joy. He tried to stand up, but his ankle prevented it. "Oh, my God! I can't believe it's you."

"Yeah, it's me," he gasped. The reunion with Edwards was so unexpected that Payne didn't know what else to say. "What are you doing here?"

"I was kidnapped. We were all kidnapped." Edwards clutched Payne's hand to make sure he wasn't dreaming. "And what about you? What are you doing here?"

"I heard the island served a nice buffet." Joking was the only way he could reel his emotions back to where they needed to be. "Actually, I'm searching for Ariane. Is she here?"

Edwards nodded. "Not on the boat, but somewhere on the island. I haven't seen her today, though." He took a deep breath of air. "I haven't seen Tonya, either. I hope to God she's all right. The baby, too."

Payne winced. He had no idea that Ariane's entire family was on the Plantation. What kind of bastards would drag a family, one with a pregnant woman, into this type of situation?

"Do you have any idea where they are?"

"I don't know," he sobbed. "They might be in the cabins, but I don't know."

"No, they aren't. I already checked there." Payne glanced at the other nine slaves. "Does anyone know where the others are?"

All of the prisoners shook their heads.

"Damn!" He had hoped that someone would be able to direct him to Ariane, but it was obvious that the two groups had been kept apart. "One last question, can you tell me how many captives I should be looking for?"

Edwards shrugged. "Ten, maybe more. They rotated us around quite a bit."

"Okay, I'll take it from here. But before I leave, I'd like to make a small suggestion. Why don't you guys go home? Does that sound all right to you?"

Ten sets of eyes got misty.

Payne continued, "Before you can leave, we need to get rid of those bombs on your legs."

"But how?" shrieked one of the women. "The lead guard said they would explode if we tried to take them off. He said all of them would burst, one after another."

"And he was right. They would've exploded if you pried them off." Payne reached into his shoulder bag and retrieved Ndjai's keys. "That's why we'll use this instead."

The lady smiled in gratitude as he handed her the anklet key.

"Carefully remove the bombs, then place them gently in this bag when you're done."

While waiting for the bag to be filled, Payne walked over to the boat's instrument panel, assuming that he'd have to hot-wire it. He was pleasantly surprised to see a key in the ignition. "Hey, Robbie, how are your navigational skills? Are you any good?"

"Not too bad. I've taken you water skiing a few times, remember?"

Payne should've remembered. He and Ariane had visited Edwards in Colorado on more than one occasion. "That's right. Good, then I'm making you the captain." He placed his arm around the injured man and helped him to the wheel. "I want you to pull out of here very slowly."

"Slowly?" called out one of the kids. "Why slowly?"

Payne didn't have time to explain, but he knew he'd better do it anyway. The last thing he needed was a mutiny on the escape vessel.

"The area around the island is surrounded by fallen trees. It's a pretty thick swamp, clogged with all kinds of logs. If he goes too fast and hits one, the boat could sink." He smiled for the child's benefit. "And that would be bad."

The kid nodded his head in agreement.

Payne turned back to Edwards. "When you steer, make sure you have some people looking out into the water. They can help you avoid some of the larger obstacles. Got it?"

"Jon, I want to help," he assured him. "But Tonya is still here. I'm not going anywhere without her."

"Trust me," Payne said, "I'd feel the same way if I were you. But with your injury, you're in no shape to fight. Hell, you're not even in shape to walk. So I need you to stay on this boat and help all of these people get to safety. If you do that for me, I'll do everything in my power to rescue your wife. . . . Okay?"

Edwards nodded reluctantly. "What should I do when we get to the sea? Do you have backup waiting for us?"

"No, there's no backup. It's just me and my partner on this mission, no one else."

The looks on the prisoners' faces said it all. They couldn't believe that Payne and Jones had done so much—and risked so much—on their own.

"Once you hit the gulf, open it up to full speed and go north toward the closest set of lights. Don't stop for anyone unless it's the Coast Guard. When you hit land, call the police, NASA, anyone! The sooner I get some help around here the better."

CHAPTER 48

THE leaves and branches would have covered Jones completely, if not for the small gap near his eyes. It was the only spot that he risked showing, for it gave him his only view of the world. And if his mission was to be a success, Jones needed to know when someone was coming.

The shadow lurking in the distance told him that somebody was.

As he waited, Jones wrapped his fingers around the polymer handle of his gun, readying himself for action. If possible, he would eliminate the target from his current hiding place. If necessary, Jones was prepared to do it on the move. It was the first thing he learned with the MANIACs. Be ready for *anything*.

Jones watched as the shape moved closer, slipping past the tall trees with a graceful stride, using the darkness of the woods to his advantage. The lack of moonlight made things difficult, but in time Jones learned to distinguish his target from his surroundings. He wore black clothes, black leather boots, and a mask. A gun dangled from his right hand.

A grin appeared on Jones's face.

The more guards he killed, the better. It would make

things easier when they rescued Ariane and the other prisoners. So far, by his count, he had been a part of twenty deaths—thirteen in the ambush, six more on the boat, at least one at the armory—and the number would continue to grow. Hell, number twenty-one was currently approaching.

Without making a sound, Jones shifted his weight slightly, sticking the barrel of his gun through his thick bed of camouflage. He would fire when he had a clean shot and not a second before. No sense wasting a bullet on a maybe.

"Come to Papa," Jones whispered. "Take another step. Come on. Come on!"

His target finally came into view, no more than fifteen feet in front of him.

But before Jones had a chance to squeeze the trigger, the man whistled softly—a sound that had a meaning only to Jones. This man wasn't a guard. It was Payne.

"Jon," he called softly.

Covered in dark mud from the swamp, Payne glanced around, hunting for the source of the sound. He was supposed to rendezvous with Jones in this part of the woods, but his friend's concealment techniques made him undetectable. There was no way he would find Jones unless he accidentally stepped on him.

"Ollyollyoxenfree."

A large chunk of the forest's floor moved as Jones climbed to his knees. To Payne, it looked like an elevator rising from the Earth's core.

"You're lucky you whistled. I was going to try to kill you for the second time today."

Payne shrugged. It seemed like everyone was trying to kill him. "Actually, you're the lucky one. If you'd killed me, you'd have to fly coach on the way home."

"Good point. How'd the boat mission go?"

"Just like you planned. I took out the remaining guards without any problems and got the boatload of slaves off the island."

"That's great, isn't it?" Jones studied Payne's face and could tell he wasn't happy. "What's wrong? We just saved several lives. You should be thrilled."

"Not only did we save several lives, but we knew one of the survivors."

Jones's eyes widened with surprise. "Ariane was on the boat?"

Payne shook his head. "The Posse kidnapped her entire family. Her brother-in-law, Robbie, was one of the captives on board."

"What?" He had met Ariane's family on several occasions. "Was Tonya on the boat, too?"

"No. They still have her somewhere, and if you remember, she's pregnant." Payne paused as he thought about the situation. He knew Tonya was very close to her due date. "That is, if all this trauma hasn't brought on childbirth."

Jones could tell his buddy was hurting—it might be a future nephew or niece that he was talking about—so he tried to get Payne's mind back on the mission. "What did you learn about the others?"

"Not much, but something strange is going on. That boat was filled with families. Moms, dads, kids. These weren't strangers picked at random. These groups were chosen on purpose."

"But why?"

"I don't know."

"And where were they taking them?"

"I don't know that, either."

Jones forced a chuckle. "Shit, you don't know too much, do you?"

"I guess not," Payne admitted. "But I do know this. If ten of the captives were on the verge of leaving this place, then there's a good chance that the second group will be leaving shortly."

"If that happens, our odds of finding them goes down significantly."

"You got that right." Payne checked the ammo in his

Glock. "So tell me, Mr. Jones, you're the brilliant military strategist. What do you recommend we do?"

"That's easy. Let's go save some people."

HOLMES and Greene were ready to enter Ariane's room when Jackson's voice emerged from Holmes's radio. They had left Jackson five minutes before, and he was already calling.

"What the hell do you want now?" Holmes barked.

"Well, hello to you, too!" Jackson replied. "Sorry to disturb you, but we just heard a bunch of gunshots by the western dock."

"Damn!" Greene cursed. "They're going after the boat!" In the back of his mind, he was glad that he'd left his babysitting job when he did. He didn't want to face Payne and Jones until the odds were more in his favor. "We have to stop these guys before they ruin everything."

"How do we do that?" Holmes demanded. He had the most military experience of any of them, but he was clueless when it came to Payne and Jones. They were playing in a different league. "You know these guys better than I do. Do they have any flaws that we can exploit?"

Without speaking, Greene pointed to the door in front of him. As far as he knew, their only weakness lay inside the room.

Holmes considered the information, then pushed the button on his radio. "Harris, we're coming out with the two girls. In the meantime, gather up all the guards and arm them with the best weapons we have. As soon as I get outside, we're gonna storm the dock."

"You got it!" Jackson's voice was a mixture of excitement and concern. "I'll see ya soon."

Greene raised his eyebrows in surprise. "Do you think an all-out attack is gonna work on these guys? Won't they see us coming a mile away?"

"Definitely, but that's exactly what I want. I'll have our guys make as much noise as possible, and I guarantee that Payne and Jones will try to slip through a crack and come to the house." Holmes pointed to the door. "If she means as much to them as you say, they're just killing time until we leave the home front open. As soon as we make a move, they'll seize the opportunity."

Greene nodded in agreement. The plan made perfect sense. "So, while the guards are in the weeds, what are we gonna do with her?"

Holmes grinned sadistically. "We'll use her to set a trap of our own."

CHAPTER 49

JUST as Holmes had expected, Payne and Jones could hear the guards approaching, but it wasn't because of their military training. All it took was a good set of ears, for the African guards did everything in their power to make as much noise as possible. They'd been told to drive Payne and Jones toward the dock site, where they'd eventually be trapped against the water. Their technique might've been successful if they were hunting a man-eater or some other type of game. But Payne and Jones were far more intelligent than a lion. Much more dangerous, too.

"Uh-oh," Jones joked. "I think somebody's coming."

Using the night as their ally, the ex-MANIACs slipped past the squadron of guards without difficulty. They had the opportunity to kill a few men if they had wanted to, but they decided the risk wasn't worth it. They figured it was probably better if the guards continued their search in the woods while they crept unnoticed toward the main house. No sense rattling their cage if they didn't have to.

Once the duo reached the edge of the plantation house grounds, Jones asked Payne to stop. He had something on his mind, and he needed to voice it before it was too late.

"You realize, of course, that there's a very good chance that this is a setup."

"Yep."

"And if Ariane is inside, she's probably surrounded by armed guards."

"Mm-hmm."

"And there's a pretty good chance that we'll get killed doing this."

Payne frowned. "You think so?"

"No, but I wanted to make sure you were listening. You tend to block me out sometimes."

"What was that?"

Jones laughed. "Okay, let's do this."

The two men hustled to the nearest cabin and used it as temporary shelter. Then, by repeating the process several times, they slowly made their way up the row of cabins until they found themselves crouching near the blackened remains of Jones's blast site.

"Now what?" Payne asked.

From this point on, he knew their cover was limited. With the exception of a few oak trees covered in Spanish moss, there was nothing between their current position and the house.

"Front door or back?"

Jones studied the outside of the plantation house and shrugged. He'd never been inside the white-pillared mansion and had no idea what kind of security it had. Everything from here on out would be blind luck.

"It's your girlfriend, you decide."

Payne didn't even bother to reply as he made his way toward the rear of the house. Jones stayed close behind, scouting for potential trouble as he did. When they reached the back of the structure, they noticed something that made their choice a good one. Bennie Blount was sticking his head out of a downstairs window, trying to get their attention.

"Pssst," he called. "Over here!"

The duo raised their weapons in unison, then hustled over to Blount.

"What the hell are you doing?" Payne demanded.

"I was waiting for you. I watched your approach behind the cabins and saw you pause by the burned shed. That's when I realized you were coming to the house."

Payne and Jones looked at each other, puzzled. Something didn't seem right about Blount, but they couldn't figure out what it was.

"How'd you see us from that far away?" Jones wondered. "It's pretty dark out here, and you're in the back of the house."

"Security cameras. The Plantation has them everywhere."

"Cameras?" Payne's interest was piqued. He realized that they could be quite useful if he used them properly. "Where are they?"

"All over. I can't tell you where, though, because they're very well concealed. I wouldn't have even known about them if I didn't break into the security office to hunt for you guys. That's when I saw all of the monitors."

Payne glanced at Jones and grimaced. Something was wrong, definitely wrong. He could sense it. He couldn't quite put his finger on it, but it was there, like a word on the tip of his tongue. Jones noticed it, too, and he showed his displeasure by frowning. Something was up.

"Gentlemen," Blount said, grinning, "is something amiss? You seem strangely distressed by our conversation. Perhaps it was something I said?"

Finally, both men figured it out. Blount was no longer talking in the backwater language of a buckwheat. He was using the proper diction of a scholar instead.

"What the . . . ?" Payne couldn't believe what he was hearing. "You sneaky son of a bitch!"

"Now, don't be goin' on like that about my mama. She ain't no bitch, I tell ya!"

Jones's mouth fell wide open. He'd been completely fooled by Blount's act. As he stood there staring at the dreadlocked servant, he couldn't help but feel foolish. "The Academy Award for Best Actor in a Criminal Conspiracy goes to—"

Payne cut him off. They didn't have time for humor at the moment.

"Bennie, or whatever the hell your name is, look me in the eyes and tell me which side of this war you're on." Payne raised his gun and put it under Blount's chin. "I ain't shittin' you. Tell me right now, or you'll die like the rest of the Posse."

Jones laughed to himself. "You best tell him, Master Bennie. He ain't bluffin' none."

Blount responded in perfect English. "I'm with you guys, I swear! I'm not part of the Posse. I've just been biding my time and gathering information. I swear to God!"

"Information for what?" Payne demanded, pressing the gun deeper into Blount's throat.

"Tells him, Bennie! Master Payne gots himself a nasty temper and an itchy trigga finga. And that ain't no good combination."

Blount shuddered as Jones's words sank in. "I've been gathering information for the authorities. I'm trying to get this place shut down, but I can't do it in both continents without the proof to back it up. No one will listen to me until then."

"What do you mean, *both continents*?"

"The Plantation isn't just a torture site. It's a lot more complicated than that." Blount tried to swallow, but the gun pressed against his throat made it difficult. "This is business, big business! The Posse has ties all over the world, and if I want to shut everything down, I have to learn the names of the other people. That's the only way to do it properly. Get everybody at once."

Payne looked into Blount's eyes, and he appeared to be sincere. But in this case, *appeared* was the operative word. For the longest time, Blount had appeared to be an uneducated country boy, and Payne had trusted him completely. Now Blount appeared to be telling the truth a second time, and he was asking Payne to believe him again. But how could he? Blount was such an incredible actor there was no way Payne could separate his bullshit from reality.

"I'm still not sold. You're going to have to tell me something to convince me."

"Like what?" he whimpered. "I'll tell you anything, just don't kill me!"

Jones stepped forward. "What kind of business is the Posse in?"

"You guys should know. You're holding some of their products in your hands."

"Guns?" Payne remarked. "But that doesn't make sense. Why bring all of these innocent people to this island if you're going to smuggle guns? There has to be more than that."

"There is," he grunted. "But you're going to like that even less."

Payne's eyes flared with anger, causing the pressure on his gun to increase. "Why's that, Bennie? Why am I not going to like it?"

"Because you're white."

"Okay, you racist bastard, what does that have to do with anything?"

"Hey, I'm not racist, but the Posse is."

Payne smirked. "No shit! I kind of figured that out. What does racism have to do with the Posse's business? Racism can't be sold, you know."

Blount stared Payne directly in the eyes. He wanted to make sure that Payne recognized the truth of his words. "That's true, but slaves *can* be sold. White slaves."

The concept made Payne shiver. If Blount was telling the truth, it meant that these people weren't just being tortured. They were being broken—housebroken—for their new masters. "And how do you know this?"

"I just know! I've been walking around this place for several weeks and have heard stuff. Everybody treated me like an idiot, so they tried to talk over me. Nobody knew that I could put all of the pieces of the puzzle together. But I could. I've just been waiting for the right moment." Blount took a breath. "And that moment is here. It's finally here!"

"Why's that?" Jones wondered.

"Because of you two. You've killed most of the Plantation guards, you have the masters running for their lives, and as far as I can tell, you got rid of the cargo ship. This is the time to finish them off! We can end the Posse right here, right now."

"And why should we trust you?" Payne demanded. "You already dicked us once."

"But I couldn't help that! I couldn't risk blowing my cover to help you out. I couldn't! I tried to make it up to you, though. You know that! If it wasn't for me, you would've died in the box."

Payne shook his head. "You're going to have to do better. I wouldn't have been in that damn box if it wasn't for you."

"I know you don't trust me, but without my help you won't be able to save your girlfriend from a life of slavery. I can help you find her, and you know it. But we can't wait much longer."

The comment staggered Payne. With all of the fighting and arguing that was going on, Payne had forgotten about the one thing that mattered most: Ariane.

"How can you help?"

"I know the island much better than you. I can be your guide and an extra gun. Whether you know it or not, Ariane means an awful lot to me, too."

Payne pressed the gun even harder into Bennie's neck. He interpreted Blount's comment as some kind of sexual insult.

"Why is that, you skinny bastard? And trust me, if your answer isn't a good one, I'll splatter your dreadlocks all over the wall!" Payne took a deep breath to control his fury, but it didn't work. He was still fuming. "Why is Ariane important to you?"

"Why?" he stuttered. "Because she's my cousin."

CHAPTER 50

ARIANE could hear heavy footsteps in the hall, but she had no idea who was out there until the door burst open. Two large figures entered the room.

"Well, well, well." Greene laughed. "If it isn't the troublemaker's bitch!"

Holmes followed him into the room. "All tied up and lookin' good! If we had a little more time, I'd be tempted to play with her."

Greene shook his head. "Unfortunately, we don't. And all because of Payne."

The sound of his name made her heart beat faster. "Is he here?" she tried to ask, but it came out mumbled.

"Wow, I think she's trying to talk." Holmes stared at her jaw, which had been broken by Harris Jackson. "A good-looking bitch who can't talk. It's like a dream come true."

"Tease her later," Greene suggested. "We gotta move before the two soldier boys find us."

Two soldier boys? The sound was music to her ears. That meant Jones was probably with Payne, which only made sense. They did everything together, especially when it came to the military. But how in the world did they find her so quickly?

Were they brought to the island the same time as her, or did they find her on their own?

Truthfully, it didn't matter. As long as they knew where she was, she had a chance.

"Okay," Holmes said. "I'm going to untie you from the bed now, but I expect you to be on your best behavior. Understood?"

Ariane nodded, even though it hurt her jaw to do so.

Holmes reached for the knot near her left wrist, but before he got ahold of it, a frantic voice came out of his radio. "Jesus! Is that Jackson? What does he want now?"

"Don't worry about it," Greene muttered. "You take care of the girl. I'll take care of Harris." Greene pushed the reply button on his own radio. "Harris? Is that you?"

"Levon," Jackson answered, "we've got a major problem here!"

Greene frowned. "What's going on?"

"I went down to the dock to check on the boat and . . . it's gone!"

"What are you talking about?"

"All the guards are dead, and the boat is gone!"

"What about the slaves?" Greene demanded. "Where are the slaves?"

"They're gone, too! I don't know how, but the boat is gone!"

"Fuck!" Greene shouted. "I don't believe this!"

Ariane watched Greene carefully, waiting to see what he was going to do next. She sensed that he might take his anger out on her. Thankfully, that never came to pass.

"What should we do?" he asked Holmes.

Holmes shrugged as he unfastened Ariane's rope. "Your call."

Greene gave it some thought before answering. "Just wait for us at the dock. We'll be there shortly. And try to find Theo if you can. I think it would be best if we all stuck together."

"Sounds good," Jackson replied. "Make it quick. I'm in the open down here."

Greene turned off his radio. "I can't believe this shit! How can two guys cause this many problems?"

Holmes grinned at the comment. "You'd be surprised what two men can accomplish if they put their minds to it. . . . Like us, for instance."

"What are you getting at?"

"I realize you've known Harris and Theo forever, but under the circumstances, we need someone to take the blame for all of this. If the feds get a couple of suspects in custody, they won't be as likely to hunt for anyone else. At least not immediately."

Greene's interest was piqued. "What are you proposing?"

"How much would it bother you if we left them behind? Why don't we get off this island while we still have a chance?"

"Interesting," Greene muttered. However, after giving it some thought, he detected a flaw in the plan. "But we can't leave them here."

"Why not? We have the opportunity to flee, and you're not willing to seize it because of them. My God! They'd leave your ass behind in a minute!"

"Wait a second!" he yelled back. "I don't mind leaving them, but we can't. They'll name us, say we were the force behind everything, and preach their innocence. I guarantee they'll frame their stories to suit their needs, and because of Harris's knowledge of the law, they'll come out sitting pretty. Hell, they might even be given immunity to testify against us."

Holmes grimaced at the thought. "Damn, you're right. So what do you recommend?"

Greene smiled at Ariane, then glanced at his new partner. "We should leave the island ASAP. But before we do, we need to silence Theo and Harris—permanently."

BLOUNT'S comment was absurd, completely asinine. Perhaps the most outrageous, preposterous, nonsensical thing that Payne had ever heard. But that was why he was tempted to believe it. It wasn't the type of thing that someone would make up to save his own ass.

"Okay, Bennie, my interest is aroused. But I promise you, if I smell bullshit at any point of your explanation, *boom!* Understood?"

Blount nodded. "As you know, I'm not a dumb hick, but I *am* a local. My family has lived in these parts for generations. In fact, when this place was owned and operated by the Delacroix family, my ancestors worked the land as slaves."

Payne signaled for him to speed it up.

"For the past few years I've been working on my master's degree at LSU and recently started work on my thesis. I planned to show the effect that the abolition of slavery had on black families, using my family tree as an example."

"And?"

"A few months ago, I came to this island to look around. This place had been abandoned for the longest time, and I thought a few photos would look good in my project."

"What happened?"

"I bumped into a team of black men doing all kinds of work. I assumed that someone had bought the estate after Hurricane Katrina and was going to move in. So I went up to a brother to ask him a few questions about the new owner and discovered that he couldn't speak English. Actually, none of them could. These guys were right off the boat from Africa."

Jones asked, "Everyone?"

Blount nodded, then turned his attention back to Payne. "I didn't want to get anybody into trouble, including myself, so I left quickly. It's a good thing, too, because if one of the owners had seen me, I would've never been allowed to come back later."

"Why'd you want to come back?"

"I wanted to see what they were going to do to the place, and I thought it could help my research. You see, during the course of my studies, I came across a family journal from the 1860s. It was like finding gold. It gave me a firsthand account of slave life on this plantation from a distant grandmother. Simply fascinating stuff."

"I'm sure," Payne said, "but I'm beginning to get impatient here."

"You want me to get to Ariane, don't you?"

"Is it that obvious?"

Blount nodded. "During the course of the journal, my distant grandmother admits to having an affair with Mr. Delacroix, her master. She said she did it for special treatment, but eventually, it turned into more than that. She fell in love with Delacroix and allowed him to impregnate her on several occasions. Shortly after that, the Civil War ended and the journal entries stopped."

"That's it?" Payne demanded. "What does any of that have to do with Ariane?"

"At the time, I didn't know, but I was determined to talk with someone from the Delacroix family so I could get a look at their family tree. I figured if I was a direct descendant of Mr. Delacroix, then I would technically be related to all of his white offspring."

Payne started to see where this was going, and his eyes filled with acceptance. He knew that Blount was telling the truth and couldn't wait to see how Ariane fit in.

"I went to the local courthouse and tried to find his relatives, but every path I found ended in death. I swear, the Delacroix family must've been cursed because everyone in that family died so young. Anyway, when I came back here to look around again, I hoped the new owners had bought the property from a distant relative of mine and would be willing to give me an address."

"Makes sense," Payne added.

"But when I came back, I got the shock of my life. The old plantation was back in business. Not just as a farm, but as an *actual* plantation. Crops in the ground and slaves in the field, but this time, unlike the 1800s, the slaves were white."

"What did you do?" Jones wondered as he watched for unwanted company.

"I tried to leave. I wanted to tell somebody what I saw out here, but before I could get my boat out of the swamps, a big man named Octavian Holmes blocked my passage and

demanded information from me at gunpoint. I didn't want to
tell him the truth, obviously. If he knew that I had been digging around, he would've killed me. So I decided to play
dumb. At that moment, I became a buckwheat by the name
of Bennie Blount."

"Go on," Payne said.

"I convinced Master Holmes that I'd be useful around
here. I could cook, clean, and show him around the local
swamps. One thing led to another, and he decided to hire
me. I figured it was perfect. I could roam around the Plantation while I got to the bottom of things."

"Did you?"

Blount nodded. "Up until recently, the Posse was bringing
random groups of people onto the island, mostly homeless
people. They'd beat them, train them, then ship them overseas for big money. It's a lucrative business. But all of that
changed with this last group of slaves. The people that were
selected were no longer random. These people were brought
here for a reason. They were brought here for revenge."

"What kind of revenge?"

"Revenge for the black race. Theo Webster, the brains
behind the operation, traced the roots of the Plantation's four
founders and determined their family origins. Three of the
men came from slave backgrounds, but Levon Greene didn't.
His family came to America after slavery had been abol-
ished. Anyway, Webster determined the names of the slave
owners that had once owned the ancestors of the other three
men. Then, tracing their family trees to the present day, he
located the modern-day relatives of those slave owners."

"And the people that were kidnapped were the relatives?"

Blount nodded. "Ariane and her sister are distant relatives of Mr. Delacroix, my great-great-great-great-grandfather.
That's why they were brought here, and that's why I'm related. I realize it doesn't make her my first cousin, but she is
my relative. I even have the data to back it up."

Payne shook his head. "Don't worry. I actually believe
you."

"Great," muttered a relieved Jones. "Now that this Ebony

and Ivory reunion is over, do you mind if we get out of here? We got some people to save and not much time to do it."

Payne lowered his gun from Blount's chin. He was finally convinced that Bennie was on his side to stay. "Mr. Blount, would you please show us the way inside the house?"

Bennie grinned. It was the first time in his life that a white man had ever called him mister.

CHAPTER 51

WHEN the truck arrived at the western dock, Harris Jackson breathed a sigh of relief. Even though he realized he wasn't safe until Payne and Jones were caught, he felt a lot better with Holmes and Greene by his side.

"Hey, Harris," Holmes called, "where's Theo? I thought he was supposed to meet us here."

"He'll be here any minute. He said he had to go to the house for something."

Holmes nodded as he searched the dock for a trace of the missing boat. There were no clues except for a number of dead guards that littered the ground.

"These guys are good," he admitted.

"So, what are we gonna do?" Jackson wondered. "The boat's gone, half the slaves have escaped, and Payne and Jones are still running around killing our men. Is there any way we can salvage this?"

Greene gave Holmes a quick smile before speaking. "Sure we can. Remember, that's the reason we wore our masks at all times. None of the slaves can identify our faces, so they won't be able to give the cops our description. Once we leave this place, we're home free."

A flash of panic crossed Jackson's mind. He had revealed his face to Ariane Walker and Susan Ross when he tied them up inside the house.

Holmes noticed the tension in Jackson's eyes. "What's wrong? You look upset."

"I took my mask off in the bedrooms, and two of the whores saw my face."

"You idiot!" Greene blurted. "Thinking with your wrong head again, huh?"

Annoyed, Jackson took a step toward Greene. Even though Greene outweighed him by sixty pounds, he wasn't about to back down. He had to stand his ground now, or Greene would tease him forever. "What's your problem, man? Why do you have to ride me so damn hard?"

"Because I feel like it."

"And why's that? What's your problem with me?"

Greene stood his ground, reveling in the thought of a confrontation. "Here's my problem. I'm fed up with all your perverted games, your groping and raping. That shit is wrong, and it's gotta stop."

"Oh, yeah? And who's gonna stop me?"

"Who's gonna stop you?" Greene smiled at Holmes. They had discussed this moment back at the house, and Greene had volunteered for the duty. "Me, my Glock, and I."

Greene pulled his trigger and the thunderous blast echoed off the water and the surrounding trees. The bullet struck Jackson in his forehead and plowed into his brain with the finesse of a bulldozer. Then, as if in slow motion, Jackson slumped to the edge of the dock and hung there for just a second before he tumbled into the water with a loud splash.

"Nice shot," Holmes remarked. His nonchalant tone suggested that Greene had just made a free throw in a game of HORSE. "Try to keep your elbow in more. It'll improve your accuracy."

"Thanks. I'll have to remember that the next time I kill someone."

Holmes glanced at his watch and realized time was running short. "That might be sooner than you think. We have to take care of Webster before we leave. Why don't you give him a call and see what's keeping him?"

Greene nodded. The adrenaline from killing Jackson surged through him, practically making him giddy. "Breaker, breaker, one nine," he said, laughing. "Theo, do you read me?"

There was a slight delay before Webster answered. "I'm here, Levon."

"Where's here, Theo? We've been waiting for you at the dock."

Another pause. "I'm up at the house. I figured we'd have to flee, and I wanted to pack a few things before we left."

"No problem." This would work out well for Holmes and Greene. They needed to stop by the house before they left the island anyway. "I'll tell ya what, why don't we swing by the mansion and help you out with your things?"

Relief filled Webster's voice. "That would be great. I wasn't looking forward to going down to the dock by myself. I'm not very good with guns."

A wide grin returned to Greene's face. "Don't worry, Theo. I am."

PAYNE patted Webster on his head, then took the radio from his hands. "You did great. You sounded very natural."

But he refused to speak. Instead, he slumped in his chair and pouted about getting caught.

"What now?" Jones asked as he chewed on his first food in what felt like days. "We got them coming here, but what are we going to do with them when they arrive?"

Payne flicked Webster on his ear. "I say we make a trade. I'll gladly give up Theo here if they give us Ariane. As far as I'm concerned, anything we get after that will be icing."

Jones swallowed a mouthful of apple and decided it was the best goddamned piece of fruit he had ever eaten. "Speaking of icing," he said as he searched the pantry for anything that resembled cake. A box of Twinkies was the only thing he could find. "Once we get Ariane to safety, will we have time to hunt down Levon?"

"I don't care what we do as long as you understand that she's the number one priority here. After that, I'll back you on anything that your heart desires."

"Cool," he mumbled as he stuffed half a Twinkie into his mouth.

While Jones chewed the yellow cake, Blount entered the kitchen from the security office. "They'll be here any second. I just saw 'em pull their truck onto the road from the dock."

Webster stared at Blount in disbelief. It was the first time he'd heard Bennie speak normally.

"What kind of truck?" Payne wondered.

"Flatbed. Both guys are in the front, but it appears they have some hostages in the back."

Payne prayed one of them was Ariane. "Were they guys or girls?"

Blount shrugged. "Kind of looked like females, but don't quote me on it."

Jones continued eating Twinkies as he ran several different scenarios through his mind. Finally, he came across one that he liked. "Okay, fellas, this is how we'll play it. Instead of picking these guys off from a distance—which I could do with my eyes closed—I think it'd be best if we dealt with them up close and personal."

"Why's that?" Payne demanded.

"First of all, if I kill these guys long-range, there's no one to stop their speeding truck. I mean, the last thing we want is for Ariane to smash into a tree with a bomb strapped to her leg."

"Good point."

"Secondly, I get the feeling Holmes has been running things, and if that's the case, it'd be foolish to kill him without interrogating him first. There's no telling where he has slaves stored, and if we shoot him, there's a chance we won't be able to find them for a very long time."

Payne groaned at the possibilities. "Isn't a face-to-face confrontation kind of risky?"

"Definitely. And if you'd prefer, I'm still willing to pick these guys off with a scope. Of course, keep this in mind: Ariane *might* be one of those hidden slaves."

THEY drove straight to the house, across the grass of the main yard. Once they had stopped, Holmes honked the horn, hoping Webster would come to the front door. It worked. He immediately swung the door open, sticking his head out of the narrow crack.

"Can you guys come inside and give me a hand? I'm not strong enough to carry this stuff."

Greene looked at Holmes and frowned. He didn't have a clean shot from his current position, and by the time he raised his weapon, Webster would be able to duck inside the house.

"Before we do," Greene countered, "we want you to give us a hand with something."

"Really? What do you need?"

Greene glanced at Holmes and shrugged. He hadn't thought that far ahead.

Holmes jumped to his rescue with the first thing that popped into his head. "The guards have Payne and Jones cornered by the swamp, and we need help flushing 'em out. You're the smartest guy here, so we figured you could come up with something."

A grimace filled Webster's face. He didn't know what to make of Holmes's comment, but he realized something strange was going on. "Guys, I'd hate to waste my time going all the way down to the swamp for nothing. Are you sure you have them cornered?"

"Oh, yeah," Greene claimed. "We got 'em trapped all right. I made the identification myself. Now we just need some help flushing 'em out."

Payne, who was hiding behind the door, sensed Webster's

desire to make a break for the truck, so he tightened his grip on him before he could move.

"Don't even think about it," he whispered. "Tell them you can't leave until they come inside and give you a hand. Insist if you have to."

Webster obeyed. "Guys, I can't help you right now. I've got other things to worry about *inside*." He tilted his head toward the door in an effort to signal Holmes and Greene, but they didn't understand what he was pointing to. "I think it would be best if you gave me a hand."

Greene growled softly as he watched Webster twitch his head. He couldn't believe how swiftly he was becoming unglued. "I don't know what your deal is, but we need you in the truck right now. Time is running out, so let's go."

"Come on!" Holmes shouted. "We need your help immediately!"

Webster tried to move toward the truck but wasn't strong enough to tear away from Payne. In fact, the only thing that he managed to do was piss him off.

"Do that again and I'll bite off your fucking ear."

"Come on," Holmes repeated. "Let's go! Now!"

"I can't come," Webster assured him. "I'd like to, but I can't. I really can't."

Greene had heard enough. The cops were probably on their way, and the only thing that stood between him and freedom was a 150-pound computer geek. Angrily, Greene threw his door open and climbed out. "I'm sick of this. Come out here now before you really piss me off."

He accented his statement with a slam of the truck door.

And that was what Jones and Blount had been waiting for. They quietly opened their windows on the second floor of the plantation house and thrust their weapons outside. Once they had settled into comfortable positions, they aimed their guns at their targets. Jones focused on Greene. Blount pointed at Holmes, who remained inside the truck.

After counting to five, Payne threw the front door open while using Webster as a shield. "Show me your hands!" he shouted. "Show me your fucking hands!"

Greene stopped dead in his tracks and slowly raised his two closed fists into the air.

"Surprised to see us?" Jones teased from above. "You must be, since we're currently trapped down by the swamps. That's why you're turning white, isn't it?"

"Something like that."

"Don't turn too white," Payne muttered, "or someone around here might make you a slave."

Greene tried to take a breath, but his chest was too tight to inhale. "What do you guys want?"

"Revenge!" Jones shouted as he cracked his neck. "A shitload of revenge!"

Payne wrapped his arm around Webster's neck and pulled him closer. "You know what I want. I want Ariane."

"Then this is your lucky day," Greene assured him. "She's in the back of our truck with another girl. Why don't you come over and see for yourself?"

Payne shook his head. "No, thanks. I kind of like it where I'm standing now. But my partner can take a look. Hey, D.J.?"

"Yeah, chief."

"Can you see into the back of the truck?"

"Sure can. Looks like a couple of chicks to me. Not sure who they are, though. They're tied up, and their heads are covered."

"Do they look alive?"

"They sure do. I see lots of squirming."

Payne returned his attention to Greene. "So, what's next?"

"You're obviously in control. You've got a gun pointed at my heart, and your arm wrapped around Theo's neck. You tell me, how do you want to resolve this?"

"I say we shoot him," Jones suggested. "Then we can just take the girls."

Greene chuckled. "Oh, you could do that, but if you shoot me, Octavian is gonna speed off before you have a chance to grab them."

"No, he won't," Blount yelled. "Before he travels ten feet, I'll pump him like a porn star."

Greene glanced at the other end of the house and saw Blount's unobstructed view of Holmes. "That's a pretty colorful image, especially from a hick like yourself. That English of yours sounds remarkably better."

"Thanks. I borrowed your *Hooked on Phonics* tape."

Greene smiled, trying to remain as calm as possible. He had played football in front of millions of fans on TV, so he was used to keeping his nerves during times of pressure. "Hey, Octavian! Do you have a clear shot at Ariane?"

Holmes thrust his muscular arm out the back of the cab and pointed his gun at the tied-up hostages. "Definitely! There's not much that can stop a bullet from three feet away."

"That's true," Payne remarked. "But the same can be said about my distance. And I promise you, I won't miss."

"I believe you," Greene said. "But you know what? I've got a strange feeling that you're not going to shoot me. You know why? 'Cause if you do, a lot of people are gonna die!"

"Really! And how do you expect to pull that off?"

"Oh, it's not what I'm gonna *pull*. It's what I'm gonna *push*!"

Greene lowered his left hand and revealed the tiny detonator that he'd been concealing in his palm. "One touch of this button, and every anklet on this island goes *boom!*"

He accented his statement by making the sound of a large explosion, then followed it with a defiant smile. "So, let me ask you again. How do you want to resolve this?"

Payne remained stoic, showing Greene the ultimate poker face. He didn't laugh, grin, or frown. "It's simple, as far as I'm concerned. I get my girl, and you get your bitch." He tightened his grasp on Webster's neck. "Simple swap."

"What's to prevent you from shooting us the minute you get her?"

"Nothing," Payne admitted. "But what prevents you from doing the same? Remember, you're the one with the history of reneging."

"That's right," Jones cracked. "You're a re-*nigger*."

Greene allowed his eyes to float upward. He saw nothing

but the barrel of Jones's gun. "You know if you weren't black, I'd kick your ass for that comment."

"Yeah, but you'd put me in handcuffs before you even tried."

Greene lowered his gaze back to Payne. "So, you want to make a trade, huh? Tell me how to do it, and I shall oblige."

"First of all, I need to make sure that's Ariane."

Greene clicked his tongue a few times in thought. "That's gonna be tough. She's currently gagged, and I'm not about to let you near her."

"Not a problem, Levon. Just let me see her face. If it's her, we can continue. If it isn't, D.J. is going to show you his Lee Harvey Oswald impersonation."

"Don't worry," Greene assured him. "You can trust me on this one. I'll remove her hood, and you'll see that it's her. Okay? Just don't shoot me."

As Greene strolled toward the rear of the truck, he studied the upstairs window out of the corner of his eye. He hoped that Jones would relax for just a moment, giving him enough time to make his move, but Jones was too good of a soldier to slip up. The barrel of his gun followed Greene wherever he went.

"That's far enough," Jones ordered. He was afraid that Greene would sneak to the far side of the truck, and if he did, he would no longer have a clean shot at him. "Climb into the bed from the back bumper. If you flinch, you die!"

"Bennie," Payne called, "how's your shot at the driver?"

"Clear."

"Stay on him, Bennie. Never let him leave your sight."

Greene stepped onto the back bumper as directed, then pulled himself up with a quick tug of his arm. After stepping over the hatch, he moved toward Ariane, keeping his eyes on Jones while looking for a chance to get free.

"D.J.," Payne shouted, "you still got him?"

"No problem. In fact, I'm tempted to take him now, just for the hell of it."

Despite the boast, Payne felt uneasy about the situation.

There was something about the cocky look in Greene's eyes that made him nervous. Payne wasn't sure what was going on, but his gut told him that something bad was about to happen. As a precaution, he moved forward, keeping the hostage directly between himself and Greene.

"Do this nice and slow," Payne ordered. "No mistakes."

Greene nodded as he pulled Ariane into a sitting position. Next, he placed his right hand on the hood that was tied around her neck while crouching down behind her.

"D.J.?" Payne screamed.

"Don't worry. On your command, I can put a hole in his brain."

Payne felt temporarily better, but his anxiety returned when Greene started working on the rope around her throat. "Careful!"

"You gotta chill," he growled. "If I hurt her, you'll hurt Theo. And trust me, I don't want you to do that. Why? Because I want to do it myself!"

Using Ariane as a shield, Greene pulled a gun from the back of his belt and fired two shots toward Payne. As he did, Holmes punched the gas pedal hard, sending Ariane and Greene tumbling backward in a tangle of body parts, an act that kept Jones from shooting. Sure, he could've fired, but the risk of hitting Ariane was simply too high for his taste. Instead, he figured he'd rely on his backup.

"Bennie," Jones screamed, "get the driver!"

But Blount reacted too late. He fired a number of shots at the front windshield, yet the only thing that hit Holmes was shards of broken glass.

Jones cursed as the truck continued forward. He did his best to stop it by shooting at the back right tire, but the angle of the flatbed protected it like armor. He shifted his aim to the rear window, hoping to nail the driver in the back of the head, but Holmes made a sudden turn toward the side of the house.

"Son of a bitch!" Jones yelled. He couldn't believe that so many unexpected things had happened. Greene's hidden gun, his lack of compassion for Webster, the detonator, and Ariane's unintentional interference. Jones abandoned his position and ran toward the front steps, where he came across Blount in the hallway. The two of them sprinted down the stairs together, hoping to hit the truck with a long-distance shot, but when they burst out the front door, they noticed something that changed their priorities.

Two bodies were sprawled on the columned porch.

One was Webster; the other was Payne.

Both were covered in blood, and neither was moving.

CHAPTER 52

WHILE Blount ran for a first-aid kit, Jones tended to Payne, carefully probing his unconscious friend. Unfortunately, Payne's black clothes made it tough to find his injuries.

"Bennie! Get out here! I need your help!"

Blount returned a moment later, medical supplies in hand.

"Help me get his shirt off. I need to figure out where he was hit."

Expecting the worst, they carefully cut off the bloodied garment, exposing Payne's chiseled but scarred torso. Thankfully, his chest and stomach were free of new wounds.

"The blood must've been Webster's," Blount said, relieved.

"Not all of it." Jones pointed to a gaping hole in Payne's arm. One of Greene's bullets had torn through Webster's body and embedded itself in Payne's left biceps. "It's not life threatening, but I have to patch him up before he bleeds too much."

"What do you need me to do? Get you some towels? Boil some water?"

Jones frowned. "He's not having a baby. He's been shot."

Blount nodded. "Does that mean I can't do anything?"

"Actually, you can. I won't leave Jon until I treat him, but the moment he wakes up he'll want to find Ariane. Can you find us some transportation?"

"Consider it done."

While waiting for Blount's return, Jones tried to focus on Payne. Under these conditions, there wasn't much he could do other than sterilize the wound and wrap it, but he realized that might be enough to save Payne's life. Right now the two biggest concerns were blood loss and infection. A good field dressing would stop either from happening.

As Jones prepared the bandages, Payne opened his eyes. Still groggy, he blinked a few times, absorbing his surroundings. He studied Jones as he scoured through the first-aid kit.

"Excuse me, Miss Nightingale? I think you need to reapply your makeup."

A smile crossed Jones's lips. He didn't care what Payne said as long as he was able to talk. "How are you feeling?"

"Not great." He blinked a few times, trying to remember what happened. "I think my arm hurts."

"That might have something to do with the bullet that's in it. And when you fell, I think you hit your head on the steps. That's why you blacked out."

Payne winced as he touched the back of his head. A large bump was emerging from his scalp. "Where's Ariane?"

Jones frowned. He didn't want to upset his friend before his wound was treated, but he wasn't willing to lie. "To be honest, Jon, I don't know. They all got away."

"What?" He immediately tried to sit up, but Jones restrained him. "How did that happen? I thought you had a shot at Levon."

"I did, but Ariane blocked it. When the truck started to move, she tumbled on top of him. I couldn't risk pulling the trigger."

"What about the driver? Did he get hit?"

"Bennie hit the front windshield more than once, but Holmes kept driving." He paused for a moment as he considered the events. "I don't know if he hit him or not."

Payne took a deep breath, trying to calm his rage. He wasn't mad at Jones or Blount—considering the circumstances, they'd done their best—but he was upset at the unfortunate turn of events. Ariane was within reach, but he had blown his chance to retrieve her.

"We have to catch them before they leave the island. If they get away, there's no telling where they'll go."

Jones saw the desperation on Payne's face. It showed in the color of his cheeks and the glare in his eyes. But that wasn't all he noticed. He could also see his pain. There was something about the tightness of his jaw and the grimace on his lips that revealed Payne's physical agony.

"Let's take care of you first. Then we'll worry about them."

"D.J., I'm fine." He tried to sit up a second time, but Jones pushed him down again.

"Jon, we can't chase them until we get a vehicle, and Bennie's getting us one right now. So just calm down and let me patch you up while we wait for our limo."

Jones cleaned and wrapped the wound in less than five minutes. Then, as he put the last layer of elastic tape around the sterile gauze, he heard the rumble of an approaching motor. He gazed across the field, trying to identify the motorist, but was unable to.

"We better take cover."

Both men climbed to their feet and waited in the nearby bushes until they spotted Blount. They realized it was him when they saw his dreadlocks flapping in the breeze. As he pulled up on an ATV, Payne and Jones reemerged on the porch.

"Jon! You're okay!"

"Yeah, I'm all right." He glanced at the green and black Yamaha Grizzly and realized it was too small for three people. "Is this all you could find?"

"Actually, there are two more where I found this. If one of you comes with me, we can figure out a way to bring them both back."

Jones looked at Payne. "Let me go. You should rest up."

"No arguments from me."

As Blount and Jones sped away, Payne scanned the immediate vicinity, making sure that no one was watching from the trees. When he was confident that he was alone, he walked toward Webster, staring at his face. In the aftermath of the shooting, he never thought to ask about Webster's condition— he just assumed that he was dead—but one glance proved that he wasn't. Even though his eyes were closed and his lips were blue, blood pulsated from the two wounds that were visible in his upper torso.

Blood flow meant that Webster's heart was still beating.

Payne crouched next to him and examined his injuries, but Webster's wounds were too severe to be fixed with a Band-Aid. There was nothing Payne could do except offer him comfort—something he was reluctant to do, considering his role in Ariane's abduction.

"Theo," he said in a soothing voice, "can you hear me?"

Unexpectedly, Webster opened his eyes.

"Hey," Payne whispered, "how are you feeling?"

"P-p-p—" Webster was trying to say something, but his lack of strength made it difficult to pronounce the words. "Come . . . here."

Before he moved closer, Payne checked Webster for weapons—the last thing he needed was a knife in his gut. But Webster was unarmed. "I'm here, Theo."

"Paw . . . paw," he stuttered. "Paw . . ."

He looked into Webster's eyes. They were glassy and starting to droop. Payne knew he didn't have much time left. "Theo, you have to repeat that. I can't understand you."

"Paw . . . paw . . . it," he managed to mutter. "Paw . . . it."

"*Paw it*? What does that mean? Theo? What's *paw it*?"

But this time there was no reply.

The bastard died before he could finish his final message.

ON the eastern side of the island, far from the plantation house and the western dock, lay a small inlet, filled with warm water from the nearby gulf. At first glance, it seemed like an impassable marsh. Bald cypress trees clogged the waterway in sporadic groves. Jagged stumps and fallen timber, remnants of Hurricane Katrina, rose from the water like icebergs, waiting to shred any boat that dared to float by. But appearances were sometimes misleading. In this case, the water wasn't impassable. It was actually a path to freedom.

"Where the hell are we going?" Greene screamed from the back of the truck. "There's nothing back here but swampland."

Holmes answered cryptically. "It seems that way, doesn't it?"

"So why are we going here?"

"You'll see soon enough."

Greene didn't like the sound of that, but he realized he didn't have much choice. Holmes was currently in control of the situation, and he was just along for the ride. "Fine, but keep something in mind. I'm armed."

"I know that, Levon. And so do Theo and Harris."

Greene grinned as he thought about his two fallen partners, but his smile turned to a grimace when he felt the truck slowing. "Why are we stopping?"

"I want to show you something," he said through the back window. "But before I do, I think you and I need to reach some kind of an understanding."

Greene instinctively raised his gun. "The ball's in your court, huckleberry. Just make your move, and we can dance."

"I'm not talking about violence. I'm talking about our partnership. If we're going to stick together, we need to discuss what each of us is able to contribute."

"Contribute? What exactly does that mean?"

Holmes got out of the truck to explain. "For this to work, each of us has to contribute something of value. I, for instance, am going to get us off of this island and out of the country. Once we get to Africa, I'll be able to provide us with a wide network of contacts that will set us up with fake identities and a place to stay." He paused for a few seconds to let Greene absorb all of the information. "What about you?"

"Me? What the hell *can* I contribute? All my money is tied up in my house and this place, and I'm gonna have to abandon both of them."

"True, but you'll be able to get some of your cash back."

Greene grimaced. "How do you figure?"

"You never did anything illegal in your house, did you?"

"No."

"Then the FBI won't be able to take it. When Payne and Jones tell them that you were involved, they'll be able to search your house, but they won't be able to seize it. A year from now you'll be able to sell it through a local Realtor and have all of the money wired overseas. Several million, if I'm not mistaken."

Greene hadn't thought of that, and the realization that he still had some assets made him happy. "But this investment is down the tubes, right?"

"Not necessarily. If you play your cards right, you might be able to collect insurance money."

"Insurance money? For what? The burned log cabin? My deductible is more than that thing was worth."

Holmes shook his head. He'd planned for this contingency from day one. "I'm not talking about the cabin. I'm talking about the entire house. You'll be able to collect on that."

Greene raised his eyebrows. "How do you figure? With the exception of a bullet hole or two, that place is in great shape."

"If you want an explanation, just follow me." Holmes walked into a grove of trees and removed a small metal box from underneath an azalea. "Take a look inside. It'll answer most of your insurance questions."

Greene held the box with childlike fascination. He couldn't imagine what Holmes had stored so far away from the house in a tiny crate. "Actually, I'm not really in a trusting mood." He laughed. "Why don't you open it?"

Holmes grabbed the box and pulled out a small radio transmitter, one that was commonly used for mining detonations. "Think about it, Levon. We wore masks the entire time we were here, but we didn't always wear gloves. Our fingerprints are all over that house. If we don't do something about it, the FBI will be able to gather enough evidence to put us at the top of their hit list." He shook his head decisively. "And there's no way I'm gonna let that happen."

"But won't it happen anyway? With Payne, Jones, and Blount still alive, won't they be able to tell the FBI everything?"

"Yeah, but without physical evidence, there's no way they'll be able to convince an African government to extradite us. At least that's what Harris told me. He said the testimony of witnesses won't mean dick in a situation like that. Plus, if you follow all of the safeguards that I'm going to teach you, the American government won't even know where we are. We'll disappear from their radar forever."

Greene smiled. He liked the sound of that. "What about the money? Won't they find me when I try to collect on my house?"

"Not a chance. Theo set up a number of offshore accounts using the names of bogus corporations. If you use them to filter all of the funds, the FBI won't be able to touch you."

"Are you sure? That sounds risky, especially without Theo to walk me through it."

"Hey, it's your money, not mine. But if I were in your shoes, I'd try to collect every cent that I could. If you don't, you're gonna be forced to work for the rest of your life."

Greene grimaced at the thought. He was accustomed to a life of luxury and didn't relish the thought of returning to the workforce—especially the one in Africa.

"Either way," Holmes continued, "I'm blowing this joint up. The explosives are set, and I can do it with a touch of a button."

"Bullshit," Greene growled. "I paid for it, so *I* get to blow it up. At least I'll get some enjoyment out of this place."

Holmes smiled. He was glad Greene wasn't going to fight him on this. "Good! You can do it in a minute, but before you do you still need to answer my earlier question. I need to know what you're gonna contribute to this partnership."

Greene rolled his eyes. "You're obviously looking for something, so just tell me. What do you need from me? Money?"

Holmes nodded. "I was expecting us to make millions off the current batch of slaves." He turned back toward the truck and pointed to Ariane and Susan. "Now we're down to two. Granted, they're exceptional and will get top dollar, but it won't be enough to live on for the rest of my life. That's why I want some guarantees from you, right here, right now."

"Octavian, if you expect me to give you millions, you can fuck off. But if we're talking about a reasonable settlement for getting me to safety, then there's no problem. We're good."

Holmes extended his hand, and Greene shook it eagerly.

"There is one thing, though, that confuses me. As far as I can tell, we still have almost a dozen slaves left in storage. Why don't we take them with us? It would net us a lot of cash."

Holmes signaled for Greene to follow him again, and he did so willingly. The two men walked ten feet farther into the woods, where Greene saw their getaway vehicle buried under some brush. It was a hydroplane, capable of seating no more than four people at one time.

"If we had a way to transport them, I'd be all for it. But at this point, we'll have to settle for what we have. My boat for escape and your money to live on."

CHAPTER 53

SEVERAL minutes passed before Blount and Jones returned to the house with three ATVs. Blount drove his unattached while Jones lagged behind, towing the third one.

"What took you guys so long?" Payne asked. "I thought maybe you ran into trouble."

Jones shook his head. "It just took a while to figure out a towing system."

"Well, while you were busy playing engineer, I was stuck here talking to Webster. You should've told me he was still alive before you left."

Blount and Jones exchanged glances, then looked at the dead body near the porch. Webster was lying in the same position as before. "Jon, are you feeling all right? You took a blow to the head. I think you might be hallucinating."

Payne denied the suggestion. "I'm fine, D.J. My arm hurts, but my head's fine."

"You talked to him?"

"Yes!"

"And he talked back?"

"Yes! He was alive, for God's sake. I swear!"

"You know," Blount admitted, "we never checked. I think both of us just assumed that he was dead."

"He wasn't dead," Payne insisted. "I'm telling you, he was alive."

Jones removed the towing cable while he considered Payne's statement. "So, what did Lazarus have to say? Is the light as bright as they claim?"

Payne ignored the sarcasm and answered the first question. "That's the strange part. He kept repeating the same thing over and over, but it didn't make any sense."

Intrigued, Blount spoke. "Maybe it will make sense to me. What did he say?"

Payne frowned as he thought back on the urgency of Webster's statement. "*Paw it*. He kept repeating the phrase *paw it*. Does that mean anything to you?"

"Not off the top of my head, but give me a second."

"Are you sure he didn't say *Rosebud*?" Jones joked, recalling the mysterious word whispered in the famous death scene of the movie *Citizen Kane*. "Maybe *Paw It* was the name of his sled."

"I doubt it," Blount countered. "Louisiana isn't known for its snow. Heck, I can't even remember the last time I had to put my hands in my pockets, let alone a pair of gloves."

Blount's statement triggered a smile on Payne's face. In a moment's time, he had gone from confused to enlightened, and all because of Bennie. "I'll be damned! I think I got it."

"Got what?" Jones questioned.

"The point of the message! I bet Webster was trying to say *pocket* but couldn't pronounce it! I bet he has something in his pocket that he wanted me to see!"

Blount was the closest to the body, so he reached into the dead man's clothes, looking for anything of value. Even though it was soaked with blood and tattered with holes, he probed the garment for clues, trying to avoid the liquid that saturated it.

"Nope," he said. "Nothing."

"If you want to be completely thorough," Payne added, "check to see if he's wearing an undershirt with a pocket. He might've kept something there for safekeeping."

Blount slowly unbuttoned Webster's dress shirt, pulling back the blood-soaked garment like he was peeling a bright red apple. Once he exposed the undershirt, he placed his hand on the pocket and felt for anything of value. "I think there's something in here!" With newfound excitement, Blount reached into the pocket's inner lining and removed a portable hard drive, which was two inches long and a half inch wide. "I'll be damned! You were right! He wanted you to go into his pocket."

Jones, who'd just finished his work on Payne's ATV, rushed over to Blount's side. He was eager to see what had been found.

Blount stared at the object in the dim light. A look of absolute joy engulfed his face. "It's his computer drive. One day I overheard him talking about it. I walked into his office while he was on the speakerphone. He said if anything ever happened to him, he wanted the guy on the phone to search through his belongings and look for his travel drive." Blount showed it to Payne and Jones. "He said the drive would contain financial records that were crucial to their business."

Blount stared at the drive for a few more seconds then handed it to Jones. "The other guy, whoever he was, asked him what type of records he was referring to, but Theo assured him that the information would only be important if he died."

Jones studied it, making sure that the blood from Webster's wounds hadn't seeped inside. "Well, if Bennie's right, then we hit the jackpot, because one of these drives can hold a couple gigabytes of information. There's no telling what we might get from it."

Payne smiled, finally understanding the significance of the find. If they were lucky, they had just acquired the evidence they needed to nail anyone who was associated with the Posse. Holmes, Greene, Jackson, Terrell Murray, and the slave buyers themselves.

All of them could be linked to the crimes of the Plantation through Webster's data.

AS he drove the truck across the island, Octavian Holmes shook his head at his own stupidity. He couldn't believe that Greene had convinced him to trade passengers for their journey to freedom. They already had enough money to live on for the rest of their lives. If they had left the Plantation immediately, they would have escaped from the island. So why take the chance of getting caught? To him, it just didn't make any sense.

But Greene was passionate about it. In fact, he wouldn't take no for an answer. "I'm not leaving this place without *my* prisoner," he had said. "Without him, I'm not giving you a cent."

And that had done it. Holmes's greed had taken control of his common sense and convinced him to switch Susan for Nathan. He was threatening his own life, his freedom, everything, for some extra cash. Holmes shook his head repeatedly, thinking of the mistake he was making.

"You're a greedy bastard!" he said to himself.

As he pulled his truck to a screeching halt, Holmes studied the concrete shed in front of him. It appeared to be in the same condition that he'd left it in. The door was still locked from the outside, the ground was unblemished with fresh footprints, and Ndjai's dog could be heard patrolling inside. Just like it should be.

The sound of Susan's whimpering and Holmes's jingling keys caused the dog to erupt with even more ferocity than before. The barking, which had been relatively restrained, was replaced by bloodthirsty howls as the canine flung itself against the door in an attempt to strike. Time after time, the creature repeated the process, hoping to quench its cravings with a savage battle, trying to get at the intruder before he had a chance to step inside.

The dog's effort made Holmes smile.

"Hey, Tornado, it's your Uncle O. How are ya doing?"

The Ibizan hound, which had been bred with a larger breed in order to increase its size and strength, responded quickly, going from a ferocious killer to a friendly pet in less than a second. "That's a good boy. Your daddy trained you well, didn't he?"

Holmes cracked the door slightly, allowing Tornado to smell his hand.

The inside of the structure was filled with darkness and the overwhelming stench of imprisonment, created by the bodily functions of eleven terrified prisoners. There weren't windows, vents, or toilets, which meant the unsanitary conditions were bound to get worse as the hours passed. The majority of the room was enclosed by a large cage, made from thick barbed wire and massive wooden posts, that had been placed there for two reasons: to keep the slaves from the exit and to keep Tornado away from the slaves.

Before he stepped into the room, Holmes grabbed a flashlight from above the door and shined the light into the huddled group of prisoners. He moved the beam from slave to slave, studying the dirty faces until he saw the man he was looking for. The chosen one.

Nathan was standing in the back corner of the room, far from the others, his face covered in layers of coarse facial hair. If it wasn't for the prisoner's 6'5" frame, Holmes never would've recognized him. He was a shell of his former self. His body weight had dropped by at least fifty pounds in the preceding weeks, and his face was haggard. But his failing health was easily explained. He had arrived long before the current crop of slaves and had spent most of his time within the sadistic world of the Devil's Box. It had taken longer than anyone had expected, but the harsh treatment had eventually broken him.

One look into his eyes revealed it. Nathan was no longer the same man.

The peculiar thing, though, was the reason that they had brought him to the Plantation. He wasn't kidnapped because of his ancestry or his race. He was there to fulfill one man's obsession with revenge, nothing more, and as long as the

Plantation continued to flourish, his imprisonment would never end.

And thanks to Levon Greene's orders, Nathan had never been told why.

CHAPTER 54

EVEN though he had a hole in his left biceps the size of a quarter, Payne wasn't about to give up. If he was going to rescue Ariane, he knew he had to endure whatever physical pain he was feeling. He simply had to, for he realized the agony in his arm could never approach the sorrow he would feel if he lost Ariane forever.

The body mends quickly. The mind and heart do not.

"Bennie," Payne groaned over the roar of his motor, "where do you think they took her?"

Blount started his ATV, the lead vehicle in the pack, then answered. "One day when I was exploring the island, I found a boat hidden in the weeds. I'm not sure if the Posse put it there, but I think there's a chance they did. It was in pretty good shape."

Jones started the middle Yamaha, completing the thundering chorus of engines. "That sounds like a good place to start."

With a twist of their accelerators, the three machines sprang into action, tearing up the soft ground in long strips and tossing it high into the air. After getting accustomed to his controls, Payne increased his speed until he was nearly even with Blount, choosing a position near Bennie's right shoulder. Jones, on the other hand, swung wide and settled on the opposite side, hoping to protect Blount from any outside threats.

But there was nothing he could do to prevent the explosion.

Instantaneously, a loud blast overpowered the roar of the ATV motors as an invisible force slammed into the backs of the bewildered drivers. In a moment of confusion, the three men skidded to a stop then turned to locate the source of the shock wave. It was the plantation house, and it glowed like Mount Vesuvius.

As they stared at the destruction, a second explosion tore through the remnants of the eighteenth-century structure, sending antique meteorites in all directions. Fireballs sprang into the air like popcorn, spreading the inferno to the nearby trees and cabins, igniting them like they were made out of gasoline.

"The detonation was too precise to be an accident," Payne screamed over the din of the blast. "That means either the house was on a timer or the explosion was set off by hand. And if it's the latter, that means our friends are still on the island."

Blount and Jones turned from the fireworks display and studied the surrounding terrain, using the glowing nighttime sky as a giant spotlight.

"Is that the truck over there?" Blount shouted.

Jones looked in the direction that Bennie was pointing and identified the object. "I don't know if it's the truck we want, but it's definitely a truck." Like a sheriff from the Wild West, he patted the weapon that hung from his hip. "Let's saddle up, fellas, and teach them boys a lesson."

DESPITE Tornado's barking and the loud rumble of the truck engine, Holmes heard the house's detonation and stopped to investigate. Looking back, he saw the bright orange flames as they shot toward the sky and felt the concussion of the blast as its shock wave rolled across the island like an invisible stampede.

With a smile on his face, Holmes climbed from the vehicle and strolled toward the back of the truck. Tornado emerged from the front seat as well, and the two of them gazed at the light. "Did you like that, boy?"

The dog remained silent, staring at the horizon.

"You liked that, didn't you?"

Tornado answered with a low, menacing growl. Then, after a few seconds of displeasure, it began pacing back and forth across the grass of the open field.

Holmes stared at Tornado with fascination. The only time he had seen the dog act this way was when Ndjai was preparing him for an attack. "Hey, fella, it's gonna be all right. The fire isn't gonna hurt you. It's too far away to bother us."

A guttural moan emanated from the dog's throat as it continued its movement. Back and forth. Back and forth. Again and again.

"What's spooking you, boy?"

As if answering the question, Tornado hopped onto the truck and growled at the nearby trees.

"What's wrong, boy? Is there something . . . ?"

Then Holmes heard it. Softly, just below the whisper of the wind, there was a rumble. It wasn't the sound of fire as it devoured the evidence of the plantation house. No, the sound was more man-made—like a machine. Like an engine that was headed his way.

Without delay, Holmes jumped behind the wheel of the truck and hit the accelerator. Driving as quickly as the terrain would allow, he glanced in his sideview mirror and searched the darkness for his enemies' approach. He hoped that they wouldn't be back there. He prayed that he was just being paranoid. But the mirror gave him indisputable proof.

The MANIACs were behind him, and they were gaining ground.

"Son of a bitch!" He turned back and looked at Tornado,

who was still growling fiercely at the noise. "Hang on, boy. This could get messy."

"DAMN!" Blount shouted from the lead ATV. "I think he saw us!"

Payne nodded, even though he had no idea what Blount had screamed. All of Payne's concentration was focused on the driver of the truck. Not Blount, the explosion, nor the pain in his arm. Everything—every thought, every breath, every beat of his heart—was devoted to the man that threatened Ariane. Payne would make him pay for his transgressions.

But he had to catch him first.

Little by little, second by second, Payne gained ground on the vehicle. He wasn't sure how it was possible—the pickup truck had more horsepower and quicker acceleration than his ATV—but he was getting closer.

"I'm gonna make my move," Blount yelled. "I'm gonna cut him off."

Jones nodded in understanding as Blount pulled ahead like a marathon runner using his final kick. Five feet, then ten. His lead lengthened while his dreadlocks flapped in the wind like a tattered flag. Jones stared in amazement as Blount inched closer and closer to the truck.

"He's gonna catch him!" Jones shouted. "Holy shit, he's gonna catch him!"

HOLMES looked in his sideview mirror with great displeasure. Even though he drove the fastest vehicle, the trio was still gaining on him. "Come on, truck! What's wrong with you?"

He pressed the gas pedal even harder, but it was already on the floor. There was nothing else he could do to increase his speed.

"Tornado!" he called through the back window. "Attack those men!"

The dog, who'd been watching the approach of the four-wheelers, barked in response. After locking its gaze on the nearest target, Tornado obtained top speed in three quick strides, then launched itself from the back of the truck with as much force as its legs could generate. The dog flew through the air like a white missile, aiming its sleek and powerful body at the closest threat it could find: Bennie Blount.

Tornado crashed into his face with such force that it shattered Blount's nose and cheekbones on contact, knocking him from his vehicle at a nasty angle. As he fell to the ground, his leg snagged on the underside of the handlebar, forcing his vehicle to turn sideways. The awkward movement was too extreme for his Yamaha to handle, causing the Grizzly to flip over in a series of exaggerated somersaults until the spiraling vehicle burst into a massive ball of flames.

Luckily for Blount, he was thrown free of the ATV before the explosion occurred, but his broken body skidded helplessly until it came to a stop in Jones's path.

Reacting quickly, Jones leaned hard to the left, slipping past his ally by less than a foot. Unfortunately, as he surged around Blount, he found himself heading for a different catastrophe. Blount's out-of-control vehicle, still tumbling in a pronounced spin, sprang sideways and landed squarely in front of him. The two ATVs smashed together with a metallic scream, launching Jones over the handlebars of the Grizzly and onto the hard ground beyond the fiery wreck.

Payne saw the accident out of the corner of his eye—the gruesome collision of the two vehicles and his best friend's violent spill—but realized there was nothing he could do to help. As much as he wanted to return to the crash and offer his assistance, he knew he couldn't afford to. It pained him to be so selfish, so uncaring toward Jones, but he realized if he turned around now, he might lose track of Ariane forever. And he just couldn't risk that possibility.

* * *

DESPITE the thick layer of fog that clouded his mind, Bennie Blount was able to recall many details of the accident. The truck, the ATV, the vicious impact of the dog.

God, he suddenly realized, it was a miracle that he was even alive.

While giving his body a moment to recuperate, Blount tried to clear the cobwebs in his brain but was unable to snap out of his accident-induced haze. His head throbbed with every beat of his pounding heart, and his vision came and went at unannounced intervals, making it all but impossible to concentrate. He tried to focus on something simple—the names of his family members, his childhood home, what he ate for dinner—but his concentration was distracted by the warm sensation that slowly engulfed his face.

The feeling, unlike anything he had ever experienced, started in his cheeks and gradually crawled toward his eyes at a slow rate. At first, Blount wasn't sure what was causing it. A swarm of insects? The blowing wind? A hallucination? But in time, he realized what was happening. His entire face was filling with fluid.

As he lay there, twisted and grotesquely mangled, Blount could feel his cheeks as they swelled at a hideous rate. Blood flooded his taste buds as the copper-flavored liquid surged from his nose like a waterfall and drained into his open mouth below. It quickly filled with the warm fluid. As it did, he tried to purge it with a quick burst of air but realized that he was unable to. Unfortunately, he had bitten his tongue during his fall, and the severed tip floated in his mouth like a dead fish in a crimson pond.

Blount tried to roll onto his side by using his arms and hands, but nothing happened. His limbs didn't respond, and he remained stationary. Next, he tried to pull his knees toward his chest, hoping to see or detect movement of any kind, but his legs remained planted on the ground. In a final test, Blount tried to wiggle his fingers and tap his feet, but they remained lifeless.

He wanted to prove that he was making a mistake, that he was simply overreacting and wasn't paralyzed, but his body was unwilling to cooperate.

Sadly, it kept letting him down, over and over again.

CHAPTER 55

DESPITE the agony in his arm, Payne managed to close the gap between himself and the surging truck to less than five feet. Once he matched the truck's speed, Payne pulled his right leg from the ATV and placed his foot on the vehicle's seat. After doing the same with his other leg, Payne found himself steering the Yamaha in a catcher's stance, a position that would allow him to leap onto the back of the truck.

But Holmes wasn't about to let that happen.

Using his passenger-side mirror, Holmes spotted Payne in pursuit. In an effort to thwart him, Holmes swerved the truck violently to the left, trying to shake free of the high-speed pest, but Payne adjusted quickly, gliding adjacent to the right edge of the pickup. Without delay, Holmes whipped the steering wheel to the right, trying to flatten Payne with the violent impact of the two vehicles, but the maneuver back-fired.

Since Payne was anticipating Holmes's move, he used the truck's approach to his advantage, jumping from the Yamaha a split second before impact occurred. Holmes laughed when he heard the metallic crunch of the two vehicles and glanced in his mirror to examine the wreckage, but the darkness prevented him from grasping what had really happened. The only thing he could see was the spiraling glow of the ATV's headlight as it turned over in a series of violent flips.

"It was nice bumping into you!" Holmes howled.

Little did he know that Payne was still along for the ride.

THE initial sound came from behind, and it made Blount's heart leap with fear. It wasn't a distinct noise like a bark or a howl, but Blount still knew what had produced it. It was Tornado, the hound from Hades. The bloodthirsty dog had paralyzed him and was coming back for more.

Blount knew if he remained stationary he wouldn't stand a chance against the blood-crazed beast. The dog would pin him to the ground with its thick, muscular body and thrash him to death with its razor-sharp teeth. He had seen the animal in action during its training sessions with Ndjai, so he knew what it was capable of doing. If he was to survive, Blount needed to get to his feet and find some kind of weapon to defend himself. But how? He couldn't run or even twitch. What chance did he stand against something like Tornado?

Realizing he couldn't put up a fight, Blount tried to scream for help, hoping that Payne or Jones would hear him, but his severed tongue and mouthful of blood restricted his effort. Instead of a shout, all that he could produce was a muffled whimper. And no one was close enough to hear it except Tornado, who heard the plea and sprang forward to investigate.

IF he had wanted to, Payne could have killed Holmes immediately—all it would take was a bullet to the back of his head—but there was a slight problem with that approach: Who was going to stop the truck? The vehicle was going too fast to stop on its own, and since Payne was in the back of it, the thought of it ramming into a tree or plunging into a swamp wasn't appealing.

No, if Payne was going to take out Holmes, he had to do it from close range with a great deal of finesse. It was the only way to guarantee his own safety.

Payne pulled the Glock from his belt and studied the back of the truck, hoping to find something useful. The bed was bare except for a tool chest, a tire, and a thick military blanket. Payne thought for a moment, trying to figure out how he could use any of these things to his advantage, when an idea hit him. He could use the blanket to obscure Holmes's vision.

With a quick tug, Payne slid the blanket across the bed and readied it for use. All he needed to do was toss it over the front of the—

"Oh, my God!" Payne mumbled.

He stared at the object on the other side of the truck and couldn't believe what he was seeing. How had he been so blind when he first climbed aboard? How could he have missed such a large lump under the blanket? It just didn't seem possible.

But there it was. Or more accurately, there he was. The captive who'd been pulled from the Devil's Box before Payne had been placed inside. The man was handcuffed, unconscious, and lying no more than five feet away.

Payne crawled across the truck bed and tried to examine him, hoping he was still clinging to life. His skin was red and blistered, not only from severe sunburn but also from insect bites. Even though his eyes were responsive, they were lethargic—possibly from dehydration or an illness of some kind.

"Hang in there," Payne whispered.

He glanced at the open terrain of the surrounding field and realized that he needed to make his move immediately. He didn't want to abandon the sick prisoner, but if he struck now, he knew there was no chance of the truck slamming into anything solid.

"Everything's going to be fine."

Stretching the blanket in his two hands, Payne crawled toward Holmes. Although pain ripped through his biceps as he worked, he realized that he had to use his left arm to complete the job. There was no other choice.

Taking a quick breath to ease his agony, Payne thrust his arms through the broken back window and arched the blanket over the face of the stunned driver. Holmes instantly released the steering wheel and used both of his hands to tear at the thick blanket, but Payne wasn't about to give in. In fact, he felt like a rodeo champion clinging for life on the back of an angry bull.

"Stop the truck!" he demanded. "If you want to live, stop the truck now!"

Holmes responded by pushing on the gas pedal even harder while screaming, "Fuck you!" through the rough cloth of the blanket.

The vehicle's speed continued to increase until Payne yanked on the blanket again, this time in a series of rapid bursts. "I . . . said . . . stop . . . the . . . truck . . . *now*!"

Realizing that he had to do something, Holmes finally gave in to the request, but not in the way that Payne had been hoping for. Instead of easing his foot from the gas pedal, Holmes slammed on the brakes as hard as he could, trying to free himself from his captor. The sudden shift in the truck's momentum did the trick. Payne flipped over the top of the roof like a drunken gymnast, legs and arms flailing in every direction while trying to stop his slide. But nothing could prevent him from tumbling in front of the screeching truck.

WHILE shaking off the effects of the ATV crash, Jones pulled himself to a sitting position and studied his immediate surroundings. He saw two four-wheelers, both of them damaged and overturned, and the closest one to him was on fire. Using the light from the blaze, Jones checked himself for blood but was surprised to find very little. He had an assortment of scrapes and bruises, but he didn't have any open gushers like he had feared.

After rubbing his eyes for several seconds, Jones climbed

to his feet and looked for the other driver. He wasn't quite sure who he was looking for—his head was still groggy from the accident—but reasoned if there were two vehicles, there should be two bodies.

At least, that seemed to make sense in his current state.

Jones wandered to his left and stared at the flaming wreckage, making sure that no one was on fire. "Hello? Can anybody hear me?"

There was no response.

Jones limped to the second ATV, the one that he'd been driving, and pushed it over onto its wheels. Although it was dented and scratched, Jones didn't notice any major damage. There were no obvious leaks or stray parts lying on the ground, and despite the collision the wheels seemed to be intact.

"Takes a licking and keeps on—"

A deep growl broke Jones's concentration. He immediately stared in the direction of the noise and searched for the source.

"Hello?" he shouted, but this time with a little more apprehension.

Once again, there was no response.

As he studied the darkness, Jones placed his hand on his belt and felt for the cold touch of his gun. He was thankful when his fingers curled around the rough texture of the handle. It gave him a burst of confidence.

"Who's out there?" he demanded.

Another growl. Softer, angrier.

Jones took a few steps forward, holding his gun directly in front of him. He was in no mood for games and planned on punishing the first person he came across. "If you're out there, I recommend you answer me. Otherwise, I have a bullet with your name on it."

He took another step, moving closer to the source of the sound. The light of the fire helped show him the way. In fact, he relied on it.

"I'm telling you!" he warned. "You're really pissing me—"

But Jones wasn't able to finish his statement. In fact, he nearly choked on the words as he tried to say them.

Bennie Blount was sprawled on the ground, twisted and contorted in a puddle of his own blood. Hovering above him, like a monster from another world, was Tornado, its face and claws dripping with the liquid that surged from the open wounds it had created.

When the animal saw Jones, it lifted its head and growled in an effort to protect its dinner, and when it did, chunks of flesh dropped from its mouth and fell onto the red dirt below.

The bloody display made Jones nauseous, yet it only added to his determination.

He instantly raised his Glock and pointed it at the snarling beast.

Bang! The first shot entered the animal midshank, knocking it away from Blount amidst a series of yelps. But Jones refused to stop. He wouldn't be content until this creature had died.

Bang! The next bullet ripped through Tornado's hip, sending a spurt of blood into the air and onto the ground where the dog collapsed with a loud thud.

Bang! Bang! Bang! Tornado danced spasmodically as Jones pummeled its body with shot after well-aimed shot, making sure that this beast would never breathe again.

Jones sneered. "Tell Cujo I said hello."

CHAPTER 56

WHEN Payne opened his eyes, he was unable to see anything except two blazing orbs of light, one shining on either side of him. He tried leaning forward, using his good arm to lift him from the ground, but the front bumper of the truck restricted his movement.

"Wow!" he gasped, noticing that most of his body was underneath the frame of the vehicle. "Thank God for tall wheels."

Using the grille for support, Payne scrambled backward, freeing himself from the undercarriage as quickly as possible. He realized he didn't have time to plan anything elaborate—Holmes would be looking to strike hastily—so Payne decided to follow his gut. And it told him to attack.

With quiet confidence, Payne lowered his right hand to his hip and grabbed his Glock. As his finger curled around the trigger, Payne glanced under the motionless vehicle, looking for Holmes's feet. If he had seen them, he would've blasted them immediately, but Payne's search turned up empty.

That meant that Holmes was either inside the truck or on it.

Since the front windshield was missing, Payne knew he'd have an unobstructed shot if Holmes was in the front seat. He realized, though, that the windowless space would be far more beneficial to his opponent. The gap would give Holmes more room to maneuver inside the cab and an extra way to escape. But Payne wasn't about to let *that* happen.

No, the only way that Holmes was going to get away was through Payne, not through a window. Unfortunately, that was what Holmes had in mind.

While recovering from the sneak attack, Holmes noticed Payne's silhouette on the ground ahead, created by the headlights. The shadow gave Holmes all the information he was looking for: Payne was still alive and directly in front of the truck.

Without delay, Holmes slammed his foot on the gas, launching the truck forward at full speed. Payne, using his well-honed instincts, sensed what was about to happen before it actually did. With mongooselike quickness, Payne fell backward onto the hard ground. A split second later, the truck roared above him, its high undercarriage protecting Payne from injury.

The instant the truck had passed, Payne flipped onto his belly and burst forward like a sprinter at the start of a race, but he quickly realized that the vehicle was too far ahead for him to catch it. Stopping immediately, he aimed his Glock at the truck's back tire and discharged three quick rounds in succession. The second and third bullets hit their mark, piercing the right wheel and causing Holmes to temporarily lose control of the truck. The vehicle fishtailed, skidding sideways on the dew-filled grass, but Holmes didn't panic. He coolly compensated for the loss of air pressure, allowing the back end to straighten itself out, then continued forward as fast as the vehicle could carry him.

"WHERE the hell have you been?" Levon Greene growled. He had been standing by the boat for several minutes, impatiently waiting for Holmes's return. "I was getting ready to leave you."

With a look of annoyance on his face, Holmes stepped from the heavily damaged truck. "Where the hell have I been? I've been doing your dirty work, that's where I've been!" He opened the back of the truck with a slam, then climbed onto the tailgate. "If it wasn't for your selfishness, we'd already be far from this place, somewhere in the gulf by now. But no! You just had to have your pet slave, didn't you?"

Greene moved forward, glancing into the back of the truck. He wanted to make sure that Holmes had returned with Nathan. "He's gonna fetch you a lot of money, so I don't know what you're so pissed about."

Holmes glanced down at the slave and gave him a swift kick in the midsection. He was completely fed up with Greene's shit, and he needed to take it out on somebody.

"You don't know what I'm pissed about? Well, let me tell you! You brought two MANIACs to my island, then when they got loose, you ran and hid while I was forced to deal with them!" Holmes pulled the slave toward the back of the truck and waited for Greene to take him. "I mean, this is *your* guest, not mine. So why did I have to risk my life to get him?"

Greene shook his head at Holmes's ignorance. "Because I'm the one with money. If your name was on the bank account, then I'd be doing stuff for you. But I'm the one with the cash, so you're the one with the job."

PAYNE knew he had a lot of ground to make up—probably too much to do on foot—so he decided to take a chance. He wasn't sure if his four-wheeler had survived the vicious jolt from Holmes' truck, but he decided to run back to the crash site and find out. Thankfully, the gamble paid off. The Grizzly had overturned, but it worked just fine.

After putting it on its wheels, Payne jumped on the ATV and rocketed ahead with a touch of the accelerator. The green and black vehicle reached top speed as Payne urged the machine to catch Holmes. If Ariane was taken from the island, he knew the odds of finding her would go down significantly. It wouldn't be an impossible task—hell, Payne would devote his entire life and all of his resources to finding her—but he knew it would be quite difficult.

"Come on!" he implored, digging his heels into the ATV. "Go faster!"

But the vehicle was going as fast as it could, vibrating rapidly from the strain. The darkened scenery of the Plantation whipped by in a blur. The trees, rocks, and animals were all a part of the landscape that Payne ignored. His full concentration, every thought in his throbbing head, was focused on the love of his life and the bastards that had taken her away.

Oh, they would pay. They would fucking pay!

But he had to catch them first.

IT wasn't until the hydroplane eased into the warm water of the inlet that Holmes was finally able to relax. Until that moment, he was certain that Payne or Jones would appear at the last possible moment to foil his escape. But as he glided from the marsh's rugged shoreline, his anxiety started to fade.

He had faced two MANIACs in battle and lived to brag about it.

As the boat moved farther into the swamp, passing groves of cypress trees and several curious alligators, Greene noticed the difference in Holmes's appearance. His partner's face no longer looked haggard, and his body no longer looked beaten. In fact, he actually seemed to lose years as the boat continued forward.

"What's your deal?" he wondered. "You look like a new man."

"Feel like one, too." A full smile crossed his lips for the first time in hours. "My gut told me we weren't gonna make it. I don't know why, but something warned me about Payne and Jones."

"What did it say?"

"It told me that they were gonna be our downfall." Holmes took his eyes off the water and cast a paranoid glance back at the shore. "But I guess I was wrong, huh? We beat Mr. Payne-in-the-Ass once and for all."

Greene stood from his seat and looked back as well, but the hydroplane had traveled so far he could barely see the shoreline through the trees. "What does your gut tell you now?"

Holmes pondered the question as he increased the boat's speed. There was a faint glow in the water up ahead that he had a theory about. "Actually, it tells me that we're gonna make it to Africa, and something good is going to happen along the way."

"Along the way?" Greene questioned. "Why do you say that?"

Holmes extended his finger forward, causing Greene to glance in front of the hydroplane. When his eyes focused on the scene, he couldn't believe their good fortune.

Paul and Donny Metz were standing on a fallen cypress tree, trying to push the boat into the center of the channel, but their effort was completely useless. The duo, weakened from days of labor in the field, didn't have the strength to disengage the boat by themselves, and Robert Edwards didn't have enough experience with the craft to assist them.

No, the slaves weren't about to free themselves from the tree, and now that Holmes and Greene had stumbled upon them, they wouldn't be getting free at all.

PAYNE tried to follow the truck's tire marks in the grass, but the rocky terrain near the eastern shore of the island limited his tracking ability.

Once he was on his own, forced to locate Holmes with nothing to guide him, he decided to scan the swamps in both directions, hoping to stumble upon a clue. With each passing minute, he knew the chances of finding Ariane on the island were getting smaller and smaller, but he refused to give up hope while there was still fuel in his gas tank and ground to cover.

It wasn't until he saw Holmes's truck, slowly sinking into the soft mud of the marsh, that he knew he was too late to make a difference.

The Posse had escaped from the Plantation.

"Son of a bitch!" he screamed while punching the leather seat in frustration. "I can't believe I let them escape!" He took a deep breath, trying to calm down, but it didn't work. The extra oxygen simply made him more agitated than before. "Fuck! Fuck! *Fuck!*"

After a moment of contemplation, Payne moved from his four-wheeler to the edge of the swamp. He was tempted to wade out to the sinking truck to search for clues, but the splashing of nearby gators quickly eliminated the thought.

"Think, goddamn it, think! What can I do?"

Unfortunately, there was nothing he could do except watch the vehicle—and his chances of finding Ariane—slowly disappear.

CHAPTER 57

JONATHON Payne glared at the special agent across the table. He had already answered more questions in the past few hours than he had during his entire time at the Naval Academy, and it was starting to try his patience. He was more than willing to assist the FBI with their investigation, but enough was enough. It was time to speed up the process.

Payne stood from his chair and glanced at the large mirror that dominated the wall in front of him. If he was correct, the people in charge of the investigation were standing behind the glass, watching him give his testimony about the Plantation.

"That's it," he announced. "I've reached my limit. I've done nothing wrong, yet I'm being treated like a criminal. I'm not saying another word until one of you assholes comes into this room and answers a few questions for me. Do you understand? Not another word until I get some answers!"

Payne accented his request by slamming his hand against the two-way glass—his way of driving home the intensity of his message.

His point got through because less than a minute later the door to the conference room opened and the local director of operations walked in.

Chuck Dawson was a distinguished-looking man in his mid-fifties, and the power of his position showed in the confidence of his stride and the wisdom of his weathered face. He greeted Payne with a firm handshake and studied him for a moment before telling the other agent to leave the room. It would be easier to get things done alone.

"How's the arm feeling, Mr. Payne? Can I get you something for it?"

Payne glanced at his injured biceps and shrugged. It wouldn't get better without surgery, and he didn't have time for a trip to the hospital. "A beer would be nice. You know, for the pain."

Dawson smiled at the comment. "If I had some in my office, I'd offer you a cold one. But I was thinking more along the lines of bandages or a pillow."

"Nah, your doctors patched me up pretty well when I first came in. I don't think I'm ready for the golf course yet, but I'll be okay for our chat."

"If that changes, be sure to let me know. I don't want anything to happen to a national hero while you're under my care."

Payne raised his eyebrows in surprise. The recent line of questioning suggested that he was more of a suspect than a hero. He had been drilled on everything from the murder of Jamaican Sam to his possible involvement with the Posse, and now he was being praised? "On second thought, I might need a hearing test. I could've sworn you just called me a hero."

"I did," Dawson asserted. He opened the folder that he had carried into the room and glanced at its information. "From what I can tell, you and David Jones saved the lives of eleven prisoners—actually twelve if you include Tonya Edwards's baby—while killing more than twenty criminals in the process. At the same time, you managed to prevent the future abduction of countless others by shutting down an organization that we didn't even know existed until yesterday."

Dawson spotted Payne trying to read the FBI data and hastily closed the folder.

"That makes you a hero in my book."

Payne leaned back in his chair. "Well, Chuck, that seems a bit surprising. I don't feel like a hero. In fact, I feel like a second-class citizen around here. What's up with all the questions and accusations?"

Dawson smiled, revealing a perfect set of teeth. "Come on, Jon. You're ex-military. You know the way things work."

"Yeah, you like to burn up a bunch of manpower by asking tons of worthless questions just so you have something to put in your files."

The FBI director shrugged. "It's the government's way."

Payne grinned at the comment. "Well, at least you're willing to admit it's worthless. That's more than the last agent was willing to do."

"Don't be putting words into my mouth. I never said it was worthless. The questions weren't worthless. . . . Okay, I admit some of them were a little far-fetched, but they weren't without worth. We often gather more information from a person's reaction to a question than we do from their actual answer."

Payne rolled his eyes. He couldn't believe his entire morning had been wasted on psychological games. There were so many other things he could have been doing with his time. "And that's why you've been harassing me? To see if my answers and facial expressions were consistent during the baiting process?"

"Something like that. But it isn't just self-consistency that we look for. We also check your claim against the claims of others."

"Like D.J.?"

"And Bennie Blount, and the slaves, and anyone else we can dig up. We make sure that everything checks out before we're willing to accept things at face value. It's the only way to guarantee in-depth analysis."

"Well, Chuck, now that I've passed your little test, would you please answer some questions for me? I've been trying to get some information all morning, but I keep getting shot down by your flunkies."

Dawson nodded. His men had been instructed to keep Payne in the dark, but now that they were confident in Payne's innocence, he was willing to open up. "As long as the questions don't involve confidential data, I'd be happy to fill you in. Fire away!"

It was a poor choice of expressions, but Payne was willing to overlook the faux pas if it meant getting some answers. "You just mentioned Bennie Blount. How's he doing?"

"Mr. Blount is in serious but stable condition. He lost a lot of blood from the crash and the animal attack, but your buddy did a great job keeping him alive until help arrived."

"What about his legs? Is he going to be able to walk again?"

Dawson shrugged. "I'm not a doctor, so I don't know all the facts. From what I was told, he did sustain a spinal cord injury. They don't think it's a devastating one, so, God willing, he'll be as good as new after some rest and rehab."

Payne closed his eyes in thought. For some reason, Payne was always more devastated by his partners' injuries than his own. "And what about the twenty-plus prisoners we saved? Are they all right?"

"Maybe I should ask you the same question. Are *you* all right?"

"What's that supposed to mean?"

"Twenty-plus prisoners? You must have double vision or something. Like I mentioned before, you helped save the lives of eleven captives."

"Yeah, I heard you. There were eleven people on the island when you showed up and ten on the boat that I set free several hours before. If my math is correct, that would mean over twenty."

"Shit," Dawson mumbled. He suddenly realized that Payne hadn't been informed about the missing vessel. "I'm sorry to tell you this, but we never found the slave boat that you and your partner talked about. The Coast Guard is currently conducting an all-out search of the gulf, but as of right now, we don't know what happened to it."

"You've gotta be shitting me!"

"I wish I was. But it hasn't turned up."

Payne tried to process the new information as quickly as possible, but it threw him for a temporary loop. "So the slave boat could be on the bottom of the gulf? What about Robert Edwards? Did you find Robert Edwards anywhere?"

Dawson shook his head. "He's one of the missing slaves. His wife and future baby are fine, but he's still unaccounted for."

Payne tried to make sense of the information. When he left the island, he thought he had rescued everyone except for Ariane and the unknown captive from the truck, but now he realized that he might have sent a boatload of inexperienced sailors to a watery grave.

"Jon?" Dawson whispered in a comforting voice. "Not to change the subject, but when you pounded on the mirror and called me an asshole, you implied you had a bunch of questions. Did you want me to answer anything else, or is that all for now?"

It took Payne a moment to gather himself. "With the new information that you just gave me, one suddenly leaps to mind."

"Go ahead, fire away."

Payne wished he'd stop using that expression. "How in the hell did you find us? I thought the people on the boat must've told you about the Plantation, but since they're still missing I guess they couldn't have been the ones."

Dawson nodded. "A couple of planes noticed the house explosion from the air. They, in turn, notified the local authorities. Eventually, word filtered down to us."

"And you've had no luck finding the missing slaves? What about Levon Greene and Octavian Holmes? Any luck with them?"

Dawson shook his head. "We put out an APB and flooded the airports and local islands with their pictures. Unfortunately, if they decided to head south, we'll have little chance of finding them. Hell, a guy in a sailboat can fart and propel himself to Mexico from here. We're that close to the border. It makes things kind of tough for us."

ONCE Payne was excused from the conference room, he rode the elevator to the main lobby, where he met up with Jones. The two greeted each other with a firm handshake, then walked into the bright sunlight of the Crescent City.

"How'd the questioning go?"

Jones smirked like an uncaught shoplifter. "Just peachy, and you?"

"Not too bad. When things started to get sticky, I made a big fuss, and they immediately backed down." Jones's smirk must've been contagious because it quickly spread to Payne's lips. "Did they ask you anything about the hard drive?"

Jones patted the pocket of his T-shirt and laughed. "Nope. And to be honest with you, I forgot to mention it." He stopped on the sidewalk and pretended to turn around. "Do you think I should go back and tell them? Because I could—"

"Nah, I doubt it's important. The damn thing is bound to be blank."

"Yeah, you're right. It probably won't tell us where to look for Ariane, or Levon, or the other slave owners. And even if it did, it's not like we'd care."

"Not at all," he growled. "Not one bit."

THE property in Tampico, Mexico, had been in Edwin Drake's family for four decades, but he never had any use for it until recently. After several years of dormancy, the land was now critical to Drake's slave exportation business. It served as a makeshift airport in the middle of nowhere, a place where they could load people without interference.

The boat of slaves, piloted by Octavian Holmes, reached the Tampico coast just before dawn and was greeted by two trucks full of dark-skinned guards, all chosen from Kotto's plantations in Nigeria. The Africans loaded six slaves into each truck, then drove them to Drake's property, which sat ten miles northwest of the Mexican city. When they arrived at the camp, the slaves were quickly herded into a containment building. They were stripped, hosed, deloused, and clothed, before being fed their first meal in over a day.

The slaves were then examined by Kotto's personal physician, who treated each of their injuries with urgency—these people were Kotto's property, after all—making sure that every wound was cleaned and every infection was attended to. After certifying and documenting the health of each person, the doctor gave the slaves the immunization shots they would require for their trip to their new home, Africa.

Once the medical details were taken care of, the slaves were led to Drake's homemade airfield. There the guards checked the names and ages of each.

Doubting the ability of the foreign guards, Levon Greene double-checked the list of passengers. He realized these twelve people would generate a huge payday and knew how far that money could go in Africa, so this wasn't the time to make any mistakes.

"How do things look?" Holmes asked, no longer worried about Payne or Jones. "Are the dirty dozen ready for their trip to the motherland?"

Greene nodded. "As ready as they're ever gonna be."

Holmes smiled. "To help their transition, we've selected *Roots* for their in-flight movie."

CHAPTER 58

Wednesday, July 7th
Ibadan National Railyards
Ibadan, Nigeria
(56 miles northeast of Lagos)

THE dark-skinned American looked both directions, making sure that the busy rail station was free of incoming traffic. When he was satisfied, he continued his journey forward, lifting his white cotton robe away from the grease-covered tracks. After crossing the congested railyard, he turned left, walking parallel to the far rail while trying to conceal the limp in his gait. It was the only thing about him that was the least bit conspicuous. Other than that, he blended in perfectly, resembling the rest of the peasants as they rode the trains home after a hard day of work.

"May the peace, mercy, and blessings of God be upon you," said a passing Muslim.

"And also with you," he replied in Yoruba, one of the common languages in Ibadan.

With a watchful eye, the American continued forward, searching for the designated meeting spot. He had already completed his reconnaissance of the neighborhood—checking the security around the Kotto Distribution Center, studying the building blueprints, looking for weak spots in the perimeter of the industrial plant. Overall, he was happy with his findings, but his opinion mattered little in the greater scheme of things. He was simply a pawn in a very complex game, one that he knew very little about.

But that was about to change.

At the rendezvous point, he glanced in all directions, making sure that he wasn't being followed. Everything looked clear to his well-trained eyes. Smiling confidently, he knocked on the railcar five times, the agreed-upon signal to gain access to the boxcar that had been commandeered for the current operation.

"Who is it?" called a high-pitched voice from inside.

This wasn't a part of standard protocol, but the dark-skinned man was more than willing to play along. It helped to lessen the tension of the moment. "Domino's Pizza."

"Your delivery took more than thirty minutes. I expect a large refund."

The American grabbed his crotch with both hands. "Open the door, lady. I've got your large refund, right here!"

The cargo door slid open, revealing a white soldier in full black camouflage. "Oooh," he exclaimed in a feminine voice. "And what a big refund it is!"

Both men laughed as the black soldier climbed into the railcar.

"Any problems with your recon?" asked one of the soldiers inside.

"None, except for my damn gun." He reached under his robe, removing the weapon that had been strapped to his leg. "I need to get a new leg holster or something. This thing cut off my circulation within ten minutes, and I've been limping ever since."

"Bitch, bitch, bitch!" teased a familiar voice from the back of the car. His view was obstructed by a large stack of crates, but he knew exactly who he was listening to. "You were bitching when I first trained you, and you're still bitching now. Haven't you grown up yet?"

A grin appeared on Lieutenant Shell's face. He removed his cap as a sign of respect and looked for his former commander. "I'll be damned! What are you doing here?"

"Listening to you bitch! I thought I taught you to be

tougher than that. Complaining about a cramp? Pathetic! Take two Midols and get back to work."

The two men hugged briefly, a touching reunion between MANIACs past and present.

"It's great to see you, sir. It really is. But I have to admit, ya look like shit! What happened?"

With scabs all over his face and body, Payne glanced at his left arm, dangling lifelessly in its sling. "This is what happens when you reach your mid-thirties. Your body starts to fall apart."

"Don't let him fool you," Jones interjected, moving from his hiding place on the other side of the boxcar. "He got into a disagreement with an exotic dancer, and she kicked his ass. Breast to the face . . . breast to the face . . . high heel to the nuts . . . knockout!"

Shell laughed like a little kid as he rushed to D.J.'s side. It had been a long time since they'd spoken, and the smiles on their faces revealed their love and admiration for one another. It was the type of bond that developed when two people had been through hell together—the type of stuff that the MANIACs were known for.

"How are you doing, Rocky?"

"Pretty damn good," Shell declared. He hadn't heard his nickname since Payne and Jones had left the squad. "But I'd like the right to change my opinion. I mean, if you guys are here, then something big is about to go down. Right?"

He looked at Jones, then Payne. He noticed anxiety in both sets of eyes, something that was atypical for them.

"Damn," he groaned. "How big are we talking about?"

"Pretty big," Payne admitted. He tried to smile to lessen the tension, but his effort was less than successful. "And quite personal."

The comment piqued Shell's interest. "Personal? As in, off-the-books personal? As in, the-government-doesn't-know-we're-here-but-who-gives-a-rat's-ass-about-them-anyway personal?"

Payne nodded, looking forward to Shell's response.

"Halle-fucking-lujah! Military missions are always so

boring. It's about time we got the old gang back together and had some fun!"

Jones nodded in agreement but wasn't nearly as enthusiastic. "You're right, it's been way too long. But I don't know if *fun* is the right word to describe this mission."

"Oh, yeah?" Shell laughed, still not understanding the sensitive nature of the assignment. "Then what word would you use?"

Payne took a step forward, intensity returning to his face. It was a look that Shell had seen several times before. One that meant it was time for business. "The word I'd use is *desperate*."

"Desperate?"

Payne nodded. "And once I tell you why I called you here, you'll understand why."

"You called us here?" Shell asked, dumbfounded. "How did you pull that off? Nobody's supposed to know where we are, yet you somehow managed to track us down? Don't get me wrong, it's great to see ya, but that doesn't make much sense to me."

Captain Juan Sanchez, the MANIACs current leader, cleared his throat. "It doesn't have to make sense to you, as long as it makes sense to me."

Shell sprang to attention. "Yes, sir. Sorry, sir."

Sanchez winked at Payne, his former team leader. "But since you'll bitch the rest of the night if I don't tell you, I'll be a nice guy and let you in on the secret."

"Thank you, sir. I'm all ears, sir."

"As luck would have it, I stay in touch with Captain Payne on a regular basis, which is apparently more than you. He gave me a call and briefed me on his current situation. Soon after, I offered to give up our much-needed R & R in order to help. That is, of course, if it's all right with you."

"Once a MANIAC, always a MANIAC!" Shell shouted passionately.

"You're damn right!" Sanchez growled. He quickly turned his attention from his second in command to the man he had served under for several years. "Captain Payne, at this time I would like to offer you control of the finest, fiercest fighting force ever to walk the face of this fucking planet. We are the MANIACs, and we will follow you and fight with you until death—their death—so help me, God!"

Payne nodded in appreciation.

It had taken a while, but he finally realized that everything would be all right.

THE Qur'an, the spiritual text of Islam, required all Muslim adults to pray five times a day—at dawn (*fajr*), noon (*zuhr*), midafternoon (*asr*), sunset (*maghrib*), and night (*isha*)—to prove their unyielding faith and uncompromising devotion to Allah. Unfortunately, these sessions were not assigned to a specific hour, making prayer time a difficult thing to agree upon among modern-day Muslims. In order to rectify this problem, most Islamic communities utilized a muezzin to climb the minaret of the local mosque and announce the beginning of each prayer session. When his voice was heard, echoing loudly throughout the streets of the city, all Muslims were expected to stop what they were doing and drop to their knees in prayer.

These breaks were their holy time, moments of forgiveness and thanks. But in Payne's mind, it was also their biggest weakness. It gave him five daily opportunities to catch the enemy with their guard down. Literally. And he planned to exploit it for all it was worth.

As nighttime crept over Nigeria, the MANIACs snuck along the outer perimeter of the eight-block Kotto Distribution Center, using the shadows as their cover while waiting for their signal to start the assault. Although Payne had showed them the advantages of this unconventional approach, the twelve soldiers didn't like the lengthy exposure time that they would have in the field. They were used to invading, dominating, and leaving, but rarely waiting. But in this case, they agreed that the benefits of their master plan far outweighed the negatives. In fact, if all went well, they knew their battle with Kotto's men would be over within seconds, making it the easiest mission they'd ever been on.

Unfortunately, it didn't feel very easy while they waited.

Dressed in black and trying to blend in with the landscape, the soldiers were unable to relax. They were nervous and eager, excited and scared, but not relaxed. Too many things could go wrong for them to be relaxed, especially since the start signal was in the hands of a stranger they had never worked with before.

No, not Payne. All the MANIACs followed his advice like scripture.

In actuality, they were waiting for the muezzin, the Islamic crier. They would go on his call, during the Muslims' moment of weakness—when the sun kissed the horizon and the guards least expected violence.

The voice rang out like a tormented wail, soaring from the largest mosque in the city to the smallest homes in the neighborhoods below. The muezzin's impassioned plea, like a hypnotic command from Allah himself, sent people dropping to the ground, causing all Muslims to set aside their nightly activities in order to give thanks.

And the MANIACs took advantage of it.

"Gracias," said Payne, who was thankful for the opportunity to burst into the complex with a silenced Heckler & Koch MP5 K in his hands. He knew when he reached his assigned territory, a small section in the center where the hostages were supposedly kept, that all of Kotto's guards would be on the floor, praying toward the distant land of Mecca. And once he found them, he would use them for target practice.

Payne was trailed by Jones, Shell, and Sanchez, and their path met no resistance along the way. No guards, no workers, no noise. The place was an industrial ghost town, and the lack of activity unnerved Payne. In confusion, he drew a large question mark in the air.

Responding in the silent language of the MANIACs, Shell touched his watch, made a counterclockwise motion with his finger, pointed to his eyes, then to the room straight ahead. That meant when he had come through earlier, he had seen the guards in the next room.

Payne nodded in understanding.

If Shell's reconnaissance was accurate, the massacre was about to commence, and it would take place in the chamber they were facing. Their goal was to eliminate as many guards as possible—the plant workers were already out of the building, so they didn't have to worry about innocent bystanders getting hit—and rescue the slaves from captivity.

After taking a deep breath, Payne calmly pointed to his watch, his foot, and then his own backside before glancing back at his partners. The unexpected signal brought smiles to their faces. In MANIAC-speak, it meant it was time to kick some ass.

The four men moved forward, looking for the best possible opportunity to begin their assault. And as they'd hoped, that moment occurred the instant they walked in the door. Ten guards, all assembled in the tiny area, were spread across the floor in prayer. Each was kneeling on an individual straw mat while facing Mecca.

And unluckily for Kotto's men, that direction was away from the door.

Wasting no time, Payne and Shell crept to the left while Jones and Sanchez slid to the right. Then, once everyone was in position, Payne looked at his friends and nodded. It was his signal to commence the assault.

Pfffft! Pfffft! Pfffft! Pfffft!

Fury rained upon the guards like a judgment from God, splattering their innards all over the room like a slaughterhouse floor. The tiny bursts of gunfire, muffled by the silencers, continued at a rapid pace until the MANIACs were confident that Kotto's men were dead.

Then, just to be safe, Shell and Sanchez fired some more.

No sense in taking any chances.

When target practice was over, Jones treaded through the carnage, inspecting bodies as he moved. Crouching near the door, he examined the spring lock and chose the proper pick.

"The infrared that we used earlier showed that this room was full of people. From what we could tell, there was no sign of weapons. Hopefully, they're who we're looking for."

Payne nodded anxiously, praying that Ariane was inside and unharmed.

It had been nearly a week since he had last kissed her, since he had held her in his arms and confessed his love to her. It was the first thing he was going to do when he saw her. He was going to grab her and tell her how much he cared, how much she meant to him, how lonely he had been without her. She was his world, and he was going to make damn sure she knew it.

"Got it," Jones whispered.

The sound of his partner's voice brought Payne back to reality. He moved to the left of the entrance, wrapped his finger around his trigger, and waited for Jones to turn the handle.

With a flick of his wrist, Jones swung the door open and calmly waited against the outside wall for an outburst of violence. Payne and the others waited, too, knowing that inexperienced guards often charged forward to investigate the unknown. But when the four men heard nothing—no footsteps, voices, or gunshots—they realized they were either facing an elite team or no one at all.

Payne did his best to raise his injured arm and slowly counted down for his men.

Three fingers. Two fingers. One finger. Showtime.

The MANIACs entered with precision. Jones slid in first, followed closely by Payne and the others. With guns in a firing position, the men scoured the room for potential danger, but none was present. The only thing they saw was a scared group of hostages, gagged and tied up in the center of the floor.

"Is there anyone in here?" Jones demanded. "Did they set any traps?"

The heads of the hostages swung from side to side.

Shell and Sanchez didn't take their word for it, though.

They carefully searched the corners, the walls, and the exposed pipes of the twenty-by-twenty-foot metallic room, which had the feel of a submarine mess hall, but found nothing that concerned them.

When Shell gave the word, Jones grabbed his radio and spoke rapidly, ordering the next wave of MANIACs to enter the facility.

But Payne ignored all of that. His mind was on one thing and one thing only: Ariane.

He moved into the group of hostages and instantly recognized their faces from the boat. He couldn't wait to ask them how they managed to get caught—the last thing he knew they were motoring away from the island—but that would have to wait until after he found Ariane.

Shit! Where was she? Why couldn't he find Ariane?

Out of nowhere, the face of Robert Edwards appeared in the crowd, and Payne rushed to his side. He removed his gag and asked, "Are you okay?" But before he got a response, he continued. "Have you seen Ariane?"

"No," Edwards said. "Have you seen Tonya? Have you seen my Tonya?"

At that moment, Payne could've kicked himself. Here he was worrying about his own needs when he should've been more concerned with the needs of the slaves. They were the ones who had been through the bigger ordeal. Compared to them, he'd been through nothing.

"Tonya's fine, just fine. And the baby's still inside her, right where it should be."

Relief flooded Edwards's face. "Where *he* should be. We're having a boy."

Payne smiled at the information. "Right where *he* should be."

"And Tonya? Where is she now?"

"Don't worry. She's safe. She's in New Orleans at FBI headquarters, giving a statement. And before I left town, I got her an appointment with the best obstetrician in the state. He promised me that she'd be in good hands."

"Thank God," Edwards muttered.

Payne gave him a moment to collect his thoughts and count his blessings before he continued his questioning. "Robbie, I don't mean to be rude, but . . ."

"You want to know about Ariane."

"Have you seen her?"

Edwards nodded. "She was on the plane with the rest of us, but once we landed, the two big guys grabbed her and a male slave and took them somewhere else."

"Two big guys? Was it Holmes and Greene?"

"Yeah. They grabbed her as soon as we landed."

Payne couldn't believe the news. Why did they single her out from all the others? Was it because of him? Were they planning on torturing her because of his interference? That would be a tough thing for him to handle.

"Do you have any idea where they took her?"

Unfortunately, Edwards stared at him blankly, unable to offer a single suggestion.

CHAPTER 59

Friday, July 9th
The Kotto Family Estate
Lagos, Nigeria

WITH trepidation, Ariane moved toward the large man. They had shared a boat to Mexico, a plane to Nigeria, and a train to Lagos, but he had failed to utter a single word during the entire journey—not even when he was handcuffed, drugged, or beaten. It was like his body was there, but his mind wasn't. She hoped to change that, though. She wanted to undo the damage that had been done to him. That is, if he would let her.

"I'm not going to hurt you," she whispered. "I promise I'm not going to hurt you like those other guys. I just want to know your name." She studied his face, hoping to see a blink or a smile, but there was no sign of interaction on his part. "My name's Ariane. What's yours?"

Nothing.

"I heard some of the guards refer to you as Nathan. Is that your real name, or did they just make it up?"

Still nothing.

"I like the name Nathan," she said. "So many people are named Mike or Scott that it gets monotonous. But not Nathan. That's a name that people will remember, like you. You're a big guy that people will remember, so you should have a memorable name." She gazed into his eyes, but they remained unresponsive. "What about my name? Ariane? Do you like it? I do, for the same reason that I like yours. It's different. In fact, I've never met another Ariane in my entire life. How about you? Have you ever met an Ariane before?"

For an instant, he shifted his eyes to hers, then looked away. It wasn't much, but it was so unexpected she almost took a step back in surprise.

"Well, I guess that means you haven't." She grabbed his hand and shook it. "Now you can never say that again because we just officially met."

A large smile crossed her dry lips as she tried to decide what she wanted to say next. "I'd ask for your last name, but I have a feeling that might take a little bit longer. Besides, we don't want to get too personal. This is our first date after all."

LEVON Greene sat on the edge of his bed, trying to block out the events of the past few days, but too much had happened for him to forget. Jackson and Webster were dead, murdered by his own hand. The Plantation was history, blown to bits with the touch of a button. And worst of all, he was a fugitive on the run, unable to return to the only country where he'd ever wanted to live.

Greene tried to analyze things, tried to figure what went wrong with Webster's full-proof scheme, and he kept coming up with the same answer: Payne and Jones. It was their fault. Everything could be traced back to them. If Greene had just shot them when they met at the Spanish Plaza or killed them while they slept at his house, none of this would have happened. The Plantation would still be in business, the second batch of slaves would be in Africa, and Greene would be enjoying a hot bowl of jambalaya in one of his favorite restaurants.

"Fuck," he mumbled in disgust. "I can't believe I let this happen."

With a scowl on his face, he trudged from his bedroom,

looking for something to alleviate his boredom. Kotto and all of his servants were already in bed, sleeping peacefully in their air-conditioned rooms, but Greene was still on New Orleans time, unable to rest because of the difference between the two continents.

Limping down the marble staircase, he heard the far-off mumble of an announcer's voice. He followed the sound to Kotto's living room.

"Couldn't sleep?" Holmes asked while glancing up from the game on the plasma TV.

A smile returned to Greene's lips. "It's late afternoon in Louisiana. My body won't be ready for bed for another ten hours."

Holmes nodded in understanding. As a mercenary, he had been forced to work in several different countries, so he knew about the inconveniences of travel. "Don't worry, Levon. Your internal clock will adjust to the sun. You should be fine by the end of the week."

Greene sat on the couch across from Holmes. "What about the other stuff? When will I get used to that?"

"Like what?"

"Food, culture, language, girls . . ."

"Oh." He laughed. "You mean all the stuff that makes life worth living. That will take a little bit longer, but if you're flexible, you'll learn to adapt. Every country has its advantages and disadvantages—if you know where to look."

"I'll believe it when I see it," Greene said while rubbing his knee.

Holmes instinctively glanced at Greene's left leg, staring at the gruesome scars that covered it. "Does your knee still trouble you?"

Greene didn't like talking about it, but he realized Holmes was the only American friend he had left. "The pain comes and goes, but the instability is constant. As I start to get older, my joint will deteriorate even more, meaning I'll have to get knee replacement surgery . . . Something to look forward to in my old age, I guess."

Holmes realized there was nothing he could say, so he decided to change the subject. "Levon, I've been meaning to ask you a question for a while now, and since this is the first time we've ever talked about your knee, I was wondering if I could ask it."

Greene looked at Holmes, studying his face. He knew what Holmes was going to ask even before he asked it. "You want to know about Nathan."

"If you don't mind talking about it."

"No problem. You brought him here for me."

"True, but I don't want to overstep—"

"It's fine. What do you want to know?"

A thousand questions flooded Holmes's mind. "Everything."

Greene smiled as he thought about it. He'd waited nearly three years to get back at Nate Barker, the player who had ended his magnificent football career. Thirty-three months of pain, rehab, and nightmares. One thousand days of planning and plotting his personal revenge.

"I started thinking about Barker as soon as they wheeled me off the field. It was amazing. There I was, in unbelievable pain, listening to the gasps of horror from the crowd as they replayed the incident over and over on the scoreboard, but for some reason, a great calm settled over me. You could actually see it during the TV telecast. One minute I was writhing in agony, the next minute I was serene."

Greene shook his head at the memory. To him, it felt like it had happened yesterday. "The team doctor assumed that I had gone into shock, but I'm telling you I didn't. The truth is I started thinking about Nate Barker. The bastard who did this to me was responsible for getting me through my agony. I'm telling you, one thought, and one thought alone, allowed me to get through my pain. It was the thought of revenge."

"So you knew right away that you wanted to get even?"

"Hell, yeah! He took away my livelihood. He took away my leg. You're damn right I wanted to get even. And do you know what? I've never regretted it. From the moment we seized him to the moment I locked him in the cage downstairs, I've never looked back. In fact, I view his kidnapping as the crowning achievement of my life."

A bittersweet smile appeared on Greene's lips.

"Nate Barker ruined my life. Now I'm getting a chance to ruin his."

THE loud ringing startled Kotto, causing him to flinch under his purple comforter. Nightmares had gotten the best of him lately, so he'd been sleeping in a state of uneasiness.

The damn phone just about killed him.

After turning on a nearby light, he realized what was happening and grabbed the cell phone off his nightstand. Few people had his number, so he knew that the call had to be important.

"Kotto," he mumbled, slightly out of breath.

"Hannibal?" Edwin Drake shrieked. "Thank God you're alive! When I heard the news, I thought perhaps they had gotten you, too."

"What in the hell are you talking about? Do you know what time it is?"

"Time! I can't believe you're worried about time! There are so many other things that we need to be concerned with."

Kotto glanced at his clock. It was after midnight. He would much rather be sleeping. "Have you been drinking, Edwin? You're not making any sense."

"Sense? *I'm* not making sense? You're the chap who isn't making sense—especially since the incident happened in Ibadan!"

The fog of sleep lifted quickly. There was only one thing in Ibadan that Drake would be concerned with, and the thought of an incident sent shivers down Kotto's spine.

"My God, what has happened?"

"You mean, you haven't heard? It happened at your place, for God's sake!"

"What did? What's wrong?"

"The slaves . . . they're gone!"

The four words hit Kotto like a lightning bolt, nearly stopping his heart in the process.

"Gone?" he croaked as his chest tightened. "How is that possible?"

"Don't ask me! I sent one of my men to inspect the snow, and when he got there, there was no snow! They were gone!"

"But that's not possible! If the slaves had escaped, I would've been told. My guards would've called me! These were my best men. They would've called me immediately."

Drake remained silent as he thought about the ramifications. "If those were your best men, then we are in trouble. Very grave trouble."

"Why?"

"Because your guards are dead."

Lightning bolt number two hit, causing pain in his chest and left arm.

"Dead? My men are dead?"

Drake nodded gravely. "Quite."

"And you're sure of this?"

"Of course I'm sure! I wouldn't be so panicked if I wasn't sure!" Drake tried taking a breath, but his chest was tight as well.

"I'm sorry to doubt you, but it just seems so unlikely . . . What should we do?"

"That is why I'm calling. We need to figure out some kind of plan. I am on my plane, and I'll be arriving there shortly. I was going to check the plant myself, but since you're still alive, I shall tell my pilot to land in Lagos instead of Ibadan. It will be easier to talk if we're face-to-face."

"I'll have my car and several guards meet you at the airport."

"I appreciate the gesture," Drake said, "but I doubt it will be necessary. Who in their right mind would plan a second attack so quickly after their first?"

* * *

JONES smirked as he continued to monitor Kotto's conversation from a nearby car. "These guys don't know us very well, do they?"

"No," Payne growled. "We'll have to make sure we introduce ourselves."

CHAPTER 60

EDWIN Drake opened the front door to Kotto's home without knocking. He had no time to be polite at this hour of the evening. All of his hard work was crumbling, and he was determined to save it before irreparable damage had occurred.

"Hannibal," he called, "where are you?"

The Nigerian rushed from the living room, where he'd been briefing Holmes and Greene on the slaves, and met Drake in the front parlor.

"Edwin," he said as he shook the man's hand. "I'm so sorry that this is necessary. I truly am. Obviously, I'm just as shocked about the incident as you are."

"I somehow doubt that," he replied coolly. "It seems that you have been keeping secrets."

The comment caught Kotto off guard. "Secrets? I have no secrets from you."

"No? I find that hard to believe, with the information I've just acquired. Who is Jonathon Payne, and why have you been keeping him from me?"

Octavian Holmes heard the name as he emerged from

the other room and decided to answer for Kotto. "Payne's our biggest problem. Now, before I respond to your other question, I've got an even better one for you. Who the fuck are you?"

Drake was ready to spout a nasty comeback until he saw Holmes's size. When he saw an even larger figure behind Holmes, he decided it would be best to play nice. "I'm Edwin Drake, Hannibal's financial partner. And you are?"

"Octavian Holmes, Hannibal's main supplier of slaves." He glanced over his shoulder and pointed to his large shadow. "This here is Levon Greene. He's *my* financial partner."

"Ah, the American footballer. I've heard about you." Drake studied the two men and realized he wanted to stay on their good sides. "It's certainly a pleasure to meet our U.S. connection. I'm glad to see that Hannibal wasn't exaggerating when he told me that our snow was in some rather capable hands. Now that I see you two, I realize he was right."

Kotto remained silent for a brief moment, waiting to see if Holmes responded to the obvious attempt at flattery. When he didn't, Kotto decided to ease the tension. "Edwin has flown in from South Africa in order to discuss the Ibadan incident."

"And to see how you're doing," Drake added. "I know that you've lost a lot of men. You must be in shock."

Kotto was more stunned by Drake's quick change in tone than by the incident itself. It had gone from accusatory to sympathetic in a matter of seconds. "I was shocked at first, but now that I've had some time to think about it, I'm fine. Saddened, but fine."

"Good," Drake stated. "I'm glad to—"

"Enough with the small talk," Holmes ordered. "You said something about Hannibal keeping secrets from you. What did you mean by that?"

Drake's complexion got whiter than normal. He wasn't used to being bossed around. "As I was saying, I just received some information from the States, and it seems you failed to let me know everything about the Plantation. You told me that there was some trouble, but you never told me that it was blown up."

All eyes shifted to Kotto, who squirmed under the sudden spotlight. "I wasn't keeping it from you, Edwin. I was just waiting for the appropriate moment to tell you. I didn't want to tell you on the phone. We've already discussed the danger of that. Besides, I wanted to design a backup plan and have it in place before I broke the news to you. I figured it would ease the shock of it all."

"Actually, it did quite the opposite. Instead of having time to make preparations, I am now forced to deal with everything at once. The Plantation, the missing slaves, the murdered guards! That is a bloody lot to recover from."

"I see that now. But obviously I couldn't have foreseen the incident at Ibadan. There was no way of knowing that they would find us so quickly."

Drake winced at the statement. "What do you mean by *they*? Who are *they*?"

"They," Holmes answered, "would be Jonathon Payne and David Jones. They single-handedly wiped out the Plantation. Once I heard the details of Ibadan, I assumed that they were behind that as well."

"I really doubt that," Drake uttered. "Maybe they were behind things at the Plantation—you were there, so you would know—but I don't see how they could've handled the Ibadan massacre. There was a variety of shell casings found, not just from one weapon but from several. And unless these are the type of men that would tote five weapons apiece, they couldn't have done it alone. They needed plenty of help to pull that off."

"Damn," Holmes mumbled under his breath. "I hope . . ."

"What?" Kotto demanded. "What do you hope?"

Holmes glanced at Kotto, then at Greene, and both of them were surprised by the look in his eyes. The air of confidence that used to ooze from Holmes was gone. No longer did he carry himself like he was invincible. In fact, his face seemed to suggest fear.

"I hope I'm wrong about this, but this sounds like the MANIACs."

THE semitropical landscape gave the soldiers many hiding places as they made their way across Kotto's yard. They had already eliminated a few of his guards and several of his security cameras; now they were going for his power supply. Once the electricity was cut, they would storm the house under a cloak of darkness.

"What can you see?" Payne asked Sanchez through his headset.

The captain of the MANIACs was in the midst of an infrared scan of the house, trying to determine the current number of occupants. When he was through, he lowered the high-tech device and spoke into his radio.

"I can't see anyone, sir. It's like the place is empty."

"No one?"

"That's affirmative, sir."

Payne and Jones winced, trying to figure out where everyone was. The house had been under surveillance for the last several hours, so they knew there should be people. A lot of people.

Jones whispered, "If you can't see anyone upstairs, scan the basement. Maybe there's someone down there."

"I'll try, but the moat around the house might interfere. It doesn't see well through water."

Payne crept closer to the house, trying to stay as low as possible. There was no sense risking his life before they knew if Ariane was inside. "Try closer to the drawbridge. The water might be shallower there."

"You got it."

Payne and Jones waited patiently while Sanchez attempted to get a better reading. After more than a minute of scanning, he gave them the bad news.

"He's got something in the basement, but I can't get a readout on this thing. It might be a vault or a bomb shelter of some kind, but whatever it is, it's too thick for me to see through."

"Keep us posted if anything changes."

"I will."

After switching channels on his radio, Payne tried to get an update from Shell, who was in charge of knocking out Kotto's power lines with a small explosion. He remained silent until the device was set and he had repositioned himself in the nearby trees.

Once there, Shell turned his radio to an all-inclusive frequency and spoke to the entire squad, using the tone and mannerisms of a commercial airline pilot.

"Ladies and gentlemen, this is your lieutenant speaking. In exactly thirty seconds, we will be experiencing some violent turbulence, so I would advise you to prepare your night vision and put your firearms into their locked and loaded positions." Shell smiled to himself before finishing. "And as always, thank you for choosing the MANIACs."

Twenty . . . fifteen . . . ten . . . five . . . BOOM!

The earth shook as the explosion ripped through the power station, tearing the generator to shreds in one blinding burst of heat and light. Payne and Jones were tempted to glance at the display of sparks but realized it would ruin their night vision for the next several minutes. So they waited patiently, until the shower of orange light subsided and Kotto's entire estate fell under the blanket of darkness.

When the moment felt right, Payne pushed the button on his transmitter and growled into the microphone. "Gentlemen, don't let me down."

With phenomenal quickness and stealth, the soldiers converged on the stone mansion and crawled across the structure's moat in groups of two and three, using wooden boards that they carried with them. Windows, doors, and skylights were points of entry, and the MANIACs breached them effortlessly in a series of textbook military maneuvers.

"So far, so good," Payne muttered as he watched the

assault from Kotto's yard. "I'd like to be inside, though, where all the action is."

Jones nodded his head in agreement. "Yeah, but there's no way you could've climbed over the moat with that arm of yours. And you know it."

"Actually, I *don't* know it. I think if I was given the chance, I could've—"

Jones squeezed his friend's injured biceps in order to prove his point.

"Jesus!" he grunted in agony. "You didn't have to do that!"

But Payne was thankful that Jones had, because it reminded him that he'd made the correct decision by sitting this one out. If he hadn't, he would've slowed down the team, and that was something he wasn't willing to risk. At this point the only thing that mattered to Payne was Ariane, and everything else—his soldierly pride, his lust for action, and his desire for revenge—paled in comparison.

"I hope you realize there's no reason to feel guilty. We've accomplished more in the last week than anyone, including myself, could've ever imagined."

Payne didn't respond, choosing to keep his attention on the mission instead.

"Plus, you set a good example for the squad by letting them take over. A man has to know his limits, and when he reaches them, he shouldn't be ashamed to ask for help."

"I know that. In fact, I might ask for some more help right now."

"Really?" The comment surprised Jones. "Why's that?"

Payne took a moment to adjust his night vision, then calmly pointed over Jones's left shoulder. "If I'm not mistaken, I think our targets might've found a way out of the house."

Jones turned in the direction of Payne's finger and had a hard time believing what he saw. Levon Greene was standing outside Kotto's iron fence, helping Octavian Holmes climb out of a well-concealed passageway—a tunnel that wasn't mentioned on the blueprints Jones had downloaded from a local database.

"Get on the comm," Payne said, "and tell Sanchez to send half the team out to secure the periphery. Have the others continue their sweep for the slaves, but warn them about the tunnel. I don't want Greene doubling back inside if we can help it."

Jones nodded as he reached for the radio. "And while I do this, what are you going to do?"

Payne smiled as he grabbed his Glock. "I'm going to play hero."

CHAPTER 61

USING the darkness as his ally, Payne moved quietly toward the mouth of the tunnel, hoping to eliminate Holmes and Greene before they even knew what hit them. But as he approached the tall iron fence that surrounded the estate, he soon realized that there was more going on than a simple escape. Instead of slipping away from the house unnoticed, Holmes and Greene were trying to smuggle several slaves out of Kotto's house as well.

"D.J.," Payne whispered into his headset. "What's your position? I need your input up here."

A few seconds later Jones slipped into the bushes next to him. "You rang?"

"Take a look at them. Does this make any sense to you?"

Jones watched closely as the duo pulled two cloaked slaves from the tunnel and shoved them forcibly to the ground. Then, when Greene was satisfied with their positioning, he went back to the tunnel while Holmes hovered over the first pair with a handgun.

"No sense at all," Jones answered. "They must have something up their sleeves, otherwise they'd be heading for the hills by now."

"That's what I figured, but what?"

Jones shrugged. "I don't know, but it has to be something creative. They aren't going to hold us off all by themselves."

"Something creative, huh? See, that's what I can't figure out. What the hell could these guys come up with on such short notice? I mean, it's not like they have a lot of experience with . . ."

Experience. The word sent shivers down Payne's spine, for he suddenly remembered what Holmes and Greene were experienced with. Of course! It made perfect sense. The reason they weren't leaving was because they *needed* to stay nearby in order to complete their plans—just like when they blew up the Plantation.

Without delay, Payne hit the button on his radio and spoke directly to Sanchez. "Juan, get out of the house! Do you read me? Clear the area, now!"

"But, sir, we haven't completed our objective. Do you understand? We haven't—"

"Screw your objective, Juan! The house is hot. Get out at once!"

A few seconds passed before Sanchez replied. "But, sir, Ariane might still be in here."

The notion hit Payne like a sucker punch. God, how could he have forgotten about her? How was that possible?

It took him a moment to shake off the guilt—for forgetting Ariane in her time of need *and* for the command that he was about to issue—but once he thought things through, he realized he couldn't allow his personal feelings to interfere with his duties as squad leader. No matter how much he loved Ariane and how willing he was to give up his life for hers, he knew he didn't have a choice. This wasn't *Saving Private Ryan*. He couldn't risk the lives of several men to save one person. That just wasn't acceptable, especially since they were here as a personal favor.

After taking a deep breath to clear his mind, Payne turned his radio back on and said the most painful thing he'd ever had to say. "What is it about my order that you don't understand? Get out of the house now!"

* * *

LEVON Greene helped Hannibal Kotto to his feet before giving Edwin Drake a much-needed hand. Neither of the businessmen was thrilled with sneaking to freedom through the escape tunnel that started in the mansion's basement, but once they were assured that it was the only way to get away from the MANIACs, Kotto and Drake relented.

"What now?" asked Drake as he dusted off his white cloak. "Do we make a run for it?"

Greene chuckled at the thought. "A run for it? Do you actually think we can outrun an entire platoon of soldiers? Fuck that! There will be no running from anything."

Kotto heard the comment and moved forward. "Then how are we going to escape? Is someone coming to meet us?"

"No," Greene assured him, "there's no one coming to meet us. Octavian and I are going to take care of the MANIACs all by ourselves."

"You're what?" Kotto turned toward Holmes, looking for answers. "How are you going to do that?"

Greene answered cryptically. "Well, *we're* not going to do anything. Your house is."

"My house is? What kind of rubbish is that?"

Greene smiled as he reached into his pocket and pulled out a small detonator. "Not rubbish, *rubble*—because that's what your house is gonna be in a couple of seconds. With a touch of this button, your house and our problems are going bye-bye."

PAYNE was relieved when the first wave of MANIACs made it across the moat, but they weren't the men that he was truly worried about. That group was team two, the soldiers who were looking for the secret tunnel. Since they were ordered deep within the bowels of the basement, Payne knew it would take them much longer to evacuate.

He just hoped it wouldn't take too long.

"All out," declared Shell, who was the leader of the first

team. "Should we secure the periphery as ordered, or lag here to assist the others?"

"Your orders still hold." Payne wanted everyone as far away from the house as quickly as possible. "Be advised that six people have been spotted outside the fence. Repeat, six outside the fence. And some of them could be friendly."

"Half dozen on the run: some cowboys, some Indians." Shell waved his men forward before continuing his transmission. "Don't worry, sir. We won't let you down."

Payne nodded as he turned toward Jones. "What can you see?"

He answered while peering through his night-vision goggles. "The two people on the ground seem to be slaves. Greene just kicked the one on the right."

"Can you make out their faces?"

Jones shook his head. "Their cloaks prevent it. But if I were a betting man, I'd say the one getting kicked is a man. He's way too big to be a female."

Payne cursed softly. That meant the odds of Ariane being inside the house just increased. "And what about the other?"

"No idea. It could be Ariane, but I really don't know."

"Keep me posted," he said, rising to his feet. "I'm going forward to help Sanchez's crew."

"You're what?"

"I'm going to give them a hand. I'd lend them two if I could, but all I've got is one."

Before Jones could argue, Payne sprinted full speed toward the moat. He wasn't sure what he'd be able to do once he got there, but there was no way in hell he was going to sit passively while some of his men were still in danger. His men were his responsibility, and he was going to do everything he could to guarantee their safety—even if it meant risking his own life.

Once Payne reached the edge of the moat, he cast his eyes downward and studied the fifteen-by-twelve-foot trench that extended for several hundred feet around the base of the entire mansion. The walls of the pit were made of seamless concrete and had been laid with a steep slope to impede the climb of possible intruders. To discourage unwanted visits even further, Kotto had filled the bottom of the chasm with a freshwater stream and a family of Nile crocodiles that hissed and snapped like a pack of hungry guard dogs anytime humans approached.

"Knock it off," Payne growled, "or I'll make shoes out of your ass."

Captain Sanchez heard the comment as he emerged from the house. "I hope you weren't talking to me."

Payne instinctively raised his weapon but relaxed when he realized who it was. "Sorry to disappoint you, Juan, but I don't want to do *anything* with your ass."

Sanchez smiled as he traversed the narrow plank with the ease of a tightrope walker. He'd risked his life way too many times to be worried about heights or a bunch of hungry reptiles. After reaching Payne's side, he said, "I don't want to sound disrespectful, but what are you doing here? You should be back by the fence, where it's safe."

"And let you play with the crocs by yourself? Not a chance. Besides, you know how I am on missions. I'd rather do jumping jacks in a minefield than sit around, waiting."

"But, sir, aren't you just waiting up here, too?"

Payne was tempted to lecture him on the basic concept of leadership—never put anyone in a situation that you're not willing to be in yourself—but before he could, a second MANIAC exited the house.

The soldier immediately said, "Four more behind me, but I don't know where."

Payne nodded as he got on his radio to find out. "Team two status check, team two status check. What's your twenty?"

"I'm coming out now," answered the first, and a moment later he stepped outside.

"Making my way up the stairs," replied another. "About fifteen seconds 'til daylight."

Payne waited until the second soldier arrived before he went back to the radio. "Team two status check . . . What are your positions?"

Unfortunately, the remaining members of team two didn't reply.

Confused by their silence, Payne asked Chen, the soldier who had just emerged from the house, if he knew anything about their whereabouts.

"It's tough to say, sir. That basement is a labyrinth of empty jail cells and twisting corridors. There's no telling where they are or if they can even hear you. The walls are pretty thick."

"Damn!" Payne growled. He knew if he didn't get his men out of the house immediately, they were going to die. It was as simple as that. Out of sheer desperation, Payne used their real names over the airwaves. "Kokoska? Haney? Do you read me? Squawk if you can hear me."

But the only noise that followed was the foreboding sound of silence.

CHAPTER 62

THE sound of Payne's radio disrupted the quiet of the Nigerian night, but the message didn't come from the missing MANIACs. It came from Jones, and his words were ominous.

"The Posse's taking cover. Prepare for detonation."

Without delay, Payne ordered his men from the area while he dropped to his knees to secure the wooden plank with his good arm. After locking it in place, he yelled to Chen, the soldier on the other side of the moat. "Run for it!"

The young MANIAC did as he was told and started across the temporary bridge. Unfortunately, as he neared the halfway point, the first explosion erupted and its shock wave knocked him forward with the force of a hurricane. He instinctively tried to regain his balance using his arms as counterweights, but the jolt was way too powerful to overcome.

As Chen started to fall, Payne was tempted to lunge for him but knew it wouldn't do either of them any good. Even if he'd managed to latch on, there was no way he would be able to maintain his own balance. So, instead of doing something impossible, Payne used his energy to yank the board off the far side of the moat while holding on to his end the best that he could. Agony gripped its claws into his injured biceps as the plank slammed into the water below, but he didn't have time to suffer. If he didn't get to the bottom of the chasm immediately, Chen was going to be the only human in a battle royal, and he wasn't about to let that happen.

Grabbing his Glock, Payne sat on the smooth plank, which rested at a forty-five-degree angle, and started his descent on the kiddie slide from hell. He'd gotten a third of the way down the slope when he spotted Chen, who was injured and struggling to get out of the shallow water by the far bank, and the twelve-foot crocodile that was chasing him.

With the confidence of a big-game hunter, Payne aimed his weapon at the croc's head and fired. The bullet struck his target directly below its eye, causing the reptile to roar in anguish and thrash its tail like a flag in a violent storm, but that wasn't good enough for Payne. He realized that wounded animals were often the most dangerous, so the instant his feet touched liquid he finished the job by depositing two more rounds into the angry beast.

"Holy shit!" Chen gasped from the nearby shore. "That was unbelievable."

"Not really. I practice that move in my swimming pool all the time."

"Seriously, that was awesome!"

But Payne shrugged off the praise. After all, Chen was there to do him a favor. "Are you hurt? Can you make it back up the plank?"

"Doubtful, sir. I messed up my knee pretty bad when I landed."

Payne nodded as he scouted the waist-deep water for more crocs. Thankfully, the others huddled lazily on the opposite shore. "But you'll live, won't you? I mean, I shouldn't just leave you here as an entrée, right?"

Chen smiled through his pain. "No, sir. I don't think I'd like that very much."

"Good, then let's figure a way to get you out of—"

Before he could finish, a second explosion ripped through the house, one that lit the surrounding sky with a massive ball of flame and hurled chunks of wood and metal high into the air. To escape the falling debris, Payne shoved Chen under the lip of the concrete ledge and sheltered him with his own body while waiting for things to calm down.

JONES covered his head as another blast shook the earth but refused to take his eyes off the enemy. They had settled behind a rock formation near the escape tunnel, and he figured they'd stay there as long as there were more charges to detonate. At least he hoped that was the case, because while they sat on their asses watching the fireworks, his team was moving in to finish them off.

A static-filled message trickled over Jones's radio, but he was unable to make out the voice.

"You're breaking up," Jones shouted into his mouthpiece. "Repeat."

There was a slight delay. "This . . . Payne. Can . . . me?"

"Jon?" He cupped his hand over his earpiece so he could hear better. "Is that you?"

"Of course . . . me! I can't . . . you've already forgotten . . . fucking voice!"

Jones was thrilled that Payne was bitching at him. That was his way of saying that he was fine. "Where are you, man? I was told you got caught up in the pyrotechnics."

"I did. Thankfully, Chen and . . . were . . . the moat during . . . big blast. The concrete shielded . . . getting hurt."

Jones did his best to make out the words, but the tumult and the static made it difficult. "Are you hurt? Do you need me to get you out?"

". . . banged up, but I'm . . ." Dead air filled the line for a few seconds before Payne's voice could be heard again. ". . . word on Ariane?"

"We're still not sure where she is. Shell called in and claimed he could see a female with the Posse, but that report is unconfirmed. Repeat, that is unconfirmed."

". . . about . . . oska . . . Haney?"

"No word from Kokoska or Haney. But we aren't giving up hope. Those two have been through worse."

Several more seconds passed before Jones could hear him again, and when he could, Payne was in the middle of a long message. ". . . is a hole up . . . it might be . . . way into . . . I'm going to . . . Chen . . . it out."

"Jon," he shouted, "you're breaking up. I can't understand you. Please repeat."

". . . hole . . . moat . . . a way into the . . ."

Unfortunately, nothing but static came across the line.

PAYNE wasn't sure if his message had gotten through, but he realized he couldn't waste any more time on the radio trying to find out. He and Chen were currently sitting ducks, and he knew if they stayed put, it was just a matter of time before something—an explosion, a crocodile, or an enemy soldier—took them out.

"I know you're banged up, but how does a long walk sound to you?"

Chen looked at Payne in the flickering firelight and grimaced. "You tell me, sir. How does a long walk sound?"

"It's just what the doctor ordered." Payne slipped his good arm around Chen's waist and helped him to his feet. "Don't get any wrong ideas. This isn't going to be a romantic stroll. That last blast opened a fissure in the wall, and I'm hoping it'll lead somewhere safe."

The duo trudged through the waist-deep stream for several yards while keeping a constant eye out for crocs. Luckily, the giant reptiles were just as uninterested in a skirmish as the MANIACs were, and they did their best to stay far out of the humans' way.

"Okay," Payne said once they had arrived at the crevice. "Let me check things out before we get you in there. Will you be all right for a few minutes on your own?"

Chen nodded as he slumped to the ground, exhausted.

"Just holler if something starts to eat you."

"Don't worry, I think that's probably the natural reaction."

Payne grinned as he checked his weapon then leaned inside the cavelike opening, which extended from water level to nearly three feet above his head. The darkness of the interior prevented him from seeing much, so he was forced to use one of the chemical torches that he carried in his belt. After breaking the cylinder's inner seal, he gave the liquids a quick shake, and the phosphorescent mixture filled the man-made grotto with enough light to read a newspaper.

"I'll be right back," he told Chen. "Don't go anywhere."

By using the green glow of the high-tech lantern, Payne was able to figure out what he had stumbled upon. It was the tunnel that the Posse had used for their escape. The cylindrical shaft started somewhere to his right, deep within the bowels of Kotto's basement, and continued to his left, ending somewhere outside the fence on the western flank of the estate. Or at least it used to. Due to all the recent explosions, Payne had no idea if the route was still passable. He hoped it was, since he and Chen were looking for a way out of the moat, but he realized he wouldn't know for sure until he explored the mysteries that lay farther ahead.

CHAPTER 63

HOLMES and Greene laughed with childlike enthusiasm as the first few explosions tore through the house. In their minds every blast meant a few less soldiers that they'd have to deal with, and if the second part of their plan was going to be successful, they had to keep the number of MANIACs to an absolute minimum.

"Are you sure this is going to work?" Drake wondered from his position on the ground. "If these troops are as skilled as you claim, will they really be fooled by something so simple?"

The comment knocked the smile off Holmes's face. He had known Edwin Drake for less than a few hours but had learned to despise the man. "I'll tell you what, Eddie. If you don't want to participate in phase two of my plan, you can take off your cloak and start walking. It won't make a damn bit a difference to me."

"I didn't mean to offend you," he insisted. "But—"

"But what? You call my plan *foolish*, then claim you didn't mean to offend me? Fuck that, and fuck you! If you keep it up, I'll put a bullet in your ass myself."

The smile on Greene's face got even wider because he

disliked Drake as well. "So what's it gonna be? Are you in or out? We gotta know now."

Drake glanced at Kotto for some moral support, but none was forthcoming. Kotto had just watched his house detonated for the sake of the plan, so he wasn't about to give up on Holmes and Greene's idea anytime soon.

"Fine," Drake relented. "What would you like me to do?"

"Just lie there quietly until Levon and I change our clothes," Holmes ordered. "When it's time to do something else, we'll let you know."

AFTER helping Chen inside the tunnel, Payne headed west in hopes of finding the exit but found something more exciting.

Payne traveled less than twenty yards down the concrete shaft when he noticed the artificial light of his lantern start to burn brighter than it had just seconds before. At first he figured the chemical compound in his torch was simply heating up, but after a few more steps, he realized that the added radiance wasn't coming from him. The extra burst of light was shining from somewhere up ahead.

Concerned by the possibilities, Payne hid his light in his pocket and inched silently toward the source of the phantom glow. With weapon in hand, he crept along the smooth edge of the wall until he came to a strange bend in the tunnel. For some reason the passageway turned sharply to the left, then seemed to snake back to the right almost instantly—perhaps to avoid a geological pitfall of some kind. Whatever the reason for the design, Payne concluded that the epicenter of the light was somewhere in that curve.

Pausing to collect his thoughts, Payne reached into the leather sheath that hung at his side and pulled out a nine-inch hunting knife that had once belonged to his grandfather. Even though it was nearly fifty years old, the single-edged bowie knife was sharp enough to cut through metal and sturdy enough to be used in hand-to-hand combat. In this case, though, it possessed a less obvious attribute that he hoped to take advantage of: a mirrorlike finish.

By extending the weapon forward, Payne hoped to see what was lurking around the corner without exposing himself to gunfire. Sure, he knew he wouldn't be able to see much in a simple reflection, but if he was able to get a small glimpse of what was waiting for him, he'd be better prepared to face it.

"Show me something good," he whispered to the knife.

And surprisingly, it did.

Payne couldn't tell how many people were gathered up ahead—they were huddled too close together for him to get an accurate count—but he had a feeling he knew who they were. They were escaped slaves, part of the *original* Plantation shipment that had been sent to Nigeria several weeks before Ariane had even been abducted. People who—

Wait a second, he thought. If these were actually escaped slaves, what were they doing *sitting* in this tunnel? If they'd somehow gotten free from Kotto's house, why weren't they running down this passageway toward the outside world? Common sense told him that was what they should be doing. And what was keeping them so damn quiet? Were they afraid to speak, or was there an outside factor that was keeping them silent? Something, perhaps, like an armed guard? That would explain a lot, he reasoned. Plus, it would clarify the presence of their light. Payne figured if the slaves were hiding, then they wouldn't be dumb enough to use a lantern. That would be an obvious giveaway in this deadly game of hide-and-seek.

No, the slaves' silence, coupled with their ill-advised use of a light, suggested only one thing: Someone was trying to get these people noticed.

Thankfully, Payne was way too intelligent to fall for the ploy—especially since he'd taught the maneuver to many of his men during their initial training. And since he had taught the tactic, he knew exactly how to beat it.

"Yoo-hoo!" he called loudly. "Come out, come out, wherever you are!"

Several seconds passed before Payne heard the reply he was expecting.

"Captain Payne?" shouted Haney, one of the missing MANIACs. "Is that you?"

"It sure is, princess. I've come to rescue you from the evil dungeon. Are you alone?"

"No, Kokoska's with me, but he's unconscious. He took a bump on his head during the first blast. He's been fading in and out ever since."

Despite the conversation, Payne moved forward cautiously, just in case he was overlooking a foot snare or something more diabolical. "And the prisoners? Where'd you find them?"

"In a basement cage. Can you believe that shit? They'd be buried under tons of rubble right now if we hadn't gotten to them. The assholes were just planning on leaving them in there with tiny bombs strapped to their legs."

"Tiny bombs?" he asked. "Were they silver?"

"Yeah!" Haney showed his face and held up one of the devices to prove his point. "How'd you know their color, sir?"

Payne grabbed the explosive with disgust. "They used the same thing on the Plantation."

After taking a few seconds to examine the mechanism, Payne smiled at the hostages, trying to reassure them that their lives were about to return to normalcy. None of them smiled back, which wasn't surprising. As a group, they'd been through so much in such a short amount of time that Payne knew it would take more than a smile for any of them to start trusting the world again. He realized it would take love and friendship and a shitload of therapy to get them back on track, but he hoped that they'd be able to get over this eventually.

"Sir?" Haney blurted. "What's the status topside? Did everyone make it out okay?"

Payne shook his head. "Chen's resting in the tunnel behind me. He took a nasty fall into the moat, but he'll live."

"What about Ariane? Did she get out all right?"

Payne took a deep breath. "Unfortunately, that still remains to be seen."

"Sir?" he asked, slightly confused.

"Don't get me wrong. I'm confident she made it out before the blast. But my guess is there are still some loose ends that need to be taken care of before she'll be completely free." Payne paused in thought. "Thankfully, loose ends are my specialty."

JONES tried to reestablish contact with Payne but met with little success. With no more time to waste, Jones decided to change his priorities and forge ahead without him.

"Team one," Jones uttered into his headset, "what's your status?"

Shell answered. "We've got the Indians surrounded. We can move on your word."

"What's the risk to the cowboys?"

"Higher than it was a moment ago."

The comment bothered Jones, who had lost visuals on Holmes and Greene a few minutes before. "Please explain."

"Everyone's dressed the same. Long white cloaks with hoods that cover their faces."

"Give me the numbers, Lieutenant. How risky are the odds?"

"I wouldn't bet my dog on 'em, sir." Shell paused to speak to one of his men before he continued his transmission. "By our count we're looking at three black and three white, and one of the whites is definitely a woman. And two of the blacks are supersized."

"The big ones are probably Holmes and Greene. They're the ones we want the most."

"Maybe so, but there's a problem. Their size doesn't stand out anymore."

"Why not?"

"The six have gathered in a tight cluster, so it's tough to tell where one person ends and the next begins."

"In a cluster? How badly do they blend?"

"They look like a giant marshmallow, sir."

Jones cursed before he spoke again. "What are you telling me? No go on the snipers?"

"That's affirmative, sir—unless you can put out the fire. It's messing up our ability to see."

"How so, Lieutenant? It didn't bother my sightline."

"That's because it's at your back, sir. The frontal glare prevents our night vision from working properly. Without 'em, our snipers don't have enough light to shoot."

Jones couldn't believe what he was hearing. Each man was equipped with enough optical equipment to see a lightning bug fart from a half mile away, but they couldn't see a 275-pound man in the light of a raging inferno. "Let me get this straight: You're telling me it's too bright and too dark for you at the *exact same time*?"

Shell grinned at the paradox. "Ain't it a fucked-up world we live in?"

WHEN Payne reached the end of the passageway, he gazed through the thick wall of vines that had obscured the tunnel's presence from the outside world and studied the scene before him. The six people who had escaped through the corridor were now dressed identically and standing in a compact huddle—their arms around each other's shoulders and their heads tilted forward in order to obscure each other's height.

"Damn!" he growled. Even from point-blank range, there was no way he could risk a shot.

"D.J.," he whispered into his radio, "where are we positioned?"

Jones smiled at the sound of Payne's voice. He knew his best friend would pop up eventually. It was just a matter of when. "We're in a semicircle with a radius of twenty yards. We'd surround them completely, but the fence cuts off their route to the east, so there's no need."

"Have they attempted to make contact?"

"No, which is kind of puzzling. They obviously know

we're out here, but they haven't come forward with any demands."

"That is kind of strange," Payne admitted. "Almost as strange as their formation. I've never seen anything like it before."

"Me, neither . . . Out of curiosity, where are you right now?"

"Me? I'm about ten feet to their rear, watching them from the door to the escape tunnel."

"Did you say you're *in* the tunnel?" Jones shook his head in amazement, stunned at Payne's ability to turn up in the damnedest of places. "How did you pull that off?"

"Long story. Oh, and just for the record, I stumbled upon our missing brethren. They're a little banged up but very much alive."

"Thank God! I was worried about them. Any need for emergency evac?"

"Nah, they'll be fine until this crisis is over. By the way, how are you planning on ending it?"

Jones laughed at Payne's choice of words. Both of them knew who was going to put an end to things, and it certainly wasn't going to be Jones. "Thankfully, that's not my decision, Jon. Now that you're back as team leader, I can sit back, relax, and watch you work your magic."

"It's funny you should mention magic, because that's exactly what I had in mind. With a little help from you, I think we can make the Posse disappear."

CHAPTER 64

JONES waited for Payne's go-ahead before he walked toward the enemy. Jones continued forward while doing nothing to conceal himself. In fact, he so desperately wanted to be seen by Holmes and Greene that he fired his weapon into the air just to get their attention.

"You know," he exclaimed, "you guys are pretty damn bad at taking hostages. For this tactic to work, you're *supposed* to issue a crazy list of demands. I've been waiting for several minutes now, and I haven't heard a peep."

Greene's bass-filled voice emerged from the center of the huddle. "That's because we've been waiting for you. Now that you're here, I guess we can start this shit."

"Oh, goody!" Jones mocked. "But before we begin, I think it's only fair if I introduced the rest of my negotiating team. Fellas, why don't you come out and say hello?"

Like ghosts emerging from a sea of fog, the MANIACs simply materialized out of nothingness. One second they weren't visible to the naked eye, and the next they were standing with weapons raised, like Spartans waiting for an approaching horde.

"As you can see," Jones continued, "we outnumber you by a large margin."

"What, is that supposed to scare us?" Holmes screamed, his head bobbing ever so slightly as he did. "You might outnumber us, but there's no way you can shoot us without endangering the hostages. And trust me, if you guys come any closer, I'll kill one of them myself."

Jones smiled at the threat while taking another step forward. "I don't believe that for a second. Why? Because if you hurt anyone, you'll be killed. I know it, and you know it. Hell, everyone here knows it. So why even bother to threaten us? It's just so clichéd."

"Maybe so, but it's the truth! I wonder how Payne would feel if I sliced up that tasty bitch of his? How do you think he'd like that?"

"That's a good question. Why don't you ask him yourself?"

"I would, if he showed his face. Where's that pussy hiding?"

Payne answered the question by tapping Holmes on the shoulder. "Right behind you."

Like a well-orchestrated magic trick, Payne had used his assistant to lure everyone's attention forward while the key maneuvering was being done in the background. Of course, now that the deception was over, Payne needed to finish the performance in grand style. He did so by sliding his knife across his enemy's throat with assassinlike perfection. Crimson gushed from Holmes's carotid artery, staining the front of his cloak like a wounded deer in the snow, but that wasn't good enough for Payne. He immediately tossed Holmes over his shoulder and finished him off by falling backward and slamming his elbow into the bridge of his nose. The maneuver drove Holmes's nasal bone into his brain with brutal efficiency.

Death was instantaneous.

With his first rival vanquished, Payne sprang to his feet and searched the huddle in front of him for his next target.

Unfortunately, despite his speed, Payne was still too slow for Greene, who had latched onto Ariane's throat at the first sign of trouble. He was currently shoving a .45-caliber pistol against the side of her head.

"Stay back!" Greene demanded as he dragged her toward the tunnel. "I swear to God, if you come any closer, I'll kill her."

"Calm down!" Payne pleaded. "Don't do anything stupid. Just relax."

But Payne knew that would be tough, because he was having a difficult time doing it himself.

He had been a rock—poised and relaxed—when he crept up on Holmes, but some of his composure disappeared when he got his first real glimpse of Ariane since this ordeal had started.

One look and his heart started racing.

"Are you all right?" Payne asked.

"Been better," she mumbled with her swollen jaw. "And you?"

"Pretty damn good," he lied. "I've been trying to get ahold of you for a while. You're a difficult girl to track down."

"Sorry about that. I've been doing some traveling."

"Traveling?" Payne took a step closer, looking for an opening. "Come on, why don't you just admit it? You'll do anything to get out of an ass-kicking on the golf course."

"Darn, you finally figured me out. All of this has been—"

"Will you shut the fuck up?" Greene yelled. "Your lovesick banter is driving me *crazy*." To prove his point, he tightened his grip on Ariane's neck, nearly cutting off her airway. "This is my time to talk, not yours! Do you got that, Payne? My time!"

"Okay, okay, I'm sorry. Go ahead and talk. I'm listening. I swear."

Greene took a deep breath. "First of all, tell your men to get back. When I get anxious, my muscles start to contract, and if that happens, I'm liable to break her fuckin' neck!"

"Not a problem, Levon. But first you gotta ease up just a little bit. Let her breathe, my man. Just let her breathe."

"I'm serious, Jon. Get them back!"

"I will, I promise, but only if you stop hurting her." Payne took another step forward, trying to get as close to Greene as possible. "Come on, Levon, why don't you just put down your gun and walk away from this? If you do that, I promise we won't kill you."

"Great! So, what are you going to do? Cart me back to the U.S., where I'll be viewed like Michael Vick times a million? Screw that! I get out of this free, or I get slaughtered right here! There's no quit in me! You should know that. I don't quit!"

Another step forward. "It's not quitting, Levon. It's simply doing the smart thing."

"Stay where you are, or I'll kill her! I mean it!"

Payne threw his hands up in acceptance. "I won't move from here, okay? I just want to talk to you. Don't do anything stupid. I just want to discuss things."

"Then tell your men to back off! If all you wanna do is talk, there's no reason to have them so close!" The tension in his voice proved that he was close to losing it. "What difference is it gonna make if they back up? They'll still be close enough to kill me if I make a move, so get them to back up!"

Payne looked at Jones and reluctantly nodded. "Not too far, but ease the grip slightly."

"You heard the captain," Jones told the men. "Give them ten more feet of breathing space. But if Greene even sneezes, take him out with everything you've got."

The men followed their orders, dropping back several steps but never taking their aim off Greene. When they reached their mark, Jones shouted for them to stop.

"Is that better?" Payne asked. "I did like you wanted, as a sign of good faith. I didn't have to, but I did. Now, why don't you do the same for me? Why don't you give me something?"

"Like what? The only thing you want is the girl, and do

you know what? I can see why she means so much to you. I had a chance to check her out in the shower, and let me tell you, she's one tasty piece of ass."

Normally, Payne would've gone after somebody who made a comment like that, but in this case he all but welcomed it. He realized it was an opportunity that he could use to his advantage.

"Jeez," he said to Ariane, "you should consider yourself lucky! You've always wanted to hook up with an NFL player, and he sounds pretty interested. This might be your big chance."

Calmly, as if she wasn't in a life-or-death struggle, Ariane turned her attention to Greene. She wasn't sure why, but she knew that she was supposed to distract him with conversation. "You played in the NFL? Oh, my God, that is so cool! What's your name?"

But before Greene could speak, Payne answered for him. "That's Levon Greene. I told you about him, remember? He's the linebacker I met while playing basketball. You know, the one with the bad left knee."

"You have a bad knee?" she groaned. "How horrible! That's one thing I always hated about sports. The moment a player gets hurt, their opponents take advantage of it."

And then she proved her point.

Slowly, she lifted her left foot until it was directly in front of Greene's knee. Then, she thrust it backward with as much strength as she could, ramming it into his kneecap at a perfect angle. The pain from the blow caused Greene to howl in agony, but more importantly, it caused him to loosen his grip on her neck, which gave her the chance to get away.

The instant she dove to the ground Payne raised his weapon like a quick-draw artist and fired. Jones did the same from farther back, and the two of them filled Greene with enough bullets to take down a polar bear. Shot after shot entered his chest and neck, causing his body to dance to the rhythm of gunfire. It continued to do so until both of them had emptied their entire clips into the man they had once considered a friend.

When the firing stopped, the MANIACs charged forward to deal with Kotto and Drake and the slaves that remained in the tunnel, but Payne wasn't worried about any of them. His only concern was Ariane, and he ran to her side to see if she was all right.

"I'm so happy to see you."

"I love you so much," she insisted, crying tears of joy on Payne's shoulder as they sat on the ground. "I can't believe that you found me." She sobbed for an entire minute, clinging to him like a favorite stuffed animal. "But what took you so long? I thought you were supposed to be like Rambo or something."

Payne laughed loudly, thankful for a girl who was able to keep her sense of humor despite all that she had been through. "Hey, you said you were looking forward to the long weekend, so I figured I should take my time in getting here."

"A long weekend is one thing, Jonathon, but an entire week is quite another."

He smiled, wiping away her tears with the cloth of her cloak. "Look on the bright side. It's already Friday, so by the time we get back to America, it will actually be the weekend again."

Ariane sighed as she pulled him against her chest.

She never wanted to let go of him.

Jones was hesitant to break up the tender moment, but he needed Payne to decide what they were going to do with Kotto and Drake. "If you don't mind," he said, "I'd like to borrow Jon for a minute before you two start shagging on the damn ground."

Ariane glanced at Jones and gave him a warm smile. She knew that he'd risked his life on several occasions during the past week and wanted him to realize how much she appreciated it.

"He's all yours, D.J. There'll be no shaggin' until I get

cleaned up." She stood from the ground and dusted herself off. "Besides, I wanted to check on someone."

Payne raised his eyebrows. "Did you make a friend in prison? How cute!"

She smiled again, despite her sore jaw. "I think his name's Nathan, but that's all I really know. He doesn't talk too much because of all the torture."

"Big guy, lots of scars? He was in the Devil's Box before me. Hakeem said he'd left him in the device for several weeks. Unfortunately, I have no idea who he is, though."

"I do," interjected Sanchez, who'd been listening to their reunion. "I'm from San Diego, so I should know who he is."

All three turned toward him, looking for information.

"His name's Nate Barker, and he plays for the Chargers. According to ESPN, he's been missing for a few months now, simply disappeared from his house one night."

"Are you sure?" Payne asked. It seemed risky for the Posse to kidnap someone who was famous. "Why would they grab a high-profile guy like that?"

Sanchez offered an explanation. "If I remember correctly, he's the player that hurt Levon's knee. Snapped it like a twig up in Buffalo."

Payne glanced at Barker and studied his haggard appearance. He certainly had the height to be a football player, even though it was painfully obvious that he'd lost a lot of weight during the past several weeks. "This was all done for revenge? My God, what a sick bastard Levon turned out to be! I would've never guessed it before all of—"

"Sirs!" Shell shouted urgently. He was on his knees near Greene's body, and the look on his face suggested that something was wrong. "Get over here, sirs!"

Payne, Jones, and Sanchez dashed forward while Ariane chose to stay behind.

"It's Greene," Shell said. "He's still alive. He was wearing a vest under his cloak."

"Are you serious?" Payne sank to the ground next to Shell and looked into Greene's eyes. They were open and, considering his current condition, fairly active. "Levon, can you hear me?"

Greene nodded his head slightly, as blood gushed from the wounds in his neck and shoulders. "You got me, Payne. You got me good."

"I didn't get you, Levon. You got yourself. I can't believe you did all this shit for revenge."

Greene closed his eyes to escape the agony but managed to turn his lips into a large smile. "No regrets," he groaned. "I got no regrets."

Payne was ready to lecture him further when he suddenly sensed a large presence hovering behind him. Looking up, he was surprised to see the battered body of Nate Barker.

"Levon," the lineman croaked. His throat was dry and cracked from severe dehydration.

Greene reopened his eyes and stared into the face of his enemy.

Barker leaned closer, letting Greene see his face. "That play," he said. "That play where you got hurt? I didn't try to hurt you. I swear, I didn't."

But Greene wouldn't accept it. He closed his eyes and shook his head in denial.

It wasn't something that he'd ever believe.

"Honestly," Barker continued. "I've never hurt anyone on purpose in my entire life. I swear to God, I haven't." Then suddenly, without warning, he placed his foot on Greene's left knee and anchored it with his body weight. "That is, until now!"

With all of his remaining strength, Barker grabbed Greene's lower leg and pulled it upward, tugging and yanking on the limb until the weakened joint literally exploded from the excess stress. The loud popping of tendons and cartilage was quickly accented by Greene's screams of pain, which sent shivers down the spines of everyone in the area.

But Barker was far from done. With a devious grin on his face, he lifted his foot off of Greene's knee and slammed it into the middle of Greene's throat. He'd been put through so much over the past several weeks that there was no way he was going to stop. No fucking way.

Not until *his* revenge was complete. Not until *he* felt vindicated for *his* pain.

And no one in the area had any desire to stop him.

EPILOGUE

THE door was closed and the room was dark, but that didn't stop Payne and Jones from entering. They'd broken so many laws in the past few weeks that they weren't about to let visiting hours—or the heavyset nurse at the front desk—stand in their way.

Not with something as important as this to take care of.

"So," Payne growled as he approached the bed, "did you actually think we were going to forget about your role in this?"

The injured man didn't know what to say, so he simply shrugged his shoulders.

"You can't be that stupid!" Jones said. "What, are you a buckwheat or something?"

The comment brought a smile to Bennie Blount's heavily bandaged face. "I haven't known what to think," he whispered. "I haven't seen you guys since my accident."

Payne placed his hand on Blount's elbow and gave it a simple squeeze. "We're sorry about that. We would've been here *much* sooner, but we've been tied up in red tape. Of course, that tends to happen when you sneak into a foreign country and kill a bunch of people."

Jones shook his head in mock disgust. "The Pentagon and all its stupid policies. Please!"

Blount laughed despite the pain it caused in his cheeks.

Payne said, "I hear the swelling around your spinal cord has gone down. How's your movement?"

"Pretty good. I'm still a little wobbly when I walk, but the doctors think I'll be fine."

"That's great news, Bennie! I've been worried sick about you."

"Me, too," added Jones.

"Now my biggest concern is my face. That crazy dog did a lot of damage."

Payne gave Blount's elbow another squeeze. "Well, stop worrying about it. I'm flying in the world's best plastic surgeons to treat you. They'll have you back to your old self in no time."

Jones nodded. "Unless, of course, your old self isn't good enough. They could make you look like Denzel, or Will Smith, *or* give you a nice set of D-cups. Whatever you want."

Payne frowned. "Do you think his frame could support D-cups? I'd say no more than a C."

"Really? I think he'd look good with—"

"Forget the tits." Blount laughed. "My old self would be fine, just fine. But . . ."

"But what?" Payne demanded. "If you're worried about the money, don't be. All of your hospital bills have already been taken care of."

"What?" he asked, stunned. "That's not necessary."

"Of course it is! After all you've sacrificed, I wouldn't have it any other way."

"Listen to him, Bennie. Even with a truckload of insurance, you'd still have tons of out-of-pocket expenses."

"Yeah, but—"

"But, nothing!" Payne insisted. "Furthermore, you'll never see another tuition bill for the rest of your life. As soon as you're feeling up to it, you can head back to school, compliments of the Payne Industries Scholarship Fund. We'll take care of everything—including a monthly stipend for beer and hookers."

Blount shook his head. "Jon, I couldn't. Seriously."

"Hey," Jones added, "that's not all. We have one more surprise for you, something that's more valuable than money."

"Guys, enough with the gifts."

"Hang on," Payne insisted. "You'll really like this one. We saved the best for last."

Then, with his typical flash of showmanship, Payne threw the door aside to reveal the most attractive woman Blount had ever seen.

Dark brown hair. Dark brown eyes. Unbelievable figure. Simply dazzling.

She stood there for several seconds, speechless, unsure of what to do next. Finally, with her composure regained, she grabbed Payne's arm and glided across the room to meet the family member she'd never even known she had.

"Bennie," Payne said with a lump in his throat, "I'd like to introduce you to someone who's very special to me. This is your cousin Ariane."

Author's Note

While conducting my research for this novel, I read hundreds of journal entries that detailed the ungodly horrors that occurred on many nineteenth-century plantations. And *not* just the accounts of ex-slaves. In order to keep my research as balanced as possible, I studied just as many narratives from slave owners as I did from the slaves themselves. And do you know what? I'm glad I did, because it wasn't until I read the firsthand accounts of these brutal men that I started to understand how malicious and sadistic some of them really were.

Sure, it was unsettling to read about the sting of a bullwhip from a slave's point of view, but not nearly as disturbing as the words of one overseer who described the process of whipping his workers in near-orgasmic terms. "The delicious crack of leather on flesh fills my hand with delight and sends my body a shiver."

Chilling, indeed.

It was those types of quotes that convinced me to include the graphic sequences that I did, scenes that are so full of carnage and torture (the Devil's Box, the Listening Post, etc.) that some readers have complained to me about nightmares. Well, I'm sorry for your loss of sleep. But if I didn't stress the gore and bloodshed of plantation life, then I would have been the one losing sleep. Because my story would have been less than accurate.

And now a special excerpt
from Chris Kuzneski's

THE LOST THRONE

Coming soon in hardcover from
G. P. Putnam's Sons!

PROLOGUE

Christmas Day 1890
Piazza della Santa Carità
Naples, Italy

THE greatest secret of ancient Greece was silenced by a death in Italy.

Not a shooting or a stabbing or a murder of any kind—although dozens of those would occur later—but a good old-fashioned death. One minute the man was strolling across the Piazza della Santa Carità, pondering the significance of his discovery; the next, he was sprawled on his stomach in the middle of the cold square. People rushed to his side, hoping to help him to his feet, but one look at his gaunt face told them that he needed medical attention.

Two policemen on horseback were flagged down, and they rushed him to the closest hospital, where he slipped in and out of consciousness for the next hour. They asked him his name, but he couldn't answer. His condition had stolen his ability to speak.

The man wore a fancy suit and overcoat, both of which revealed his status. His hair was thin and gray, suggesting a man in his sixties. A bushy mustache covered his upper lip.

Doctors probed his clothes, searching for identification, but found nothing of value. No papers. No wallet. No money. If they had only looked closer, they might have noticed the secret pocket sewn into the lining of his coat, and the mystery would have ended there. But as hospital policy dictated, no identification meant no treatment. Not even on Christmas morning.

With few options, the police took him to the local station house, an ancient building made of brick and stone that would shelter him from the bitter winds of the Tyrrhenian Sea. They fed him broth and let him rest on a cot in an open cell, hoping he would regain his voice.

In time, he regained several.

Starting with a whisper that barely rose above the level of his breath, the sound slowly increased, building to a crescendo that could be heard by the two officers in the next room. They hurried down the corridor, expecting to find the stranger fully awake and willing to answer their questions. Instead they saw a man in a semicatatonic state who was babbling in his sleep.

His eyes were closed and his body was rigid, yet his lips were forming words.

One of the officers made the sign of the cross and said a short prayer while the other ran for a pencil and paper. When he returned, he pulled a chair up to the cot and tried to take notes in a small journal. Maybe they'd get an address. Or if they were really lucky, maybe even a name. But they got none of those things. In fact, all they got was more confused.

The first words spoken were German. Then French. Then Portuguese. Before long he was mixing several languages in the same sentence. Dutch followed by Spanish and Latin. English layered with Greek and Russian. Every once in a while he said something in Italian, but the words were so random and his accent so thick that they made little sense. Still, the officer transcribed everything he could and before long he noticed some repetition. One word seemed to be repeated over and over. Not only in Italian but in other languages as well.

Il trono. Le trône. El trono.

The throne.

This went on for several minutes. Language after language from one man's mouth. Like the devil speaking in tongues. Then, just as quickly as it started, it stopped.

No more words. No more clues.

The man would never speak again.

Two days later, after he had been identified, newspapers around the globe reported his death. Yet there was no mention of his strange behavior. Nothing about his ramblings or the throne he kept describing. Instead, reporters focused on the colorful details of his life—his wealth, his accomplishments, his discoveries. All the things that made him famous.

Of course, if they had known the truth about his final days, what he had finally found after years of searching, they would have written a much different story.

One of fire, deception, and ancient gold.

One that wouldn't have an ending for two more centuries.

CHAPTER 1

Present day
Saturday, May 17th
Metéora, Greece

THE monk felt the wind on his face as he plummeted to his death, a journey that started with a scream and ended with a thud.

Moments before, he had been standing near the railing of the Moni Agia Triada, the Monastery of the Holy Trinity. It was one of six monasteries perched on natural rock pillars near the Pindus Mountains in central Greece. Known for their breathtaking architecture, the monasteries had been built two thousand feet in the air with one purpose in mind: protection.

But on this night, their sanctity was breached.

The intruders had crossed the valley and climbed the hillside with silent precision. They carried no guns or artillery, preferring the weapons of their ancestors. Swords stored in scabbards were strapped to their backs. Daggers in leather sheaths hung from their hips. Bronze helmets covered their entire heads except for their eyes and mouths.

Centuries ago the final leg of their mission would have been far more treacherous, requiring chisels and ropes to scale the rock face. But that was no longer the case—not since 140 steps had been carved into the sandstone, leading to the entrance of Holy Trinity. Its front gate was ten feet high and made of thick wood, yet they breached it easily and slipped inside, spreading through the compound like a deadly plague.

The first to die was the lookout who, instead of doing his job, had been staring at the twinkling lights of Kalampáka, the small city that rested at the base of the plateau. Sadly, it was the last mistake he ever made. No questions were asked, no quarter was given. One minute he was pondering the meaning of life, the next his life was over.

No bullets. No blades. Just gravity and the rocks below.

One of the monks inside the church heard his scream and tried to warn the others, but before he could, the intruders burst through both doors. Brandishing their swords, they forced all the monks into the center of the room, where the holy men were frisked and their hands were tied.

Seven monks in total. A mixture of young and old.

Just as the intruders had expected.

For the next few minutes, the monks sat in silence on the hard wooden pews. Some of them closed their eyes and prayed to God for divine intervention. Others seemed reconciled to their fate. They knew the risks when they accepted this duty, what their brotherhood had endured and protected for centuries.

They were the keepers of the book. The chosen ones.

And soon they would be forced to die.

With the coldness of an executioner, the leader of the soldiers strode into the church. At first glance he looked like a moving work of art: muscle stacked upon muscle in statuesque perfection, a gleaming blade in his grasp. Unlike the others who had entered before him, his helmet was topped with a plume of red horsehair, a crest that signified his rank.

To the monks, he was the face of death.

Without saying a word, he nodded to his men. They sprang into action, grabbing one of the monks and dragging him toward the stone altar. Orthodox tradition prevented the brethren from trimming their facial hair after receiving tonsure—a symbolic shaving of their heads—so his beard was long and gray, draping the front of his black cassock like a hairy bib.

"What do you want from us?" cried the monk as he was shoved to his knees. "We have done nothing wrong!"

The leader stepped forward. "You know why I'm here. I want the book."

"What book? I know nothing about a book!"

"Then you are no use to me."

He punctuated his statement with a flick of his sword, separating the monk's head from his body. For a split second the monk's body didn't move, somehow remaining upright as if no violence had occurred. Then suddenly it slumped forward, spilling its contents onto the floor.

Head on the left. Body on the right. Blood everywhere.

The monks gasped at the sight.

"Bring me another," the leader ordered. "One who wants to live."

CHAPTER 2

THE phone rang in the middle of the night, sometime between last call and breakfast. The time of night reserved for two things: emergencies and wrong numbers.

Jonathon Payne hoped it was the latter.

He rolled over in the hotel bed and reached for the nightstand, knocking something to the floor in his dark room. He had no idea what it was and wasn't curious enough to find out. Still feeling the effects of his sleeping pill, he knew if he turned on a light he would be awake until dawn. Of that he was certain. He had always been a problem sleeper, an issue that had started long before his career in the military and had only gotten worse after.

Then again, years of combat can do that to a person.

And he had seen more than most.

Payne used to lead the MANIACs, an elite special forces unit composed of the top soldiers from the Marines, Army, Navy, Intelligence, Air Force, and Coast Guard. Whether it was personnel recovery, unconventional warfare, or counter-guerrilla sabotage, the MANIACs were the best of the best. The boogeymen that no one talked about. The government's secret weapon.

Yet on this night, Payne wanted no part of his former life.

He just wanted to get some sleep.

"Hello?" he mumbled into the hotel phone, expecting the worst.

A dial tone greeted him. It was soft and steady like radio static.

"Hello?" he repeated.

But the buzzing continued. As if no one had even called. As if he had imagined everything.

Payne grunted and hung up the phone, glad he could roll over and go back to sleep without anything to worry about. Thrilled it wasn't an emergency. He'd had too many of those when he was in the service. Hundreds of nights interrupted by news. Updates that were rarely positive.

So in his world, wrong numbers were a good thing. About the best thing possible.

Unfortunately, that wasn't the case here.

SEVERAL hours later Payne opened the hotel curtains and stepped onto his private veranda at the Renaissance Vinoy in downtown St. Petersburg. Painted flamingo pink and recently restored to its former glory, the resort was a stunning example of 1920s Mediterranean Revival architecture. The type of grand hotel that used to be found all over Florida yet was quickly becoming extinct in the age of Disneyfication.

The bright sunlight warmed his face and the sea breeze filled his lungs as he stared at the tropical waters of Tampa Bay, less than ten miles from many of the best beaches in America. Where the sand was white and the water was turquoise. Where dolphins frolicked in the surf. Born and raised in Pittsburgh, Payne rarely got to see dolphins in his hometown—only when he went to the aquarium or when the Miami Dolphins played the Steelers at Heinz Field.

In many ways, Payne looked like an NFL player. He was 6'4", weighed 240 pounds, and was in remarkable shape for a man in his late thirties. Light brown hair, hazel eyes, and a world-class smile. His only physical flaws were the bullet holes and scars that decorated his body. Although he didn't view them as flaws. More like medals of honor because each one stood for something.

Of course, he couldn't tell their stories to most people because the details were classified, but all of the scars meant something to him. Like secret tattoos that no one knew about.

The droning of a small aircraft caught Payne's attention, and he watched it glide across the azure sky and touch down at Albert Whitted Airport, a two-runway facility on the scenic waterfront, a few blocks away. It was the type of airfield that handled banner towing and sightseeing tours. Not large commuter jets. And certainly not the tactical fighters that he had observed during the last forty-eight hours. They required a lot more asphalt and much better pilots.

Every few months Payne visited U.S. military installations around the globe with his best friend and former MANIAC, David Jones. They were briefed on the latest equipment, and they offered their opinions to top brass on everything from training to tactics. Even though both soldiers were retired from active duty, they were still considered valuable assets by the Pentagon.

Part expert, part legend.

Their latest trip had brought them to Florida, where Mac-Dill Air Force Base occupied a large peninsula in the middle of Tampa Bay—eight miles south of downtown Tampa and nine miles east of St. Petersburg. All things considered, it wasn't a bad place to be stationed. Or to visit. Which is why Payne and Jones always looked forward to their next consulting trip.

They picked the destination and the military picked up the tab.

"Hey!" called a voice from below. "You finally awake?"

Payne glanced down and saw David Jones standing on the sidewalk, staring up at him. Jones was 5'9" and roughly forty pounds lighter than Payne. He had light brown skin, short black hair, and a thin nose that held his stylish sunglasses in place. Sadly, the rest of his outfit wasn't nearly as fashionable: a green floral shirt, torn khaki cargo shorts, and a pair of flip-flops.

"I'm starving," Jones said. "You want to get some chow?"

"With you? Not if you're wearing *that*."

"Why? What's wrong with it?"

"Honestly? It looks like Hawaiian camouflage."

Jones frowned, trying to think of a retort. "Yeah, well . . ."

"Well, what?"

"Maybe I'm looking to get *leid*."

Payne laughed. It wasn't a bad comeback for a Sunday morning. "I'll meet you in the lobby."

TEN minutes later the duo was walking along Bayshore Drive. The temperature was in the mid-seventies with low humidity. Gentle waves lapped against the stone wall that lined the harbor while palm trees swayed in the breeze. Payne wore a golf shirt and shorts, an outfit considered dressy in Florida, where many people wore T-shirts or no shirts at all.

As they turned onto Second Avenue NE toward the St. Petersburg Pier, Payne and Jones spotted a parked trolley-bus called the Looper. It was light blue and filled with tourists who were taking pictures of a tiny brick building with a red-tiled roof. A senior citizen tour guide, wearing a beige Panama hat and speaking with a Southern drawl, explained the building's significance over the trolley's loudspeaker system. They stopped to listen to his tale.

"You are looking at the fanciest public restroom in America, affectionately known as Little St. Mary's. Built in 1927 by Henry Taylor, it is a scaled-down replica of St. Mary Our Lady of Grace, the gorgeous church he built on Fourth Street that we'll be seeing soon. Both buildings are typical of the Romanesque Revival style, featuring several colors of brick, arched windows, and topped with a copper cupola. This one's approximately twenty feet high and fifty feet wide."

Cameras clicked as the tour guide continued.

"As the legend goes, the local diocese offered Taylor a large sum of money to build the octagonal church that he finished in 1925. However, for reasons unknown, they chose not to pay him the full amount. Realizing that he couldn't win a fight with the church, he opted to get revenge instead. At that time the city was taking bids to build a comfort station, a fancy term for bathroom, somewhere near the waterfront. Taylor made a ridiculously low bid, guaranteeing that he would get the project. From there, he used leftover materials from the church site and built the replica that you see before you, filling it with toilets instead of pews."

The tour guide smiled. "It was his way of saying that the Catholic Church was full of crap!"

Everyone laughed, including Payne and Jones, as the Looper pulled away from the curb and turned toward the Vinoy. Meanwhile the duo remained, marveling at the stone-carved columns and the elaborate tiled roof of Little St. Mary's.

"Remind me to go in there later," Jones said. "And I mean that literally."